This is my Funniest

LEADING SCIENCE FICTION WRITERS
PRESENT THEIR FUNNIEST STORIES EVER

EDITED BY

Mike Resnick

BENBELLA BOOKS, INC.

Dallas, Texas

Introduction © 2006 by Mike Resnick

"Space Rats of the CCC" © 2001 by Harry Harrison

"The Lemon-Green Spaghetti-Loud Dynamite-Dribble Day" © 1967 by William Tenn, reprinted from *Cavalier*

"Dick W. and His Pussy, or Tess and Her Adequate Dick" © 1997 by Jane Yolen, reprinted from *A Dick for a Day: What Would You Do If You Had One?*

"Night of the Cooters" © 1987 by Omni Publications Int., Ltd., reprinted from *Omni*

"A Delightful Comedic Premise" © 1974 by Mercury Press, reprinted from *The Magazine of Fantasy and Science Fiction*

"The Capo of Darkness" © 2002 by Laura Resnick, reprinted from *Vengeance Fantastic*

"Franz Kafka, Superhero!" © 1993 by David Gerrold, reprinted from *Alternate Warriors*

"Too Hot to Hoot" © 1996 by Spider Robinson, reprinted from *Callahan's Legacy*

"Amanda and the Alien" © 1983 by Agberg, Ltd., reprinted with permission of author and Agberg, Ltd.

"Faith" © 1989 by James Patrick Kelly, reprinted from *Asimov's Science Fiction*

"The Growling" © 1994 by Jody Lynn Nye, reprinted from *Chicks in Chainmail*

"Alien Radio" © 1993 by Nick DiChario, reprinted from *Christmas Ghosts*

"Primordial Chili" © 1999 by Tom Gerencer, reprinted from *SF Age*

"The Dog Said Bow-Wow" © 2001 by Michael Swanwick, reprinted from *Asimov's Science Fiction*

"Sweet, Savage Sorcerer" © 1990 by Esther Friesner, reprinted from *Amazing Stories*

"The Hanging Curve" © 2002 by Gardner Dozois, reprinted from *The Magazine of Fantasy and Science Fiction*

"Deus Tex" © 1996 by Cryptic, Inc., reprinted from *Realms of Fantasy*

"The Flim-Flam Alien" © 1982 by Creativity, Inc., reprinted from *Amazing Science Fiction Stories*

"Present" © 2004 by Kristine Kathryn Rusch, reprinted from *The Retrieval Artist and Other Stories*

"You'll Catch Your Death of Colds" © 1996 by Bill Fawcett & Associates, reprinted from *Don't Forget Your Spaceship, Dear*

"The Usurper Memos" © 2001 by Josepha Sherman, reprinted from *Villains Victorious*

"Patent Infringement" © 2002 by Nancy Kress, reprinted from *Asimov's Science Fiction*

"Ickies in Mirrorshades" © 2004 by David Brin

"Ligdan and the Young Pretender" © 1987 by Walter Jon Williams, reprinted from *There Will Be War*

"A !Tangled Web" © 1981 by Joe Haldeman, reprinted from *Analog*

"Revolt of the Sugar Plum Fairies" © 1992 by Mike Resnick

"Myth Manners' Guide to Greek Missology #1: Andromeda and Perseus" © 1999 by Harry Turtledove, reprinted from *Chicks 'N Chained Males*

"The Soul Selects Her Own Society" © 1996 by Connie Willis, reprinted from *War of the Worlds: Global Dispatches*

"Cordle to Onion to Carrot" © 1971 by Robert Sheckley, reprinted from *Playboy*

BenBella Books, Inc.
6440 N. Central Expressway, Suite 617
Dallas, TX 75206
www.benbellabooks.com
Send feedback to feedback@benbellabooks.com

Printed in the United States of America
10 9 8 7 6 5 4 3 2

Library of Congress Cataloging-in-Publication Data

This is my funniest : leading science fiction writers present their funniest stories ever / edited by Mike Resnick.
    p. cm.
  ISBN 1-932100-95-4
  1. Science fiction, American. I. Resnick, Michael D.

  PS648.S3T47 2006
  813'.0876208—dc22

2006014201

Proofreading by Stacia Seaman and Zachary Settle
Cover design by Laura Watkins
Cover art by Ralph Voltz
Text design and composition by John Reinhardt Book Design
Printed by Victor Graphics, Inc.

Distributed by Independent Publishers Group
To order call (800) 888-4741 • www.ipgbook.com

For special sales and media inquiries contact Yara Abuata at yara@benbellabooks.com

Contents

Contents

Introduction

MIKE RESNICK

~~~~~~~~~~~~~~

SCIENCE FICTION WRITERS LIKE TO LAUGH.

Maybe it's because so much science fiction is dystopian—after all, by definition, no one can create more than one Utopia—but whatever the reason, the fact remains that no field of fiction has as long and rich a track record of publishing humorous stories as science fiction. I don't think there's ever been a magazine or anthology editor who would refuse to buy a good story simply because it was funny, and sooner or later just about every practitioner takes a shot (or five, or thirty) at writing a humorous story.

We have a long and respected tradition of it. Back in the earlies, we had Stanton A. Coblentz, who at least thought he was funny, and Edgar Rice Burroughs, who was never subtle but often funny (usually on purpose). Move the calendar ahead and we had Fredric Brown, Henry Kuttner, Eric Frank Russell, and Fritz Leiber, none of them writing humor exclusively (or even predominantly), but each writing enough to make a reputation as a humorist (or, more accurately, as a humorist *too*.)

Then, starting at the halfway mark of the century, the humor and the humorists started coming fast and thick—Robert Sheckley, William Tenn, Harry Harrison, and their contemporaries. Then came John Sladek and George Alec Effinger and *their* contemporaries. Even Isaac Asimov got in on the act with his books of limericks and *The Sensuous Dirty Old Man*.

These days we've got Connie Willis and Esther Friesner, and we've got some humorists like Douglas Adams and Terry Pratchett who live on the bestseller lists. The next generation has already made its appearance in the person of young Tom Gerencer.

The most frustrating part of editing this book was explaining to the

1

dozen or so writers who asked for input that the title was *This is my Funniest* and not *Mike Resnick Thinks This is my Funniest*. More than once I had to forcibly restrain myself from asking for *my* favorite rather than *their* favorite. (I did break down once and tell the late Bob Sheckley which one I hoped he'd choose. To his credit, he stuck with the one he liked best.)

So here they are, a broad cross section of our very finest writers, some whom are known for their humor, and some of whose appearance here will surprise you (until you read their stories and then wonder why the hell they don't do it more often).

Enjoy. And maybe even giggle here and there.

In the beginning there were many pulp magazines—of great variety. But only in the SF pulps could you find all the heady delights of space opera.

Delightful, that is, if you were a prepubescent male with no literary taste whatsoever. Oh, how we adored those garish magazines with their exploding covers, the heroes stronger than strong, the zapping spaceships, and the nonstop action. The dismal grammar, the childish plots, and the endless, senseless conflicts.

Still, I do miss space opera, miss the simplicity of it all, the dream-making mythos. I miss the emotional impact, but of course I can't bear to read it anymore. I read it as it was being published in the pulps, never doubting the talent of E. E. Smith, Ph.D., Edmond Hamilton, and the young John Campbell. Now those ancient magazines have flaked themselves into oblivion; probably a good thing.

But it's a bad thing in that there are writers working today attempting to become modern practitioners of the ancient craft of space opera. To them I say *No*! Let the super-strong heroes and mile-long spaceships rest and rust in peace. It had its day, its place in time, its importance to the juvenile and developing field of science fiction.

When I read some of the attempts to reestablish space opera I was aghast. A mistake—let it remain in its peaceful grave. In an attempt to point out the illiteracy, the false characterization, the general clumsiness of the field, I wrote this parody. If readers—and writers—could be induced to laugh at this bygone field of literary endeavor, then perhaps they would cease attempts to revive it.

If you love space opera, you will hate me.

If you don't know it—why, I think that you can still enjoy the story.

—Harry Harrison

Space Rats of the CCC

HARRY HARRISON

~~~~~~~~~~

THAT'S IT, MATEY, PULL UP A STOOL, sure, use that one. Just dump old Phrnnx onto the floor to sleep it off. You know that Krddls can't stand strong drink—much less drink flnnx, and that topped off with a smoke of the hellish krmml weed. Here, let me pour you a mug of flnnx, oops, sorry about your sleeve. When it dries you can scrape it off with a knife. Here's to your health and may your tubeliners never fail you when the kpnnz hordes are on your tail.

No, sorry, never heard your name before. Too many good men come and go, and the good ones die early aye! Me? You never heard of me. Just call me Old Sarge, as good a name as any. Good men I say, and the best of them was—well, we'll call him Gentleman Jax. He had another name, but there's a little girl waiting on a planet I could name, a little girl that's waiting and watching the shimmering trails of the deep-spacers when they come, and waiting for a man. So for her sake we'll call him Gentleman Jax, he would have liked that, and she would like that if only she knew, although she must be getting kind of gray, or bald by now, and arthritic from all that sitting and waiting but, golly, that's another story and by Orion it's not for me to tell. That's it, help yourself, a large one. Sure the green fumes are normal for good flnnx, though you better close your eyes when you drink or you'll be blind in a week, haha!, by the sacred name of the Prophet Mrddl!

Yes, I can tell what you're thinking. What's an old space rat like me doing in a dive like this out here at galaxy's end where the rim stars flicker wanly and the tired photons go slow? I'll tell you what I'm doing, getting drunker than a Planizzian pfrdffl, that's what. They say that drink has the power to dim memories and by Cygnus I have some memories that need dimming. I see you looking at those scars on my hands.

5

Each one is a story, matey, aye, and the scars on my back each a story and the scars on my...well, that's a different story. Yes, I'll tell you a story, a true one by Mrddl's holy name, though I might change a name or two, that little girl waiting, you know.

You heard tell of the CCC? I can see by the sudden widening of your eyes and the blanching of your space-tanned skin that you have. Well, yours truly, Old Sarge here, was one of the first of the Space Rats of the CCC, and my buddy then was the man they know as Gentleman Jax. May Great Kramddl curse his name and blacken the memory of the first day when I first set eyes on him....

"Graduating class...ten-SHUN!"

The sergeant's stentorian voice bellowed forth, cracking like a whiplash across the expectant ears of the mathematically aligned rows of cadets. With the harsh snap of those fateful words a hundred and three incredibly polished boot heels crashed together with a single snap, and the eighty-seven cadets of the graduating class snapped to steel-rigid attention. (It should be explained that some of them were from alien worlds, different numbers of legs, and so on.) Not a breath was drawn, not an eyelid twitched a thousandth of a milliliter as Colonel von Thorax stepped forward, glaring down at them all through the glass monocle in front of his glass eye, close-cropped gray hair stiff as barbed wire, black uniform faultlessly cut and smooth, a krmml weed cigarette clutched in the steel fingers of his prosthetic left arm, black gloved fingers of his prosthetic right arm snapping to hat-brim's edge in a perfect salute, motors whining thinly in his prosthetic lungs to power the Brobdingnagian roar of his harshly bellowed command.

"At ease. And listen to me. You are the hand-picked men—and hand-picked things too, of course—from all the civilized worlds of the galaxy. Six million and forty-three cadets entered the first year of training, and most of them washed out in one way or another. Some could not toe the mark. Some were expelled and shot for buggery. Some believed the lying Commie pinko crying liberal claims that continuous war and slaughter are not necessary, and they were expelled and shot as well. One by one the weaklings fell away through the years, leaving the hard core of the Corps—you! The Corpsmen of the first graduating class of the CCC! Ready to spread the benefits of civilization to the stars. Ready at last to find out what the initials CCC stand for!"

A mighty roar went up from the massed throats, a cheer of hoarse masculine enthusiasm that echoed and boomed from the stadium walls. At a signal from von Thorax a switch was thrown, and a great shield of imperviomite slid into place above, sealing the stadium from prying eyes and ears and snooping spyish rays. The roaring voices roared on enthusiastically—and many an eardrum was burst that day!—yet were stilled in an instant when the Colonel raised his hand.

"You Corpsmen will not be alone when you push the frontiers of civilization out to the barbaric stars. Oh no! You will each have a faithful companion by your side. First man, first row, step forward and meet your faithful companion!"

The Corpsman called out, stepped forward a smart pace, and clicked his heels sharply, said click being echoed in the clack of a thrown-wide door and, without conscious intent, every eye in that stadium was drawn in the direction of the dark doorway from which emerged....

How to describe it? How to describe the whirlwind that batters you, the storm that engulfs you, the spacewarp that en-warps you? It was as indescribable as any natural force!

It was a creature three meters high at the shoulders, four meters high at the ugly, drooling, tooth-clashing head, a whirlwinded, spacewarped storm that rushed forward on four piston-like legs, great-clawed feet tearing grooves in the untearable surface of the impervitium flooring, a monster born of madness and nightmares that reared up before them and bellowed in a soul-destroying screech.

"There!" Colonel von Thorax bellowed in answer, blood-specked spittle mottling his lips. "There is your faithful companion, the mutacamel, mutation of the noble beast of Good Old Earth, symbol and pride of the CCC—the Combat Camel Corps! Corpsman, meet your camel!"

The selected Corpsman stepped forward and raised his arm in greeting to this noble beast, which promptly bit the arm off. His shrill screams mingled with the barely stifled gasps of his companions who watched, with more than casual interest, as camel trainers girt with brass-buckled leather harness rushed out and beat the protesting camel with clubs back from whence it had come, while a medic clamped a tourniquet on the wounded man's stump and dragged his limp body away.

"That is your first lesson on combat camels," the Colonel cried huskily. "Never raise your arms to them. Your companion, with a newly grafted arm will, I am certain, ha-ha!, remember this little lesson. Next man, next companion!"

Again the thunder of rushing feet and the high-pitch gurgling, scream-like roar of the combat camel at full charge. This time the Corpsman kept his arm down, and the camel bit his head off.

"Can't graft on a head, I am afraid," the Colonel leered maliciously at them. "A moment of silence for our departed companion who has gone to the big rocket pad in the sky. That's enough. Ten-SHUN! You will now proceed to the camel training area where you will learn to get along with your faithful companions. Never forgetting that each has a complete set of teeth made of imperviumite, as well as razor-sharp claw caps of this same substance. Dis-MISSED!"

The student barracks of the CCC was well known for its "no frills" or rather "no coddling" decor and comforts. The beds were impervitium slabs—no spine-sapping mattresses here!—and the sheets of thin burlap. No blankets of course, not with the air kept at a healthy four degrees centigrade. The rest of the comforts matched so that it was a great surprise to the graduates to find unaccustomed comforts awaiting them upon their return from the ceremonies and training. There was a shade on each bare-bulbed reading light and a nice soft two-centimeter-thick pillow on every bed. Already they were reaping the benefits of all the years of labor.

Now, among all the students, the top student by far was named M____. There are some secrets that must not be told, names that are important to loved ones and neighbors. Therefore I shall draw the cloak of anonymity over the true identity of the man known as M____. Suffice to call him "Steel," for that was the nickname of someone who knew him best. "Steel," or Steel as we can call him, had at this time a room-mate by the name of L____. Later, much later, he was to be called by certain people "Gentleman Jax," so for the purpose of this narrative we shall call him "Gentleman Jax" as well, or perhaps just plain "Jax." Jax was second only to Steel in scholastic and sporting attainments, and the two were the best of chums. They had been roommates for the past year and now they were back in their room with their feet up, basking in the unexpected luxury of the new furnishings, sipping decaffeinated coffee, called koffee, and smoking deeply of the school's own brand of denicotinized cigarettes, called Denikcig by the manufacturer but always referred to, humorously, by the CCC students as "gaspers" or "lungbusters."

"Throw me over a gasper, will you, Jax," Steel said, from where he lolled on the bed, hands behind his head, dreaming of what was in store for him now that he would be having his own camel soon. "Ouch!" he chuckled as the pack of gaspers caught him in the eye. He drew out one of the slim white forms and tapped it on the wall to ignite it, then drew in a lungful of refreshing smoke. "I still can't believe it..." he smoke-ringed.

"Well it's true enough, by Mrddl," Jax smiled. "We're graduates. Now throw back that pack of lungbusters so I can join you in a draw or two."

Steel complied, but did it so enthusiastically that the pack hit the wall and instantly all the cigarettes ignited and the whole thing burst into flame. A glass of water doused the conflagration but, while it was still fizzling fitfully, a light flashed redly on the comscreen.

"High priority message," Steel bit out, slamming down the actuator button. Both youths snapped to rigid attention as the screen filled with the iron visage of Colonel von Thorax.

"M____, L_____, to my office on the triple." The words fell like leaden weights from his lips. What could it mean?

"What can it mean?" Jax asked as they hurtled down a drop-chute at close to the speed of gravity.

"We'll find out quickly enough," Steel snapped as they drew up at the "old man's" door and activated the announcer button.

Moved by some hidden mechanism the door swung wide and, not without a certain amount of trepidation, they entered. But what was this? This! The Colonel was looking at them and smiling, smiling, an expression never before known to cross his stern face at any time.

"Make yourselves comfortable, lads," he indicated, pointing at comfortable chairs that rose out of the floor at the touch of a button. "You'll find 'gaspers' in the arms of these servochairs, as well as Valumian wine or Snaggian beer."

"No koffee?" Jax open-mouthedly expostulated, and they all laughed.

"I don't think you really want it," the Colonel susurrated coyly through his artificial larynx. "Drink up, lads, you're Space Rats of the CCC now, and your youth is behind you. Now look at that."

That was a three-dimensional image that sprang into being in the air before them at the touch of a button, an image of a spacer like none ever seen before. She was as slender as a swordfish, fine-winged as a bird, solid as a whale, and as armed to the teeth as an alligator.

"Holy Kolon," Steel sighed in open-mouthed awe. "Now that is what I call a hunk o' rocket!"

"Some of us prefer to call it the *Indefectible*," the Colonel said, not unhumorously.

"Is that her? We heard something...."

"You heard very little, for we have had this baby under wraps ever since the earliest stage. She has the largest engines ever built, new improved MacPhersons[1] of the most advanced design, Kelly drive[2] gear that has been improved to where you would not recognize it in a month of Thursdays—as well as double-strength Fitzroy projectors[3] that make the old ones look like a kid's pop-gun. And I've saved the best for last...."

"Nothing can be better than what you have already told us," Steel broke in.

"That's what you think!" The Colonel laughed, not unkindly, with a sound like tearing steel. "The best news is that, M____, you are going to be Captain of this spacegoing super-dreadnought, while Lucky is Chief Engineer."

"Lucky L____would be a lot happier if he were Captain instead of king of the stokehold," he muttered, and the other two laughed at what they thought was a joke.

"Everything is completely automated," the Colonel continued, "so it can be flown by a crew of two. But I must warn you that it has experimental gear aboard so whoever flies her has to volunteer...."

"I volunteer!" Steel shouted.

---

[1] The MacPherson engine was first mentioned in the author's story "Rocket Rangers of the IRT" (*Spicy-Weird Stories*, 1923).

[2] Loyal readers first discovered the Kelly drive in the famous book *Hell Hounds of Coal Sack Cluster* (Slimecreeper Press, Ltd., 1931), also published in German as *Teufelhund Nach der Knockwurst Exspres*. Translated into Italian by Re Umberto, unpublished to date.

[3] A media breakthrough was made when the Fitzroy projector first appeared in "Female Space Zombies of Venus" in 1936 in *True Story Confessions*.

"I have to go to the terlet," Jax said, rising, though he sat again instantly when the ugly blaster leaped from its holster to the Colonel's hand. "Ha-ha, just a joke. I volunteer, sure."

"I knew I could count on you, lads. The CCC breeds men. Camels too, of course. So here is what you do. At 0304 hours tomorrow you two in the *Indefectible* will crack ether headed out Cygnus way. In the direction of a certain planet."

"Let me guess, if I can, that is," Steel said grimly through tight-clenched teeth. "You don't mean to give us a crack at the larshnik-loaded world of Biru-2, do you?"

"I do. This is the larshniks' prime base, the seat of operation of all their drug and gambling traffic, where the white-slavers offload, and the queer green is printed, site of the flnnx distilleries and lair of the pirate hordes."

"If you want action that sounds like it!" Steel grimaced.

"You are not just whistling through your back teeth," the Colonel agreed. "If I were younger and had a few less replaceable parts this is the kind of opportunity I would leap at...."

"You can be Chief Engineer," Jax hinted.

"Shut up," the Colonel implied. "Good luck, gentlemen, for the honor of the CCC rides with you."

"But not the camels?" Steel asked.

"Maybe next time. There are, well, adjustment problems. We have lost four more graduates since we have been sitting here. Maybe we'll even change animals. Make it the CDC."

"With combat dogs?" Jax asked.

"Either that or donkeys. Or dugongs. But it is my worry, not yours. All you guys have to do is get out there and crack Biru-2 wide open. I know you can do it."

If the stern-faced Corpsmen had any doubts they kept them to themselves, for that is the way of the Corps. They did what had to be done and the next morning, at exactly 0304:00 hours, the mighty bulk of the *Indefectable* hurled itself into space. The roaring MacPherson engines poured quintillions of ergs of energy into the reactor drive until they were safely out of the gravity field of Mother Earth. Jax labored over his engines, shoveling the radioactive transvestite into the gaping maw of the hungry furnace, until Steel signaled from the bridge that it was "change-over" time. Then they changed over to the space-eating Kelly drive. Steel jammed home the button that activated the drive and the great ship leaped starward at seven times the speed of light.[4] Since the drive was fully automatic Jax freshened up in the fresher, while his clothes were automatically washed in the washer, then proceeded to the bridge.

"Really," Steel said, his eyebrows climbing up his forehead. "I didn't know you went in for polka-dot jockstraps."

"It was the only thing I had clean. The washer dissolved the rest of my clothes."

"Don't worry about it. It's the larshniks of Biru-2 who have to worry! We hit atmosphere in exactly seventeen minutes and I have been thinking about what to do when that happens."

"Well, I certainly hope someone has! I haven't had time to draw a deep breath, much less think."

"Don't worry, old pal, we are in this together. The way I figure it we have two choices. We can blast right in, guns roaring, or we can slip in by stealth."

"Oh, you really have been thinking, haven't you."

"I'll ignore that because you are tired. Strong as we are, I think the land-based batteries are stronger. So I suggest we slip in without being noticed."

"Isn't that a little hard when you are flying in a thirty-ton spacer?"

"Normally, yes. But do you see this button here marked *invisibility*? While you were loading the fuel they explained this to me. It is a new invention, never used in action before, that will render us invisible and impervious to detection by any of their detection instruments."

"Now that's more like it. Fifteen minutes to go, we should be getting mighty close. Turn on the old invisibility ray...."

"Don't!"

"Done! Now what's your problem?"

"Nothing really. Except the experimental invisibility device is not expected to last more than thirteen minutes before it burns out."

Unhappily, this proved to be the case. One hundred miles above the

---

[4] When the inventor Patsy Kelly was asked how the ships could move at seven times the speed of light when the limiting velocity of matter, according to Einstein, was the speed of light, he responded in his droll Goidelic way, with a shrug, "Well—sure and I guess Einstein was wrong."

barren, blasted surface of Biru-2 the good old *Indefectible* popped into existence.

In the minutest fraction of a millisecond the mighty spacesonar and superradar had locked grimly onto the invading ship while sublights flickered their secret signals, waiting for the correct response that would reveal the invader as one of theirs.

"I'll send a signal, stall them. These larshniks aren't too bright," Steel laughed. He thumbed on the microphone, switched to the interstellar emergency frequency, then bit out the rasping words in a sordid voice. "Agent X-9 to prime base. Had a firefight with the patrol, shot up my code books, but I got all the SOBs, ha-ha! Am coming home with a load of eight hundred thousand long tons of the hellish krmml weed."

The larshnik response was instantaneous. From the gaping, pitted orifices of thousands of giant blaster cannon there vomited forth ravening rays of energy that strained the very fabric of space itself. These coruscating forces blasted into the impregnable screens of the old *Indefectible* which, sadly, was destined not to get much older, and instantly punched their way through and splashed coruscatingly from the very hull of the ship itself. Mere matter could not stand against such forces unlocked in the coruscating bowels of the planet itself so that the impregnable imperialite metal walls instantly vaporized into a thin gas which was, in turn, vaporized into the very electrons and protons (and neutrons too) of which it was made.

Mere flesh and blood could not stand against such forces. But in the few seconds it took the coruscating energies to eat through the force screens, hull, vaporized gas, and protons, the reckless pair of valiant Corpsmen had hurled themselves headlong into their space armor. And just in time! The ruin of the once-great ship hit the atmosphere and seconds later slammed into the poison soil of Biru-2.

To the casual observer it looked like the end. The once-mighty queen of the spaceways would fly no more, for she now consisted of no more than two hundred pounds of smoking junk. Nor was there any sign of life from the tragic wreck to the surface crawlers who erupted from a nearby secret hatch concealed in the rock and crawled through the smoking remains with all their detectors detecting at maximum gain. Report! the radio signal wailed. No sign of life to fifteen decimal places! snapped back the cursing operator of the crawlers before he signaled them to return to base. Their metal cleats clanked viciously across the barren soil, and then they were gone. All that remained was the cooling metal wreck hissing with despair as the poison rain poured like tears upon it.

Were these two good friends dead? I thought you would never ask. Unbeknownst to the larshnik technicians, just one millisecond before the wreck struck down two massive and almost indestructible suits of space armor had been ejected by coiled steelite springs, sent flying to the very horizon where they landed behind a concealing spine of rock, which, just by chance, was the spine of rock into which the secret hatch had been built that concealed the crawlway from which the surface crawlers with their detectors emerged for their fruitless search, to which they returned under control of their cursing operator who, stoned again with hellish krmml weed, never noticed the quick flick of the detector needles as the crawlers reentered the tunnel, this time bearing on their return journey a cargo they had not exited with as the great door slammed shut behind them.

"We've done it! We're inside their defenses," Steel rejoiced. "And no thanks to you, pushing that Mrddl-cursed invisibility button."

"Well, how was I to know?" Jax grated. "Anyways, we don't have a ship anymore but we do have the element of surprise. They don't know that we are here, but we know they are here!"

"Good thinking...hssst!" he hissed. "Stay low, we're coming to something."

The clanking crawlers rattled into the immense chamber cut into the living stone and now filled with deadly war machines of all description. The only human there, if he could be called human, was the larshnik operator whose soiled fingertips sprang to the gun controls the instant he spotted the intruders, but he never stood a chance. Precisely aimed rays from two blasters zeroed in on him and in a millisecond he was no more than a charred fragment of smoking flesh in the chair. Corps justice was striking at last to the larshnik lair.

Justice it was, impersonal and final, impartial and murderous, for there were no "innocents" in this lair of evil. Ravening forces of civilized vengeance struck down all that crossed their path as the two chums rode a death-dealing combat gun through the corridors of infamy.

"This is the big one," Steel grimaced as they came to an immense door of gold-plated impervialite before which a suicide squad committed suicide under the relentless scourge of fire. There was more feeble resistance, smokily, coruscatingly, and noisily exterminated, before this last barrier went down and they rode in triumph into the central control, now manned by a single figure at the main panel. Superlarsh himself, secret head of the empire of interstellar crime.

"You have met your destiny," Steel intoned grimly, his weapon fixed unmovingly upon the black-robed figure in the opaque space helmet. "Take off that helmet or you die upon the instant."

His only reply was a slobbered growl of inchoate rage, and for a long instant the black-gloved hands trembled over the gun controls. Then, ever so slowly, these same hands raised themselves to clutch at the helmet, to turn it, to lift it slowly off....

"By the sacred name of the Prophet Mrddl!" the two Corpsmen gasped in unison, struck speechless by what they saw.

"Yes, so now you know," grated Superlarsh through angry teeth. "But, ha-ha, I'll bet you never suspected."

"You!!" Steel insufflated, breaking the frozen silence. "You! You!! YOU!!!"

"Yes, me, I, Colonel von Thorax, Commandant of the CCC. You never suspected me and, ohh, how I laughed at you all of the time."

"But...." Jax stammered. "Why?"

"Why? The answer is obvious to any but democratic interstellar swine like you. The only thing the larshniks of the galaxy had to fear was something like the CCC, a powerful force impervious to outside bribery or sedition, noble in the cause of righteousness. You could have caused us trouble. Therefore we founded the CCC, and I have long been head of both organizations. Our recruiters bring in the best that the civilized planets can offer, and I see to it that most of them are brutalized, morale destroyed, bodies wasted, and spirits crushed so they are no longer a danger. Of course, a few always make it through the course no matter how disgusting I make it—every generation has its share of super-masochists—but I see that these are taken care of pretty quickly."

"Like being sent on suicide missions?" Steel asked ironly.

"That's a good way."

"Like the one we were sent on—but it didn't work! Say your prayers, you filthy larshnik, for you are about to meet your maker!"

"Maker? Prayers? Are you out of your skull? All larshniks are athe-ists to the end...."

And then it was the end, in a coruscating puff of vapor, dead with those vile words upon his lips, no less than he deserved.

"Now what?" Steel asked.

"This," Jax responded, shooting the gun from his hand and imprison-ing him instantly with an unbreakable paralysis ray. "No more second best for me—in the engine room with you on the bridge. This is my ball game from here on in."

"Are you mad!" Steel fluttered through paralyzed lips.

"Sane for the first time in my life. The superlarsh is dead, long live the new superlarsh. It's mine, the whole galaxy, mine."

"And what about me?"

"I should kill you, but that would be too easy. And you did share your chocolate bars with me. You will be blamed for this entire debacle—for the death of Colonel von Thorax and for the disaster here at larshnik prime base. Every man's hand will be against you, and you will be an outcast and will flee for your life to the farflung outposts of the galaxy where you will live in terror."

"Remember the chocolate bars!"

"I do. All I ever got were the stale ones. Now...GO!"

You want to know my name? Old Sarge is good enough. My story? Too much for your tender ears, boyo. Just top up the glasses, that's the way, and join me in a toast. At least that much for a poor old man who has seen much in this long lifetime. A toast of bad luck, bad cess I say, may Great Kramddl curse forever the man some know as Gentleman Jax. What, hungry? Not me—no—NO! Not a chocolate bar!!!!!

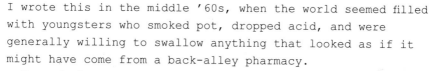

I wrote this in the middle '60s, when the world seemed filled with youngsters who smoked pot, dropped acid, and were generally willing to swallow anything that looked as if it might have come from a back-alley pharmacy.

Two of them, college students who came to our home for dinner late in one of those years, were astonished to discover that Greenwich Villagers like the pair of us had never so much as turned on in our entire lives.

"Don't you want your consciousness expanded?" one of them asked my wife.

"No," Fruma replied. "If anything, I want it contracted."

—*William Tenn*

The Lemon-Green Spaghetti-Loud Dynamite-Dribble Day

WILLIAM TENN

~~~~~~~~~

Testimony of Witness No. 5671 before the Special Presidential Investigative Commission. Leonard Drucker, thirty-one years old, unmarried, of 238 West 10th Street, New York City, Borough of Manhattan, employed as a salesman by the Har-Bern Office Partition Company of 205 East 42nd Street, New York City, Borough of Manhattan. Witness, being placed under oath, does swear and depose:

WELL, I DON'T KNOW, the telephone woke me up about eight A.M. on that Wednesday morning. I grabbed at it, half falling out of bed, and finally managed to juggle it up to my ear. A girl's voice was saying, "Hello, Lennie? Is that you, Lennie? Hello?"

After a couple of seconds, I recognized the voice. I said, "Doris? Yeah, it's me. What's the matter?"

"You tell me, Lennie!" She sounded absolutely hysterical. "Have you been listening to the radio? I called up three people already and they're just as bad as the radio. You sure you're all right?"

"I'm fine. Hey, it's eight o'clock—I had another fifteen minutes' sleep. And my coffee—it's in the percolator. Let me turn the—the—"

"You too!" she screeched. "It's affected you too! What's the matter with everybody? What's happening?" And she hung up.

I put down the phone and shuddered. Doris was a girl I'd been seeing, and she'd looked very normal. Now it was obvious she was just another kooky Village chick. I may live in the Village, but I hold down a good job and I dress conservatively. Usually, I stay far away from kooky Village chicks.

There was no point in going back to sleep, so I flipped the switch gizmo on my electric percolator and turned it on. That, I guess, is the crucial part of this testimony. You see, I always set up my coffee percolator the night before and fill it with water. When I get up in the morning, I'm too blind and dopey to cook anything.

Because of Doris's call, I also flicked on the radio before I went into the bathroom. I splashed some cold water on my face, rinsed out my toothbrush, and put some toothpaste on it. It was halfway to my mouth when I began listening to the radio. I put it down on the sink and went out and sat next to the radio, really fascinated. I never brushed my teeth: I was one lucky son of a bitch all around.

The radio announcer had a warm, sleepy voice. He was enunciating carefully: "...forty-eight...forty-nine...*forty!* Forty-one...forty-two... forty-three...forty-four...forty-five...forty-six...forty-seven...forty-eight...forty-nine...*forty!* Forty-one...."

I stayed with that voice, I don't know, for a long time. It didn't ever get up to fifty. The coffee had finished perking, so I poured myself a cup and sat and twirled the dial. Some of the stations—they were the Jersey ones, I found out later—sounded pretty much as usual, but most of the broadcasts were wild. There was a traffic report, I remember, that just gripped me.

"...and on the Major Deegan Expressway, traffic is moderate to spaghetti-loud. All dynamite-dribbles are reported moving smoothly. The Cadillacs are longer, the Continentals are thinner, and the Chrysler Imperials have mostly snapped in two. Five thousand Chevrolet convertibles are building a basketball court in one uptown lane of the Franklin D. Roosevelt Drive...."

While I was having another cup of coffee and some cookies, I happened to glance at my watch, and I realized almost an hour had slipped by with that damn radio! I gave myself a one-two-three shave with the electric razor, and started dressing frantically.

I thought of calling Doris back to tell her she was right, but I thought, better not, better get to work first. And you know something? I never saw or heard from Doris again. I wonder what happened to *her* on that day. Well, she wasn't the only one. Right?

There was hardly anyone on the street, just a few people sitting on the curb with funny expressions on their faces. But I passed that big garage between my apartment house and the subway station, and there I stopped dead. It's one of the most expensive car hangars in the Village and it looked like, I don't know, a junkyard soufflé.

In the dimness, I could see cars mashed against cars, cars mashed against walls. Broken glass mixed in with strips of torn-off chrome. Fenders ripped off, hoods sprung open and all twisty.

Charlie, the attendant, came dragging out of his cubicle and kind of grinned at me. He looked as if he'd tied one on last night.

"Wait'll your boss sees this," I told him. "Man, you'll be dead."

He pointed at two cars locked together nose to nose near the entrance. "Mr. Carbonaro was here. He kept asking them to go on making love. When they wouldn't, he said to hell with them, he was going home. He was crying just like a milk bottle."

It was turning into one weird morning. I was only half surprised when there was no one on duty in the subway change booth. But I had a token on me. I put it in the turnstile and clunked through.

And that's when I first began to get scared—on the platform of the subway station. Whatever else is going on in the world, to a New Yorker the subway is a kind of man-made natural phenomenon, routine and regular as the sun coming up. And when the routine and regularity stop in the subway, you sure as hell notice it.

Like the guy on his hands and knees at one end of the platform staring up a woman's dress, she rocking on high heels and singing a song to the ceiling. Or this pretty young Negro girl, sitting on a wooden bench, crying her heart out and wiping her eyes with great big newsprinted sheets of that morning's *Times*. Or the doctor-lawyer type miming a slalom in and out of the iron pillars of the platform. He was chanting, "Chug, chug, chug-azoom, chug, chug, chug-azoom." And nobody in the station being startled, or even looking worried.

Three trains in a row came in and went right on through without stopping, without even slowing down. The engineer of the last one was a big, white-haired guy who was laughing his head off as he flashed past. Then a fourth train came in, and this one stopped.

Only two of us on the platform made a dash for it: me and a young fellow in khaki pants and a brown sweater. The doors opened and shut, *zip-zip*, practically in the same motion. The train took off without us.

"What's going on?" the young fellow whined at me. "I'm late for work—I had to run out of the house without any breakfast. But I can't get a train. I paid my fare. Why can't I get a train?"

I told him I didn't know, and I left him and went upstairs. I was very scared. I got into a phone booth and tried to call my office. The phone rang for a long time: no answer.

Then I wandered around on that corner near the subway station for a while, trying to decide what I should do next, trying to figure out what was happening. I kept calling the office. No luck. That was damn funny—it was way after nine o'clock. Maybe no one at all had come in today? I couldn't imagine such a thing.

I began noticing that the people going by on the street had a funny sort of stare, a kind of pop-eyed, trancy look. Charlie, the garage man, he'd had it. But the kid in the brown sweater on the subway platform, he didn't have it. I saw a mirror in a store window and looked at myself. I didn't have it.

The store was a television repair place. They had a television set in the window, tuned into a program, and I got all involved in watching it. I don't know what the program was—two men and a woman were standing around talking to each other, but the woman was doing a slow strip. She was talking and peeling off her clothes at the same time. She had trouble with the garter belt and the men helped her. No pantyhose—I guess she was an old-fashioned type.

Next door, there was a liquor store. People were going in and out, buying a lot of liquor. But then I saw that buying wasn't exactly the right word. What they'd do, they'd walk in, shoot a quick, suspicious look at the owner, grab up a couple of bottles—and walk out. The owner was watching them do this with a big, beaming smile.

A guy came out with a couple of fifths, a stinking, dirty guy, strictly a Bowery type. He was all happy—you know, the millennium.

We both saw the other didn't have the pop-eyed look. (This was the first time, but all that day I had a lot of those flashes of recognition. You immediately noticed someone without the pop-eyed look.)

"It's great, hah?" he said. "All over town. Help yourself, fella, help yourself to the sauce. You know whatsa-matter with 'em, hah?"

I stared at his maybe three, maybe five teeth. "No. What?"

"They've been drinking water. It's finally caught up with them. Poison, pure poison. I always said it. You know the last time I had a glass of water? You know, hah? Over twelve years ago."

I just turned my back and took off and left him standing there.

Walking fast, uptown on Sixth, I said to myself, where the hell am I going? I decided to go to my office on 42nd Street. It's like when there was a subway strike. I still belonged at the office.

For a while I looked out for a taxi, but you know, there were damn few cars going up the avenue, and most of them were traveling very, very slowly. Once in a while, there'd be one going fast, highway speed or beyond. Plenty of accidents.

The first accident I saw, I ran over to see if I could help. But the driver had already crawled out. He looked at the fire hydrant he'd knocked over, he looked at it spouting and shook himself and staggered away. After that I passed up the accidents. I just kept an eye out to see that no cars were coming up on the sidewalk after me.

But that geyser of water made me think of what the bum had said. Was it something in the water? I'd had coffee, but I'd set up the percolator the night before. And I hadn't had time to brush my teeth. Doris, the guy in the brown sweater in the subway, they hadn't eaten breakfast yet, they hadn't touched water. Neither had the bum. It had to be the water.

I didn't know anything then about that bunch of LSD kids, you know, one of them being the daughter of a Water Supply engineer and getting her hands on her father's charts and all the other stuff that's come out. That poor guy! But I knew about enough to stay away from anything that used water from a tap. So, just in case, I stopped in at a self-service grocery and got a six-pack of soda, you know, cans with pull-open tops.

The clerk was looking at the back wall in a trance. He had such a scared expression on his face it almost made my hair stand up. I waited for him to start screaming, but he didn't. I walked out and left a dollar on the counter.

A block further on, I stopped to watch a fire.

It was in one of those small, scabby loft buildings that line lower Sixth. There were no flames visible, just a continuous balloon of smoke coming out of a third-floor window. A crowd of sleepy, dopey-looking people were in front of the place, mixed in with a bunch of bored, dopey-looking firemen. The big red fire engine was all the way up on the sidewalk with its nose inside the smashed window of a wholesale florist's. And a hose that someone had attached to a fire hydrant was just lying there, every once in a while coughing up a half gallon of water like a snake with tuberculosis.

I didn't like the idea of there being people inside, maybe burning to death very quietly. So I pushed through the crowd. I got up to the first floor landing and the smoke there was already too thick and smothery for me to go any higher. But I saw a fireman sitting comfortably against the wall on the landing, his fire helmet slid down over the front of his face. "No beer," he was saying to himself. "No beer and no steam room." I took him by the hand and led him downstairs.

There was a light rain going on, and I felt like getting down on my knees and saying Thank You to the sky. Not that the rain put out this particular fire, but, you know, without the occasional drizzles we had all that day keeping the city damp, there wouldn't have been much of New York left.

Right then, I had no idea that what was going on was limited to New York City. I remember wondering, as I took shelter in a hallway across the street, if all this was some kind of sneak enemy attack. And I wasn't the only one thinking that, as I found out later. I mean the nationwide alert, and the hotline, and Moscow frantically trying to get in touch with its delegate at the U.N. I just read about the treaty the Russian delegate signed that day with the delegates from Paraguay and Upper Volta. No wonder the Security Council had to declare everything that happened at the U.N. in those twenty-four hours null and void!

When the rain stopped, I began to work my way north again. There was another crowd in front of a big Macy's window on 34th Street near Sixth Avenue. A half-dressed guy and a naked girl were on a couch—the window display was advertising furniture that week—and they were making it.

I stood in the middle of all those trance-like stares and I just couldn't pull myself away. A man next to me with a good leather briefcase kept murmuring, "Beautiful, beautiful. A pair of lemon-green snowflakes." Then the Herald Square clock, the one where those two statues with hammers bang away at a great big bell, that clock began to sound off the strokes of twelve noon. I shook myself and pushed out of the crowd. The guy and the girl were still making it.

A woman on the edge of the crowd, a very pleasant, gray-haired woman in a black dress, was going from person to person and taking their money away. She'd take wallets away from the men and little money purses out of the women's pocketbooks, and she'd drop them in a large paper shopping bag. If anyone made the least sign of annoyance while she robbed him, she'd leave him alone and go on to the next one. The shopping bag was hanging kind of heavy.

She suddenly realized I was watching her, and she looked up. Like I said, we non-zombies recognized each other in a flash all that day. She blushed a deep blush, all the way to the roots of her gray hair. Then she turned and ran away at top speed, her heels going clack-clack-clack, the pink slip under her black dress flashing up and swirling around. She held on to the shopping bag as she ran.

The things people must have been pulling that day! Like those two Hoboken guys who heard on the radio that Manhattan had gone crazy. They put on a couple of gas masks and drove through the Holland Tunnel—this was maybe an hour before it was closed to all vehicular traffic—and went down to Wall Street to rob themselves a bank. They weren't even carrying weapons: they figured they'd just walk in and fill their empty suitcases with cash. But what they walked into was a street gun duel between two cops from a radio car who'd been hating each other for months. I saw a lot of things like that which I can't remember now while I'm testifying.

But I do recall how the tempo seemed to be picking up. I'd headed into Broadway, giving up completely on the idea of going to the office. There were a lot more traffic accidents and a lot more people sitting on curbs and smiling into space. And going through the upper thirties, I saw at least three people jump out of windows. They came down in a long blur, *zonk-splash,* and nobody paid any attention to them.

Every block or so, I'd have to pull away from someone trying to tell me about God or the universe or how pretty the sunlight was. I decided to, I don't know, kind of withdraw from the scene for a while. I went into a luncheonette near 42nd Street to get a bite to eat.

Two countermen were sitting on the floor, holding hands and crying their hearts out. Five girls, secretary-types, were bent over them like in a football huddle. The girls were chanting, "Don't buy at Ohrbach's, Ohrbach's is expensive. Don't buy at Ohrbach's, Ohrbach's is expensive."

I was hungry: by this time that sort of thing didn't even make me sweat. I went behind the counter, found packaged bread and cheese, and I made myself a couple of sandwiches. I ignored a bloody knife lying near the bread-board. Then I sat down at a table near the window and opened a couple of my cans of soda.

There were things to see—the tempo was picking up all the time. A schoolteacher trotting by with a wooden classroom pointer in her hand, waving it and singing "Little Red Wing." Behind her about twenty or thirty pudgy eight-year-olds carrying bus stop signs, one bus stop sign to every two or three kids. An old woman trundling half a dozen dead-looking cats in a brand-new, bright green wheelbarrow. A big crowd marching along and singing Christmas carols. Then another, smaller crowd singing something else, I don't know, a foreign national anthem, I guess. But, you know, a lot of singing, a lot of people suddenly doing things together.

When I was ready to leave, another light drizzle started, so I had to sit tight for an hour or so more. The rain didn't stop the five secretary-types, though. They snake-danced out into it, yelling, "Everybody—let's go to Fifth Avenue!" They left the crying countermen behind.

Finally, it was clear and I started off again. All over the street there were clumps of people, arms locked, yelling and singing and dancing. I didn't like it one bit: it felt like the beginnings of a riot. At the Automat near Duffy Square, there was a bunch of them spread out on the sidewalk, looking as if they were having an orgy. But when I got closer, I saw they were only lying there caressing each other's faces.

That's where I met those newlyweds who'll be testifying after me—Dr. and Mrs. Patrick Scannell from Kosackie, Indiana. They were standing outside the Automat whispering to each other. When they saw I didn't have the pop-eyed, zombie look, they fell all over me.

They'd come into New York late the night before and registered at a hotel. Being, you know, honeymooners, they hadn't climbed out of the sack until almost two in the afternoon. That's what saved them. Months before, when they'd been planning their honeymoon, they'd bought tickets to a Broadway show, a matinee, Shakespeare's *Macbeth*, and they'd charged out of the hotel room fast not to miss it. They'd run out without breakfast or anything, just a candy bar Mrs. Scannell was carrying in her purse.

And from the way they described it, that production of *Macbeth* was like nothing else anybody ever saw on land or sea. Four actors on the stage, only one of them in costume, all of them jabbering away in speeches from *Macbeth, Hamlet, A Streetcar Named Desire, Oedipus Rex,* and *Who's Afraid of Virginia Woolf?* "It was like an anthology of the theater," Mrs. Scannell said. "And not at all badly done. It hung together in a fascinating way, really."

That reminds me. I understand a publishing house is bringing out a book of the poetry and prose written in New York City on this one crazy LSD day. It's a book I sure as hell intend to buy.

But interesting or fascinating or what, that oddball show in a professional Broadway theater scared the pants off them. And the audience, what there was of it, scared them even more. They'd walked out and gone looking around, wondering who dropped the bomb.

I shared my soda with them, using up the last of the six-pack. And I told them how I'd figured out it was in the water. Right away. Dr. Scannell—he was a dentist, I found out, not a medical doctor—right away, he snapped his fingers and said, "Damn it—LSD!" I bet that makes him the first man in the country to guess it, right?

"LSD, LSD," he repeated. "It's colorless, odorless, tasteless. One ounce contains 300,000 full doses. A pound or so in the water supply and— Oh, my God! Those magazine articles gave someone the idea!"

The three of us stood there drinking our soda and looking at the people screaming, the people chuckling, the people doing all kinds of crazy things. There were mobs now heading east and yelling, "Everybody to Fifth Avenue. Everybody to Fifth Avenue for the big parade!" It was like a kind of magic had spread the word, as if the whole population of Manhattan had gotten the same idea at the same time.

I didn't want to argue with a professional man, you know, but I'd also read a lot of those magazine articles on LSD. I said I hadn't read about people doing some of the things I'd seen that day. I mean, I said, take those crowds chanting like that?

Dr. Scannell said that was because of the cumulative feedback effect. The *what?* I said. So he explained how people had this stuff inside them, making them wide open psychologically to begin with, and all around them the air was full of other LSD reactions, going back and forth, building up and up. That was the cumulative feedback effect.

Then he talked about drug purity and drug dosage—how in this situation there was no control over how much anyone got. "Worst of all," he said, "there's been no psychological preparation. Under the circumstances, anything could happen." He stared up and down the street at the crowds going chant-chant-chant, and he shivered.

They decided to get some packaged food and drink, then go back to their hotel room and hole up until it was all over. They invited me along, but, I don't know, by this time I was too interested to go into hiding; I wanted to see the thing through to the end. And I was too scared of fires to go and sit in a fourteenth-floor hotel room.

When I left them, I followed the crowds that were going east as if they all had an appointment together. There were thick mobs on both sides of Fifth; across the avenue, I could see mobs of people coming west toward it. Everyone was yelling about the big parade.

And there really was a parade, that's the funny part. I don't know how it got organized, or by whom, but it was the high point, the last word, the ultimate touch, to that damn day. What a parade!

It was coming up Fifth Avenue against the one-way traffic arrows—although by this time there was no traffic anywhere—it was coming up in bursts of fifty or a hundred people, and in between each burst there'd be a thin line of stragglers that sometimes wandered off and got mixed in with the people on the sidewalk. Some of the signs they carried were smeary and wet from being recently painted; some of them looked very old as if they'd been pulled out of a trunk or a storage bin. Most of the paraders were chanting slogans or singing songs.

Who the hell can remember all the organizations in that parade? I mean, you know, the Ancient Order of Hibernians, the CCNY Alumni Association, the Untouchables of Avenue B, Alcoholics Anonymous, the NAACP, the Anti-Vivisection League, the Washington Heights Democratic Club, the B'nai B'rith, the West 49th Street Pimps and Prostitutes Mutual Legal Fund, the Hungarian Freedom Fighters, the Save-the-Village Committee, the Police Holy Name Society, the Daughters of Bilitis, the Our Lady of Pompeii Championship Basketball Team. All of them.

And they were mixed in together. Pro-Castro Cubans and anti-Castro Cubans marching along side by side, singing the same mournful Spanish song. Three cops, one of them without shoes, with the group of college students carrying placards, "Draft Beer, Not People." A young girl wearing a sandwich sign on which was scribbled in black crayon, "Legalize Rape—Now!" right in the middle of a bunch of old men and old women who were singing "Jay Lovestone is our leader, We shall not be moved . . ." The County Kerry band playing "Deutschland über Alles" followed by the big crowd of men in business suits, convention badges in their lapels, who were teaching two tiny Italian nuns to sing, "Happy birthday, Marcia Tannenbaum, happy birthday to you." The nuns were giggling and hiding their faces in their hands. And behind them, carrying a huge white banner that stretched right across Fifth Avenue, two grizzled-looking, grim-faced Negro men about seventy or eighty years old. The banner read: "Re-elect Woodrow Wilson. He kept us out of war!"

All through the parade, there were people with little paint cans and brushes busily painting lines up the avenue. Green lines, purple lines, even white lines. One well-dressed man was painting a thin red line in the middle of the marchers. I thought he was a Communist until he painted past me and I heard him singing, "God save our gracious queen. . . ." as he walked backward working away with the brush. When his paint ran out, he joined a bunch from Local 802 of the Musicians Union who had come along holding up signs and yelling, "Abolish Folk Songs! Abolish All Forms of Rock! Save Tin Pan Alley!"

It was the best parade I ever saw. I watched it until the Army paratroops who'd landed in Central Park came down and began herding us to the Special Rehabilitation Centers they'd set up.

And then, damn it, it was all over.

I don't do bawdy.

No, I lie.

I don't do bawdy in public. But in private...that's a different story.

So there I was, at a friend's apartment in New York, and she a writer of some renown in literary circles, and she tells me she is doing a short story for a new feminist anthology called (I kid you not) *Dick for a Day*.

And she challenged me. Doubled dared. Well, she looked at me funny, which was the same thing.

So I went home and thought, I can do this! But sometimes making leaps like that are scary.

So I wrote in a mode I was familiar with—the fairy tale. "Dick W" is what came out. The anthologist bought the story. Without a single change. Honest. I'm a writer. Would I lie?

—Jane Yolen

31

Dick W. and His Pussy, or Tess and Her Adequate Dick

JANE YOLEN

~~~~~~~~

O NCE UPON A TIME—I say that up front so you will know this is a fairy tale and not just another wish-fullfilment fantasy—there was a boy named Adequate Dick. Unfortunate, but true. His mother, being no better than she should have been, but a beauty nonetheless, named him after that which had brought her much fame though little fortune.

When she saw that having a child narrowed her client base, she abandoned him. Simply dropped him off at the nearest dock: Whittington Pier. If she had dropped him *off* the dock instead of *at* it, this story would have been considerably shorter.

Adequate Dick knocked about the port for quite some time, about fifteen years to be exact, eventually taking the dock's name as his own after much pier counseling. He was a handsome boy; in that he took after his mother. But in all other ways he was like his dad. Adequate.

At last one day he was hired by a kind merchant who was always on the lookout for cheap labor.

"Will you come and work for me, Adequate Dick Whittington Pier?" asked the merchant.

"I will," said Adequate Dick.

They shook hands but signed no papers. In those days no one could write, though most had handshakes down pat.

Now the boy quickly came to the attention of the merchant's pretty daughter, Tess, who had a fondness for lower-class Dicks. She gave him money and considerable other favors which Adequate Dick, being well named, and handsome, but not particularly favored in the brain department, took as a compliment.

He took a few other things as well: her silver ring, a glass vase, a small nude portrait done on ivory. He didn't take Tess's virtue. She had none left for him to take.

The merchant knew that cheap labor has a way of drifting, and so to keep his servants happy and at home, he gave them certain allowances. He allowed them once a year to give him something of theirs to take on his voyage, something the merchant might sell to make their fortunes. None of them ever got rich this way, of course. But, as if it were a sixteenth-century lottery, the chance of becoming millionaires overnight kept all the servants trying and at home. *Very* trying and *quite* at home.

Adequate Dick had nothing to give the merchant but a cat named Pussy (and the things he had taken from Tess, but those he would not part with). But when it was his turn, he handed over his pet without a thought. *Pussy could make my fortune*, he thought, thereby proving himself his mother's boy. The vegetable does not fall very far from the tree.

Tess could have warned him that his chances for a fortune were slim at best. But she didn't want him leaving anyway. *Why waste a perfectly adequate Dick*, was her motto.

So far—I can hear you saying—this sounds like a folk tale, what with the merchant and his pretty daughter, a servant and his cat. Or maybe it sounds like the plot of an eighteenth-century picaresque novel. Or a grainy, naughty black-and-white French film. But how can it be a *fairy* tale? It has no fairies in it. Or magic.

And you would be right. Right—but impatient.

Wait for it.

The merchant's ship ran aground on a small island kingdom and he was thought lost to the world. The household, like a boat, began to founder; the servants to look for other work. Adequate Dick, being last hired was first fired, so he went off toward the familiar docks to seek his fortune. Without—of course—his Pussy. Either one.

So what of Tess?

She tried to take over her father's firm. She was the merchant's only child, after all. But the men who worked for her complained.

"She has," they said, "no adequate Dick. And who can run a business without one?" It was true. Her Adequate Dick had gone back to his piers.

Then a miracle!

You must allow me a miracle.

Surely miracles will do in a tale when magic is nowhere to be found. Miracles *are* magic processed by faith and a lack of a scientific imagination.

The merchant returned home unexpectedly, but just in time it seems, with much gold in his ship's hold. The island kingdom where he had run aground had itself been overrun by rats. That he had Pussy to sell was a great fortune. Or a miracle. Or a serendipity. Or a fairy tale. Or the kind of luck a Donald Trump would envy. (Speaking of adequate Dicks.)

So he sold Dick's Pussy. But little did he know the consequences of such a sale. For miracles are not singular. They lean on one another, like art on art. No sooner was Pussy sold, than Tess—far away in London—found herself changed beyond measure. That is—she could measure the change. It occurred between her legs.

Was she surprised? Not really. It was merely form following function.

The merchant returned home rich beyond counting.

"Where is that Adequate Dick?" he asked when he entered the door.

"Oh, father!" Tess cried. "He has gone. But something rare has occurred. Something better than Adequate."

Her father did not listen. He was not a man to believe in the miraculous beyond the swelling of a purse. "Better get him back then," her father said. "He has wealth and treasure."

As do I, thought Tess, pausing to spit accurately by the doorstoop. Then she ran down the road to call Adequate Dick home, crying: "Turn again Whittington Pier." She had never called him by his first name outside of her bedroom.

He heard her and he turned.

And returned.

Now that he was rich, Tess could marry him, though, given the circumstances, she never slept with him again. He was no longer of the lower classes and he was—after all—only an *adequate* Dick.

She had better.

When Mike Resnick contacted me about being in this book, I got in a quandary. I don't write *stories* to be funny; it's the non-fiction I write for *that* effect. There's humor in my serious stories (*that's* a lot like real life—funny stuff happens in the middle of battles and other life-and-death situations). Thurber, Damon Runyan, and those guys and girls know that, which is why their stuff has lasted. (There's *nothing* so dead as topical humor from the '20s and '30s....)

But then I thought: I've written one story where a pretty humorous fellow gets caught up smack dab in the middle of the biggest crisis ever faced (in the nineteenth century, in literature anyway) by mankind. Maybe that will fill the bill....

A short, compressed background about the writing of "Night of the Cooters":

Late August 1985: I'd been fishing for a month in Colorado with the late, great, sorely missed Chad Oliver. The only reading material I'd taken to the cabin was Frank McConnell's *The Critical Edition of War of the Worlds*. I knew I had to write *this* story. We left *rising trout* to make the two-and-a-half-day drive back to Austin—because that's where the NASFIC (the big alternate convention held in the U.S. when the World SF Convention is overseas) was—and Chad was Toastmaster and I was on many, many panels AND I had to read a new story....

We got in Wednesday morning to find that 1) my reading was 3 P.M. *Thursday* 2) my most recent ex-girlfriend was in the hospital for emergency surgery and 3) my housemate's fourteen-year-old dog had *just* died. ("It's a lot like having bees live in your hat."—The Firesign Theater)

Well, I helped out my inconsolable housemate as best I could; I went to the hospital around 8 P.M.—lots of people

from the convention were there to see my friend. She had
to make Gardner Dozois leave the room as he was making
her laugh so hard she thought she'd busted her stitches.
Eventually I got home and got what I laughingly refer to as
"a little sleep."

Seven A.M. Thursday I got up and started writing *this*.
At some point I took a shower, at some point I got a ride
to the convention; I borrowed somebody's room around 2 P.M.
(I *think* it was Pat Cadigan's, although that may have been
another convention, another story. . . .) to write on that
little desk-thing nobody uses in hotel rooms. I finished the
story (quite literally) coming off the elevator at 3 P.M.,
where I read it to about 150 people. (That was twenty years
ago, when I was too old for such shenanigans; I'm way too
old for it now, though I occasionally find myself *still* doing
it. . . .)

A few days after the convention, after I got some *real*
sleep, I typed it up and sent it off to Ellen Datlow at
Omni; she bought it and published it. It was up for a Nebula
or Hugo or something, lost handily, and was the title of my
third collection.

When (quite independently, years later) Kevin J. Anderson
came up with *War of the Worlds: Global Dispatches* (published
on the hundredth anniversary of *War of the Worlds*), he did
me the signal honor of picking this up as the *only* reprint
in what was otherwise an original anthology.

I hope this one's funny enough to keep company with the
other stories collected around it here. . . .

—Howard Waldrop

Night of the Cooters

HOWARD WALDROP

This story is in memory of Slim Pickens (1919–1983).

SHERIFF LINDLEY WAS ASLEEP ON the toilet in the Pachuco County courthouse when someone started pounding on the door.

"Bert! Bert!" the voice yelled as the sheriff jerked awake.

"Gol Dang!" said the lawman. The Waco newspaper slid off his lap onto the floor.

He pulled his pants up with one hand and the toilet chain on the waterbox overhead with the other. Chief Deputy Sweets stood before him, a complaint slip in his hand.

"Dang it, Sweets!" said the sheriff. "I told you never to bother me in there! It's the hottest Thursday in the history of Texas! You woke me up out of a hell of a dream!"

The deputy waited, wiping sweat from his forehead. There were two big circles, like half-moons, under the arms of his blue chambray shirt.

"I was fourteen, maybe fifteen years old, and I was a Aztec or Mixtec or somethin'," said the sheriff. "Anyways, I was buck-naked, and I was standin' with one foot up on one wall, and they was presentin' me to Moctezuma. I was real proud, and the sun was shinin', but it was real still and cool down there in the Valley of Mexico. I looks up at the grandstand, and there's Moctezuma and all his high muckety-mucks with feathers and stuff hangin' off 'em, and more gold than a circus wagon. And there was these other guys, conquistadors and stuff, with beards and rusty helmets, and I-talian priests with crosses you coulda barred a livery-stable door with. One of Moctezuma's men was explainin' how we was fixin' to play ball for the gods and things.

"I knew in my dream I was captain of my team. I had a name that

39

sounded like a bird fart in Aztec talk, and they mentioned it and the name of the captain of the other team, too. Well, everything was goin' all right, and I was prouder and prouder, until the guy doing the talkin' let slip that whichever team won was gonna be paraded around Tenoch-titlán and given women and food and stuff like that, and then tomorrow A.M. they was gonna be cut up and simmered real slow and served up with chilis and onions and tomatoes.

"Well, you never seed such a fight as broke out then! They was a-yellin', and a priest was swingin' a cross, and spears and axes were flyin' around me like it was an Irish funeral.

"Next thing I know, you're a-bangin' on the door and wakin' me up and bringin' me back to Pachuco County! What the hell do you want?"

"Dr. De Spain wants you to come over to his place right away."

"He does, huh?"

"That's right, Sheriff. He says he's got some miscreants he wants you to arrest."

"Everybody else around here has desperadoes. De Spain has miscre-ants. I'll be so danged glad when the town council gets around to movin' the city limits fifty foot to the other side of this place, I won't know what to do! Every time anybody farts too loud, he calls me."

Lindley and Sweets walked back to the office at the other end of the courthouse. Four deputies sat around with their feet propped up on desks. They rocked back and forth respectfully and watched as the sher-iff went to the hat pegs.

On one of the dowels was a sweat-stained hat with turned-down points at front and back. The sidebrims were twisted in curves. The hat angled up to end in a crown that looked like the business end of a Phillips screwdriver. Under the hat was a holster with a Navy Colt .41 that looked like someone had used it to drive railroad spikes all the way to the Continental Divide. Leaning under them was a 10-gauge pump shotgun with the barrel sawed off just in front of the foregrip.

On the other peg was an immaculate new round-top Stetson of brown felt with a snakeskin band half as wide as a fingernail running around it.

The deputies stared.

Lindley picked up the Stetson.

The deputies rocked back in their chairs and resumed yakking.

"Hey, Sweets!" said the sheriff at the door. "Change that damn calendar on your desk! It ain't Wednesday, August seventeenth; it's Thursday, August eighteenth."

"Sure thing, Sheriff."

Lindley went down the courthouse steps onto the rock wall. He passed the two courthouse cannons he and the deputies fired off three times a year—March second, July Fourth, and Robert E. Lee's birthday. Each cannon had a pyramid of ornamental cannonballs in front of it.

Waves of heat came off the cannons, the ammunition, the telegraph wires overhead, and, in the distance, the rails of the twice-a-day spur line from Waxahachie.

The town was as still as a rusty shovel. The 45-star United States flag hung like an old, dried dishrag from its stanchion. From looking at the town you couldn't tell the nation was about to go to war with Spain over Cuba, that China was full of unrest, and that five thousand miles away a crazy German count was making airships.

Lindley had seen enough changes in his sixty-eight years. He had been born in the bottom of an Ohio keelboat in 1830; was in Bloody Kansas when John Brown came through; fought for the Confederacy, first as a corporal, then as a sergeant major, from Chickamauga to the Wilderness; and had seen more skirmishes with hostile tribes than most people would ever read about in a dozen Wide-Awake Library novels.

It was as hot as under an upside-down washpot on a tin shed roof. The sheriff's wagon horse seemed asleep as it trotted, head down, puffs hanging in the still air like brown shrubs made of dust around its hooves.

There were ten, maybe a dozen people in sight in the whole town. Those few on the street moved like molasses, only as far as they had to, from shade to shade. Anybody with sense was asleep at home with wet towels hung over the windows, or sitting as still as possible with a funeral-parlor fan in their hands.

The sheriff licked his big droopy mustache and hoped nobody nodded to him. He was already too hot and tired to tip his hat. He leaned back in the wagon seat and straightened his bad leg (a Yankee souvenir) against the boot board. His gray suit was like a boiling shroud. He was too hot to reach up and flick the dust off his new hat.

He had become sheriff in the special election three years ago, to fill out Sanderson's term when the governor had appointed the former attorney general. Nothing much had happened in the county since then.

"Gee-hup," he said.

The horse trotted three steps before going back into its walking trance.

Sheriff Lindley didn't bother her again until he pulled up at De Spain's big place and said, "Whoa, there."

The black man who did everything for De Spain opened the gate.

"Sheriff," he said.

"Luther," said Lindley, nodding his head.

"Around back, Mr. Lindley."

There were two boys—raggedy town kids, the Strother boy and one of the poor Chisums—sitting on the edge of the well. The Chisum kid had been crying.

De Spain was hot and bothered. He was only half dressed, with suit pants, white shirt, vest, and stockings on but no shoes or coat. He hadn't maccasered his hair yet. He was pointing a rifle with a barrel big as a drainpipe at the two boys.

"Here they are, Sheriff. Luther saw them down in the orchard. I'm sure he saw them stealing my peaches, but he wouldn't tell me. I knew something was up when he didn't put my clothes in the usual place next to the window where I like to dress. So I looked out and saw them. They had half a potato sack full by the time I crept around the house and caught them. I want to charge them with trespass and thievery."

"Well, well," said the sheriff, looking down at the sackful of evidence. He turned and pointed toward the black man.

"You want me to charge Luther here with collusion and abetting a crime?" Neither Lindley's nor Luther's faces betrayed any emotion.

"Of course not," said De Spain. "I've told him time and time again he's too soft on filchers. If this keeps happening, I'll hire another boy who'll enforce my orchard with buckshot, if need be."

De Spain was a young man with eyes like a weimaraner's. As Deputy Sweets said, he had the kind of face you couldn't hit just once. He owned half the town of Pachuco City. The other half paid him rent.

"Get in the wagon, boys," said the sheriff.

"Aren't you going to cover them with your weapon?" asked De Spain.

"You should know by now, Mr. De Spain, that when I wear this suit I ain't got nothin' but a three-shot pocket pistol on me. Besides"—he looked at the two boys in the wagon bed—"they know if they give me any guff, I'll jerk a bowknot in one of 'em and bite the other'n's ass off."

"I don't think there's any need for profanity," said De Spain.

"It's too damn hot for anything else," said Lindley. "I'll clamp 'em in the *juzgado* and have Sweets run the papers over to your office tomorrow mornin'."

"I wish you'd take them out one of the rural roads somewhere and flail the tar out of them to teach them about property rights," said De Spain.

The sheriff tipped his hat back and looked up at De Spain's three-story house with the parlor so big you could hold a rodeo in it. Then he looked back at the businessman, who'd finally lowered the rifle.

"Well, I know you'd like that," said Lindley. "I seem to remember that most of the fellers who wrote the Constitution were pretty well off, but some of the other rich people thought they had funny ideas. One of the things they were smart about was the Bill of Rights. You know, Mr. De Spain, the reason they put in the Bill of Rights wasn't to give all the little people without jobs or money a lot of breaks with the law. Why they put that in there was for if the people without jobs or money got upset and turned on *them*, they could ask for the same justice everybody else got."

De Spain looked at him with disgust. "I've never liked your homespun parables, and I don't like the way you sheriff this county."

"I don't doubt that," said Lindley. "You've got sixteen months, three weeks, and two days to find somebody to run against me. Good evening, Mr. De Spain."

He climbed onto the wagon seat.

"Luther."

"Sheriff."

He turned the horse around as De Spain and the black man took the sack of peaches through the kitchen door into the house.

The sheriff stopped the wagon near the railroad tracks where the houses began to deviate from the vertical.

"Jody. Billy Roy." He looked at them with eyes like chips of flint. "You're the dumbest pair of squirts that ever lived in Pachuco City! First off, half those peaches were still green. You'd have got bellyaches, and your mothers would have beaten you within an inch of your lives and given you so many doses of Black Draught you'd shit over tin-rail fences all week.

"Now listen to what I'm sayin', cause I'm only gonna say it once. If I ever hear of *either* of you stealing anything, anywhere in this county, I'm going to put you *both* in school."

"No, Sheriff, please, no!" Their eyes were wide as horses'.

"I'll put you in there every morning and come and get you out seven long hours later, and I'll have the judge issue a writ keeping you there till you're *twelve years old.* And if you try to run away, I'll follow you to the ends of the earth with Joe Sweeper's bloodhounds, and I'll bring you back."

They were crying now.

"You git home."

They were running before they left the wagon.

Somewhere between the second piece of cornbread and the third helping of snap beans, a loud rumble shook the ground.

"Goodness' Sakes!" said Elsie, his wife of twenty-three years. "What can that be?"

"I expect that's Elmer, out by the creek. He came in last week and asked if he could blast on the place. I told him it didn't matter to me as long as he did it between sunup and sundown and didn't blow his whole family of rug-rats and yard-apes up.

"Jake, down at the mercantile, said Elmer bought enough dynamite to blow up Fort Worth if he'd a mind to—all but the last three sticks in the store. Jake had to reorder for stump-blowin' time."

"Whatever could he want with all that much?"

"Oh, that damn fool has the idea the vein in that old mine what played out in '83 might start up again on his property. He got to talking with the Smith boy, oh, hell, what's his name—?"

"Leo?"

"Yeah, Leo, the one that studies down in Austin, learns about stars and rocks and all that shit...."

"Watch your language, Bertram!"

"Oh, hell! Anyway, that boy must have put a bug up Elmer's butt about that—"

"Bertram!" said Elsie, putting down her knife and fork.

"Oh, hell, anyway. I guess Elmer'll blow the side off his hill and bury his house before he's through."

The sheriff was reading a week-old copy of the *Waco Herald* while Elsie washed up the dishes. He sure missed *Brann's Iconoclast*, the paper he used to read, which had ceased publication when the editor was gunned down on a Waco street by an irate Baptist four months before.

The Waco paper had a little squib from London, England, about there having been explosions on Mars ten nights in a row last month, and whether it was a sign of life on that planet or some unusual volcanic activity.

Sheriff Lindley had never given volcanoes (except those in the Valley of Mexico) or the planet Mars much thought.

Hooves came pounding down the road. He put down his paper. "*Sheriff, Sheriff!*" he said in a high, mocking voice.

He strode to the door and opened it.

"Tommy, what's all the hooraw?"

"Jimmy. Sheriff, something fell on our pasture, tore it all to hell, knocked down *the tree*, killed some of our cattle, Tommy can't find his dog, Mother sent—"

"Hold on! Something fell on your place? Like what?"

"I don't know! Like a big rock, only sparks was flyin' off it, and it roared and blew up! It's at the north end of the place, and—"

"Elsie, run over and get Sweets and the boys. Have them go get Leo Smith if he ain't gone back to college yet. Sounds to me like Pachuco County's got its first shootin' star. Hold on, Jimmy, I'm comin' right along. We'll take my wagon; you can leave your pony here."

"Oh, hurry, Sheriff! It's big! It killed our cattle and tore up the fences—"

"Well, I can't arrest it for *that*," said Lindley. He put on his Stetson. "And I thought Elmer'd blowed hisself up. My, my, ain't never seen a shooting star before...."

"Damn if it don't look like somebody threw a locomotive through here," said the sheriff.

The Atkinson place used to have a sizable hill and the tallest tree in the county on it. Now it had half a hill and a big stump and beyond, a huge crater. Dirt had been thrown up in a ten-foot-high pile around it.

There was a huge, rounded, gray object buried in the dirt and torn caliche at the bottom. Waves of heat rose from it, and gray ash, like old charcoal, fell off it into the shimmering pit.

Half the town was riding out in wagons and on horseback as the news spread. The closest neighbors were walking over in the twilight, wearing their go-visiting clothes.

"Well, well," said the sheriff, looking down. "So that's what a meteor looks like."

Leo Smith was already in the pit, walking around.

"I figured you'd be here sooner or later," said Lindley.

"Hello, Sheriff," said Leo. "It's still too hot to touch. Part of a cow's buried under the back end."

The sheriff looked over at the Atkinson family. "You folks is danged lucky. That thing coulda come down smack on your house or, what's worse, your barn. What time it fall?"

"Straight up and down six o'clock," said Mrs. Atkinson. "We was settin' down to supper. I saw it out of the corner of my eye; then all tarnation came down. Rocks must have been falling for ten minutes!"

"It's pretty spectacular, Sheriff," said Leo. "I'm going into town to telegraph off to the professors at the University. They'll sure want to look at this."

"Any reason other than general curiosity?" asked Lindley.

"I've only seen pictures and handled little bitty parts of one," said Leo. "But it doesn't look usual. They're generally like big rocks, all stone or iron. The outside of this one's soft and crumbly. Ashy, too."

There was a slight pop and a stove-cooling noise from the thing.

"Well, you can come back into town with me if you want to. Hey, Sweets!"

The chief deputy came over.

"A couple of you boys better stay here tonight, keep people from falling in the hole. I guess if Leo's gonna wire the University, you better keep anybody from knockin' chunks off it. It'll probably get pretty crowded. If I was the Atkinsons, I'd start chargin' a nickel a look."

"Sure thing, Sheriff."

Kerosene lanterns and carriage lights were moving toward the Atkinsons' in the coming darkness.

"I'll be out here early tomorrow mornin' to take another gander. I gotta serve a process paper on old Theobald before he lights out for his chores. If I sent one o' you boys, he'd as soon shoot you as say howdy."

"Sure thing, Sheriff."

He and Leo and Jimmy Atkinson got in the wagon and rode off toward the quiet lights of town far away.

There was a new smell in the air.

The sheriff noticed it as he rode toward the Atkinson ranch by the south road early the next morning. There was an odor like when something goes wrong at the telegraph office.

Smoke was curling up from the pasture. Maybe there was a scrub fire started from the heat of the falling star.

He topped the last rise. Before him lay devastation the likes of which he hadn't seen since the retreat from Atlanta.

"Great Gawd Almighty!" he said.

There were dead horses and charred wagons all around. The ranch house was untouched, but the barn was burned to the ground. There were crisscrossed lines of burnt grass that looked like they'd been painted with a tar brush.

He saw no bodies anywhere. Where was Sweets? Where was Luke, the other deputy? Where had the people from the wagons gone? What had happened?

Lindley looked at the crater. There was a shiny rod sticking out of it, with something round on the end. From here it looked like one of those carnival acts where a guy spins a plate on the end of a dowel rod, only this glinted like metal in the early sun. As he watched, a small cloud of green steam rose above it from the pit.

He saw a motion behind an old tree uprooted by a storm twelve years ago. It was Sweets. He was yelling and waving the sheriff back.

Lindley rode his horse into a small draw, then came up into the open.

There was movement over at the crater. He thought he saw something. Reflected sunlight flashed by his eyes, and he thought he saw a rounded silhouette. He heard a noise like sometimes gets into bobwire on a windy day.

He heard a humming sound then, smelled the electric smell real strong. Fire started a few feet from him, out of nowhere, and moved toward him.

Then his horse exploded.

The air was an inferno, he was thrown spinning—

He must have blacked out. He had no memory of what went next. When he came to, he was running as fast as he ever had toward the uprooted tree.

Fire jumped all around. Luke was shooting over tree roots with his pistol. He ducked. A long section of the trunk was washed over with flames and sparks.

Lindley dove behind the root tangle.

"What the ding-dong is goin' on?" he asked as he tried to catch his breath. He still had his new hat on, but his britches and coat were singed and smoking.

"God damn, Bert! I don't know," said Sweets, leaning around Luke. "We was out here all night; it was a regular party; most of the time we was on the lip up there. Maybe thirty or forty people comin' and goin' all the time. We was all talking and hoorawing, and then we heard something about an hour ago. We looked down, and I'll be damned if the whole top of that thing didn't come off like a Mason jar!

"We was watching, and these damn things started coming out—they looked like big old leather balls, big as horses, with snakes all out the front—"

"What?"

"Snakes. Yeah, tentacles Leo called them, like an octy-puss. Leo'd come back from town and was here when them boogers came out. Martians he said they was, things from Mars. They had big old eyes, big as your head! Everybody was pushing and shoving; then one of them pulled out one of them gun things, real slow like, and he just started burning up everything in sight.

"We all ran for whatever cover we could find—it took 'em a while to get up the dirt pile. They killed horses, dogs, anything they could see.

Fire was everywhere. They use that thing just like the volunteer firemen use them water hoses in Waco!"

"Where's Leo?"

Sweets pointed to the draw that ran diagonally to the west. "We watched awhile, finally figured they couldn't line up on the ditch all the way to the rise. Leo and the others got away up the draw—he was gonna telegraph the University about it. The bunch that got away was supposed to send people out to the town road to warn people. You probably would have run into them if you hadn't been coming from Theobald's place.

"Anyway, soon as them things saw people were gettin' away, they got mad as hornets. That's when they lit up the Atkinsons' barn."

A flash of fire leapt in the roots of the tree, jumped back thirty feet into the burnt grass behind them, then moved back and forth in a curtain of sparks.

"Man, that's what I call a real smoke pole," said Luke.

"Well," Lindley said. "This just won't do. These things done attacked citizens in my jurisdiction, and they killed my horse."

He turned to Luke.

"Be real careful, and get back to town, get the posse up. Telegraph the Rangers and tell 'em to burn leather gettin' here. Then get ahold of Skip Whitworth and have him bring out The Gun."

Skip Whitworth sat behind the tree trunk and pulled the cover from the six-foot rifle at his side. Skip was in his late fifties. He had been a sniper in the War for Southern Independence when he had been in his twenties. He had once shot a Yankee general just as the officer was bringing a forkful of beans up to his mouth. When the fork got there, there was only some shoulders and a gullet for the beans to drop into.

That had been from a mile and a half away, from sixty feet up a pine tree.

The rifle was an .80-caliber octagonal-barrel breechloader that used two and a half ounces of powder and a percussion cap the size of a jawbreaker for each shot. It had a telescopic sight running the entire length of the barrel.

"They're using that thing on the end of that stick to watch us," said Lindley. "I had Sweets jump around, and every time he did, one of those cooters would come up with that fire gun and give us what-for."

Skip said nothing. He loaded his rifle, which had a breechblock lever the size of a crowbar on it, then placed another round—cap, paper cartridge, ball—next to him.

He drew a bead and pulled the trigger. It sounded like dynamite had gone off in their ears.

The wobbling pole snapped in two halfway up. The top end flopped back into the pit.

There was a scrabbling noise above the whirring from the earthen lip. Something round came up.

Skip had smoothly opened the breech, put in the ball, torn the cartridge with his teeth, put in the cap, closed the action, pulled back the hammer, and sighted before the shape reached the top of the dirt.

Metal glinted in the middle of the dark thing.

Skip fired.

There was a *squeech*; the whole top of the round thing opened up; it spun around and backward, things in its front working like a daddy longlegs thrown on a roaring stove.

Skip loaded again. There were flashes of light from the crater. Something came up shooting, fire leaping like hot sparks from a blacksmith's anvil, the air full of flames and smoke.

Skip fired again.

The fire gun flew up in the air. Snakes twisted, writhed, disappeared.

It was very quiet for a few seconds.

Then there was the renewed whining of machinery and noises like a pile driver, the sounds of filing and banging. Steam came up over the crater lip.

"Sounds like a steel foundry in there," said Sweets.

"I don't like it one bit," said Bert. "Be danged if I'm gonna let 'em get the drop on us. Can you keep them down?"

"How many are there?" asked Skip.

"Luke and Sweets saw four or five before all hell broke loose this morning. Probably more of 'em than that was inside."

"I've got three more shots. If they poke up, I'll get 'em."

"I'm going to town, then out to Elmer's. Sweets'll stay with you awhile. If you run outta bullets, light up out the draw. I don't want nobody killed. Sweets, keep an eye out for the posse. I'm telegraphing the

Rangers again, then goin' to get Elmer and his dynamite. We're gonna fix their little red wagon for certain."

"Sure thing, Sheriff."

The sun had just passed noon.

Leo looked haggard. He had been up all night, then at the telegraph office sending messages to the University. Inquiries had begun to come in from as far east as Baton Rouge. Leo had another, from Percival Lowell out in Flagstaff, Arizona Territory.

"Everybody at the University thinks it's wonderful," said Leo.

"People in Austin would," said the sheriff.

"They're sure these things are connected with Mars and those bright flashes of gas last month. Seems something's happened in England, starting about a week ago. No one's been able to get through to London for two or three days."

"You telling me Mars is attacking London, England, and Pachuco City, Texas?" asked the sheriff.

"It seems so," said Leo. He took off his glasses and rubbed his eyes.

"'Scuse me, Leo," said Lindley. "I got to get another telegram off to the Texas Rangers."

"That's funny," said Argyle, the telegraph operator. "The line was working just a second ago." He kept tapping his keys and fiddling with his coil box.

Leo peered out the window. "Hey!" he said. "Where's the 3:14?" He looked at the railroad clock. It was 3:25.

In sixteen years of rail service, the train had been four minutes late, and that was after a mud slide in the storm twelve years ago.

"Uh-oh," said the sheriff.

They were running out of Elmer's yard with a wagonload of dynamite. The wife and eleven of the kids were watching.

"Easy, Sheriff," said Elmer, who, with two of his boys and most of their guns, was riding in back with the explosives. "Jake sold me everything he had. I just didn't notice till we got back here with that stuff that some of it was already sweating."

"Holy shit!" said Lindley. "You mean we gotta go a mile an hour out there? Let's get out and throw the bad stuff off."

"Well, it's all mixed in," said Elmer. "I was sorta gonna set it all up on the hill and put one blasting cap in the whole load."

"Jesus. You woulda blowed up your whole house and Pachuco City, too."

"I was in a hurry," said Elmer, hanging his head.

"Well, it can't be helped, then. We'll take it slow."

Lindley looked at his watch. It was six o'clock. He heard a high-up, fluttering sound. They looked at the sky. Coming down was a large, round, glowing object throwing off sparks in all directions. It was curved with points, like the thing in the crater at the Atkinson place. A long, thin trail of smoke from the back end hung in the air behind it.

They watched in awe as it sailed down. It went into the horizon to the north of Pachuco City.

"One," said one of the kids in the wagon, "two, three—"

Silently they took up the count. At twenty-seven there was a roaring boom, just like the night before.

"Five and a half miles," said the sheriff. "That puts it eight miles from the other one. Leo said the ones in London came twenty-four hours apart, regular as clockwork."

They started off as fast as they could under the circumstances.

There were flashes of light beyond the Atkinson place in the near dusk. The lights moved off toward the north where the other thing had plowed in.

It was the time of evening when your eyes can fool you. Sheriff Lindley thought he saw something that shouldn't have been there sticking above the horizon. It glinted like metal in the dim light. He thought it moved, but it might have been the motion of the wagon as they lurched down a gully. When they came up, it was gone.

Skip was gone. His rifle was still there. It wasn't melted but had been crushed, as had the three-foot-thick tree trunk in front of it. All the caps and cartridges were gone.

There was a monstrous series of footprints leading from the crater down to the tree, then off into the distance to the north where Lindley thought he had seen something. There were three footprints in each series.

Sweets's hat had been mashed along with Skip's gun. Clanging and banging still came from the crater.

The four of them had made their plans. Lindley had his shotgun and pistol, which Luke had brought out with him that morning, though he was still wearing his burnt suit and his untouched Stetson.

He tied together the fifteen sweatiest sticks of dynamite he could find.

They crept out, then rushed the crater.

"Hurry up!" yelled the sheriff to the men at the courthouse. "Get that cannon up those stairs!"

"He's still coming this way!" yelled Luke from up above.

They had been watching the giant machine from the courthouse since it had come up out of the Atkinson place, before the sheriff and Elmer and his boys made it into town after their sortie.

It had come across to the north, gone to the site of the second crash, and stood motionless there for quite a while. When it got dark, the deputies brought out the night binoculars. Everybody in town saw the flash of dynamite from the Atkinson place.

A few moments after that, the machine had moved back toward there. It looked like a giant water tower with three legs. It had a thing like a teacher's desk bell on top of it, and something that looked like a Kodak roll-film camera in front of that. As the moon rose, they saw the thing had tentacles like thick wires hanging from between the three giant legs.

The sheriff, Elmer, and his boys made it to town just as the machine found the destruction they had caused at the first landing site. It turned toward town and was coming at a pace of twenty miles an hour.

"Hurry the hell up!" yelled Luke. "Oh shit—!" He ducked. There was a flash of light overhead. The building shook. "That heat gun comes out of the box on the front!" he said. "Look out!" The building glared and shook again. Something down the street caught fire.

"Load that sonofabitch," said Lindley. "Bob! Some of you men make sure everybody's in the cyclone cellars or where they won't burn. Cut out all the damn lights!"

"Hell, Sheriff. They know we're here!" yelled a deputy.

Lindley hit him with his hat, then followed the cannon up to the top of the clock-tower steps.

Luke was cramming powder into the cannon muzzle. Sweets ran back down the stairs. Other people carried cannonballs up the steps to the tower one at a time.

Leo came up. "What did you find, Sheriff, when you went back?"

There was a cool breeze for a few seconds in the courthouse tower. Lindley breathed a few deep breaths, remembering. "Pretty rough. There was some of them still working after that thing had gone. They were building another one just like it." He pointed toward the machine, which was firing up houses to the northeast side of town, swinging the ray back and forth. They could hear its hum. Homes and chicken coops burst into flame. A mooing cow was stilled.

"We threw in the dynamite and blew most of them up. One was in a machine like a steam tractor. We shot up what was left while they was hootin' and a-hollerin'. There was some other things in there, live things maybe, but they was too blowed up to put back together to be sure what they looked like, all bleached out and pale. We fed everything there a diet of buckshot till there wasn't nothin' left. Then we hightailed it back here on horses, left the wagon sitting."

The machine came on toward the main street of town. Luke finished with the powder. There were so many men with guns on the building across the street it looked like a brick porcupine. It must have looked that way for the James Gang when they were shot up in Northfield, Minnesota.

The courthouse was made of stone. Most of the wooden buildings in town were scorched or already afire. When the heat gun came this way, it blew bricks to dust, played flame over everything. The air above the whole town heated up.

They had put out the lamps behind the clock faces. There was nothing but moonlight glinting off the three-legged machine, flames of burning buildings, the faraway glows of prairie fires. It looked like Pachuco City was on the outskirts of hell.

"Get ready, Luke," said the sheriff. The machine stepped between two burning stores, its tentacles pulling out smoldering black horse tack, chains, kegs of nails, then heaving them this way and that. Someone at the end of the street fired off a round. There was a high, thin ricochet off the machine.

Sweets ran upstairs, something in his arms. It was a curtain from one of the judge's windows. He'd ripped it down and tied it to the end of one of the janitor's long window brushes.

On it he had lettered in tempera paint COME AND TAKE IT.

There was a ragged, nervous cheer from the men on the building as they read it by the light of the flames.

"Cute, Sweets," said Lindley, "too cute."

The machine turned down Main Street. A line of fire sprang up at the back side of the town from the empty corrals.

"Oh, shit!" said Luke. "I forgot the wadding!"

Lindley took off his hat to hit him with. He looked at its beautiful felt in the mixed moonlight and firelight.

The thing turned toward them. The sheriff thought he saw eyes way up in the bell-thing atop the machine, eyes like a big cat's eyes seen through a dirty windowpane on a dark night.

"Gol Dang, Luke, it's my best hat, but I'll be damned if I let them cooters burn down my town!"

He stuffed the Stetson, crown first, into the cannon barrel. Luke shoved it in with the ramrod, threw in two thirty-five-pound cannon balls behind it, pushed them home, and swung the barrel out over Main Street.

The machine bent to tear up something.

"Okay, boys," yelled Lindley. "Attract its attention."

Rifle and shotgun fire winked on the rooftop. It glowed like a hot coal from the muzzle flashes. A great slather of ricochets flew off the giant machine.

It turned, pointing its heat gun at the building. It was fifty feet from the courthouse steps.

"Now," said the sheriff.

Luke touched off the powder with his cigarillo.

The whole north side of the courthouse bell tower flew off, and the roof collapsed. Two holes you could see the moon through appeared in the machine: one in the middle, one smashing through the dome atop it. Sheriff Lindley saw the lower cannonball come out and drop lazily toward the end of burning Main Street.

All six of the tentacles of the machine shot straight up into the air, and it took off like a man running with his arms above his head. It staggered, as fast as a freight train could go, through one side of a house and out the other, and ran partway up Park Street. One of its three legs went higher than its top. It hopped around like a crazy man on crutches before its feet got tangled in a horse-pasture fence, and it went over backward with a shudder. A great cloud of steam came out of it and hung in the air.

No one in the courthouse tower heard the sound of the steam. They were all deaf as posts from the explosion. The barrel of the cannon was burst all along the end. The men on the other roof were jumping up and down and clapping each other on the back. The COME AND TAKE IT sign on the courthouse had two holes in it, neater than you could have made with a biscuit-cutter.

First a high whine, then a dull roar, then something like normal hearing came back into the sheriff's left ear. The right one still felt like a kid had its fist in there.

"Dang it, Sweets!" he yelled. "How much powder did Luke use?"

"Huh?"

Luke was banging on his head with both his hands.

"How much powder did he use?"

"Two, two and a half cans," said Sweets.

"It only takes half a can a ball!" yelled the sheriff. He reached for his hat to hit Luke with, touched his bare head. "I feel naked," he said. "Come on, we're not through yet. We got fires to put out and some hash to settle."

Luke was still standing, shaking his head. The whole town was cheering.

It looked like a pot lid slowly boiling open, moving just a little. Every time the end unscrewed a little more, ashes and cinders fell off and into the second pit. There was a piled ridge of them. The back turned again, moved a few inches, quit. Then it wobbled, there was a sound like a stove being jerked up a chimney, and the whole back end rolled open like a mad bank vault and fell off.

There were 184 men and 11 women all standing behind the open end of the thing, their guns pointing toward the interior. At the exact center were Sweets and Luke with the other courthouse cannon. This time there was one can of powder, but the barrel was filled to the end with everything from the blacksmith-shop floor—busted window glass, nails, horseshoes, bolts, stirrup buckles, and broken files and saws.

Eyes appeared in the dark interior.

"Remember the Alamo," said the sheriff.

Everybody, and the cannon, fired.

When the third meteor came in that evening, south of town and thirteen minutes past six, they knew something was wrong. It wobbled in flight, lost speed, and dropped like a long, heavy leaf.

They didn't have to wait for this one to cool and open. When the posse arrived, the thing was split in two and torn. Heat and steam came up from the inside.

One of the pale things was creeping forlornly across the ground with great difficulty. It looked like a thin gingerbread man made of glass with only a knob for a head.

"It's probably hurting from the gravity," said Leo.

"Fix it, Sweets," said Lindley.

"Sure thing, Sheriff."

There was a gunshot.

No fourth meteor fell, though they had scouts out for twenty miles in all directions, and the railroad tracks and telegraph wires were fixed again.

"I been doing some figuring," said Leo. "If there were ten explosions on Mars last month, and these things started landing in England last Thursday week, then we should have got the last three. There won't be any more."

"You been figurin', huh?"

"Sure have."

"Well, we'll see."

Sheriff Lindley stood on his porch. It was sundown on Sunday, three hours after another meteor should have fallen, had there been one.

Leo rode up. "I saw Sweets and Luke heading toward the Atkinson place with more dynamite. What are they doing?"

"They're blowing up every last remnant of them things—lock, stock, and asshole."

"But," said Leo, "the professors from the University will be here tomorrow, to look at the ships and the machines! You can't destroy them!"

"Shit on the University of Texas and the horse it rode in on," said the sheriff. "My jurisdiction runs from Deer Piss Creek to Buenos Frijoles, up to the Little Clear Fork of the North Branch of Mud River, back to the Creek, and everything in between. If I say something gets blowed up, it's on its way to Kingdom Come."

He put his arms on Leo's shoulders. "Besides, what little grass grows in this country's supposed to be green, and what's growing around them things is red. I *really* don't like that."

"But, Sheriff! I've got to meet Professor Lowell in Waxahachie tomorrow morning...."

"Listen, Leo. I appreciate what you done. But I'm an old man. I been kept up by Martians for three nights, I lost my horse and my new hat, and they busted my favorite gargoyle off the courthouse. I'm going in and get some sleep, and I only want to be woke up for the Second Coming, by Jesus Christ Himself."

Leo jumped on his horse and rode for the Atkinson place.

Sheriff Lindley crawled into bed and went to sleep as soon as his head hit the pillow.

He had a dream. He was a king in Babylon, and he lay on a couch at the top of a ziggurat, just like the Tower of Babel in the Bible. He surveyed the city and the river. There were women all around him, and men with curly beards and golden headdresses. Occasionally someone would feed him a great big fig from a golden bowl.

His dreams were not interrupted by the sounds of dynamiting, first from one side of town, then another, then another.

This is the story even people who don't like my stories like.

Self-mockery can take you places ferocity never can; it works passably well on convention panels and it works very well here. "Hold nothing up to scorn but yourself," the Talmud says—or if it doesn't, it should. "Make jest of yourself, not your enemies, and so you will in the deeper sense leave them without the weapon of insult," the Talmud adds—or if it doesn't, it should.

The Malzberg who lives, breathes, forages, and begs in these pages is not quite this Malzberg with whom I make circumstance every day, but he is close. As Robert Redford's line at the end of *The Sting* goes, "It's not enough...but it's close." Giggle. "It is close."

This story happened because Ed Ferman said, "Can you write a funny story? Just once I'd like to publish a funny story of yours." There are people who felt in the 1970s that I should be expunged from science fiction the way that Wisk was supposed to expunge ring around the collar, and even they seemed to like this story fine. As always, there is a moral to be taken, a lesson (a Talmudic lesson) to be applied, but, as always, I am unable to extract it.

—Barry Malzberg

A Delightful Comedic Premise

BARRY MALZBERG

~~~~~~~~~

Dear Mr. Malzberg:

I wonder if you'd be interested in writing for us—on a semicommissioned basis, of course—a funny short story or novelette. Although the majority of your work, at least the work which I have read, is characterized by a certain gloom, a blackness, a rather despairing view of the world, I am told by people who represent themselves to be friends of yours that you have, in private, a delightful sense of humor which overrides your melancholia and makes you quite popular at small parties. I am sure you would agree that science fiction, at least at present, has all the despair and blackness which it or my readers can stand, and if you could come in with a light-hearted story, we would not only be happy to publish it, it might start you on a brand-new career. From these same friends I am given to understand that you are almost thirty-four years of age, and surely you must agree that despair is harder and harder to sustain when you move into a period of your life where it becomes personally imminent; in other words, you are moving now into the Heart Attack Zone.

Dear Mr. Ferman:

Thank you very much for your letter and for your interest in obtaining from me a light-hearted story. It so happens that you and my friends have discovered what I would like to think of as My Secret...that I am not a despairing man at all but rather one with a delicious if somewhat perverse sense of humor, who sees the comedy in the human condition and only turns out the black stuff because it is now fashionable and the word rates, at all lengths, must be sustained.

I have had in mind for some time writing a story about a man, let me

call him Jack, who is able to re-evoke the sights and sounds of the 1950s
in such a concrete and viable fashion that he is actually able to *take* people back into the past, both individually and in small tourist groups.
(This idea is not completely original; Jack Finney used it in *Time and
Again*, and of course this chestnut has been romping or, I should say,
dropping around the field for forty years, but hear me out.) The trouble with Jack is that he is not able to re-evoke the more fashionable and
memorable aspects of the 1950s, those which are so much in demand
in our increasingly perilous and confusing times, but instead can recover only the failures, the not-quite-successes, the aspects-that-never-
made-it. Thus he can take himself and his companions not to Ebbets
Field, say, where the great Dodger teams of the 1950s were losing with
magnificence and stolid grace but to Shibe Park in Philadelphia, home
of the Athletics and Phillies, where on a Tuesday afternoon a desultory
crowd of four thousand might be present to watch senile managers fall
asleep in the dugout or hapless rookies fail once again to hit the rising
curve. He cannot, in short, recapture the Winners but only the Losers:
the campaign speeches of Estes Kefauver, recordings by the Bell Sisters
and Guy Mitchell, the rambling confessions of minor actors before the
McCarthy screening committee that they once were Communists and
would appreciate the opportunity to get before the full committee and
press to make a more definitive statement.

Jack is infuriated by this and no wonder; he is the custodian of a
unique and possibly highly marketable talent—people increasingly love
the past, and a guided tour through it as opposed to records, tapes, rambling reminisces would be enormously exciting to them—but he cannot
for the life of him get to what he calls the Real Stuff, the more commercial and lovable aspects of that cuddly decade. Every time that he thinks
he has recaptured Yankee Stadium in his mind and sweeps back in time
to revisit it, he finds himself at Wrigley Field in Chicago where Wayne
Terwilliger, now playing first base, misses a foul pop and runs straight
into the stands. What can he do? What can he do about this reckless
and uncontrollable talent of his, which in its sheerest perversity simply
will not remit to his commands? (It is a subconscious ability, you see;
if he becomes self-conscious, it leaves him entirely.) Jack is enraged. He
has cold sweats, flashes of gloom, and hysteria. (I forgot to say that he
is a failed advertising copywriter, now working in Cleveland on display

advertising mostly for the Shaker Heights district. He needs money and approbation. His marriage, his *second* marriage is falling apart. All of this will give the plot substance and humanity, to say nothing of warm twitches of insight.) He *knows* that he is on to something big, and yet his clownish talent, all big feet and wide ears, mocks him.

He takes his problem to a psychiatrist. The psychiatrist takes some convincing, but after being taken into the offices of *Cosmos* science fiction to see the editor rejecting submissions at a penny a word, he believes everything. He says he will help Jack. This psychiatrist, who I will call Dr. Mandleman, fires all of his patients and enters into a campaign to help Jack recover the more popular and marketable aspects of the fifties. He too sees the Big Money. He moves in with Jack. A psychiatrist in his own home: together they go over the Top 40 charts of that era, call up retired members of the New York football Giants, pore through old Congressional Records in which McCarthy is again and again thunderously denounced by two liberal representatives....

Do you see the possibilities? I envision this as being somewhere around 1,500 words but could expand or contract it to whatever you desire. I am very busy as always but could make room in my schedule for this project, particularly if you could see fit to give a small down payment. Would fifty dollars seem excessive? I look forward to a work from you.

Dear Mr. Malzberg:
I believe that you have utterly misunderstood my letter and the nature of the assignment piece.

There is nothing *funny* in a fantasy about a man who can recapture only the ugly or forgotten elements of the past. Rather, this is a bitter satire on the present which you have projected, based upon your statement that "people love their past," with the implication that they find the future intolerable. What is funny about *that*? What is funny about failure too? What is funny about the Philadelphia Athletics of the early nineteen fifties with their ninety-four-year-old manager? Rather, you seem to be on the way to constructing another one of your horrid metaphors for present and future, incompetence presided over by senescence.

This idea will absolutely not work, not at least within the context of a delightful comedic premise, and as you know, we are well-inventoried with work by you and others which will depress people. I cannot and will not pay fifty dollars in front for depressing stuff like this.

Perhaps you will want to take another shot at this.

Dear Mr. Ferman:

Thanks for your letter. I am truly sorry that you fail to see the humor in failure or in the forgettable aspects of the past—people, I think, must learn to laugh at their foibles—but bow to your judgment.

Might I suggest another idea which has been in mind for some time. I would like to write a story of a telepath, let me call him John, who is able to establish direct psionic links with the minds, if one can call them "minds," of the thoroughbreds running every afternoon except for Sundays and three months a year at Aqueduct and Belmont race tracks in Queens, New York. John's psionic faculties work at a range of fifty yards; he is able to press his nose against the wire gate separating paddock from customers and actually get *inside* the minds of horses. Dim thoughts like little shoots of grass press upon his own brain; he is able to determine the mental state and mood of the horses in turn as they prance by him. (Horses of course do not verbalize; John must deduce these moods subverbally.)

Obviously John is up to something. He is a mind reader; he should, through the use of his talent, be able to get some line on the outcome of a race by knowing which horses feel well, which horses' thoughts are clouded by the possibility of soporifics, which other horses' minds show vast energy because of the probable induction of stimulants. Surely he should be able to narrow the field down to two or three horses anyway which *feel good* and, by spreading his bets around these in proportion to the odds, assure himself of a good living.

(I should have said somewhat earlier on, but, as you know, am very weak at formal outlines, that John's talents are restricted to the reading of the minds of *animals*; he cannot for the life of him screen the thoughts of a fellow human. If he could, of course, he would simply check out the trainers and the jockeys, but it is a perverse and limited talent, and John must make the best of what God has given him, as must we all—for instance I outline poorly.)

The trouble is that John finds there to be no true correlation between the prerace mood or thoughts of horses and the eventual outcome. Horses that feel *well* do not necessarily win, and those horses from whom John has picked up the most depressing and suicidal emanations have been known to win. It is not a simple reversal; if it were, John would be able to make his bets on the basis of reverse correlation and do quite well this way; rather, what it seems to be is entirely *random*. Like so much of life, the prerace meditations of horses appear to have no relationship to the outcome; rather, motives and consequences are fractured, split, entirely torn apart; and this insight, which finally comes upon John after the seventh race at Aqueduct on June 12, 1974, when he has lost fifty-five dollars, drives him quite mad; his soul is split, and his mind shattered; he runs frantically through the sparse crowds (it is a Tuesday, and you know what OTB has done to race track attendance anyway) shouting, screaming, bellowing his rage to the heavens. "There's no connection!" he will scream. "Nothing makes sense, nothing connects, there is no reason at all!" and several burly Pinkertons, made sullen by rules which require them to wear jackets and ties at all times, even on this first hot day of the year, seize him quite roughly and drag him off into the monstrous computer room housing the equipment of the American Totalisator Company; there a sinister track executive, his eyes glowing with cunning and evil, will say, "Why don't you guys ever learn?" (he is a metaphor for the Devil, you see; I assure you that this will be properly planted, and the story itself will be an *allegory*) and, coming close to John, will raise a hand shaped like a talon, he will bring it upon John, he will. . . .

I propose this story to be 25,000 words in length, a cover story in fact. (You and Ronald Walotsky will see the possibilities here, and Walotsky, I assure you, draws horses very well.) Although I am quite busy, the successful author of fifteen stories in the field, two of the novels published in *hardcover*, I could make time in my increasingly heavy schedule to get the story to you within twelve hours of your letter signifying outline approval. I think that an advance of fifty dollars would be quite reasonable and look forward to hearing from you by return mail, holding off in this meantime from plunging into my next series of novels which, of course, are already under lucrative contract.

Dear Mr. Malzberg:

We're not getting anywhere.

What in God's name is *funny* about a man who perceives "motives and consequences to be entirely fractured...torn apart?" Our readers, let me assure you, have enough troubles of their own; they are already quite aware of this or do not *want* to be aware of it. Our readers, an intelligent and literate group of people numbering into the multiple thousands, have long since understood that life is unfair and inequitable, and they are looking for entertainment, release, a little bit of *joy*.

Perhaps we should forget this whole thing. There are other writers I would rather have approached, and it was only at the insistence of your friends that I decided to give you a chance at this one. We are heavily inventoried, as I have already said, on the despairing stuff, but if in due course you would like to send me one of your characteristic stories, *on a purely speculative basis*, I will consider it as a routine submission.

Dear Mr. Ferman:

Please wait a minute or just a few minutes until you give me another chance to explain myself. I was sure that the two story ideas you have rejected, particularly the second, were quite funny; but editorial taste, as we professional writers know, is the prerogative of the editor; and if you *don't* see the humor, I can't show it to you, humor being a very rare and special thing. I am however momentarily between novels, waiting for the advance on the series contract to come through and *would* be able to write you a story at this time; let me propose one final idea to you before you come to the wrong conclusion that I am not a funny writer and go elsewhere, to some wretched hack who does not have one-quarter of the bubbling humor and winsomely comprehensive view of the human condition that I do.

I would like to write a story about a science fiction writer, a highly successful science fiction writer but one who nevertheless, because of certain limitations in the field and slow payment from editors, is forced to make do on an income of three thousand four hundred and eighty-three dollars a year (last year) from all of his writings and, despite the pride and delight of knowing that he is near or at the top of his field, finds getting along on such an income, particularly in the presence of a wife and family, rather difficult, his wife not understanding entirely (as she *should* understand) that science fiction is not an ultimately lucrative field for most of us but repays in satisfaction, in *great* satisfactions. This writer, who we shall call Barry, is possessed after a while by his fantasies; the partitions, in his case, between reality and fantasy have been sheared through by turmoil and economic stress, and he believes himself in many ways to be not only the creator but the receptacle of his ideas, ideas which possess him and stalk him through the night.

Barry is a gentle man, a man with a gracious sense of humor, a certain *je ne sais quoi* about him which makes him much celebrated at parties, a man whose occasionally sinister fictions serve only to mask his gay and joyous nature... but Barry is seized by his fantasies; people do not truly understand him, and now at last those aforementioned walls have crumbled; he takes himself to be not only the inventor but the *hero* of his plot ideas. Now he is in a capsule set on Venus flyby looking out at the green patch while he strokes his diminutive genitals and thinks of home; now again he is an archetypal alien, far from home, trying to make convincing contact with humanity; now yet again he is a rocket ship, an actual physical rocket ship, a phallic object extended to great length and power, zooming through the heavens, penetrating the sky.

I'll do this at 1,500 words for five dollars down. Please let me hear from you.

Dear Mr. Malzberg:
This was a doomed idea from the start. I hope you won't take this personally, but you need help.

Dear Mr. Ferman:
My husband is at Aqueduct today, living in a motel by the night, and says he will be out of touch for at least a week, but I know he would have wanted me to acknowledge your letter, and as soon as he returns I assume he'll be in touch with you.

I assume also that in saying that he needs "help" you are referring to the fact that, as he told me, you were commissioning a story from him with money in front, and I hope that you can send us a check as soon as possible, without awaiting his return. He said something about a hundred or a thousand dollars, but we'll take fifty.

—Joyce Malzberg

I wrote "The Capo of Darkness" for a DAW Books anthology editor Denise Little invited me into. This story combines my longtime interests in the Mafia and religion, both of which I should no doubt take more seriously.

—Laura Resnick

The Capo of Darkness

LAURA RESNICK

THE DAY THEM TWO POLENTA-EATING bums from Eden came to the Underworld began like any day down here. Just another Eternity of hellfire and brimstone, nothing special. Business as usual. I checked in on the wailing of the damned, acknowledged blood sacrifices from 17,459 politicians, brokered the souls of a few no-talent international movie stars, called in a marker on Wall Street, culled some vig from a shipment of virtue headed for Our Lady of Perpetual Chastity School For Girls in Yonkers, and made sure that every IRS agent who'd ever lived and died was still engulfed in the inferno of Everlasting Suffering where they belonged.

Like I said, nothing special.

Then *they* showed up.

I knew who they was right away, of course. Who else in all of Creation wears fig leaves, for Chrissake? (I can say that name down here. It's *upstairs* that you gotta be careful about taking it in vain.) Okay, fine, the two of them screwed up and had to be thrown outta the outfit. I get that. A boss can't go soft and let his crew get away with disobeying orders. But Mister Yahweh went too far, giving them nothing but fig leaves to wear when He kicked them out of Eden. And don't think I didn't say so to His face back when I used to work for Him.

Yeah, that's right. I used to be an enforcer for the Big Guy, Yahweh, Jehovah, the Lord of Hosts, the Head Honcho, the *capo di tutti capi* in all of Creation. The Supreme Being who started the whole show. And although we had a pretty serious falling out when He damned me for all Eternity and sent me to Hell, you won't never catch me making no disrespectful remarks about Mister Yahweh. What He done to me was business. Nothing personal. And whatever I done back to Him since then ain't personal, neither.

Sure, I had a rough time after being kicked outta Heaven, but things worked out pretty good for me in the end. Mister Lucifer saw my potential and offered me a little work. Next thing you knew, I was a made guy on his crew. Didn't take me long, neither, to work up to the job I held the day *they* arrived.

It was the woman who spoke to me first. Of *course*. Hey, she was the one who ate the forbidden fruit first, too, you know what I'm saying? She had a rep as a sassy broad, and she seemed like she was still living up to it after all these millennia; but I knew the Dark Prince had fond memories of her, from way back when they was all in Eden, so I figured I could let the attitude roll off me when she demanded, kinda snooty-like, "Who's in charge here?"

"The Boss," I said. "Who'd ya think?"

She frowned. "Who are you?"

"I'm his *consigliere*. You want a favor from Mister Lucifer, you gotta talk to me."

"*Consigliere*?" the guy with her asked.

"Yeah," I said, "I'm the *capo's* right-hand soul around here now."

"*You're* seated at the right hand of the father?" he asked, looking sorta stupid.

"No, you're thinking of a different boss, kid." *The* boss, if truth be known; but, hey, I knew it wasn't smart to say so down here. Then, because people made this kind of mistake all the time, I asked, "Are you sure you're in the right place? Heaven's way up—"

"We're not going to Heaven. We *can't* go." The broad straightened her fig leaf and added, "But you already know that, don't you?"

"Yeah," I said, maybe seeing a little of what Lucifer had liked about her back when they was both in Paradise, "I do. I used to be with that outfit." I shrugged. "Cherubim talk. I heard things."

She looked startled. "You used to be in Heaven? And now you're working for the Lord of Flies?"

"He don't go by that title no more. He didn't like the novel, thought it showed him in a bad light. And don't call him 'Beelzebub,' neither," I advised, figuring it wouldn't hurt to give these underdressed kids a little help. "He's gotten real sensitive about it. He thinks it makes him sound like a character in an English comedy."

I shouldn't have wasted my breath. She rolled her eyes and said, "I told him that more than five thousand years ago."

"Yeah, right, sweetheart. Hell is full of women who say 'I told you so.' We keep 'em here to torment the men who welshed on bets and ratted to the Feds."

"We're wasting time," she said.

"You're right," I agreed. "What business you got down here?"

"That's for us to discuss with the Dark Lord."

"You're asking for a sit-down with Satan?"

"Yes."

"This goes against protocol," I warned her.

"It's important," she insisted.

"It better be. He gets cranky if I waste his time. And when the boss gets cranky, I get mean, sister. You understand what I'm saying?"

She leaned closer—*real* close—and suddenly the fig leaves kinda appealed to me, being so skimpy. "I didn't back down when Yahweh got in my face in Eden, so I'm certainly not going to let the likes of you scare me, buster."

I grinned. "You can call me Vito."

Okay, so I like a broad with huevos. So sue me.

"Vito?" The guy went a little pale. "Not... Vito 'The Knuckles' Giacalone?"

"The very same." So they'd heard of me. Well, lotsa people have, I don't deny it.

"You were pretty high up in the Heavenly Choir," he said.

I shrugged. "I don't sing. Never did."

The broad looked a little impressed now. "They say Yahweh didn't make a move without consulting you."

"No, no, He was His own deity," I insisted modestly. "Always. Sometimes He just, you know, liked a little feedback, that's all."

"They say you're the one who cleaned up the Road of Good Intentions for Him."

"They?"

She shrugged. "Like you said, cherubim talk."

"So I guess they talked about why I left, too."

The two of them exchanged a glance, then she said, "You were sending Lucifer a cut of the souls on the Road to Salvation. When Yahweh found out you'd been skimming off the top and not giving Him any vig, He condemned you to Eternal Damnation."

I nodded. "The Big Guy's got a hell of a temper."

"Hey, you don't need to tell *us*," the guy said.

"In fact," the woman added, "that's why we're here."

"Oh?"

She met my eyes, square and direct. In that moment, she didn't look like she was made from Adam's rib. She looked like razor-sharp steel. "We want to take out a contract on Yahweh."

"Adam and Eve to see you, boss," I said to Lucifer.

Old Nick had had a thing for Eve millennia ago, as everyone knows, so I wasn't surprised to see his eyes shoot flames of hellfire when she and Adam entered his diabolical presence.

"You're looking well," the Dark Prince said to her.

"Thanks," Adam said.

We all looked at him. After a moment, he turned red and fumbled for a chair.

"You don't sit until the devil invites you to, kid," I advised him.

"Oh! Um...." Adam got even redder. "Sorry. We've been, you know, outcast and exiled for so long, I've forgotten...."

"Your manners?" Lucifer murmured, making the air quiver hotly with his terrible voice.

"He's just nervous," Eve said, giving the boss a pointed look. "Leave him alone."

What *is* it about women? The Prince of Darkness, the only *capo* in Creation who's ever given Yahweh a run for His money, apologized to her and invited them both to take a seat.

Being a very busy omnipotent archdemon, Lucifer decided to get right down to business. "Vito tells me you want my help whacking out Yahweh."

"That's right."

"Out of the question."

"We're ready to pay whatever price you demand," Eve said, looking steely again.

"No."

"Our eternal souls are yours for the asking."

"Are you listening to me, Eve? I said—"

"It's not as if you haven't killed others."

"No!" Lucifer thundered, getting impatient.

Adam bleated, "It was all her idea! I had nothing to do with it!"

"Yeah?" I said. "That's just the excuse I'd expect from the guy who said, when Yahweh asked why he ate the fruit, 'The woman made me do it.'" What a pansy the Supreme Deity had picked to be the father of all mankind.

Adam got hot under the fig leaf. "I couldn't lie to *God*!"

"Some stand-up guy you are," I said. "Back when I was still alive, you know what we did to guys like you? First we cut off their—"

"This is really beside the point, Vito," Lucifer said.

"Yes, boss."

"And we can't whack Yahweh," he added to Eve, "regardless of what happened in Eden."

"I would have thought," Eve said, "that you, of all entities, would have the guts—"

"He's an eternal being," Lucifer said. "*The* eternal being. I could whack Him out all day every day from now until the end of time, and He wouldn't die. It just doesn't work that way." He sighed and added morosely, "Trust me on this."

Eve gasped. "You mean you've already tried it?"

"*Hull-o-o-o!*" Lucifer said. "Did the whole war between Good and Evil which has existed ever since I got cast out of Heaven completely escape your attention?"

"I got the memo," she snapped back. "I guess I just missed the footnote about you trying to bump off the Maker of All Things."

"Yahweh kept it quiet," I said. "Getting whacked out gave Him a terrible migraine, and He didn't want anyone else getting ideas and following Mister Lucifer's example."

"So you're saying it can't be done?" Eve asked, looking sort of despairing.

"That's what I'm saying," Lucifer confirmed.

"But. . . . But. . . . We want vengeance!" Eve cried.

"My dear girl," Lucifer said, "if you've got grievances with Yahweh, I suggest you go lay them at His feet, not at my hooves."

"Grievances? You can call what He did to us a mere grievance?"

"We disobey one little order," Adam added. "We taste one little piece of fruit, which didn't taste good anyhow, and—"

"Ingrates!" Lucifer said, steamed now. "That wasn't just a 'little piece of fruit' that I gave you! That was the fruit of the tree of knowledge!"

"It was sort of sour," Adam insisted.

"More like bitter," Eve opined.

"Didn't care for it at all," Adam added.

"And the aftertaste," Eve said. "Yech."

The two of them made identical faces. I seen Carmine Corvino make a face like that just before he keeled over from the strychnine a hitman from the Matera family put in his minestrone.

"It wasn't intended to be a gastronomic experience." His satanic majesty sounded real grumpy. "The fruit of knowledge made you self-aware and gave you the freedom to choose between Good and Evil."

"I was burping for hours," Adam confided.

"Choice! Self-determination! Free will!" the boss shouted, making the halls of Hell quiver. "I told Yahweh that you, His greatest and finest creation, were worthy of these gifts! But did He listen to me? Noooooo! He knew best. He *always* knew best." Lucifer sneered. "He had no need to listen to a mere archangel."

"So why was the tree there in the first place?" I asked. "I always did wonder."

"Yahweh and I were playing poker, and—"

"He used to play poker?" Adam asked.

"Don't interrupt the devil, kid," I said.

"Sorry."

"He was *terrible* at it," Lucifer said. "Vito, you never saw anyone so bad at a bluff. It was almost tragic." He shrugged the magnificent red-and-black wings whose feathers had been singed off eons ago in his fiery descent from Heaven. "I probably could have gambled my way back into Heaven long ago—as if anyone would want to—except that He quit cards altogether after what happened in Eden."

"I get it, boss. You're saying that He lost a pot to you that had the tree of knowledge in it."

"Seven-card stud. He was trying to make me think He had pulled to an inside straight. Like even being the Supreme Deity could make *that* happen." The boss snorted with ribald amusement. Adam jumped out of his chair a second before Satan's fiery breath singed it. "When He called my hand, I showed Him my four aces. I thought He'd burst into tears."

Eve guessed, "You cheated."

"That's such a low word. Let's just say I employed certain skills which are not necessarily observed within the strictest canon of the game."

"And the result," Eve said, "was that you tempted me—"

"And then *she* tempted *me*," Adam added.

"Petulance is so unbecoming to the father of mankind," Lucifer chided.

"And we've been outcasts ever since!"

"So have I," the boss pointed out, "but I've made something of myself. You two, on the other hand, appear to have been moping around ever since Eden."

"Yahweh threw us into Limbo!" Eve looked pretty pissed off.

"Limbo?" I frowned. "No way. I'd have known."

"Oh, yes, you were skimming off Limbo, too, I know that." Now she *sounded* pretty pissed off, too.

"Just making sure certain people who didn't really belong there got out before too many millennia passed." I said to the boss, "Boy, and people thought Purgatory was bad. Did I ever tell you what a mess Limbo was until the Big Guy finally closed it down?"

"Let me guess," Lucifer said to Eve. "Yahweh imprisoned you there, but He kept it off the books—even the second set of books."

"You know Him so well," Eve said coldly.

"So *that's* why I didn't know you was there." I didn't mention that I'd never even known there'd been a second set of books. I got a rep to maintain, after all.

"So when they closed Limbo. . . ." Lucifer prodded.

"We tried the Road to Redemption," Eve said, "but Yahweh's heart was still hard. So laying our grievances at His feet, as you suggest, Mephisto, won't do any good."

I took a quick look at the boss. Using that old pet name. . . . Oh, yeah. I could see it had just the effect Eve wanted it to have. This broad knew how to play *her* cards, even if Yahweh didn't.

But Lucifer had a rep to think about, too, so the *capo* of Darkness merely raised one terrible claw to his toothy mouth, faked a yawn, and said, "Ho-hum, so Yahweh condemned you unfairly, locked you up in the most boring place in Creation without telling anyone, and now He won't let you back on His—if I may be excused for saying so—notoriously dull team. Why should I care?"

"Because it's your fault!" Eve shouted.

"Don't shout at the devil," I said.

"My dear girl," the Evil One said, "*you're* the one who ate the fruit of knowledge. I merely suggested you might be a trifle hungry."

"You did more than that, and you damn well know it," she said between gritted teeth. "You coaxed me. You convinced me. You cajoled me."

Adam added, "Yeah!" Such a help.

"You *seduced* me!" Eve accused.

"Yeah!" Adam paused. "Um . . ." He looked at Eve. "Seduced? You never told me that."

"You owe me, Lucifer," she said.

"Seduced?" Adam repeated. "How, exactly?"

"I still wouldn't know what that damn tree was for, if you hadn't told me," Eve continued.

"You told me he 'talked' you into it, Eve. Seduced? No, you never said *that*. I would remember."

"And as for my voluntarily biting into a fruit that smelled the way that one did. . . . It never would have happened if not for you," Eve said.

"Eve, you want to explain to me about the *seduction* you forgot to mention the five million other times we've discussed this?"

"Jesus H. Christ, Adam!" Eve suddenly caught herself and looked at us. "Uh, can I say that here?"

We both nodded.

"Jesus H. Christ, Adam! It was eons ago! Could we please focus on the problem at hand?"

"Oh, excuse me if I'm just a little sensitive about this, but as I recall, Yahweh made you for *me*. Me! *My* companion. *My* partner. *My* mate. And now I find out that the first time another entity came along—"

"This is why I never told you! I knew this is exactly how you'd react! 'Mine, mine, mine!'"

"Oh, as if *you* didn't get jealous about Lilith!"

The infernal temperature suddenly seemed to drop a few hundred degrees.

"*I told you*," Eve said to Adam, in a voice I'd never even heard a federal judge use, "*never to say that name in my presence again*."

"I'm glad you advised this sit-down, Vito," Lucifer said to me. "This is getting interesting."

Adam went all red again. Eve was as white as the Pearly Gates.

"Do go on," the Prince of Darkness urged them.

"We'll discuss this later," Eve said to Adam.

"We certainly will," he replied.

She faced the monarch of Hell. "Even if you don't feel you're at all responsible for what happened—"

"No, no, I take full credit," he said. "I just don't feel guilty about it."

"Yes, well, rumor has it that no one with the capacity to feel guilt winds up here," she said.

"No, we've got some Jews here." A moment later I admitted, "Well, okay, only the ones who were lawyers."

"Mephisto," she said, pouring it on now. "You've had your differences with Yahweh, too. Don't you want to help us for your own sake?"

"For evil's sake?" He sighed. "Hmmm...."

"Or just," she said, moving in for the kill, "for the fun of it?"

"The fun of it? Ah, it *would* be fun," he admitted, "but since He can't be whacked out—"

"So let's torment Him instead of killing Him."

"Do you happen to have a plan?"

She nodded. "What would send Yahweh into a depression for centuries?"

"A growth in Hinduism," Lucifer said promptly. "That whole nirvana thing always bugged the shit out of Him. He said Eternal Paradise was a waste if people were going to strive for sheer nothingness, and he got really—"

"No." Eve sounded impatient. "Not Hinduism. Let's try this another way. What does He value most?"

"Mankind?" Lucifer guessed.

Eve rolled her eyes, then said to me. "I'll bet you know."

"His rep," I said without hesitation. "Mister Yahweh's very big on His rep. Doesn't like it messed with."

"Exactly!" Eve smiled.

"So you want us to mess with His rep?" I asked, stunned.

"That's what I want."

Wow. I was right, this broad had huevos.

"He'll take it hard," I told Lucifer, "that's for sure."

"Oooh! This does sound like fun," the Dark One said, rubbing his claws together.

"How we gonna do it?" I asked.

Eve explained, "Lucifer will endow thoroughly unprincipled and morally bankrupt men with tremendous powers of charisma and persuasion, then provide them with opportunities to humiliate Yahweh before millions of people and thoroughly undermine His credibility in their eyes."

"What an interesting concept," Lucifer said. "I'm in."

And that's how televangelism was born.

It went exactly the way we planned. Guys you wouldn't loan five bucks to or leave alone with your daughter were going on TV every week and convincing millions of people to send them charitable donations in Yahweh's name. Next thing you knew, these goombata would be caught using the money to pay for their mansions, their private jets, their underage girlfriends in hotel rooms with jacuzzis, their personal playgrounds, their booze, their drugs. Whatever.

It was brilliant, and we was incredibly pleased with how good it was going. We figured that any minute, Yahweh would have a nervous breakdown.

Of course, you've probably already figured out what we overlooked. When trying to smear Yahweh's rep, we completely forgot one of the things He's best known for: giving people second chances. It's a trait He passed on to his favorite creation, mankind, and they emulated His endless benevolence by forgiving a bunch of these goons, go figure. And these bums getting forgiven, well, it made them come to love Yahweh, which in turn made everyone else love Yahweh even more, too. And next thing we knew, Yahweh's polls were at an all-time high, and He was feeling so benevolent that He decided He'd been too hard on Adam and Eve—whom He forgave and let into Heaven.

"Which," Lucifer said grimly to me, "was probably Eve's plan all along." He sighed, wafting fire and smoke through the halls of Hell. "I'd forgotten how damn clever that woman is. I'll bet you anything she nibbled of the fruit of knowledge before I ever came along."

"You think, boss?"

"I'll bet she only pretended I'm the one who talked her into it, so she could blame me when Yahweh asked her about it."

"Guess it backfired," I said, thinking of her millennia in Limbo.

Lucifer nodded. "She didn't know about the poker game. He was always so sensitive about little things like that."

We sat in silence for a while, both feeling pretty gloomy.

Finally he said, "You know what this means now, don't you?"

"Yeah, I think so, boss." I was the one who advised the sit-down with Adam and Eve. So now I was the one who had to take the fall for it.

"It's not personal, Vito."

I nodded. "I know. Just business."

"I'd bump you off if I could," he assured me.

"I appreciate the thought, Mister Lucifer."

"But, seeing as how you're already dead...."

"Guess I'm exiled?"

"I'm afraid so, Vito."

"Well.... No point in hanging around, then. It's been a privilege working for you, boss."

"I know," he said.

And that's how I wound up leaving Hell, all on account of Yahweh's rep being the best deserved rep in Creation, and Lucifer being maybe a little too overconfident.

I ain't bitter, though. Like the boss said, it was business, nothing personal. And I'm sure Mister Yahweh will be businesslike about it, too, when I go to Him now and explain about how I helped invent televangelists all in an attempt to earn my way back into Heaven.

I think it'll work. After all, Yahweh's very big on giving people second chances.

It all happened in one of those middle-of-the-night frenzied bursts of creativity that left me exhausted and feeling like a giant cockroach the next morning. But that's all anyone ever knows about Kafka: the damn cockroach story. You get it in high school—if they're still teaching literature in high school. Otherwise you get it in college lit.

The first time I read the story it disturbed me—not the idea of someone turning into a cockroach, because that happens all the time in my neighborhood—but that as a story, it violated so many of "rules" of storytelling. At least the rules that I'd been taught. Worst of all, it didn't seem to have a point (like "don't take candy from strangers" and "never play pool with anyone named after a city"); but maybe that was the real point of it after all, that there was a whole other way of looking at things, a non-Aristotelian, non-Freudian genre of absurdist-surrealism that would trouble even the dreams of Charles Dodgson.

Kafka is not a guy you read for the fun of reading. Kafka is a guy you read so you can say you read Kafka. He's hard work. His most frustrating tale is *The Trial*, about a guy who's on trial, but he doesn't know why, what he's been charged with, when or where the trial is, or even what the ultimate outcome will be. It's a metaphor for life, right? (Everything is a metaphor for life, but more so with Kafka.)

The point is, when you actually "get" Kafka, you get that *everything* is absurd and surreal, not just Kafka. That's why Franz Kafka is a superhero. Merely by existing, he changes the world he exists in.

And, of course, his archenemy is obvious.

—David Gerrold

83

Franz Kafka, Superhero!

DAVID GERROLD

~~~~~~~~~~

HE RATTLE OF THE RED ROACH PHONE—a noise like an angry cicada—brought him to instant wakefulness. He rolled out of bed in a single movement, scooped up the handset, and held it to his ear. He didn't speak.

The familiar voice. The words crisp and mellifluous. "One-thirty-three. How soon can you leave?"

He bent to the nightstand and switched on the lamp with a loud click. He opened the World Atlas that lay directly under the glow to page 133. A map of Vienna. He glanced to the clock. The minute hand had long since fallen off, but he'd become fairly proficient at telling the time by the position of the hour hand alone. "I'll be on the ten-thirty train."

"Good," said the voice. The line clicked and went silent.

He undid the laces tying up the throat of his nightshirt, letting the wide neck of the garment fall open and away. He began shrugging it down off his shoulders, pulling it down to his waist, shedding it like an insect pushing its way out of its cocoon, all the while darting his eyes about the room in quick, nervous little glances. It fell forgotten to the floor. He stepped out of it, pink, naked, and alert. A whole new being. His eyes glistened with anticipation and excitement.

He dressed quickly, efficiently. He put on a shiny black suit. He selected a matching black tie. He buttoned his dark red vest meticulously. He wound his watch and tucked it into his vest. He opened the top drawer and selected his two best handkerchiefs; then, after a moment's consideration, he selected a third one as well—his *silk* handkerchief, the one he only used for special occasions.

He pulled on his heavy wool overcoat. He grabbed his carpet bag from the closet, already packed. He was ready to go.

As he walked, he considered. Fifteen minutes to the train station. Five minutes to buy a ticket. Twenty minutes to spare before the train arrived. Yes. He could purchase a newspaper and have a coffee and a croissant in the cafe while he waited. Good.

He could feel the power in his step. He was ready for battle. His mind was clear. This time, he would confront the arch-fiend PsycheMan in his lair. Yes! The enemy would know the taste of ashes and despair before *this* day was through.

In his ordinary life, he pretended to be just another faceless dark slug—sweaty, confused, trapped by circumstance. He moved through the maze of twisty gray streets, almost unnoticed. If by chance he did attract the attention of another being, they would see him only as a squat dark shape, brooding, uncommunicative.

In his ordinary life, he pretended to be a writer of grotesque fantasies, a mordant storyteller of obscure, deranged, and unpublishable dreads. His visions were tumbled and stifling—almost repulsive in their queerness. People avoided the possibility of close contact, which was exactly what he wanted and needed—

—Because in his *extra*ordinary life, he was Bug-Man! *The human insect!*

Transformed by a bizarre experiment in Marie Curie's laboratory—accidentally exposed to the life-altering rays of the mysterious element *radium*—he had become a *whole new kind of being.* A strange burst of power had expanded throughout his entire body, shredding the very cells of his flesh.

For a single bright instant, he comprised the entire universe, he knew *everything,* understood *everything.* His skin glowed white as the very essence of life itself infused his whole being. For just that single instant, he became a creature of *pure energy!* And then the transforming bath of radioactive power ebbed and the entire cosmos collapsed again, down into a single dark node at the bottom of his soul. When his vision cleared, he realized that the insect specimen he had been holding had vanished completely, its essence subsumed throughout his flesh.

That night, under the intoxicating rays of the full moon, he discovered a new plasticity to his flesh. His bones had become malleable. His muscles could be used to pull his body into a shape that was at first painful and frightening, then curious, and finally invigorating and powerful. His skin toughened like armor. He turned and saw himself in the mirror as something strange and beautiful. A shining black carapace. Glistening faceted eyes. Trembling antennae. He could taste symphonies in the air that he had never known before. He could hear colors previously undreamt. The strength in his limbs was alarming! Thrilling! He had become a master *of metamorphosis.* Franz Kafka, superhero!

In the days that followed, he learned to control his new powers, leaping from buildings, tunneling, biting, scrabbling through the earth in the dead of night. The cost of his ability to metamorphosize was a ferocious hunger. He satisfied it by preying on the predators of society. He became a force to be reckoned with, seeking out those who preyed on the weak, snapping them in two, and feeding on their flesh. Soon, the dark underworld elements of Austria learned the fury of his appetites. The word spread. *The night belonged to Bug-Man.*

Soon he became an ally to the great governments of Europe, battling arch-fiends all over the continent. His exploits became world-famous. His twilight battles were the stuff of legend. Where evil spread its nefarious claws, the cry would soon go up: "This is a job for Bug-Man!"

Now, he hurried to Vienna, eager for the final confrontation with the greatest monster of them all: the terrible master of confusion, Sigmund Freud—more commonly known to the League Of United Superheroes Everywhere as *PsycheMan!*

The evil Dr. Freud terrorized his victims by summoning up the monsters of the id. He used their own fears against them, plundering their treasures, and leaving them feeble and empty. Freud's victims babbled in languages of their own, meaningless chatter. They capered like monkeys, simpered like idiots, grinning and drooling; he filled the asylums with his victims. Franz Kafka could not wait to catch this monster on his own overstuffed couch. He dabbed at his chin with his handkerchief, lest someone observe him drooling in anticipation.

The train lurched and rattled and crawled across the Austrian countryside. By the time it finally clattered into the Vienna station, it was nearly four in the afternoon. Dusk would be falling soon, and with it would come his terrible hunger. No matter, tonight he intended to feed well. He would soon suck the marrow from the bones of Dr. Freud. He could hardly wait to sink his gleaming pincers into the soft white flesh of the little Viennese Jew, injecting him with his venom, then tasting the liquefied flesh, inhaling its aroma, taking it hungrily into his meta-morphosed self, refreshing himself, invigorating his energies. He would turn the monster's very flesh into fuel for his own divine crusade against evil!

Wiping his mouth again, covering his excitement with his now-sod-den handkerchief, Kafka hurried to the post office window and asked if a letter had been left for him. The squint-eyed clerk handed it across without comment. Kafka shoved it into his coat pocket without look-ing at it and scuttled away out of the glare of the bright lights overhead. At last he flattened himself into a dark corner and opened the envelope quickly. Inside was a small square of paper with an address neatly typed on it. Kafka repeated the address to himself three times, memorizing it, then wadded up the paper and shoved it into his mouth, chewing fran-tically. It was several moments before he was able to swallow the wad, and during the entire time his little dark eyes flicked back and forth, watching for suspicious strangers. But no, nobody had noticed the dark little creature in the corner.

Kafka swallowed the last of the paper and left the station, relieved to be away from the screech of the trains and the crush of so many peo-ple. He headed north, walking briskly, but not so fast as to call attention to himself. He headed directly for the address on the paper. He had to see the house before the sun set. The narrow cobbled streets of Vienna echoed with his footsteps.

All the buildings clustered like newborn wedding cakes, close and or-nate. The streets and alleys between them were already sunk in roman-tic gloom, and the first smells of the evening meal were already filling the streets. He passed open shop doors and restaurants. His heightened senses told him of the spices in the sausages, the honey in the pastries, the butterfat in the cream. A horse-drawn wagon clattered by, dragging with it the animal scent of manure and sweat. Smoke from the chim-neys climbed up into the oppressive sky. The heavy flavor of coal per-vaded everything.

Kafka found the street he was looking for and turned left into it as if he was a long-familiar resident. He slowed his pace and studied the houses on the opposite side of the avenue, one at a time, examining each as if none of them held any specific interest for him. They were tall, narrow structures, each hiding behind a wrought-iron fence. The high peaked roofs offered multiple opportunities to hide and possible easy access through the gabled windows, but Kafka ignored them. He let his attention wander to the cobbled street itself, the sewers and the drains. If he was satisfied with what he saw, he gave no sign. He continued on down the street toward the end.

At the end of the block, he turned right, crossed the street, and headed up toward the next block. He turned right and headed up the row of houses looking thoughtfully at each one. As luck would have it, the building directly behind Dr. Freud's suspected lair was a small hotel for retired gentlemen.

He climbed up the front steps, entered, and rang the bell at the registration desk. Shortly, a wizened old clerk appeared and Kafka inquired politely if there were a quiet room available in the back of the inn. There was, and he immediately secured it for two days. He would need a private place in which to accomplish his metamorphosis, and time to recover afterward. He considered himself extremely fortunate to be so close to his quarry.

Wiping his chin, he let himself into the room, put down his carpet bag just inside the door, turned, and locked the door behind him. At last! He was so close to his arch-enemy, Freud, he could almost taste his blood! He crossed to the window and parted the curtains. Across a narrow garden, he could see the shuttered rear windows of Dr. Freud's house. He wondered what nefarious deeds were going on behind those walls.

He'd know soon enough; the moon was already visible above the rooftops. He pulled the curtains aside and opened the window, the better to admit the healing rays of moonlight. He began pulling off his clothes, almost clawing his way out of them, exposing his pallid flesh to the intoxicating luminance.

He opened the carpet bag and began laying out the equipment that he would need. A large rubber sheet—he spread it across the floor. A large block of wood—battered, chipped, and scarred; he placed that carefully on the sheet.

The transformation began slowly. He felt the first twinges in his shoulders and in his knees. He began to twitch. The long hours cooped up in the train had left him stiff and uncomfortable; this metamorphosis would be a painful one. Good! A flurry of little shudders shook his body; he grabbed hold of a chair for support until the seizure eased. He knew he had to be careful, he knew he didn't dare risk losing consciousness; he had to stay awake and deliberately shape himself for the battle ahead.

His head. Most important. His mandibles—

His teeth began to lengthen in his mouth, pushing his jaw painfully out of its sockets. He shoved his fingers into his mouth and started pulling his teeth painfully forward, shaping them into the digging and grinding tools that he would shortly need.

Next, his skull. He put his right hand under his chin and his left hand on top of his head and pressed them toward each other as hard as he could. The bones of his skull creaked and gave. His head began to flatten. His chin spread, his eyes bulged sideways, his jaw widened out, his teeth splayed forward, his eyebrows sprang out like antennae—blood began to pour from his nose. He pressed harder and harder, until the pain became unbearable, but still he pressed until he no longer had the strength in his arms or the leverage with which to press.

Already his spine was softening, could no longer support his weight. He dropped to the floor, grunting as the air was forced from his lungs. His arms flopped wildly. He pulled his knees up and grabbed hold of his feet as hard as he could. As he straightened his legs again, his arms began to lengthen. His elbows popped, the bones pulling out of their sockets—he screamed with pain; rolled over and grabbed the block of wood in his mouth, bit it as hard as he could. He did this again and again, stretching his arms into long, black, hairy appendages.

Yes, the hair! It was sprouting all over his arms and legs. His legs were softening now. He pulled his knees up to his chest, and now, grabbing them again with his hardening arms, he pulled at his knees until the sockets popped and now his legs could lengthen naturally. He clutched his feet, working them into clawlike shapes, stretching his toes, pulling at them mercilessly, grunting with the pain, and still continuing to pull. And yes, now the side appendages were large enough to grab, to pull, to stretch. He worked his muscles savagely, massaging them into shape, strengthening them. Yes, this was going to be one of the best! The more pain he experienced, the better the transformation!

He rolled around on the floor, rubbing his back and sides against the rubber sheet, hardening his carapace. He wiped at his multifaceted eyes with his front legs, cleaning them of bloody residue. His antennae twitched. He was almost done. Almost there—and yes, in a final spasm of completion, he *ejaculated*! Spurt after spurt after spurt of sickly yellow-looking ichor. The shaft of his metallic-looking penis retreated again inside his chitiny shell, and Bug-Man raised himself aloft on his six exquisite legs, chittering with satisfaction and joy!

Bug-Man was a simple being. He had no knowledge of anything but the blood of his enemy. He cared nothing for Franz Kafka or the League Of United Superheroes Everywhere. He knew little of trains and croissants and newspapers. Bug-Man was a creature of hunger and rage. He knew only the ferocious desire for vengeance. He lived for the hot red fulfillment of delicious gluttony. His mandibles clattered in soft anticipation. He drooled with excitement. He wanted one thing only—the flesh of PsycheMan! He could not rest until he'd crunched the skull of Sigmund Freud between his diamond-hard teeth!

He leapt to the window, flinging it open, pulling himself out onto the balustrade, poising himself, stretching himself up into the darkness and the holy glow of the full moon above. Across the way, he heard a gasp, and then the sound of a window slamming. A light vanished. He heard the sounds of running footsteps. He ignored them all. He leapt.

He landed lightly on the soft black earth of the garden below. Instantly, he began digging, down and down into the deep delicious soil, his six legs working frantically, flinging the dirt, backward and upward, scattering it in every direction. His mandibles chewed and cut. In moments, he was gone, sliding into the cool dark space beneath the lawn, tunneling his way toward the house of Sigmund Freud, the monster.

The night fell silent. The moon rose higher and higher until it was directly overhead, casting its lambent radiance down across the gabled old houses of sleeping Vienna. And then a noise....

The sound of something creaking, cracking, crackling as it broke—

The ancient floorboards came away in ragged chunks. The hole widened. Something was chewing up through the ground, widening the hole in quick, malicious bites. And then it was climbing up and into the cellar of the house. Bug-Man was here! Inside the house of his arch-enemy! He scrabbled purposefully across the floor, sniffing the air with his antennae. He slid up the stairs, not bothering to open the door at the top, breaking through it instead like a flimsy construction of cardboard.

He was in the pantry! The overwhelming pantry, reeking with conflicting flavors and aromas—all the spices and ingredients of a thousand different meals, coffee-chocolate-butter-garlic-sausage-cheese-pepper-bread—they all repulsed him now. He moved swiftly to the kitchen, to the dining room, to the stairway in the hall, and up the stairs, breaking away the banister as he climbed to give himself room.

There was no dark at the top of the stairs. The light came on abruptly. Someone was moving up there. Bug-Man's glistening multifaceted eyes caught the image in a shattered reality. There—silhouetted against the glare of the electric lamp beyond—stood the terrible demonic form of Sigmund Freud, the *PsycheMan!*

He stood alone, wearing only a nightshirt, a robe, and fuzzy blue slippers. He rested one hand on the top of the broken banister to support himself. He looked incredibly frail, but his eyes gleamed with turquoise power! His high forehead bulged abnormally; the fringe of white hair around it was not enough to conceal its freakish expanded shape. His predatory chin was concealed by the long white beard. His bony knees stuck out from beneath the hem of his garment like awkward chicken legs.

The transformed Kafka lifted himself up, as if about to leap. He uttered a low sound, a moan of anticipatory lust, a growl of warning, a challenge, a chittering of danger.

"Ach!" said Freud. "It's only you. Well, come in, come in. I've been expecting you. You're late again." He waggled his finger warningly. "You superheroes, you think you can come calling any time, day or night, without an appointment—"

He started to turn away, then suddenly, turned back toward Bug-Man, his eyes blazing with red fire! *"Well, I won't have it!"* He knocked the ash off his cigar into his hand and carefully pocketed the residue. Then he lifted the cigar like a baton, holding it outstretched toward the man-bug. With his other hand he stroked the cigar, once, twice, a third time—suddenly the cigar emitted a crackling bolt of blue-white lightning down the staircase. Bug-Man ducked his head just in time. The blast of fire splattered off his back singing the walls, scorching the wallpaper, striking little fires among the chips and sawdust of the broken banister all the way down and leaving the air stinking of ozone.

Kafka was stunned. For a moment, he almost forgot that he was

Bug-Man. Freud was much stronger than he thought. He must have been gaining converts faster than they had realized, far more than they had estimated. He must have been draining the life force of hundreds, perhaps thousands of hapless souls, distilling their very being down into his own evil essence.

Bug-Man recovered himself then. He stopped thinking, stopped considering, stopped caring—he remembered his purpose. To *feed on the flesh of Sigmund Freud!* He charged up the stairs after the monstrous little man. But Freud's frail demeanor was only another deceit. The old man scampered away like an animated elf, disappearing into the darkness at the far end of the hall.

Bug-Man followed relentlessly, his six long hairy legs scrabbling loudly on the hardwood floor. His claws left nasty scratches in the polished surface. He plunged into the darkness—

And found himself in a maze of twisty little passages, all alike. A maze. The maze. Twisty little passages. A twisty little maze. All alike.

His eyes swiveled backward and forward—and he hesitated. For a moment, he had to be Kafka again. Had to rely on his innate human intelligence instead of his insect instinct. Reminded himself, *Freud has no power of his own. He borrows the power of others. He summons monsters from the id and lets them fight his battles for him. But it's all illusion. You will destroy yourself fighting empty manifestations of your own fears. Ignore the illusions. Concentrate on what's real!*

Bug-Man's hesitation stretched out forever. His chitiny shell began to soften. His mandibles clattered in confusion. *But—but how do I know what's real?* he wondered. *Everything that a being can know is ultimately experiential. I have no way to stand apart from the experiential nature of existence! So how can I access what is real and distinguish it from illusion?*

It seemed as if all time was standing still. Kafka's mind raced, his thought processes accelerated. *Be who you are!* he shouted to the Bug-Man! *Don't let him define you! He is a walrus. You are the Bug-Man! You are the greatest superhero ever! Ignore the lies! Anything that contradicts the Bug-Man is a lie! Remember that!*

The Bug-Man snarled. Unconfused. He knew himself again, submerged himself once more in crimson fury and fire; the hunger and rage suffused his body like a bath of acid. He clicked his mandibles, reached out with his pincers and started pulling down the ugly twisty little walls and their dripping veins and wires, started pulling down the twisty little maze of darkness and fury, sending creatures of indeterminate shape scuttling out into the fringes, started pulling down the twisty little passages all alike, pulling and chewing and breaking through—

He was in a tunnel. Blackness behind him. Blackness ahead.

The tunnel slanted downward into the bottomless dark. The walls were straight; they were set wide apart, but the ceiling was low. Everything was cut from dark wet stone. The water dripped from the walls and slid downward into the gloom ahead. His eyes refocused. What little light there was seeped into the air from no apparent source.

Far in the distance below, something moved. He could smell it. His antennae quivered in anticipation. He lifted his pincers. He readied his stinger, arching his tail high over his head. His venom dripped.

The thing ahead was coming closer. In the blackness below, a formless form was growing. It opened its eyes. Two bright red embers, glowing ferociously! The eyes were screaming toward him now!

Stinger?!

Bug-Man remembered just in time. *Ignore the lies!*

The red eyes went hurling past him, vanishing into darkness. The screams of rage faded into distant echoes that hung in the air like dreadful memories—

I could have stung myself, right behind the brain case—he realized. And then, realizing again how narrowly he had escaped the trap of the Freudian paradigm, he warned himself again. *You are the Bug-Man! Don't let him define you or your reality! Monsters from the id aren't real!*

The Bug-Man headed down the tunnel. Its angle of descent increased abruptly, getting steeper and steeper, until he was slipping, sliding, skidding, tumbling—

—onto the hard-baked surface of a place with no sun, no moon, no sky, and no horizon. Tall black cylinders surrounded them, leaping up into the gloom and disappearing overhead. They looked like the bars of a cage.

Freud stood beside one of the bars, surveying him thoughtfully. "You are resisting the treatment," he said. "I can't help you if you do not want to be helped." He waggled his finger meaningfully. "*You must really want to change!*"

Bug-Man roared in fury. It consumed him like volcanic fire. He became a core of molten energy. The blast of emotion overwhelmed him. Enraged, he charged.

Bug-Man galloped across the space between them, tearing up the floor with his six mighty claws. He thundered like a bull, hot smoke streaming from the vents of his nostrils. The black leviathan leapt—

—and abruptly, Freud was gone!

Bug-Man smashed against the bars of the cage like a locomotive hitting a wall, his legs flailing, his body deforming, the air screaming out from his lungs like a steam whistle. He shrieked in rage and frustration and pain. He fell back, legs working wildly, righted himself, whirled around, eyes flicking this way and that, focusing on Freud again. The *PsycheMan* waited for him on the opposite side of the cage. The Bug-Man didn't hesitate! He charged again—

—and again, he came slamming up against the bars. Helpless for an instant, he lay there gasping and wondering what he was doing wrong. Transformed Kafka shuddered in his shell. But he pushed the thought aside, levered himself back to his feet, focused again on his target, readied his charge, sighted his prey—

This time, he would watch to see which way the *PsycheMan* leapt. He would snatch him from the air. He held his pincers high and wide. Instead of charging, he advanced steadily, inexorably, closing on his elusive prey like some ghastly mechanical device of the industrial revolution gone mad. His mandibles clicked and clashed. His eyes shone with unholy fury. A terrible guttural sound came moaning up out of his throat—

—came slamming hard against the bars of the cage as if he'd been fired into them by a cannon. The discontinuity left him rolling across the floor in pain, clutching at his aching genitals and crying in little soft gasps. He pulled himself back to his knees, his feet, trying to solidify his form again. He stood there, wavering, almost whimpering.

"What's wrong?" he asked himself. "What am I doing wrong?"

Kafka looked across the cage. Freud stood there grinning nastily. The old man laughed. "You battle yourself!" he said thickly. "The rigidity of your constructed identity cannot deal with events occurring outside of its world view. You become confused and you attack shadows and phantoms!"

Kafka took a deep breath. Then another, and another. "I am Franz

Kafka, superhero!" he said to himself. "I am here to destroy the evil paradigm of Dr. Freud! I will not be defeated."

No!—he realized abruptly. *That way doesn't work! I am the master of metamorphosis. I must metamorphose into something that the doctor cannot defeat!* At first he thought of giant squids and vampire bats, cobras and bengal tigers, raging elephants, bears, dragons, manticores, goblins, trolls—Jungian archetypes! *But, no*—he realized. *That would be just more of the same! Just another monster! To fight a monster I must change into something ELSE—*

He stood there motionless, staring across the cage at his fiendish opponent, considering. His mind worked like a precision machine, a clockwork device ticking away at superfast speed. His thoughts raced, exploring strange new possibilities he had never conceived before.

Ego cogito sum—he considered. *I have been reacting to his manipulations. Reactive behavior allows him to control the circumstance. Proactive behavior puts me in control. I should attack him, but attacking him is still reaction. Yet, if I don't attack him, I cannot defeat him. How can I be proactive without being reactive?*

Bug-Man wavered. His confusion manifested itself as a softening of his shell, a spreading pale discoloration of his metallic carapace. His mandibles began to shrink. His arms and legs began to plump out, seeking their previous shape. *No!* he shrieked to himself. *No! Not yet! I haven't killed him yet!*

Bug-Man felt himself weakening, growing ever more helpless in the face of his enemy. He felt shamed and embarrassed. He wanted to scuttle off and hide in the woodwork. His bowels let loose, his bladder emptied. His skin became soft and pallid again. He stood naked before Freud. Franz Kafka, superhero. But the Bug-Man was defeated, discredited—

No! said Kafka. *No! I won't have it. I am Franz Kafka, superhero! I don't need to be a giant cockroach to destroy the malevolence of Freud! I can stop him with my bare hands.*

—And then he knew!

"Your paradigm is invalid," Kafka said. "It's powerful, yes, but ultimately, it has no power over those who refuse to give it power; therefore, it is not an accurate map of the objective reality, only another word-game played out in language." Freud's eyes widened in surprise. Kafka took two steps toward him. "You're just a middle-aged Viennese Jew, who smokes too much, talks too much, and suffers from—your word—*ago-raphobia.* You can't even cross the street without help!" Freud held up a hand in protest, but Kafka kept advancing, continued his unflinching verbal assault. "You're a dirty old man. You can't stop talking about sex, you want to kill your father and copulate with your mother—and you believe that everybody else feels the same thing, too! You're despicable, Sigmund Freud!"

Freud's chin trembled. "You—you don't understand. You're functioning as a paranoid schizophrenic with psychotic delusions. You've constructed a worldview in which explanations are impossible—"

"That won't work, Siggie. It's just so much language. It's just a load of psyche-babble. The distinctions you've drawn are arbitrary constructions that only have the meaning that we as humans invest them with. Well, I withdraw my investment. Your words are meaningless. I will not be *psychologized.* You are just a disgusting little man who likes to talk about penises!"

The old man made one last attempt to withstand the withering assault of Kafka's logic. "But if you withdraw all meaning from the paradigm—" he protested, "—what meaning can you replace it with?"

"That's just it!" exulted Kafka, delivering the death blow. *"Life is empty and meaningless!"*

Horrified, Freud collapsed to the floor of his parlor, clutching at his chest.

Kafka stood over him, triumphant. *"It's meaningless, you old fart!"*

Freud moaned—

"It doesn't mean anything! And it doesn't even mean anything that it doesn't mean anything! So we're free to make it up any way we choose!"

"Please, no. Please, stop—"

But Kafka wasn't finished. "Your way is just a possible way of being, Sigmund—but it isn't the only way! The difference between you and me is that because I know the bindings of my language, I also know my freedom within those bindings! You have been focusing on the bindings, you old asshole, *not the freedom."*

Freud was shuddering now, impaled on Kafka's impeccable truths. He trembled uncontrollably on the patterned rug, sick and despairing at the chaotic darkness gathering around him. The broken shards of his shattered paradigm had sliced his soul mercilessly, leaving the poor defeated man twitching in the growing puddles of his own terminal *weltschmerz*. "Forgive me, please. I didn't know what I was doing."

Kafka knelt to the floor, gathered Freud up in his arms, held him gently, cradling him like a child. He placed one soft hand on the old man's forehead. "It's all right now, Siggie," he soothed. "It's all over. You can stop. You can rest."

Freud looked up into Kafka's calm expression, questioning, hoping. He saw only kindness in the superhero's eyes. Reassured, he let himself relax; he allowed peace to flood throughout his body. All stiffness fled. Sigmund Freud rested securely in Franz Kafka's arms. "Thank you," he whispered. "Thank you."

"No," said Kafka. "On the contrary. It is *I* who should thank *you*." And with that he plunged his needle-sharp teeth into Sigmund Freud's pale exposed neck, ripping it open. He bent his head and fed ferociously. The hot rush of blood slaked his incredible thirst, and he moaned in delirious ecstasy.

Triumph was delicious.

The immortal storyteller Alfred Bester once said that the way to tell a story is to begin with a disaster and then build to a climax. I'd like to—believe me, I'd like to—but this particular story happened just the other way round.

—*Spider Robinson*

Too Hot to Hoot

SPIDER ROBINSON

I T WAS A GOOD CLIMAX, AT LEAST.

Well, okay, maybe that's a silly statement. Perhaps you feel that there is no such thing as a *bad* climax; that some are better than others, is all. I could argue the point, but I won't. Let's just agree with Woody Allen that "The worst one I ever had was right on the money," stipulate that they're all at least okay, and try to quantify the matter a bit.

On a scale of ten, then, rating "the least enjoyable orgasm I've ever had" as a One, and "reaching the culmination of hours of foreplay with the sexiest partner imaginable after years of celibacy" as a Ten, the climax I'm speaking of now was probably about a Nine-Five.

This despite the fact that every one of the ingredients I've named for a Ten were present. The foreplay had been so extensive and inventive (*Groucho, leering*: "...and the *aft*play wasn't so bad either....") that the sun was coming up by the time I was going in the other direction; my partner was the sexiest woman on the planet, my darling Zoey Berkowitz; and she was my first real lover (as opposed to mere sexer) in more years than I cared to think about. True, we had already been lovers for several months, by then...but the honeymoon was by no means over. (In fact, it still isn't. The way I see it, our relationship is really just a single continuous ongoing act of lovemaking, a dance so complex and subtle that we often disengage bodies completely for hours at a time.) My father used to say, "Familiarity breeds content," and that's always been my experience.

No, what brought the meter down as low as Nine-Five was merely a matter of mechanics. Zoey has never been a small woman, not since the sixth grade, anyway, and she was nine and a half months months pregnant at the time all this happened, in the late fall of 1988.

101

Indeed, if I could travel in time like Mike Callahan, and went far enough back into hominid history, I think I could prove my theory that pregnancy is responsible for the evolution of Man As Engineer. (This might help explain why there are so few female engineers.) A man who has successfully managed the trick with a mate in the latter stages of pregnancy possesses most of the insights necessary to build a house—and a strong motivation in that direction, as well. If inventing math were as much fun, we'd probably own the Galaxy by now.

But I digress....

As I was saying, Zoey and I had solved the Riddle of the Sphinx together one more time, just as enough dawnglow was sneaking past the edges of the curtains to let us see what we already knew, and neither of us was paying attention to any damn imaginary scoring judges—we were both well content, if a little fatigued. By the time we had our breath back, the day was well and truly begun: birds had begun warbling somewhere outside, and traffic was building up to the usual weekday-morning homicidal frenzy out on Route 25A (*why* are they all in such a hurry to get to a place they hate and do things they don't care about?), a combination of sounds that always puts me right to sleep. That's probably just where I'd have gone if Zoey hadn't poked me in a tender spot and murmured drowsily, "...'cha *snickering* about?"

I hadn't realized I was. In fact, I wasn't. "I'm not," I said. "I'm chuckling."

She shook her head. "Unh-unh. I like Snickers better'n Chuckles."

I considered a couple of puns having to do with the physical characteristics and components of the candy named, but left them unspoken. Sexual puns are funnier *before* you come. "Chortling, then," I said. "Definitely not a snicker."

Zoey grimaced, her eyes still glued shut. "But *why*? Are you."

"Oh, it's just this silly mental picture I get after we make love," I admitted. "I keep seeing little Nameless floating in there, startled awake by this rhythmic earthquake... then staring in fascination as all these millions of confused, exhausted, disappointed little wigglers show up, looking everywhere for an egg. I'll bet they tickle. The little tyke must get a chuckle out of it."

"Or a chortle," she agreed, chortling sleepily. "I will too—f'now on. Thanks. Neat image."

She yawned hugely then, so of course I did too, and we did the little bits of physical backing and filling necessary to move from Cuddling to Snuggling, and we'd probably both have been comfortably asleep together in only another minute or two. But we had forgotten about the Invisible Machines of Murphy.

The universe is full of them, and many of them seem to be simple pressure-switches. For instance, there's one underneath most toilet seats: your weight coming down on the seat somehow causes the phone to ring. (Unless you've brought the phone in with you: in that case the switch cues a Jehovah's Witness to knock on your door.) There's another one built into most TV remote controls, wired into the channel-select button: if you try to browse, it somehow alerts every station on the the air to go to commercial. The most maddening thing about these switches is that, being of Murphy, they're unreliable: you can't be sure whether or just when they will function, except that it will usually turn out in retrospect to have been at the most annoying possible moment. So the tiny pair of switches under my eyelids, sensing that I was just about to drop off to sleep, picked now to send out the signal that causes my alarm clock to ring. Excuse me—I mean, to:

BZZZZZZZZZZZZZZZZZZZZZZZZ!!!!!

For the past two weeks that damned thing had been going off at just this ungodly hour—set by mine own hand and with Zoey's foreknowledge and consent—and every single time it came as a rude and ghastly surprise. Neither of us could get used to it. I had been a professional musician for a quarter of a century until I gave it up to tend bar; Zoey still was one—or had been right up until carrying both a baby and a bass guitar got to be too much for her; it had been decades since either of us had willingly gotten up at dawn. Dawn was what you occasionally stayed up as late as. Sunlight gave you the skin cancer, everybody knew that. *Civilians* got up at dawn, for heaven's sake.

Well, so do nine-and-a-half-month-pregnant women. And their partners. No matter what their normal sleep-cycle is.

Being more than nine months pregnant may mean nothing at all. Not even when you get up to nine and a half months, and the kid hasn't even dropped yet. Maybe you just guessed wrong on the conception date. We don't want you to worry, Ms. Berkowitz. But maybe, just maybe something is wrong in there. Maybe little Nameless doesn't *want* to come out and play, ready or not. If so, it is a bad decision, however one might sympathize—because once Nameless *is* ready, he or she will begin to do what all fully formed babies do best: excrete. And, polluting the womb, will die. And possibly take you along for company. The chances of this are indeterminate...but it might be wisest if you just checked into the hospital now, Ms. Berkowitz, and allowed us to induce labor with a pitocin drip....

Zoey had awarded that offer an emphatic "Fuck you very much, Doctor," and I was behind her a hundred percent. At the time. We had both devoured most of the available literature on birthing as a subversive activity, and were determined to Do This Naturally—not with drugs and episiotomies, like postmodern drones, but the way our primitive ancestors did it in the caves: with a trained Lamaze partner, a camcorder, and a physician standing by just in case. As far as we were concerned, Nameless could emerge in his or her own good time.

The hospital had seen all too many zealots like us; they sighed and agreed to let us wait as long as we could stand it, against advice...provided we were willing to furnish daily proof that Nameless was not in fact dying in there. In the form of a maternal urine sample. Which they would need first thing in the morning. Every morning. Wherefore:

BZZZZZZZZZZZZZZZZZZZZZZZZ!!!!!

As far as I can see, the biggest disadvantage to having a pregnant lady around the home is that it's always your turn to get up. I said a few words, and Zoey stuck an elbow in my ribs, saying, "Not in front of the baby!" So I said some more words, but in my head, and got up out of bed. As I went around the bed, I confirmed by eye that her chamber pot was placed where she would be able to conveniently straddle it, and went to the bathroom to get another specimen container from the package under the sink. (If you think ten yards is too short a walk to the bathroom for a chamber pot to be necessary, you've never been nine and a half months pregnant.) And then...well, it got complicated.

I bent over, see, and took the package by a scrap of torn flap at the top, and straightened up, intending to rummage inside the thing for a specimen container once I got it up to around waist level. But Zoey had been pregnant for nine months and thirteen days, and those damn packages hold a dozen... so it was empty... and since it was empty, it didn't weigh anything... and since I was expecting it to weigh at least *something*, and was more than a little groggy... well, I overbalanced and landed ass-first in the bathtub, whanging my head against the tile wall.

It could have happened to you, okay? Sure, it didn't, and never will... but it *could* have. And if it had, I wouldn't have laughed at *you*.

Oh all right, I'm lying. Go ahead.

Zoey had apparently decided to rest her eyes until I got back, and *then* get up into a sitting position, when there was someone there to help. But her love was true: I believe the combination of my piteous wail and the loud reverberating *boom* were probably enough to cause at least one of her eyes to open, perhaps as much as halfway. "You alive, hon?" she murmured.

I was dazed, and not honestly sure of the answer, but I could not ignore the concern in her voice. "Depends on what you call living," I temporized, trying with little success to get out of the tub.

Her reply was a snore.

My struggles triggered another of those invisible Murphy Switches: the shower-head's built-in bombsight detected the presence of an unsuspecting human in its target area, and cut loose with the half-cup or so of ice-water it keeps handy for such occasions, scoring a direct hit on my groin. That got me up out of the bathtub, at least, though I can't explain exactly how; all I know is, an instant later I was standing up and drawing in breath to swear. Loudly. With a great effort I managed to squelch it. The useless empty paper sack that should have held specimen jars was still in my hand; I flung it angrily toward the wastebasket beyond the toilet bowl. But of course it had poor aerodynamic characteristics for a projectile: it fluttered and flapped and curled over and fell short, square into the toilet bowl. Two points. This time I was not entirely successful in suppressing my bark of rage; it emerged as a kind of moan. I turned angrily on my heel, and walked straight into the edge of the open bathroom door. The sun went nova, and when it had cooled, I found that I was sitting again, on the cold tile floor this time. The front of my head now hurt as much as the back, and my buttocks hurt twice as much.

Outside in the bedroom, Zoey snored again.

For the third time, my lungs sucked in air... and then let it out again, very slowly. If I woke Zoey with screamed curses, I'd have to explain why—and then refrain from strangling her while she giggled. Or chortled. I got up, rubbed the places that hurt, and turned my attention to the problem of improvising an alternate urine container. If it had been for myself or another male, no problem—but females need a wider aperture. I shuffled past the sleeping Zoey and left the bedroom, searching for inspiration.

By the time I found it, I had left our living quarters completely and wandered out into Mary's Place proper.

Living in back of a tavern has been a lifelong dream of mine, and the reality has turned out to be even better than I imagined. There, for instance, ranked in rows behind the bar, were a plethora of acceptable receptacles. (Say that three times fast with marbles in your mouth and you'll never need a dentist again.) Before selecting one, I punched a combination into The Machine and set a mug upright on its conveyor belt, which hummed into life and whisked the mug away into the interior. Less than a minute later it emerged from the far side of The Machine, filled now with fresh hot Tanzanian Peaberry coffee adulterated to my taste. I took it and the specimen container I had chosen back into the bedroom.

There are few things a very pregnant woman will wake up for, but peeing is definitely one of them. Getting Zoey to a sitting position on the side of the bed (without tipping over the chamber pot) was probably less difficult than portaging a piano. The smell of coffee must have helped. She took a long sip of it, then came fully awake when she recognized the receptacle I was offering her.

"Jake, I am *not* peeing into a stein."

"Oh hell, Zoey, what's its religion got to do with anything? It's wide enough, it's been sterilized, it's got a lid I can tape shut after, we're out of specimen jars, just go ahead and get it over with, okay? Whoever it is today will be here any minute."

My best friends in the world—a.k.a.: my regular clientele—had organized what they insisted on calling a Pee Pool: each morning one of them took a turn at coming by Mary's Place to pick up the day's specimen and ferry it to the hospital for analysis. I had no idea whose turn it was today, and was too groggy to figure it out, but the way things were going I suspected it would be one of the rare prompt ones.

Zoey thought it over, and relaxed to the inevitable. She set the coffee down where I couldn't reach it without stepping over her, deployed the stein above the thundermug, and cut loose.

Sure enough, just as she finished, there was a thunderous knocking. A *distant* thunderous knocking—at the bar's front door.

That irritated me. Whoever it was could have just as easily come around to *this* side of the building and knocked on the much-closer *back* door. As a gesture of my irritation, I tossed aside the underpants I had just managed to locate, snatched the filled stein out of Zoey's hand, and set off to answer the knock stark naked. "Jake—" Zoey called after me, and I snarled, "Whoever it is has it coming," over my shoulder. For the second time that day I padded out of the living area and into the bar, went through the swinging doors into the foyer, and flung open the outside door with a flourish.

And was vouchsafed a vision.

It had to be a vision. Reality, even the rather plastic kind I've learned to live with over the years, simply could not—I felt—produce a sight like that. Nor was it a mere hallucination: I had not had a drink in many hours, or a toke in several days. The thing was so weird that it took me a full second or two to learn to see it: at first my brain rejected what it was given and searched for plausible alternatives.

This object is a fireplug—no, a fireplug's older brother—over which someone has draped a very used painter's dropcloth, and onto the top of which someone has placed the severed head of a pitbull. No, wait, pitbulls don't have mustaches. Perhaps this is the secret midget son of Buddy Hackett, wearing a paint-spattered toga as part of his fraternity initiation. No, I have it now: this is R2-D2 dressed for Halloween. Or maybe—

We gaped at each other for a good five seconds of silence, the vision and I, before I tentatively—and correctly—identified it as the ugliest woman I had ever seen. The moment I did so, I screamed and jumped back a foot—and at the exact same instant, she did the exact same thing.

The difference was, I was holding a nearly full stein.

The lid flew open when I started, and a glog of the contents sailed out into the air: an elongated fluid projectile, like a golden version of the second, liquid-metal-model Terminator. It caught her amidships and splattered, the splat-sound overpowered by the *clop!* of the stein lid slamming shut again.

There was a short pause, and then she barked.

I mean barked, like a dog. In fact, *yapped* is closer to the sound she made—but doesn't begin to convey the impact. Even "barked" isn't strong enough. Maybe "bayed." Imagine a two-hundred-pound Pekingese with a bullhorn, and you've only started to imagine that sound. It was something like all the fingernails in the world being drawn across all the blackboards in Hell and then amplified through the Madison Square Garden sound system at maximum gain.

I shivered rather like a dog myself, blinked rapidly without effect, and felt my testicles retreating into my trunk.

The vision barked again, louder—a sound which you can duplicate for yourself if you wish by simply inserting a power drill into each ear simultaneously. As its echo faded, I heard the distant sounds of Zoey approaching to investigate. She pushed the swinging doors open and joined me in the foyer—stopped short and gaped.

The...I was finally beginning to believe it was a human woman, or something like one...gaped back at the two of us, staring from the naked hairy man to the extremely pregnant woman in the ratty bathrobe. She opened her mouth to bark again, paused, blinked, looked down at the damp stain on her chest, sniffed sharply—the sight of her hirsute nostrils flaring will go with me to my grave—glared up at me, then at the stein in my hand, then back at me, then down at the stain on her chest again, then one more time at Zoey, and finally she threw back her head and *howled.*

A couple of glasses burst behind the bar.

I heard them just before my hearing cut out completely, as though God had accidentally overloaded the automatic level control on my tape deck. I know I tried to scream myself, but don't know whether I succeeded. I also tried to jam my fingers into my ears, to stop the pain that continued long after actual hearing had fled. Not only didn't it help a bit, the stein I had abandoned to do so landed squarely on my bare right foot, with a crunch that I *did* hear, by bone conduction, and sprayed the last of its contents onto the creature's behaired shins, pilled socks, and orthopedic shoes.

A pity, for it caused her to sustain her howl longer than she might have otherwise, and to shake at me a fist like a small wrinkled ham.

Horrible as that shriek was—and it was, even without being audible—the end of it was worse, for now she had to draw in breath for the *next* one, and so I saw her teeth. I can see them now. My eyes sent my brain an urgent message asking how come *they* had to stay on duty when my ears had already bugged out.

With that, my Guardian Idiot snapped out of his stupor, and reminded me that I did not have to endure this trial any longer than I chose to. I closed the door quietly but firmly in her face.

Then I stood on one leg and cradled my mashed foot in both hands and hopped in pain. Then I lost my balance and fell down, for the third time that morning, on my bare ass, banging my head again too. (For those of you who are connoisseurs of anguish, a hardwood floor is perceptibly harder than either tub or tile.)

Zoey, bless her, did the only thing she could: she burst out laughing.

I did not join her. Not right away. I tried a withering glare—but if age cannot wither nor custom stale my Zoey, no glare of mine is going to do the trick. Then I thought about kicking her, somewhere that wouldn't endanger Nameless—but now was not a good time to get beat up. Next I opened my mouth to say something—deeming it safe because I assumed she was still as deafened as me by the vision's banshee cry.

But before I could, I realized that the deafness must have worn off: I could hear Zoey's hoots of helpless hysteria, now, and the distant and fading sound of that monstrous barking outside. So I closed my mouth, prepared a slightly less offensive speech, opened my mouth again...and clearly heard the sound of knocking.

Distant knocking. Not here—but at the back door, back in the bedroom...where one of my friends must be waiting to receive the daily beaker of piss.

Now I joined Zoey in laughing.

I just had to. It was that or go mad. The louder and more urgent the distant knocking became, the harder we laughed. Finally I got up, collected the empty stein, and went, still laughing, to answer the knock.

"What the *hell* was that?" Zoey asked as we walked back toward our quarters, wiping away tears of laughter.

"I think it was a person," I said. "I'm pretty sure it was a life form of some kind, anyway."

"If you say so. I wonder what in God's name she wanted. What language was that she was speaking?"

"I'm not sure she was evolved that far. Come on, hurry up, or—"

Needless to say, by the time we got to the back door to answer the knock, the knocker—Noah Gonzalez—had given up and gone round to the front door. I left Zoey there and retraced my steps through the entire building—for the third time, before coffee—and got to the front door moments after Noah had given up and gone round to the *back* door again.

That's it, I thought, *I quit.* I went as far as the bar, made a second cup of coffee and vowed not to move another step until I had finished drinking this one. Zoey and Noah must have connected, and worked out for themselves the awkward business of him waiting in the bedroom while she waddled into the bathroom and refilled the stein for him. (No problem for a pregnant lady.) By the time she came out to find me, carrying my bathrobe, I was putting the finishing touches on the lyrics of a new song.

It goes like this:

God has a sense of humor, but it's often rather crude
What He thinks is a howler, you or I would say is rude
But cursing Him is not a real productive attitude
Just laugh—you might as well, my friend,
'cause either way you're screwed
　I know: it sounds so simple, and it's so hard to do
　To laugh when the joke's on you

God loved Mort Sahl, Belushi, Lenny Bruce—He likes it sick
Fields, Chaplin, Keaton... anyone in pain will do the trick
'Cause God's idea of slapstick is to slap you with a stick:
You might as well resign yourself to stepping on your dick
　It always sounds so simple, but it's so hard to do
　To laugh when the joke's on you

　You can laugh at a total stranger
　When it isn't your ass in danger

And your lover can be a riot
—if you learn how to giggle quiet
But if you want the right to giggle, that is what you gotta do
when the person steppin' on that old banana peel is you

A chump and a banana peel: the core of every joke
But when it's you that steps on one, your laughter tends to choke
Try not to take it personal, just have another toke
as long as you ain't broken, what's the difference if you're broke?
  I know: it sounds so simple, but it's so hard to do
  To laugh when the joke's on you

It can be hard to force a smile, as you get along in years
It isn't easy laughin' at your deepest secret fears
But try to find your funny-bone, and have a couple beers:
If it don't come out in laughter, man, it's comin' out in tears
  I said it sounds so simple, but it's so hard to do
  To laugh when the joke's on you

The barking vision did not return. Within ten minutes, Zoey and I had crawled back into bed, where we would enjoy a sound and undisturbed sleep, and nothing else awful or astonishing was to happen after that until well after sundown.

But—had we but known it—the ending of Mary's Place had already begun.

California, where I have made my home the past three-and-a-half decades, is a goofy place with great weather and gorgeous scenery. I love the scenery and the weather, am not so fond of the goofiness.

In "Amanda and the Alien," I turned a dangerous alien life form loose about twenty miles east of where I live and set out to see how my fellow Californians would cope with it. I meant the results to be comic, but even after all this time on the West Coast I'm not sure from day to day whether what goes on all around me out here is comic or tragic.

—Robert Silverberg

Amanda and the Alien

ROBERT SILVERBERG

AMANDA SPOTTED THE ALIEN LATE Friday afternoon outside the Video Center, on South Main. It was trying to look cool and laid-back, but it simply came across as bewildered and uneasy. The alien was disguised as a seventeen-year-old girl, maybe a Chicana, with olive-toned skin and hair so black it seemed almost blue, but Amanda, who was seventeen herself, knew a phony when she saw one. She studied the alien for some moments from the other side of the street to make absolutely certain. Then she walked over.

"You're doing it wrong," Amanda said. "Anybody with half a brain could tell what you really are."

"Bug off," the alien said.

"No. Listen to me. You want to stay out of the detention center, or don't you?"

The alien stared coldly at Amanda and said, "I don't know what the crap you're talking about."

"Sure you do. No sense trying to bluff me. Look, I want to help you," Amanda said. "I think you're getting a raw deal. You know what that means, a raw deal? Hey, look, come home with me, and I'll teach you a few things about passing for human. I've got the whole friggin' weekend now with nothing else to do anyway."

A flicker of interest came into the other girl's dark, chilly eyes. But it died quickly, and she said, "You some kind of lunatic?"

"Suit yourself, O thing from beyond the stars. Let them lock you up again. Let them stick electrodes up your ass. I tried to help. That's all I can do, is try," Amanda said, shrugging. She began to saunter away. She didn't look back. Three steps, four, five, hands in pockets, slowly heading for her car. Had she been wrong, she wondered? No. No. She could be wrong about some things, like Charley Taylor's interest in spending

115

the weekend with her, maybe. But not this. That crinkly haired chick was the missing alien for sure.

The whole county was buzzing about it: Deadly nonhuman life form has escaped from the detention center out by Tracy, might be anywhere, Walnut Creek, Livermore, even San Francisco, dangerous monster, capable of mimicking human forms, will engulf and digest you and disguise itself in your shape. And there it was, Amanda knew, standing outside the Video Center. Amanda kept walking.

"Wait," the alien said finally.

Amanda took another easy step or two. Then she looked back over her shoulder.

"Yeah?"

"How can you tell?"

Amanda grinned. "Easy. You've got a rain slicker on, and it's only September. Rainy season doesn't start around here for another month or two. Your pants are the old Spandex kind. People like you don't wear that stuff anymore. Your face paint is San Jose colors, but you've got the cheek chevrons put on in the Berkeley pattern. That's just the first three things I noticed. I could find plenty more. Nothing about you fits together with anything else. It's like you did a survey to see how you ought to appear and then tried a little of everything. The closer I study you, the more I see. Look, you're wearing your headphones, and the battery light is on, but there's no cassette in the slot. What are you listening to, the music of the spheres? That model doesn't have any FM tuner, you know.

"You see? You may think that you're perfectly camouflaged, but you aren't."

"I could destroy you," the alien said.

"What? Oh, sure. Sure you could. Engulf me right here on the street, all over in thirty seconds, little trail of slime by the door, and a new Amanda walks away. But what then? What good's that going to do you? You still won't know which end is up. So there's no logic in destroying me, unless you're a total dummy. I'm on your side. I'm not going to turn you in."

"Why should I trust you?"

"Because I've been talking to you for five minutes and I haven't yelled for the cops yet. Don't you know that half of California is out searching for you? Hey, can you read? Come over here a minute. Here." Amanda tugged the alien toward the newspaper vending box at the curb. The headline on the afternoon *Examiner* was

BAY AREA ALIEN TERROR MARINES TO JOIN NINE-COUNTY HUNT
MAYOR, GOVERNOR CAUTION AGAINST PANIC

"You understand that?" Amanda asked. "That's you they're talking about. They're out there with flame guns, tranquilizer darts, web snares, and God knows what else. There's been real hysteria for a day and a half. And you standing around here with the wrong chevrons on! Christ. Christ! What's your plan, anyway? Where are you trying to go?"

"Home," the alien said. "But first I have to rendezvous at the pickup point."

"Where's that?"

"You think I'm stupid?"

"Shit," Amanda said. "If I meant to turn you in, I'd have done it five minutes ago. But, okay, I don't give a damn where your rendezvous point is. I tell you, though, you wouldn't make it as far as San Francisco rigged up the way you are. It's a miracle you've avoided getting caught until now."

"And you'll help me?"

"I've been trying to. Come on. Let's get the hell out of here. I'll take you home and fix you up a little. My car's in the lot down on the next corner."

"Okay."

"Whew!" Amanda shook her head slowly. "Christ, some people sure can't take help when you try to offer it."

As she drove out of the center of town, Amanda glanced occasionally at the alien sitting tensely to her right. Basically the disguise was very convincing, Amanda thought. Maybe all the small details were wrong, the outer stuff, the anthropological stuff, but the alien looked human, it sounded human, it even smelled human. Possibly it could fool ninety-nine people out of a hundred, or maybe more than that. But Amanda had always had a good eye for detail. And at the particular moment she had spotted the alien on South Main she had been unusually alert, sensitive, all raw nerves, every antenna up.

Of course it wasn't aliens she was hunting for, but just a diversion, a little excitement, something to fill the great gaping emptiness that Charley Taylor had left in her weekend.

Amanda had been planning the weekend with Charley all month. Her parents were going to go off to Lake Tahoe for three days, her kid sister had wangled permission to accompany them, and Amanda was going to have the house to herself, just her and Macavity the cat. And Charley. He was going to move in on Friday afternoon, and they'd cook dinner together and get blasted on her stash of choice powder and watch five or six of her parents' X cassettes, and Saturday they'd drive over to the city and cruise some of the kinky districts and go to that bathhouse on Folsom where everybody got naked and climbed into the giant Jacuzzi, and then on Sunday—Well, none of that was going to happen. Charley had called on Thursday to cancel. "Something big came up," he said, and Amanda had a pretty good idea what that was, his hot little cousin from New Orleans, who sometimes came flying out here on no notice at all, but the inconsiderate bastard seemed to be entirely unaware of how much Amanda had been looking forward to this weekend, how much it meant to her, how painful it was to be dumped like this. She had run through the planned events of the weekend in her mind so many times that she almost felt as if she had experienced them. It was that real to her. But overnight it had become unreal.

Three whole days on her own, the house to herself, and so early in the semester that there was no homework to think about, and Charley had stood her up! What was she supposed to do now, call desperately around town to scrounge up some old lover as a playmate? Or pick up some stranger downtown? Amanda hated to fool around with strangers. She was half tempted to go over to the city and just let things happen, but they were all weirdoes and creeps over there, anyway, and she knew what she could expect from them. What a waste, not having Charley! She could kill him for robbing her of the weekend.

Now there was the alien, though. A dozen of these star people had come to Earth last year, not in a flying saucer as everybody had expected, but in little capsules that floated like milkweed seeds, and they had landed in a wide arc between San Diego and Salt Lake City.

Their natural form, so far as anyone could tell, was something like a huge jellyfish with a row of staring purple eyes down one wavy margin, but their usual tactic was to borrow any local body they found, digest it, and turn themselves into an accurate imitation of it. One of them had made the mistake of turning itself into a brown mountain bear and another into a bobcat—maybe they thought that those were the dominant life forms on Earth—but the others had taken on human bodies, at the cost of at least ten lives.

Then they went looking to make contact with government leaders, and naturally they were rounded up very swiftly and interned, some in mental hospitals and some in county jails, but eventually—as soon as the truth of what they really were sank in—they were all put in a special detention camp in Northern California.

Of course a tremendous fuss was made over them, endless stuff in the papers and on the tube, speculation by this heavy thinker and that about the significance of their mission, the nature of their biochemistry, a little wild talk about the possibility that more of their kind might be waiting undetected out there and plotting to do God knows what, and all sorts of that stuff. Then came a government clamp on the entire subject, no official announcements except that "discussions" with the visitors were continuing, and after a while the whole thing degenerated into dumb alien jokes ("Why did the alien cross the road?") and Halloween invader masks. Then it moved into the background of everyone's attention and was forgotten.

And remained forgotten until the announcement that one of the creatures had slipped out of the camp somehow and was loose within a hundred-mile zone around San Francisco. Preoccupied as she was with her anguish over Charley's heartlessness, even Amanda had managed to pick up that news item. And now the alien was in her very car. So there'd be some weekend amusement for her after all. Amanda was entirely unafraid of the alleged deadliness of the star being: Whatever else the alien might be, it was surely no dope, not if it had been picked to come halfway across the galaxy on a mission like this, and Amanda knew that the alien could see that harming her was not going to be in its own best interests. The alien had need of her, and the alien realized that. And Amanda, in some way that she was only just beginning to work out, had need of the alien.

She pulled up outside her house, a compact split-level at the western end of town. "This is the place," she said.

Heat shimmers danced in the air, and the hills back of the house, parched in the long dry summer, were the color of lions. Macavity, Amanda's old tabby, sprawled in the shade of the bottlebrush tree on the ragged front lawn. As Amanda and the alien approached, the cat sat up warily, flattened his ears, and hissed. The alien immediately moved into a defensive posture, sniffing the air.

"Just a household pet," Amanda said. "You know what that is? He isn't dangerous. He's always a little suspicious of strangers."

Which was untrue. An earthquake couldn't have brought Macavity out of his nap, and a cotillion of mice dancing minuets on his tail wouldn't have drawn a reaction from him. Amanda calmed him with some fur ruffling, but he wanted nothing to do with the alien and went slinking sullenly into the underbrush. The alien watched him with care until he was out of sight.

"Do you have anything like cats back on your planet?" Amanda asked as they went inside.

"We had small wild animals once. They were unnecessary."

"Oh," Amanda said, losing interest. The house had a stuffy, stagnant air. She switched on the air-conditioning. "Where is your planet, anyway?"

The alien pointedly ignored the question. It padded around the living room, very much like a prowling cat itself, studying the stereo, the television, the couches, the coffee table, and the vase of dried flowers.

"Is this a typical Earthian home?"

"More or less," said Amanda. "Typical for around here, at least. This is what we call a suburb. It's half an hour by freeway from here to San Francisco. That's a city. I'll take you over there tonight or tomorrow for a look, if you're interested." She got some music going, high volume. The alien didn't seem to mind; so she notched the volume up even more. "I'm going to take a shower. You could use one, too, actually."

"Shower? You mean rain?"

"I mean body-cleaning activities. We Earthlings like to wash a lot, to get rid of sweat and dirt and stuff. It's considered bad form to stink. Come on, I'll show you how to do it. You've got to do what I do if you want to keep from getting caught, you know." She led the alien to the bathroom. "Take your clothes off first."

The alien stripped. Underneath its rain slicker it wore a stained T-shirt that said FISHERMAN'S WHARF, with a picture of the San Francisco skyline, and a pair of unzipped jeans. Under that it was wearing a black brassiere, unfastened and with the cups over its shoulder blades, and a pair of black shiny panty-briefs with a red heart on the left buttock. The alien's body was that of a lean, tough-looking girl with a scar running down the inside of one arm.

"By the way, whose body is that?" Amanda asked. "Do you know?"

"She worked at the detention center. In the kitchen."

"You know her name?"

"Flores Concepcion."

"The other way around, probably. Concepcion Flores. I'll call you Connie, unless you want to give me your real name."

"Connie will do."

"All right, Connie. Pay attention. You turn the water on here, and you adjust the mix of hot and cold until you like it. Then you pull this knob and get underneath the spout here and wet your body and rub soap over it and wash the soap off. Afterward you dry yourself and put fresh clothes on. You have to clean your clothes from time to time, too, because otherwise they start to smell, and it upsets people. Watch me shower, and then you do it."

Amanda washed quickly, while plans hummed in her head. The alien wasn't going to last long wearing the body of Concepcion Flores. Sooner or later someone was going to notice that one of the kitchen girls was missing, and they'd get an all-points alarm out for her. Amanda wondered whether the alien had figured that out yet. The alien, Amanda thought, needs a different body in a hurry.

But not mine, she told herself. For sure, not mine.

"Your turn," she said casually, shutting the water off.

The alien, fumbling a little, turned the water back on and got under the spray. Clouds of steam rose, and its skin began to look boiled, but it didn't appear troubled. No sense of pain?

"Hold it," Amanda said. "Step back." She adjusted the water. "You've got it too hot. You'll damage that body that way. Look, if you can't tell the difference between hot and cold, just take cold showers, okay? It's less dangerous. This is cold, on this side."

She left the alien under the shower and went to find some clean clothes. When she came back, the alien was still showering, under icy water. "Enough," Amanda said. "Here. Put these clothes on."

"I had more clothes than this before."

"A T-shirt and jeans are all you need in hot weather like this. With your kind of build you can skip the bra, and anyway I don't think you'll be able to fasten it the right way."

"Do we put the face paint on now?"

"We can skip it while we're home. It's just stupid kid stuff anyway, all that tribal crap. If we go out we'll do it, and we'll give you Walnut Creek colors, I think. Concepcion wore San Jose, but we want to throw people off the track. How about some dope?"

"What?"

"Grass. Marijuana. A drug widely used by local Earthians of our age."

"I don't need no drug."

"I don't, either. But I'd like some. You ought to learn how, just in case you find yourself in a social situation." Amanda reached for her pack of Filter Golds and pulled out a joint. Expertly she tweaked its lighter tip and took a deep hit. "Here," she said, passing it. "Hold it like I did. Put it to your mouth, breathe in, suck the smoke deep." The alien dragged the joint and began to cough. "Not so deep, maybe," Amanda said. "Take just a little. Hold it. Let it out. There, much better. Now give me back the joint. You've got to keep passing it back and forth. That part's important. You feel anything from it?"

"No."

"It can be subtle. Don't worry about it. Are you hungry?"

"Not yet," the alien said.

"I am. Come into the kitchen." As she assembled a sandwich—peanut butter and avocado on whole wheat, with tomato and onion—she asked, "What sort of things do you guys eat?"

"Life."

"Life?"

"We never eat dead things. Only things with life."

Amanda fought back a shudder. "I see. Anything with life?"

"We prefer animal life. We can absorb plants if necessary."

"Ah. Yes. And when are you going to be hungry again?"

"Maybe tonight," the alien said. "Or tomorrow. The hunger comes very suddenly, when it comes."

"There's not much around here that you could eat live. But I'll work on it."

"The small furry animal?"

"No. My cat is not available for dinner. Get that idea right out of your head. Likewise me. I'm your protector and guide. It wouldn't be sensible to eat me. You follow what I'm trying to tell you?"

"I said that I'm not hungry yet."

"Well, you let me know when you start feeling the pangs. I'll find you a meal." Amanda began to construct a second sandwich. The alien prowled the kitchen, examining the appliances. Perhaps making mental records, Amanda thought, of sink and oven design, to copy on its home world. Amanda said. "Why did you people come here in the first place?"

"It was our mission."

"Yes. Sure. But for what purpose? What are you after? You want to take over the world? You want to steal our scientific secrets?" The alien, making no reply, began taking spices out of the spice rack. Delicately it licked its finger, touched it to the oregano, tasted it, tried the cumin. Amanda said, "Or is it that you want to keep us from going into space? You think we're a dangerous species, and so you're going to quarantine us on our own planet? Come on, you can tell me. I'm not a government spy." The alien sampled the tarragon, the basil, the sage. When it reached for the curry powder, its hand suddenly shook so violently that it knocked the open jars of oregano and tarragon over, making a mess. "Hey, are you all right?" Amanda asked.

The alien said, "I think I'm getting hungry. Are these things drugs, too?"

"Spices," Amanda said. "We put them in our foods to make them taste better." The alien was looking very strange, glassy-eyed, flushed, sweaty. "Are you feeling sick or something?"

"I feel excited. These powders—"

"They're turning you on? Which one?"

"This, I think." It pointed to the oregano. "It was either the first one or the second."

"Yeah." Amanda said. "Oregano. It can really make you fly." She wondered whether the alien would get violent when zonked. Or whether the oregano would stimulate its appetite. She had to watch out for its appetite. There are certain risks, Amanda reflected, in doing what I'm doing. Deftly she cleaned up the spilled oregano and tarragon and put the caps on the spice jars. "You ought to be careful," she said. "Your metabolism isn't used to this stuff. A little can go a long way."

"Give me some more."

"Later," Amanda said. "You don't want to overdo it too early in the day."

"More!"

"Calm down. I know this planet better than you, and I don't want to see you get in trouble. Trust me. I'll let you have more oregano when it's the right time. Look at the way you're shaking. And you're sweating like crazy." Pocketing the oregano jar, she led the alien back into the living room. "Sit down. Relax."

"More? Please?"

"I appreciate your politeness. But we have important things to talk about, and then I'll give you some. Okay?" Amanda opaqued the window, through which the hot late-afternoon sun was coming. Six o'clock on Friday, and if everything had gone the right way Charley would have been showing up just about now. Well, she'd found a different diversion. The weekend stretched before her like an open road leading to Mystery Land. The alien offered all sorts of possibilities, and she might yet have some fun over the next few days, if she used her head. Amanda turned to the alien and said, "You calmer now? Yes. Good. Okay, first of all, you've got to get yourself another body."

"Why is that?"

"I've reasons. One is that the authorities are probably searching for the girl you absorbed. How you got as far as you did without anybody but me spotting you is hard to understand. Number two, a teenaged girl traveling by herself is going to get hassled too much, and you don't know how to handle yourself in a tight situation. You know what I'm saying? You're going to want to hitchhike out to Nevada, Wyoming, Utah, wherever the hell your rendezvous place is, and all along the way people are going to be coming on to you. You don't need any of that. Besides, it's very tricky trying to pass for a girl. You've got to know how to put your face paint on, how to understand challenge codes, what the way you wear your clothing says, and like that. Boys have a much simpler subculture. You get yourself a male body, a big hunk of a body, and nobody'll bother you much on the way to where you're going. You just keep to yourself, don't make eye contact, don't smile, and everyone will leave you alone."

"Makes sense," said the alien. "All right. The hunger is becoming very bad now. Where do I get a male body?"

"San Francisco. It's full of men. We'll go over there tonight and find a nice brawny one for you. With any luck we might even find one who's not gay, and then we can have a little fun with him first. And then you take his body over—which incidentally solves your food problem for a while, doesn't it? And we can have some more fun, a whole weekend of fun." Amanda winked. "Okay, Connie?"

"Okay." The alien winked, a clumsy imitation, first one eye, then the other. "You give me more oregano now?"

"Later. And when you wink, just wink one eye. Like this. Except I don't think you ought to do a lot of winking at people. It's a very intimate gesture that could get you in trouble. Understand?"

"There's so much to understand."

"You're on a strange planet, kid. Did you expect it to be just like home? Okay, to continue. The next thing I ought to point out is that when you leave here on Sunday, you'll have to—"

The telephone rang.

"What's that sound?" the alien asked.

"Communications device. I'll be right back." Amanda went to the hall extension, imagining the worst: her parents, say, calling to announce that they were on their way back from Tahoe tonight, some mix-up in the reservations or something.

But the voice that greeted her was Charley's. She could hardly believe it, after the casual way he had shafted her this weekend. She could hardly believe what he wanted, either. He had left half a dozen of his best cassettes at her place last week, Golden Age rock, *Abbey Road*, and the Hendrix one and a Joplin and such, and now he was heading off to Monterey for the festival and wanted to have them for the drive. Did she mind if he stopped off in half an hour to pick them up?

The bastard, she thought. The absolute trashiness of him! First to torpedo her weekend without even an apology, and then to let her know that he and what's-her-name were scooting down to Monterey for some fun, and could he bother her for his cassettes? Didn't he think she had any feelings? She looked at the telephone as if it were emitting tads and scorpions. It was tempting to hang up on him.

She resisted the temptation. "As it happens," she said, "I'm just on my way out for the weekend myself. But I've got a friend who's staying here cat-sitting for me. I'll leave the cassettes with her, okay? Her name's Connie."

"Fine. That's great," Charley said. "I really appreciate that, Amanda."

"It's nothing," she said.

The alien was back in the kitchen, nosing around the spice rack. But

Amanda had the oregano. She said, "I've arranged for delivery of your next body."

"You did?"

"A large healthy adolescent male. Exactly what you're looking for. He's going to be here in a little while. I'm going to go out for a drive. You take care of him before I get back. How long does it take for you to engulf somebody?"

"It's very fast."

"Good." Amanda found Charley's cassettes and stacked them on the living-room table. "He's coming over here to get these six little boxes, which are music-storage devices. When the doorbell rings, you let him in and introduce yourself as Connie and tell him his things are on this table. After that you're on your own. You think you can handle it?"

"Sure," the alien said.

"Tuck in your T-shirt better. When it's tight, it makes your boobs stick out, and that'll distract him. Maybe he'll even make a pass at you. What happens to the Connie body after you engulf him?"

"It won't be here. What happens is I merge with him and dissolve all the Connie characteristics and take on the new ones."

"Ah. Very nifty. You're a real nightmare thing, you know? You're a walking horror show. Here you are, have another little hit of oregano before I go."

She put a tiny pinch of spice in the alien's hand. "Just to warm up your engine a little. I'll give you more later, when you've done the job. See you in an hour, okay?"

She left the house. Macavity was sitting on the porch, scowling, whipping his tail from side to side. Amanda knelt beside him and scratched him behind the ears. The cat made a low, rough purring sound, not much like his usual purr.

Amanda said, "You aren't happy, are you, fella? Well, don't worry. I've told the alien to leave you alone, and I guarantee you'll be okay. This is Amanda's fun tonight. You don't mind if Amanda has a little fun, do you?" Macavity made a glum, snuffling sound. "Listen, maybe I can get the alien to create a nice little calico cutie for you, okay? Just going into heat and ready to howl. Would you like that, guy? Would you? I'll see what I can do when I get back. But I have to clear out of here now, before Charley shows up."

She got into her car and headed for the westbound freeway ramp. Half past six, Friday night, the sun still hanging high above the Bay. Traffic was thick in the eastbound lanes, the late commuters slogging toward home, and it was beginning to build up westbound, too, as people set out for dinner in San Francisco. Amanda drove through the tunnel and turned north into Berkeley to cruise city streets. Ten minutes to seven now. Charley must have arrived. She imagined Connie in her tight T-shirt, all stoned and sweaty on oregano, and Charley giving her the eye, getting ideas, thinking about grabbing a bonus quickie before taking off with his cassettes. And Connie leading him on, Charley making his moves, and then suddenly that electric moment of surprise as the alien struck and Charley found himself turning into dinner. It could be happening right this minute, Amanda thought placidly. No more than the bastard deserves, isn't it? She had felt for a long time that Charley was a big mistake in her life, and after what he had pulled yesterday, she was sure of it. No more than he deserves.

But, she wondered, what if Charley has brought his weekend date along? The thought chilled her. She hadn't considered that possibility at all. It could ruin everything.

Connie wasn't able to engulf two at once, was she? And suppose they recognized her as the missing alien and ran out screaming to call the cops?

No, she thought. Not even Charley would be so tacky as to bring his date over to Amanda's house tonight. And Charley never watched the news or read a paper. He wouldn't have a clue as to what Connie really was until it was too late for him to run.

Seven o'clock. Time to head for home.

The sun was sinking behind her as she turned onto the freeway. By quarter past she was approaching her house. Charley's old red Honda was parked outside.

Amanda parked across the street and cautiously let herself in, pausing just inside the front door to listen.

Silence.

"Connie?"

"In here," said Charley's voice.

Amanda entered the living room. Charley was sprawled out comfortably on the couch. There was no sign of Connie.

"Well?" Amanda said. "How did it go?"

"Easiest thing in the world," the alien said. "He was sliding his hands under my T-shirt when I let him have the nullifier jolt."

"Ah. The nullifier jolt."

"And then I completed the engulfment and cleaned up the carpet. God, it feels good not to be hungry again. You can't imagine how tough it was to resist engulfing you, Amanda. For the past hour I kept thinking of food, food, food—"

"Very thoughtful of you to resist."

"I knew you were out to help me. It's logical not to engulf one's allies."

"That goes without saying. So you feel well fed now? He was good stuff?"

"Robust, healthy, nourishing—yes."

"I'm glad Charley turned out to be good for something. How long before you get hungry again?"

The alien shrugged. "A day or two. Maybe three. Give me more oregano, Amanda?"

"Sure," she said. "Sure." She felt a little let down. Not that she was remorseful about Charley, exactly, but it all seemed so casual, so offhanded—there was something anticlimactic about it, in a way. She suspected she should have stayed and watched while it was happening. Too late for that now, though.

She took the oregano from her purse and dangled the jar teasingly. "Here it is, babe. But you've got to earn it first."

"What do you mean?"

"I mean that I was looking forward to a big weekend with Charley, and the weekend is here. Charley's here, too, more or less, and I'm ready for fun. Come show me some fun, big boy."

She slipped Charley's Hendrix cassette into the tape deck and turned the volume all the way up.

The alien looked puzzled. Amanda began to peel off her clothes.

"You, too," Amanda said. "Come on. You won't have to dig deep into Charley's mind to figure out what to do. You're going to be my Charley for me this weekend, you follow? You and I are going to do all the things that he and I were going to do. Okay? Come on. Come on." She beckoned.

The alien shrugged again and slipped out of Charley's clothes, fumbling with the unfamiliarities of his zipper and buttons. Amanda, grinning, drew the alien close against her and down to the living-room floor.

She took its hands and put them where she wanted them to be. She whispered instructions. The alien, docile, obedient, did what she wanted.

It felt like Charley. It smelled like Charley. And after her instructions, it even moved pretty much the way Charley moved.

But it wasn't Charley, it wasn't Charley at all, and after the first few seconds Amanda knew that she had goofed things up very badly. You couldn't just ring in an imitation like this. Making love with this alien was like making love with a very clever machine, or with her own mirror image. It was empty and meaningless and dumb.

Grimly she went on to the finish. They rolled apart, panting, sweating.

"Well?" the alien said. "Did the earth move for you?"

"Yeah. Yeah. It was terrific—Charley."

"Oregano?"

"Sure," Amanda said. She handed the spice jar across. "I always keep my promises. babe. Go to it. Have yourself a blast. Just remember that that's strong stuff for guys from your planet, okay? If you pass out, I'm going to leave you right there on the floor."

"Don't worry about me."

"Okay. You have your fun. I'm going to clean up, and then maybe we'll go over to San Francisco for the nightlife. Does that interest you?"

"You bet, Amanda." The alien winked—one eye, then the other—and gulped a huge pinch of oregano. "That sounds terrific."

Amanda gathered up her clothes, went upstairs for a quick shower and dressed. When she came down, the alien was more than half blown away on the oregano, goggle-eyed, loll-headed, propped up against the couch and crooning to itself in a weird atonal way. Fine.

Amanda thought, You just get yourself all spiced up, love. She took the portable phone from the kitchen, carried it with her into the bathroom, locked the door, and quietly dialed the police emergency number.

She was bored with the alien. The game had worn thin very quickly. And it was crazy, she thought, to spend the whole weekend cooped up with a dangerous extraterrestrial creature when there wasn't going to be any fun in it for her. She knew now that there couldn't be any fun at all. And besides, in a day or two the alien was going to get hungry again.

"I've got your alien," she said. "Sitting in my living room, stoned out of its head on oregano. Yes, I'm absolutely certain. It was disguised as a Chicana girl first, Conception Flores, but then it attacked my boyfriend,

Charley Taylor, and—yes, yes, I'm safe. I'm locked in the john. Just get somebody over here fast—okay. I'll stay on the line—what happened was, I spotted it downtown outside the video center, and it insisted on coming home with me—"

The actual capture took only a few minutes. But there was no peace for hours after the police tactical squad hauled the alien away, because the media were in on the act right away, first a team from Channel 2 in Oakland, and then some of the network guys, and then the *Chronicle*, and finally a whole army of reporters from as far away as Sacramento and phone calls from Los Angeles and San Diego and—about three that morning—New York.

Amanda told the story again and again until she was sick of it, and just as dawn was breaking, she threw the last of them out and barred the door.

She wasn't sleepy at all. She felt wired up, speedy and depressed all at once. The alien was gone, Charley was gone, and she was all alone. She was going to be famous for the next couple of days, but that wouldn't help. She'd still be alone. For a time she wandered around the house, looking at it the way an alien might, as if she had never seen a stereo cassette before, or a television set, or a rack of spices. The smell of oregano was everywhere. There were little trails of it on the floor.

Amanda switched on the radio and there she was on the six A.M. news. "—the emergency is over, thanks to the courageous Walnut Creek High School girl who trapped and outsmarted the most dangerous life form in the known universe—"

She shook her head. "You think that's true?" she asked the cat. "Most dangerous life form in the universe? I don't think so, Macavity, I think I know of at least one that's a lot deadlier. Eh, kid?" She winked. "If they only knew, eh? If they only knew." She scooped the cat up and hugged it, and it began to purr. Maybe trying to get a little sleep would be a good idea. Then she had to figure out what she was going to do about the rest of the weekend.

I needed a good laugh when I wrote this story in 1988. My marriage had just fallen apart and I was a divorced single dad who hadn't had a date in seventeen years. As I look back on it now, I read it partly as a Note To Self. *Dear Jim*, it says to me, *snap out of it! Your life isn't over.* And it wasn't. Within a year I met Pam; we celebrate our thirteenth anniversary this year.

"Faith" has long been a favorite of mine to read in public, since it is accessible to folks who are convinced that they hate science fiction. In fact, this story had its world debut as a reading at the Prescott Park Arts Festival in Portsmouth, New Hampshire. I was the opening act for a summer evening's performance under the stars; the main attraction was a community theater production of *Little Shop of Horrors*. Curiously enough, the climax of this story takes place at the Prescott Park Arts Festival where an unnamed science fiction writer is opening for (gasp) *Little Shop of Horrors*.

Coincidence or conspiracy? You be the judge.

But it wasn't until ten years later that "Faith" provided me with one of the great thrills of my career. My collection *Think Like A Dinosaur* had just come out when I got a fan letter which began with the usual gratifying praise but quickly got down to business. It seemed that one Michael Ching, composer and artistic director of Opera Memphis, was a Kelly fan in general and a "Faith" fan in particular. He was writing to ask my permission to adapt it into an opera.

It took me almost an hour to peel myself off the ceiling. "Faith" debuted at the Concord City Auditorium in New Hampshire in 1999, had a three week off-off Broadway run, and was part of the programming at the Chicago WorldCon in 2000. No one was more surprised than I to discover that my funny little novelette wanted to be an opera when it grew up.

—James Patrick Kelly

Faith

JAMES PATRICK KELLY

F AITH WAS ABOUT TO CROSS CONGRESS STREET with an armload of
overdue library books when she was run over by a divorce.
There was no mistaking Chuck's cranberry BMW 325i idling
at the light—except that Chuck was supposed to be in Hartford. The woman next to him had enough blonde hair to stuff a pillow.
The light changed and the BMW accelerated through the intersection.
Chuck was crazy if he thought he could get away with a hit and run.
The blonde looked suddenly ill; she folded down in her seat like a Bar-
bie doll in a microwave. Without thinking, Faith hurled the top book
in her stack. *Whump!* It was the first time she had ever appreciated Ste-
phen King's wordiness; *The Tommyknockers* bounced off the passenger
door, denting it nicely. Chuck raced up Islington and out of her life. The
book lay open next to the curb. Its pages fluttered in the wind, waving
good-bye to fifteen years of marriage.

She had a long convalescence, during which Kleenex sales reached an
all-time high. Chuck got the Beemer, the bimbo, and the freedom to be
himself—poor bastard. She got the cape on Moffat Street and their teenager, Flip. By the time the divorce was final, she had lost her illusions
about love, half of her friends, and twenty-three pounds.

She realized she was healing one day during her lunch hour. She was
in a dressing room at Marshalls and had just wriggled into a size 10 bikini.

"Maybe I should write a book," she said. In the next stall her best
friend Betty grunted in frustration. "*The Divorce Diet*, what do you
think?" Faith spread her fingers across her tummy. Her mother's bulge
had receded until it no longer resembled the front bumper of a pickup.
"You too can cry those extra pounds off." She turned and eyed her back-
side in the mirror. "Stress: the key to tighter buns."

133

"Hell of a way to lose weight." Betty remained behind the curtain; she usually avoided mirrors like a vampire. "Liposuction is cheaper. Jesus, my thighs look like water balloons." She stuck her head out to admire Faith in the bikini. "You look great, Faith, you really do. When are you going to do something about it?"

The question nagged at Faith. What was she waiting for? Women were supposed to take what they wanted these days, not wait for men to offer it. At least, that was what the cigarette ads said. All her friends wanted to fix her up—Betty, in particular. Betty was hungry for vicarious thrills; she was married to Dave, who spent too much time on the road selling excavation equipment. As Faith rebuttoned her blouse, she wondered if she was ready now to go out.

But not with friends of friends. Not yet. Better to start with something she could abandon, if necessary, without making too much of a mess. She had been following the personals in *Portsmouth Magazine*; she thought she might run an ad.

She wrote it that afternoon at work, where it was easier to see herself objectively. After all, writing ad copy was her business. *DWF.* Faith hated that acronym. In her mind she could not help but hear DWF as dwarf. Who wanted to go out with Sneezy? Or Dopey? *DWF 35.* Now she needed some adjectives. *Attractive professional.* Okay, but there should be more. *Attractive, slender, witty, secure professional.* No, no, overkill. Delete slender. Now she needed something about her interests. What were her interests? Napping came immediately to mind. After working all day at the agency and then coming home to cook and clean and vacuum and do laundry and scrub toilets, she did not exactly have the energy to train for the decathlon or plow through *The New York Review of Books*. She made herself concentrate; there had to be something. *My favorites: the flowers at Prescott Park, jazz, the beach in the winter, candlelit dinners anywhere.* Yes, she liked that; it reeked of romance. Last came specifications for her ideal date. The problem was that she was not exactly sure what she wanted. Chuck's shabby betrayal had left her utterly confused about men. *Seeking an intellectual and emotional equal.* No, too pretentious. She was looking for some guy to split a pizza with, not applying to the University of New Hampshire. She scanned some other ads; what were her fellow dwarfs searching for? *Compassionate, warm, honest, gentle, non-drinking life partners to share soft music, moonlit walks, and a lasting friendship.* She was horrorstruck: these women all wanted to spend the night with Mr. Rogers! That decided her. She batted out a last line. Two deft keystrokes brought the brochure copy for Seacoast Cruises onto the computer screen and Faith was back in business. She pushed the ad out of her mind until just before quitting time, when she printed it without looking at it, wrote a check for a two-week run, and mailed it.

DWF 35, attractive, witty, secure professional. My favorites: the flowers at Prescott Park, jazz, the beach in the winter, candlelit dinners anywhere. Looking for someone completely different. A little generic, perhaps, but it would do for starters.

When she got home, Flip, also known as The Creature From The Eighth Grade, was conducting SDI research in the back yard. He was directing photons at a nest of communist tent caterpillars with a magnifying glass he had borrowed from Faith's Oxford English Dictionary.

"Flip, I'm home. Please don't do that; it's gross."

"Ma, I'm zapping them before they go into launch mode."

"Forget it."

"Can I set them on fire with lighter fluid, then?"

"*No.* Was there any mail today?"

"You got a check from Dad. No note, though."

"Flip, I've told you before. Don't open my mail."

"He's my father, you know."

"Yes, I know." She bit back an insult and confiscated the magnifying glass instead. "Look, I'm expecting some letters soon, okay? Addressed to me. Faith Pettingell. Open my mail again, sucker, and I'm taking a hammer to your TV."

"What the matter, Ma, you got a boyfriend or something? About time you started going out."

Sometimes Flip had all the charm of a housefly. Actually, Faith loved her son dearly and would not have hesitated to rush into a burning building after him, although then they would probably both die of smoke inhalation. Betty, who substituted at the middle school, liked to say that there was really no such a thing as a thirteen-year-old, that inside every eighth grader were a ten-year-old and a sixteen-year-old locked in mortal combat. Given enough time, the big kid would win and ask to borrow the car. Meanwhile, according to Betty, the best Faith could do was to silently chant the mother's mantra: "It's only a phase, it's only a phase."

It would have been easier if only Flip did not remind her so much of Chuck.

She got seven replies to her ad. Two she tossed immediately. One guy had handwriting like a lie detector chart; she was not even sure what language he had responded in. The other was only marginally literate. Faith considered herself a tolerant woman but she simply could not see herself with a man who could not get his subjects and verbs to agree.

She also heard from two lawyers, a plumbing contractor, and a computer programmer. Both of the lawyers played tennis; one had a sailboat. The programmer claimed to have eaten at every restaurant in Portsmouth. The plumber seemed to have had the most interesting life; he was a skydiver and had once lived in Thailand. Everyone but the programmer had been married before; the plumber was in the middle of divorce number two. They all seemed harmless enough, which left her at once pleased and vaguely disappointed. She felt like a little girl on Christmas morning just after she had opened the last present.

There was one other—strange—reply. It came from a man named Gardiner Allan. He did not offer a chatty autobiography or, indeed, any information about himself at all, other than a Post Office box number in Barrington. Instead he sent poetry.

Somewhere a stranger
is sleeping alone,
dreaming of gardens.
Roses breathe poems,
sweet sonnets of scent.
Leaves stir like green hearts.
The sun's caresses
inflame her bare skin.
But the cruel breeze sighs,
it isn't enough.
Where is the lover,
tender of flowers?
Then she spots someone
drowsing in shadow,
reaches to rouse him

and uproots herself.
Your dreams can't come true
Until you wake up.

Faith was intrigued. After all, she had advertised for someone completely different. But all this stuff about inflaming caresses and bare skin and lovers. Faith had steeled herself for many things; love was not one of them. She no longer believed in love. And what kind of name was Gardiner Allan anyway? It sounded like an alias—maybe he was an escaped pervert. He had not even given a phone number. Still, no one had ever written her a poem before.

She ended up sending a postcard she had bought at the Museum of Fine Arts in Boston. On the front was a reproduction of Mary Cassatt's painting *The Letter*. On the back she wrote,

"Dear Mr. Allan,

I enjoyed your poem. Is there more to you?"

She signed it "Faith" but gave no last name or return address. Let him get in touch with her through *Portsmouth Magazine*. If mysterious and artsy was his game, she could play too.

She began conducting what she described to Betty as experiments in dating. The results were inconclusive. She saw the lawyer with the sailboat just the once, for lunch. He was five feet one. They had not said three words to each other when he started making announcements.

"I should tell you up front that I can't stand people who smoke."

Faith smiled politely. "That's okay, I don't."

"And I don't drink either."

Her smile shrank like cheap jeans. "Oh?"

"And I don't eat red meat or refined sugar."

"You do breathe?"

"Breathe? Breathe? Everyone breathes."

She liked the other lawyer better. He had a voice like an announcer on National Public Radio. He was also a great kisser; he could do things with his lower lip that were probably against the law in Alabama. He stopped calling, though, after she beat him in straight sets: 6-4, 6-2. The programmer wore plastic shoes. He took her to dinner at the Seventy-Two but then ordered for both of them without asking her first. In a moment of weakness, she went out with him once more. This time they went to Luka's. They danced after dinner, but he never made eye contact while they were on the floor. He was too busy shopping the meat market around the bar. On the drive home he took off his shoes. His feet smelled like low tide.

The plumber was gorgeous; the only problem was that he knew it. He had a lion's mane of tawny hair and biceps the size of a meatloaf; he looked and acted at least fifteen years younger than he really was. Faith knew it was shallow of her but she could not help herself; the closer she stood to him, the tighter her underwear felt. He seemed to have been everywhere and tried everything. On one date they stood outside of Rosa's for almost an hour waiting to get in, but she hardly noticed because he was telling her how he had once had a mystical experience while on psilocybin at the Temple of Dawn in Bangkok. By the time they had reached the door, most of the women in line behind them were eavesdropping shamelessly. Faith glanced back at them in amazement; the competition was ogling her date. She kept fantasizing that Chuck would drive by and see them there.`

But somehow their relationship never got out of the shallows. The more Faith did with him, the more she realized that, with this guy, what you saw was *all* you got. He could tell some wonderful stories, yet he seemed not to have learned anything from them. And his boyishness got old fast. Not only did he know the lyrics to "Teenager in Love" but he sang them with conviction. He did not have much use for Flip; she suspected it was because her son made him feel his true age. What ended their affair, though, was his explanation of the Zen of seduction.

"Yeah, I learned it from this cartoonist I used to know in Singapore. The trick is not to want anything." He traced the line of her jaw as he spoke. "Empty the mind of all desire. If you absolutely don't care what happens, it drives them wild. They start throwing themselves at you."

"Is that what happened with us?" Faith propped herself up on her elbow.

"Maybe."

"And you don't want anything from me?"

He grinned then and kissed her. It was a perfectly good kiss, but it left a bad taste in her mouth afterward. She started using her answering machine to screen his calls, which she never returned. Eventually he got the message.

By summer, the experiments were completed. Faith had begun with low expectations and they had been met exactly. At least she had proved to herself that she could date without getting involved. Now she was going to give men a rest. The weeds were choking her garden and the house needed cleaning and she had been neglecting her son.

She worried that Flip was lonely now that school was out. Usually he would bike over to swim team practice in the morning and then maybe visit his best friend Jerry, but Jerry's family went to their place on Lake Winnisquam in July. She had put Flip on a television diet of three hours a day, so he spent most afternoons either doing chores or fooling around with his computer or reading an endless stream of comics and trashy science fiction. She left work early a few days so that they could go to the beach, but that was very hard for Faith. Flip kept staring at girls' breasts like they were cupcakes and he wanted to lick the frosting off. He's perfectly normal, she told herself as she ground her teeth. She had always assumed that Chuck would provide the necessary parental guidance about sex once Flip reached puberty. Chuck, however, was hardly a role model.

She decided it was better they should go someplace where people wore clothes. "Hey, Flip," she said one night, gallantly trying to compete with *Star Trek*; Captain Kirk was smirking at some space bimbo dressed in high heels and aluminum foil. "I just got the schedule for the Arts Festival at Prescott Park. Guy Van Duser and Billy Novick are on next Friday. How about we fry up some chicken and check them out? We could stay for the play."

"*Boring.*" At the commercial he ran for the bathroom.

"Come on." She pulled the schedule from her purse. "I thought you'd like the play. *Little Shop of Horrors.*"

"Saw the movie," Flip called. "Both movies."

"How about this? Mondays they're having a science fiction film festival at the library. *When Worlds Collide.*" She read from the schedule. "*Invasion of the Body Snatchers, Plan 9 from Outer Space.*"

"*Plan 9?* Jerry says that's the worst movie ever made. I heard it's awesome. I could see that. Yeah!"

Flip had been a science fiction fan since the third grade, a vice he had picked up from Chuck. Betty had been telling Faith for years not to worry. She claimed that science fiction was only another phase.

"Well, his father never grew out of it," Faith said.

"Live with it," said Betty. "It's better than girls, believe me. You can't catch a disease from science fiction."

"It's easy for you to say." Faith twirled the phone cord impatiently. "He's not dragging you to *Plan 9 from Outer Space.* Say, what are you doing Monday? Isn't Dave in Worcester?"

"Yes, but really, there's this Newhart rerun. . . ."

"Come on, I'll take you for ice cream afterward."

About a dozen people turned out on a hot Monday night to see the worst movie ever made. It was about stodgy aliens in silver tights who zoomed around in an art deco frisbee raising the dead. The only actor she recognized was Bela Lugosi, who looked as if he had just been raised from the dead. Betty wanted to go after the first reel but Flip was staying. While the librarian changed reels, Flip struck up a conversation with a friendly man who explained that the reason Bela looked so feeble was that he had died two days after shooting started. The director had then enlisted his wife's hairdresser as a stand-in. While her son listened, Faith idly sized the stranger up as a potential date. She had been doing that a lot lately; she was still trying to figure out her type. This one was tall, skinny, and thirtyish, and he had very blue eyes. Handsome but not tastelessly so—too bad she did not trust men with glasses. Betty caught her looking and raised an inquiring eyebrow. Faith pursed her lips slyly and scooted around to face the screen. No way a Bela Lugosi fan could be her type.

After the movie, they window-shopped up Congress Street and down Market Square. When they got to Annabelle's, Faith was surprised to see the stranger already there, working on a sandwich and a bowl of soup. He grinned at her. "We've got to stop meeting like this."

Faith smiled back. "Small town, isn't it?" It was an absurdly trite comeback, but he did not seem to mind.

She was not quite sure why, but the smile stayed on her face. It felt comfortable there. She ordered a small crunchy chocolate cone while Flip and Betty settled at a table. They left her the chair facing the affable stranger.

"What did you get, Faith?" Betty nudged her. "*Faith?*"

The stranger made eye contact.

"Uh, fine." Faith's cheeks were warm. "Lovely." It was eerie, but she *knew* he would get up. She *knew* he was going to come over to talk to her. The surprise was that she wanted him to do it.

"Excuse me for eavesdropping," he said, "but is your name Faith?"

"Yes," she said.

"I think we may have corresponded." He extended his hand. "I'm Gardiner Allan."

"Uh, Gardiner Allan, right. The poet. You never wrote back."

"But I did. You never answered my second letter."

"I never got it."

He grimaced and made a crack about raccoons running the Post Office. She wanted to say something clever but *Plan 9* had turned her brain to cottage cheese. Meanwhile, Betty was practically twitching with curiosity.

"Why don't you pull up a chair, Gardiner?" said Flip.

He glanced at Faith. "I wouldn't want to intrude...."

"Yes, please sit." She scooted her chair to make room. "It's no fun eating alone. I know. This is my friend, Betty Corriveau. My son Flip."

Betty shook his hand; Flip waved. Faith could not think of anything to say so she licked her crunchy chocolate ice cream, which was already melting. Gardiner spooned up some soup. The silence stretched. Faith realized the man was probably thinking about all those damned adjectives: *witty, secure professional.* So much for truth in advertising.

"Well, this is a coincidence." Betty to the rescue. "So you're a poet, Gardiner?"

"It's a hobby, actually. Nobody earns a living from poetry—unless they work at Hallmark."

"And what do you do when you're not writing?"

"I breed plants."

"Are you with the university?" said Faith.

"No, I'm not affiliated with anyone. I guess you'd call me a freelancer."

"That must be interesting." Betty sounded skeptical. "What kind of plants to you breed?"

"Oh, different kinds." He shrugged. "I've just developed a tetraploid *hemerocallis* I'm pretty fond of."

"*Hemerocallis*," Faith said. "Daylily, right?"

"That's it." He nodded approvingly. "Tets have twice the number of chromosomes, you know. Gives them vigor, clearer colors, better substance. But they don't breed true so you have to propagate them by division, which is slow, or tissue culture, which is expensive."

"What's that you're eating?" Flip had a low tolerance for adult chit-chat. "Looks pretty nasty."

"Tomato dill soup and a vegetarian sandwich."

"Oh, are you a vegetarian?" Betty was grilling him as if she were doing an FBI background check.

"No, I just have to watch my diet." He waved his spoon vaguely. "So, Flip, what did you think of the movie?"

They soon got to comparing favorites. Gardiner kept mentioning films that even Flip had never heard of.

"I just don't understand the attraction," Betty interrupted. "Sci Fi...it's just too weird for me."

"Weird, right," said Gardiner. "You know, weird comes from the Saxon: *wyrd*. Means fate or 'what is to come.' That's why people like science fiction, I think—kids especially. Their fate matters to them. They're still interested in what's coming. Other people bury their heads in the here and now, as if it was the only reality. Change spooks them and the future scares them silly. Since they don't understand it they refuse to believe in it. But it's just plain wrong to pretend that 2001 is some impossible fairyland like Oz. Weird or not, it's coming."

Betty was momentarily speechless.

"I didn't know anyone took science fiction so seriously," Faith said.

"Not just science fiction. Fantasy, horror—I don't know. I'm strange, I guess. Different, anyway. Some people are afraid of that." He chuckled. "Hey, Flip, how about *Forbidden Planet*?"

"Is that the one with the robot?"

"Yeah. Did you know it's a remake of Shakespeare's *The Tempest*? Robbie is Ariel and Morbius is Prospero. Read *The Tempest*?"

"Shakespeare? You've got to be kidding me. They made us read *Romeo and Juliet* in English and I just about barfed."

"Flip, you've got to give Will a chance. Great fantasy writer. *The Tempest* has magicians and monsters—it's awesome. Or read some of his horror, *Macbeth* or *Hamlet*."

Faith liked the way this man's mind worked, but she was not about to let him know that. Not yet anyway. "I'm not sure I see *Macbeth* as a horror story."

"Oh, sure. There's even a curse on it; ask any actor. They're afraid to say the name; they call it 'that Scottish play.' People have died mysteriously. They say Shakespeare used real spells for the witches' dialogue."

Flip gazed at Gardiner as if he were the second coming of Rod Serling. Betty glanced at her watch—he had lost her back at *Forbidden Planet*. Faith wiped drips of crunchy chocolate ice cream from her fingers.

"I'm sorry." Gardiner looked sheepish. "I get carried away sometimes."

"No, no," said Faith. "It's fascinating. Really. Problem is that it's almost ten and I've got to be at work early tomorrow." She pushed her chair back.

"Would you mind if I called you some time?" The way he said it suggested that he did not expect her to say yes.

"Why not?" She patted his hand. "I'd like that." He had rough skin. "I'm in the book."

"See you, Gardiner," Flip said.

"Nice to meet you."

Faith could not sleep that night. Her bed seemed very big. Very lonely. The way Gardiner had guessed her name bothered her. How many other women named Faith had he accosted? She replayed their conversation in her mind. Something was wrong.

"Damn." She sat up abruptly. "*Damn.*" How was he going to get her number when she had never told him her last name?

Flip was upstairs reading and Faith was making dinner. The phone rang. "Flip, can you get that?" She heard him bound across the upstairs hall and held herself poised for a moment, but he did not call, so she went back to her chicken salad. She chopped some leftover white meat, a stalk of celery, a thin slice of Bermuda onion, and a sliver of red pepper. She found the mayonnaise in the refrigerator but did not see the relish.

"Flip, where's the relish?" she shouted.

"I needed it," he shouted back.

"You needed it? A whole jar of relish? What for?"

"Ma, I'm on the phone if you don't mind."

She wiped her hands and picked up on the kitchen extension. "We interrupt this conversation for an important announcement...."

"*Ma!*"

"Tell your friend you'll get back to him after we settle this relish crisis."

"Ma, I forgot to mention that I ran into—"

"Hello, Faith. This is Gardiner Allan."

"—Gardiner today at the library."

"Gardiner." She felt as if she had just swallowed a brick. "Hi."

"I was going to say something at dinner."

"Flip, hang up." *Click*. "Well, Gardiner, you sure have a knack for surprising people."

"I've had years of practice. I'm sorry, is this a bad time? I could try again later."

"That's okay." She caught the handset between her chin and shoulder as she checked the corn muffins in the oven. "Just puttering around the kitchen. So, how are you?"

He chattered for a while about how Park Seed was interested in exclusive rights to his new daylily for their Wayside Gardens catalog and then she babbled about the direct mail campaign she was doing for the Fox Run Mall. They complained about the muggy weather. They agreed that Flip was a wonderful kid. She made a comment about how lucky it was that Gardiner had run into him at the library.

"Maybe it wasn't luck," said Gardiner. "Maybe it was fate."

"Weird," she said. It was the first time she had made him laugh.

The preliminaries out of the way, he asked her to dinner. However, as soon she said yes, they seemed to run out of things to talk about. They agreed on Friday night at six and then he said he had to go and hung up.

"Flip, let's eat!"

As Faith listened to her son thud downstairs like a bowling ball, she wondered whether she had done a good thing in agreeing to see Gardiner Allan. Flip set the book he had been reading beside his plate.

It was *A Midsummer Night's Dream*.

Gardiner seemed edgy; he walked Faith out to his car like a man on his way to an audit. The backseat of his Ford Escort wagon was covered with a plastic dropcloth. On it squatted an enormous plant with blue-green leaves the size of dinner plates.

"Gardiner, what a beautiful plant!"

"*Hosta seiboldiana*. A new cultivar."

Faith arched an eyebrow. "I've never been out with a perennial before."

"There's a perfectly good reason why I had to bring it, which I'd rather not go into just now." He turned the ignition key; the engine grumbled and caught.

"Does it have a name?" she asked.

"23HS."

"Pleased to meet you, Mr. S." She twisted around in her seat and touched one of the big leaves.

Gardiner said nothing.

"So where are we going for dinner?"

"We've got reservations at Anthony's for six thirty."

"Great. I love Anthony's." She teased him again. "But I didn't know they served hostas there."

Silence.

"Is something wrong?" she said. "I don't bite, you know. Or at least, not until after dessert."

"Everything's fine; it's my problem."

"I see." She considered. "You know what an oxymoron is, Gardiner? Because what you just said sounded like one."

He pulled off into an empty lot. "Faith, I like you, but there's something I've got to tell you."

She sagged against the passenger door. "Okay, I'm listening." She hated it when men started confessing things on the first date.

"I don't just blurt this out to anyone, you know. People get the wrong idea. But I like you."

"You said that already."

He grasped the steering wheel as if to anchor himself. "I talk to plants."

She waited. "That's all? You mean, you don't deal crack? You're not involved with a sixth-grader?"

"No listen, I really talk to plants. Hostas, daylilies, hibiscus—you name it. I don't understand myself exactly how I do it. But I'm not crazy, believe me. Just a little different. And I get results: I'm successful at what I do. There aren't that many independent plant breeders left in this country, you know. Most of them work for universities or corporations or else they specialize in just one species. I've registered more than twenty different cultivars in the past ten years. Anyway, sometimes

I wait to tell people—women—about this. I wait until they get to know me better. But when they find out, I end up getting hurt."

"Gardiner, I...."

"It's all right if you want to go home. I understand; it's happened before. Sometimes I don't even know why I bother. Look, I don't...I certainly don't expect you to talk to plants. I'd be pretty surprised if you did. You can think whatever you want—but just don't humor me. Okay? Because first they always say 'oh, isn't that cute, he talks to plants' and then it's 'poor guy, maybe he's been alone too long,' and the next step is 'Gardiner, have you ever thought about getting counseling?' I don't need counseling! I just need someone to trust me for a change."

Faith hesitated, then reached over and gently squeezed his arm. The muscle was knotted beneath his sleeve, as if he were ready to hit someone. But she knew, somehow, that she was not the one he was angry at. It was the same spooky way she had known at Annabelle's that he was going to introduce himself. Maybe it was body language or the crack in his voice, but she had a good feeling about this man, despite his tirade. She could not say why she trusted him, but she did. "I'm sorry I teased you." She let her hand drop and checked her watch. "Did you say our reservations are for six thirty? Come on, let's go before they give some tourist our table."

He nodded and pulled back onto Islington Street. "I thought about saying that all day."

"I'll bet."

"That wasn't the way I had rehearsed it."

She sensed he was cooling off, so she grinned. "It's all part of the agenda for a first date, you know. You need to figure out whether you're with a human being or a chimpanzee, so you make up these tests—we all do."

"A test? Maybe so." He grinned back. "So what's your test?"

"Oh, I stick to the basics," she said. "Does he show up? Is he wearing shoes? Can he speak Lithuanian?" Once she got him chuckling, she met and held his gaze. "But as long as we're being disgustingly honest...I guess I need to tell you something too. I'm glad you like me, Gardiner. But when a man keeps saying things like that, I hear something else."

"Okay." He sighed. "I understand."

By the time they reached Anthony's, the crisis had passed. With the help of a bottle of Valpolicella, they laughed their way through the antipasto. For the main course Faith ordered her favorite, the cunningly spiced fetuccine carbonara. She warned Gardiner that garlic was another test. He had eggplant something. She finally tried asking him about himself over the cappuccino.

"I grew up in Hollis," he said. "Mom taught math at Nashua High and Dad owned an apple orchard. I went to UNH for a couple of years; I was going to major in plant science and help run the orchard. But it was the '60s, you know. I took a detour and never got back to the highway. I inherited some money when Dad died, so I bought the land in Barrington. I wanted to raise pot but my girlfriend at the time was paranoid, thank goodness. So I tried my hand at growing legal stuff." He lifted his cup. "The rest is horticultural history."

"You're lucky to be doing something you're good at," Faith said. "Then again, you do have the name for it."

"Gardiner was my grandmother's maiden name. Hated it when I was a kid. I thought it a bad joke my parents played on me. Now I see it more as an omen. Turns out lots of people have names that fit. The guy who took my appendix out was Dr. Cutts. The archbishop of Manila, Cardinal Sin. Grace Kelly. We once had a governor named Natt Head."

"George Bush." Faith giggled. "Dan Quayle."

"There you go."

After dinner, they strolled through town. She told him about growing up in Philadelphia. She hated discussing her marriage because of the whine that always crept into her voice, so she told Flip stories instead. Flip and the lost ant colony. Flip meets Governor Sununu. Flip and the barbecued cat food. She talked about the agency and how she was going to ask for a promotion.

"Does *your* work make you happy?" he asked.

"I don't know what happy means anymore. I thought I was happy with Chuck and he was cheating on me. Isn't happy just our capacity for self-deception?"

"That's a dumb question." He took her hand. "As long as we're being brutally honest."

"Oh." She thought about being offended. She thought about letting go of his hand. She decided not to.

They wandered through the park at twilight. Gardiner went straight for the All-America Selection trial garden. "Front-row seats for the plant play-offs. Check out the celosias." He knelt to touch some spiky flowers that looked like burning feathers. "You're gorgeous," he said.

She folded her arms. "Well, thanks."

He glanced up at her, his face bright with pleasure. "Yeah, you too," he said.

Faith had long since decided that men were born compliment-impaired. "They smell nice, anyway."

"No, that's nicotania. The white trumpets. Another old-timer they've overimproved. They bred for more flowers and gave up most of the fragrance. In your grandmother's day you would've been able to smell that bed in Maine." He straightened up. "Ever hear of Luther Burbank?"

"No." She took his hand again.

"He introduced over 800 varieties of new plants way before anyone understood genetics. He had an instinct. They say he could walk down a row of seedlings, deciding what to thin at a glance. He knew just which ones would bear the fruit he wanted. How could he do that?"

She shook her head.

"He developed a spineless cactus. Afterward he said, 'I often talked to the plants to create a vibration of love. *You have nothing to fear*, I would tell them. *You don't need your defensive thorns. I will protect you.*' That's a direct quote. 'You have nothing to fear.' Try publishing that in a scientific journal."

"This has something to do with your hosta."

"Here's another celosia," said Gardiner. "Cockscomb."

"Looks like a brain made of red velvet," she said, "and don't change the subject."

He stopped and faced her. "It wasn't only the words that Burbank said. It was his vibration." He looked uncomfortable. "You see, 23HS is forming gametophytes, getting ready for sexual reproduction. I'm telling it that I love it and making a...friendly suggestion about the offspring. A matter of a few chromosomes. It doesn't take all that much focus; it's like driving the interstate."

"Telling it? Right now?"

He nodded. His eyes seemed to get bluer and for a moment she felt that she could see inside of him. He was afraid.

So was she. "Are you saying you're using telepathy? On a hosta?"

"Telepathy? I didn't say anything about telepathy. I said *suggestion*,

Faith." He shivered in the gloom. "I hate explaining this. It always comes out wrong. So why am I telling you?"

"I don't know." She squeezed his hand. "Because you want someone to trust you?"

He stared at the lights across the river. "Would you consider coming out to the farm? I could show you there."

"I might." She surprised herself. "I just might. Promise not to sacrifice me to the corn goddess?"

"He's a mad scientist."

"He's not a scientist. He never got his degree."

It was late on a Saturday night. Betty and Faith were at the kitchen table, drinking Carlo Rossi Rhine out of coffee cups. Flip was with his father and Betty's husband Dave was in Toledo. There were only three brownies left in the pan.

"He talks dirty to plants."

"You promised to withhold judgment until I finished the story." Faith wondered if she should have said anything at all to her. "Don't you ever talk to your plants?"

"No."

"Well, I do. Millions of people do. It's perfectly acceptable behavior." Faith was keeping Gardiner's vibrations a secret for now, which was hard because they were what worried her most.

"All right, I'm withholding. He's got wonderful compost. I'm totally impartial."

"So I went up to his place in Barrington. He owns sixty acres off Route 9. The farmhouse was built in 1834; there's an attached barn, a big greenhouse. And gardens, amazing gardens."

"Is the house nice?"

"He doesn't live in the house. He could, but it's too big for him. He has a trailer, an old-fashioned aluminum Airstream. Sort of retro. When he was a kid he thought they looked like spaceships and he always wanted to live in one when he grew up."

"When he grew up," Betty repeated, writing on an imaginary notepad.

"I met his staff; he has an older couple, John and Sue, full time and three kids from UNH for the summer. Everyone was so friendly and enthusiastic—reminded me of summer camp. They whistle a lot. And it's contagious. As we walked the grounds, I felt glad just to be there. Like I wanted to stretch out on the warm grass and make the afternoon last the rest of my life."

Betty refilled Faith's empty cup. "So when he talks to plants, what does he say?"

"He's a shameless flatterer. 'How's my jewel today? You're smothered with buds. And your lines are so graceful. What, are you reblooming already?' He uses Q-tips to cross-pollinate. 'You'll like this one,' he says, 'he blooms for weeks.' And he stuffs things in his mouth like a toddler. Bits of leaf, blades of grass, thinnings—he ate a flower. Well, so did I: rose petals in the salad. But while we were in the annual garden, he ate a nasturtium. He claims it helps him stay connected. He has this theory that plants like to be consumed. They want us to make better use of them. But the worst was when he ate a Japanese beetle."

"*Ugh.* Kind of scratchy going down."

"He said he didn't do that very often but that it reassured the plants and discouraged beetles. I think he was showing off."

"Men'll do that—don't ask me why. In college, a rugby player once swallowed a guppy for me." Betty sounded wistful. "His name was Herman."

"Oh, and he named a flower after me."

"What!"

Faith grinned. "He's been working on a new daylily and apparently it's a big deal. He just sold propagation rights to this seed company and they've been pressing him to name it because their catalog is going to the printer. So now it's going to be called 'Faith.' In the morning it's a dusty salmon but as the blossom catches the sun, it gets brighter and pinker. 'Improves with age,' he says. And fragrant, too. I mean, it was so beautiful, I wanted to cry."

"He named a flower after you on the second date! Forchrissakes, did you go to bed with him?" She said it so that Faith could take it as a joke if she wanted.

Faith's grin stretched to a smile. "After dinner, everyone else went home and we talked for a long time on the porch swing at the house and then he said, 'I'm going to kiss you now unless you stop me.'"

"I take it you didn't."

"Are you kidding? I wanted to applaud." She dissolved into laughter and then pounded her wrists against her forehead. "Betty, I don't want to do this. I can't be falling already. It's too soon...I'm still rebounding from Chuck. Aren't I supposed to wait two years or something?"

"Next you'll be drawing up a flowchart! You're allowed to feel whatever you feel."

"Whose side are you on, anyway?"

"Yours."

"I didn't think you liked him after the way you acted at Annabelle's. You couldn't wait to go."

"The only reason I acted any way at all is because I was attracted to him and wished I could do something about it." She snatched up the last brownie and squinted at Faith. "Did I just say what I thought I heard myself say?"

"You don't think he's too strange?"

"Sure he's too strange." She shrugged. "Everybody is. It's a wonder we can stand one another at all, much less fall in love. I think you already know what you want to do, Faith. But if you're asking me, I say good for you."

Faith was at a loss. She had expected Betty to try and talk her out of seeing Gardiner again. Betty's approval only made her feelings for him more credible. And more scary. She wished she could have told Betty about the vibrations—or whatever the hell they were—but that would have been too reckless a violation of Gardiner's trust. Bad enough that she had blabbered as much as she had. So she was left with what seemed to her an intractable dilemma: her new boyfriend was telepathic. How else could he have recognized Faith at Annabelle's? Or found Flip at the library? Or waited until precisely the right moment to kiss her? It was not only plants that he connected to; Faith believed Gardiner had read her mind. She doubted she could be with a man who would always know what she was thinking. How would she be able to tell if she was being manipulated into doing things that she did not really want? Maybe he did not care at all, maybe he was just using his power to seduce her. When they filmed her life, they would have to call it *Passion Slave of the Mutant*. God help me, she thought, deep into yet another sleepless night, I'm sinking to Flip's level. I'm starting to see my life in terms of "B" monster movies.

Flip and Jerry were in the backseat practicing burps. Faith had never understood why rude noises should strike such profound harmonies in the souls of thirteen-year-old boys. Soon they would move on to farts. She pulled into Betty's driveway and parked next to Dave's Taurus. Something was wrong. Betty never went out when her husband was home.

"You okay?" said Faith.

"No." The screen door slammed. "Where's Gardiner?"

"He had to work late; we're meeting him at the park. Look, are you sure you want to come? I'll call him and cancel. We could go at my place and talk."

"I don't want to talk." She marched from her house as if she never intended to return. "I've been talking ever since he came home. I'm sick of hearing myself."

"Problems?"

"No problem. All I have to do is accept the fact that I have a drive-through marriage. Just take me someplace where people are having fun, okay? The more the merrier."

A dense groundcover of blankets and lawn chairs had already spread around the outdoor stage at Prescott Park Arts Festival by the time they arrived. It had been a wet summer and many of the performances had been rained out. The penultimate show of the season had drawn a big crowd on a warm Friday night. A harpist and a science fiction writer were the opening acts for *Little Shop Of Horrors*.

They spread the blanket on the lawn between the whale sculpture and the stage. Flip and Jerry wandered off to snack, ignoring Faith's protest that the cooler was full of fried chicken and fruit salad. As the crowd filled in around them, Betty steadfastly resisted Faith's efforts to draw her out. She was about as much company as a land mine. "I'm going to stretch my legs," she said finally. "I'll be back."

Faith was sympathetic; however, she could not help but resent Betty's timing. Faith did not need to be worrying about her friend when she had to decide what to say to Gardiner. One reason she had brought Jerry and Flip along was to protect herself from a serious conversation if she lost her nerve. Now she was alone.

"What's with Betty?" He snuck up behind her, stooped, and nuzzled the back of her neck. "I saw her on the way in."

"I don't know exactly." She held out her hands to be helped up. "Funny, I was just thinking of you."

He took her weight effortlessly. "I can't stop thinking of you."

She almost came into his arms but then pushed away. "Let's take a walk." He made her feel too good.

He veered toward the garden but she maneuvered him around it as she explained that Betty was having trouble with Dave, but was not talking about it. They passed over the bridge and past the parking lots on Pierce Island, strolling in silence while Faith worked up her courage. "What am I thinking right now?" she said. "Take a guess."

He put fingers to temples and affected an air of deep concentration. "You're thinking...let's see, you're thinking that if we don't turn around soon, we'll be late for the harpist. No, no, wait—that's what *I'm* thinking."

"Gardiner, what kind of vibrations do you get from me?"

"Good, good, *good*, good vibrations," he sang in a surfer falsetto.

"Be serious. I'm asking if you can read my mind."

He made a rude noise that Flip would have loved. "Everyone asks that, sooner or later. And I always tell the truth. Which is, I don't know."

"How could you not know something like that?"

"I can't tell what you're thinking, what your cat thinks, or what a rose thinks. If anything. Sometimes I sense emotions. Anger, fear, desire; the strong ones. But so what? We all give unconscious cues to one another and it's not that hard to understand them, if you pay attention. Lots of people don't. They're so locked up inside themselves that they never see anyone else. But just because I look people in the eye doesn't mean I know what's in their hearts. I'm a sender, not a receiver."

She slipped an arm around his waist. "What does that mean exactly?"

"I have no secrets because I broadcast what I feel. The stronger the emotion, the broader the cast. If I'm happy, I'm literally the life of the party. When I'm sad, people want to cry. It's a curse, really—which is why I'd rather be with my plants. It's all so much simpler with begonias. I mean I can't hide it if I don't like someone. And when I love someone...."

"You don't love me."

"No? Think about it, Faith. I'm the one that's naked. When you're close and I brush your face like this. Can't you tell? When I whisper your name? Faith."

Their lips touched.

After a while, he pulled back. "Do you know what a feedback loop is?"

"*Gardiner*, we're kissing!"

"When sound from the speaker gets picked up by the microphone, the system howls. It feeds on itself, increasing with every cycle to maximum output." He sifted her hair through his fingers. "Maybe that's what's happening to us. My love is reflected by you back to me, which makes me think you love me, which makes me love you more, and on and on. It's happened before."

"Doesn't leave much room for my feelings, does it?"

"I wish I knew what they were, Faith. Can you tell me?"

"No. I don't know. Now I'm really confused."

"So maybe it *is* feedback. What you need to do is get far away from me so you can decide what you feel without my interference."

"We'd better go back." She poked him in the ribs. "You sure know how to ruin a kiss."

They missed the first few minutes of the harpist, who was very good. The boys were restless so during the break before the science fiction writer read, she sent them over to spit off the pier. Gardiner was restless too; he went in a different direction. Faith was afraid she had hurt him.

She knew that was wrong. She was afraid of hurting him. Hurting herself. She was too damn careful; if this kept up she would never be with anyone again. She needed to take some chances. She spotted Gardiner over by the vertical planting of impatiens. He was cruising the wall of bloom like it was the salad bar at Wendy's.

"Faith, he's here," Betty hissed.

As Faith watched, Gardiner picked a flower and then surreptitiously popped it into his mouth. Nobody saw but her. She grinned and shook her head. The man needed someone to watch out for him or he was going to get in trouble someday. And she wanted him—no question about that! He had brought her back to life; now she was ready to blossom. Why should she care how he had done it?

"And he's with someone new! I can't believe it."

Faith wondered if she was far enough away to be out of Gardiner's feedback loop. Because, from this distance, he looked very much like someone she could love. "What are you mumbling about?" Even if his kissing did need work.

"*Chuck.*"

"Chuck?" Faith was dreaming now. "Chuck who?"

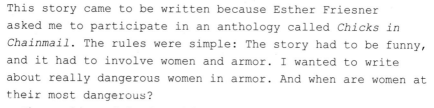

This story came to be written because Esther Friesner asked me to participate in an anthology called *Chicks in Chainmail*. The rules were simple: The story had to be funny, and it had to involve women and armor. I wanted to write about really dangerous women in armor. And when are women at their most dangerous?

The working title for this story was "Armed and With PMS." Most men don't know (and don't want to know) that when nubile women have been together for a long time, their monthly cycles synchronize. In an agrarian, warlike society where magic functions, there are bound to be some...unusual...effects caused by this phenomenon. So I wrote about them.

—Jody Lynn Nye

The Growling

JODY LYNN NYE

"**Y**OU HAVE USED UP THE last of the birch moss, Honi," Dahli complained, a frown on her heart-shaped face. She tipped up the earthenware container to prove the truth of its emptiness, then dropped it to the dirt floor. Her strong hands, used more to clenching a sword than a broom, clamped down on her hips.

"Why not? My need is the same as anyone else's," Honi pouted, flexing a bicep until her apron sleeve split, showing her bronzed arm. In a moment, the shield-sisters might come to blows over an increasingly petty argument. Their chief flung herself between them.

"Enough!" cried Shooga, her voice filling the small supply hut. "Peace between you. Since there is not enough birch moss, I order that you two shall go out and seek more, and furthermore, you shall not raise your voices again. Now, apologize," she said, patting her palms against the air as if pushing the two women together. "You are warriors and sisters in combat."

Dahli looked at Honi, who eyed her with suspicion.

"I apologize," Honi said at last.

"So do I," Dahli said, tossing back her mane of brown hair. "But you did use up the moss." Honi's face turned a deeper shade of tan.

"I needed it!"

"And what am I supposed to do? Watch where I sit for a week?" Dahli breasted up to Honi, her fists clenched. Honi went on guard with her basket, as if she was about to belabor her shield-sister over the head with it.

"Girls! Girls!" Shooga shouted, pushing them apart in truth this time. The warrior women dodged to glare at one another over her head, making faces. Shooga was fed up with the lot of them. Her back hurt, too.

The time of Growling had come again. Thank the goddesses such times were rare in the history of the village of Hee Kwal, or there would be no unity, merely widely spaced houses full of woe. The fault lay with Mother Nature herself. Women of bearing age had children, with only a few turns of the moon between birth and conceiving anew. With men gone so long, though, the last of the children had been born months ago, leaving wombs idle. It was as if all the women returned to the time of their earliest nubile season, before they had bargained between themselves for husbands. As was the way of the Mother Goddesses during the time of creation, each of the women's cycles had gradually returned, joining the pattern until they were identical in timing and duration. When the girls who had reached womanhood but never been with a man were numbered alongside the grown warriors, that made the Red Time very strong. Woe betide the unwary stranger who wandered into the village during the Growling. True, it only lasted a day or two in every moon, but it sore tried Shooga's patience.

The men of Hee Kwal had gone to the capitol of Sen Setif, to serve their year's time as honor guard to the King and Queen. Next time Shooga would see that it was the women who went to represent Hee Kwal. The men had been away so long Shooga's youngest baby was already fourteen moons old, and she was feeling the lack of male comfort. So were all the others, though they didn't precisely want them *now*. Her mate, Brohne, usually made himself scarce during this time of the moon anyway when he *was* at home, preferring to be out of range. Yet the women's patience was wearing thin at the men's absence. Their anger was never so obvious as at this time of the month. The Growling released fierce, wild, magical energies, and lent strength to female warriors' arms.

The seeress Wysacha hobbled up to them and raised her rheumy eyes to Shooga. "The Hen of Night laid the Day Egg hours ago. This argumentative one," she pointed a chipped nail at Honi, "has her appointment when the Egg reaches its highest. If she is not at my tent by the time it hatches into the red Rooster of Evening I will take the next patient."

"I will be there!" Honi said, glaring at the old woman. "You shall take away my pain, Wysacha. I receive no relief and no respect either in this village. If my husband was here...."

"If your husband was here you'd be with child, and there'd be no

Growling," Wysacha said, with a grin that showed her toothlessness. "Thank the Goddesses I'm past all that, but I thank you for the extra magic I can draw upon."

"I think the men stay away deliberately," Dahli said, shoving her dark hair behind her and working it into a rough braid. "Why resume the responsibility of home and child when they can be away, free to hunt and fight?"

"My husband will pay when he gets back, that I promise you," Honi said, hoisting her basket on her hip and tossing her golden hair. "I'll be with you very soon, Wysacha."

"Good, good," the old wizardess said, turning in a swirl of dark red robes to totter back toward her hut. "Bring some food. The Day Egg needs nourishment to grow. Huh! Goddesses pity the first man to set foot in this village: the whole place is set against you."

"The Night God spat the Gob of Light hours ago," Pex, chief of the Buh Bah admonished his spy. "How lies the land?"

The man grinned, his white teeth gleaming in the blackness of his beard. "You'll like this, chief. The whole place is empty of men, except for boys not old enough to grow peachfuzz. The women are alone, and for a long time, I wager. The village has deteriorated. Gardens are untended, and above all lies the fume of an unfamiliar smell."

"No men? Do you say so?" demanded Abbs, chief of the Ma Cho and Pex's second-in-command.

"I swear, brother," the spy said, slapping his hand on the other's well-muscled buttock in testament of a good oath.

"Hur hur hur," laughed Pex, diabolically. "It shouldn't take much to conquer them, and then—Par Tee!"

The sacred rite of Par Tee involved the consumption of much fermented spirits, followed by the ingestion of well-greased meats, and then fertility rites, the more vigorous the better. As Pex looked around at his cohort, he saw that every man's face wore a grin wide enough to swallow the ears of the man on each side.

The tribes of Buh Bah and Ma Cho had once been at war. The battling had lasted for many seasons until peace had grudgingly been proposed. It seemed that the two sides would rather sneer at one another over the bargaining table until one wise soul pointed out that if they united forces they could go and pick on smaller tribes. A treaty was suggested, and both sides agreed at once.

The most defenseless of Buh Bah's neighbors were the Sen Setif. Sen Setif males were objects of derision in both the Buh Bah and Ma Cho lands because the Sen Setif valued male and female alike, both in the arts of war and of peace. The Buh Bahs and the Ma Chos knew well that a woman's place was in a man's bed. Any woman's place. How convenient it was that they wouldn't have to fight the Sen Setif for their females.

Honi was grateful for her close-fitting leather armor as she brushed past the waist-high, stinging nettles to get close to the birch trees. She spotted a lush clump of moss and began to pull it off the white bark. Such dull work.

She heard the clink of metal near her. It must be Dahli threshing through the reeds on the bank of the stream, looking for wide lily leaves to pack the moss in. Honi wished she would hurry up. She wanted to get back to the village and have Wysacha work her magic on Honi's aching lower back. Though her skin felt as if it itched on the inside, she discovered that the irritation that had dogged her all day disappeared as soon as she set foot outside the village wall. Wysacha was right: the place was packed full of magic. Perhaps in the rite of the Third Day they could wind the whole package into a spell and send it to bring their men home safely—so she and Dahli and the others could beat them with sticks for having been gone so long.

She sighed and rested her back against the nearest tree bole. Mytee was a good man. He'd hardly know their son, who had grown up enough to walk and wield a play spear already. She'd even taught the little one to say "Surrender or die!"

Honi knelt to yank one more chunk of the absorbent moss off the handiest birch. Almost enough now for ten women, she told herself, looking down at her well-filled basket. The metallic clank came nearer. It must be Dahli. She looked up, expecting her shield-sister. Instead, she had one moment's glimpse at a tall, well-muscled, handsome, but greasy, unshaven and dirty man before hands grabbed her from behind and clamped over her eyes and mouth.

"Ow! Gods damn her, she bit me!" Gluetz howled. The eight men trying to hold onto the blonde woman paid him no mind. Their captive was refusing to cooperate. She struggled and kicked, even managing to work a fist loose now and again to punch a man in the face. Pex signalled to the warriors to drop their burden and sit on her so he could tie the woman's hands and feet. Most of them sported scratches and bruises before he was finished.

"A fine one," Abbs said, running his eyes up and down her body. "Spirited. I like that. She'll be a worthy object for the rite of Par Tee."

The female glared at them over the gag made of a wad of birch moss and her own belt. Pex grinned down at her. Suddenly, her body relaxed, and her eyes closed.

"The force of my personality," Pex said, certain that it was true. "Pick her up. Let's see if the rest of them are so easily surprised."

The men shouldered their burden, but not before Pex saw the woman's eyes open again. In them he saw hate, and the promise of retribution. That look would change to love once he gave her his personal attention.

"Soon, my pretty, soon," he said, patting her on the thigh. The woman kicked at him with both legs, almost throwing herself off Abbs's and Gluetz's shoulders.

Across the meadow, Dahli straightened up from the mass of lilies, her hands full of dripping leaves. A sharply painful impulse had hit her right in the guts. She thought it was belly cramp, returning earlier than Wysacha had promised, but no. It was a warning, the kind she felt when there was to be a battle.

"Honi?" she said out loud. Her friend didn't answer. Dahli threw away the water lilies and reached up over her shoulder for her sword.

The noise of feet threshing the reeds made her drop to one knee, on guard and out of sight.

A group of men passed her by. At first she was gladdened by the sight, thinking it was their husbands returning from their travels. The next puff of wind swiftly disabused her of the idea. These men stank like months-dead offal. Their tunics and trews bore so much soil and grease at first Dahli didn't see the rips. And besides, the garments didn't match. No Sen Setif man would let himself go so badly.

Between them, two of the men carried a struggling bundle. Honi!

Dahli thought at first of leaping up and charging in to save her friend, but realized she was well outnumbered. Better to sneak back to the village and get help.

"They've got Honi?" Shooga asked, but she was already buckling her sword harness over her black body armor. She added her favorite war hammer to a loop on her belt. "How dare they?"

"*Who* were they?" Wysacha asked, wringing her thin hands together.

"Buh Bahs," Dahli said, pacing up and back over the chief's carpets. "And Ma Chos, too, unless I mistake the smell. There's at least forty of them, all filthy."

"By the goddesses, they will pay," Shooga said, slapping one hand into the other. "Muster all the women. Put the children in the central barn with the beasts, and put a heavy guard on all the doors. Attack our village, will they?" The chief felt herself getting hot, as if the air around her had caught fire.

"Careful," Wysacha said, holding out her palms to sense the ether. "The magic is packed around us like bomb-powder. A forceful thought could set the whole place off."

Shooga stopped three paces before charging out the door and made herself calm down. The heat died away to a warning of warmth. She turned to nod at the wisewoman.

"I'll save that for the right moment, old one. In the meantime, I must see to our defense. Get to a safe place, and watch out for us."

"I'm already weaving spells," Wysacha said, tottering out the door as fast as she could.

Pex had his hand on the hilt of his sword as he swaggered into the village square, followed by his men and their captive. Nice place, this. Houses in good repair: all of them even had *roofs*. Plenty of trees to lounge beneath, lots of wood for fires. Good grass for herds. They were going to like it here. He surveyed the village as if its surrender was a mere formality.

Abbs carried a sheep he had killed. It would make a fine barbecue for the Par Tee. He threw it on the ground in front of the group and stood next to Pex. In the doorways and courtyards, women went nonchalantly about their tasks: drawing water, weaving cloth, milking cattle, pulling weeds.

"They can hardly contain their enthusiasm," Gluetz said, looking around him.

"Perhaps they haven't noticed us," Abbs whispered.

"How could they not?" Pex asked, thumping his chest mightily. "Do we not have the appearance of warriors? Do we not reek of manly musk? They ought to be grateful to us for coming. Look around you. These might not have had a man in months. Some will feel the lack."

"And how good could a Sen Setif man be anyhow," Delts snickered, "with his foolish ideas about equality? A woman gets just as much pleasure from a rough tumble as she does from slow wooing."

"Hah!" Gluetz said, slapping his leg. "And a man can get in three or four women in so much time. Why waste a nice, warm day like this one getting all hot over a single roll in the straw?"

"Hur hur hur," Pex laughed. "So true. Ladies!" He raised his hands on high, turning so every woman could look upon his masculine splendor. The women turned disinterested eyes toward the group in the center of the grassy square. "Greetings! I am Pex of the Buh Bah! You will be glad to see us. My men and I here claim title to this land and everything that grows or walks on it. We are your conquerors! Surrender to us easily, and you may even enjoy our attentions. We are bold and experienced lovers, and I promise none shall go without. What do you say?" He stood with his hands outstretched and a broad smile on his face, waiting for the gratitude of the village maidens.

"Aaaaaaaaaaaaahhhhhhhhhh!" The voices from a third of a hundred female throats were raised in a shrill war cry that caused the hair on the nape of his neck to stand straight out. From behind looms, from under milking stools, from flower baskets, from the folds of dresses came swords, spears and maces. The loose robes fell away, revealing armor and ringmail.

For just a moment, the Buh Bah were paralyzed. Then Pex swept his sword out of its scabbard just in time to meet a blow aimed at his head.

"Oh ho! So you want it rough?" Pex chortled, beating back the attack with ease. "Wonderful! My men prefer it that way."

Dahli led the first wave of ten Hee Kwals. At her side was Timayta, Honi's younger sister, eager to redress the wrong done to her family's honor. Eight of them charged straight into the midst of the men, forming a shield for the two who swung bludgeons at the knees of the men guarding Honi. While the erstwhile guards were jumping up and down clutching their legs, Dahli's squad surrounded Honi, cut her bonds, and guided her out again. As soon as her hands were free, the blonde warrior drew her own sword and waded in against the invaders.

"Cooperation," Shooga had said over and over again, when teaching tactics. "Cooperation—and hit them where they live."

Meanwhile, the other two waves of ten closed in on the mob of Ma Chos from both sides. Dahli, the last to withdraw, took a swipe at Pex himself. He disengaged her blade expertly, and countered with a hard blow that vibrated her arm to the shoulder. Gritting her teeth, she swung again. He laughed, parrying her sword and Timayta's with a single cunning move.

Dahli let out a frustrated scream between her teeth and rained blows on him from every angle, only to meet a counterstroke each time. Her own sword turned in her grip, and she had to hold it with both hands. She couldn't hold out long against such a forceful attack. An arm encased in black leather slid past her and caught the next blow on the shaft of a war hammer. Shooga shouted at her.

"Together, now!"

Dahli nodded shortly. Around them, men and women battled fiercely. Dahli saw with despair that the women were not up to their best fighting trim. It had been so long since they'd had a genuine conflict that they'd let themselves go soft. She vowed to the Mother Goddesses that if they survived this battle she'd train her muscles every day, instead of twice or thrice a week. As she began to tire, she recalled Wysacha nagging her to follow the Way of Ayrao Bix, the first and most tireless of Hee Kwal's female warriors. How she wished she had heeded that advice.

"Are you all right?" Timayta asked Honi, as the two of them hammered on the sword and shield of a black-bearded male.

"My hands are numb, my back aches, and the smell is making me sick to my stomach," Honi said, punctuating each phrase with a sound strike on their enemy's sword or leather shield. "Other than that, I am fine."

"Don't get yourselves all tired out," the man said, leering at them over the edge of his shield. "You should be looking forward to the Par Tee."

"Par Tee? With you?" Timayta cried. "How barbaric!"

"Yeah," the man grinned. "Ain't it great?"

Honi was infuriated by the big man's arrogance. She struck again and again at him, but knew her blows were not connecting with flesh. He turned them all back; not easily, but steadily. She was good, but where skills were evenly balanced, weight and height would always win. Honi was suddenly afraid that her village would fall to these disgusting invaders. They would...touch them. She panted with fury, and was made even more angry when the man watched her breathe with open admiration. Honi saw red.

She didn't know at first whether there was something in her eyes, or if the whole world was disappearing in a crimson mist. Around her, fellow warriors were falling, and the men, with fewer opponents to face, were ganging up on single women. Warriors were vanquished one after another, knocked out or tied up by the invaders. She tried to fight her way toward them, but it was getting harder and harder to see. The sun was a red lens in the sky.

Pex turned away the puny blows of the females. His men wielded the greater strength, and their cause was just. It was only a matter of time before they had worked all the fight out of the women. When they were exhausted, they'd be that much easier to convince to serve the Buh Bah. And the Ma Cho. This equal sharing stuff was too advanced for him. Normally he would just tell his men to take the ones they wanted, and leave the rest for the other tribe. Numbers weren't his strong suit, but even he could see there weren't enough women to go around.

"Don't kill any of them!" he shouted. The big woman in black and the sexy woman in ring armor pressed their attack on him as if they really knew what they were doing. For a moment he felt sorry for their fathers. If these girls had been sons, he could have made warriors out of them.

Suddenly Abbs and Delts were beside him, a redheaded woman slung between them, unconscious.

"How goes the day, brothers?" Pex asked, parrying a double blow with both hands on his sword hilt. The woman in black showed all her teeth, and slammed a hammer blow at his arm. He shrugged it off with the edge of his hide shield.

"Over soon," Abbs said, cheerfully. "This is number ten plus two to go down. Only some more to go!" Abbs wasn't too good with numbers either, but he was a good judge of a battle.

"Fine," Pex said. "I'll just finish off these two." His brother chief pushed by behind him, leaving Pex with his opponents. The women were tiring at last. He was pleased to see that the fire in their eyes was undiminished. The Par Tee would be a good one.

And yet, Pex thought, it was strange. The day had been fair, but now there was a low cloud gathering around the battle like rising mist. It wasn't dust; no one was coughing. Besides, the dirt here wasn't red.

With a skilled twist of his sword, he disarmed the big woman of her hammer. She reached over her head for the sword on her back. Pex chopped at her arm, and connected with the tricep muscle. It didn't cut through the leather, but he could tell it hurt by the tears that sprang to the woman's eyes.

"Give up now," he suggested, almost kindly. "Save us all some time."

"Never," the woman gritted. She shrugged her sword free, and engaged him again. The cloud around them grew more palpable, cutting off the sight of the other warriors around them. She slashed at his chest with the point of her blade. Pex turned it away, but just barely.

The chief of the Buh Bah began to think something was very wrong. The women should have been getting weaker, but instead, they seemed to be drawing strength from somewhere. And he, puissant fighter, felt himself growing tired. How could such a thing be? The woman in black was saying something.

"How *dare* you invade our village!" she shrieked, chopping deeply into his shield. "How *dare* you capture one of my warriors and truss her up like a roast! How dare you kill one of our prize ewes! How dare you offer to rub your greasy, smelly bodies against ours! How dare you insult us and the honor of our husbands!"

With every slash of her sword, Pex found himself retreating a step. He blundered backward over a loom. Another woman joined the attack on him, her eyes ablaze.

"You ruined my weaving!" she shrieked. "A moon's work, destroyed!" She brought a mace crashing down on him, but only hit him in the head. A mere scratch.

"You should be glad we offered to conquer you," Pex pointed out to the three women confronting him. "We will appreciate your beauty, and you won't have to wear those confining garments any longer."

"You arrogant cretin," the woman in ringmail snarled. The thrust she aimed at him actually passed through Pex's defense and rammed him in the chest. If the sword had had a point, he'd have been done for. That thought struck him just as he bumped into something.

"That you, chief?" Abbs's voice asked.

"What is happening?" Pex asked, dumbfounded, turning his head just enough to see his fellow chief, at bay. His arm was moving mechanically, parrying one blow after another. Out of the corner of his eye Pex saw that every one of their men was now back to back in the center of the village square, fighting for their lives against a brood of women. "This is impossible!"

The invaders were overwhelmed by the circle of female fighters. One by one, the men dropped, and the women clustered around the next warrior, beating him until he submitted or fell unconscious. Soon, there were only a few standing: Pex, Abbs, Delts and Gluetz.

"And, now," cried the blonde woman that they had captured out in the field, "*kill!*" She raised her sword arm over her head, and charged.

The women, only just visible through the red fog that now blanketed the village square, responded with their shrill war cry. The four invaders, as one, cowered and dropped to the ground with their arms over their heads.

"No!" a little old crone shrieked, appearing out of one of the houses. She pushed herself into the midst of the women and stood in front of the chiefs. "Don't kill. The power of the Growling will rebound back on you the way their attacks have on them!"

"Then I've already paid for this!" Honi said, striding forward to Pex. She grabbed a handful of his greasy hair and hauled him to his feet. There was incredible strength in her slender arm. Pex couldn't have stayed down if he'd wanted to.

"This is for sitting on me," Honi cried.

"I'd hate to see what would happen if your men were here," Pex said, weaving back and forth. He tried to lift his hand to brush her away, but it was too heavy.

"If our men were here," Honi said, cocking back her gloved fist and aiming carefully, "they'd watch and applaud!"

With the full force of the Growling magic behind her, Honi swung. Her fist connected with the man's chin. He flattened out on the air, and sailed a dozen yards over the heads of his men before crashing into a tree. Curious birds, disturbed from their nest, sailed down to fly around his head in a circle, chirping to one another.

As soon as the last of the invaders was defeated, the air cleared. The red mist vanished, leaving the sky a pure and sparkling blue.

"The Growling is over," Wysacha said, with a pleased nod, as if she had arranged the whole matter herself.

"Thank the Goddesses," Shooga said. She reached up to sheathe her sword and stopped in surprise. "My back has stopped hurting!"

"All you needed was some exercise," the old woman said, coming over to pat the chief on the back. "I have told you this before. Exercise and good nutrition, just as it is said the great one Ayrao Bix practiced."

"Is this the answer?" Shooga asked, only half joking. "Next time the Growling comes, we should go looking for a fight?"

"No, no," Wysacha chided her gently. "By then I hope the men are back again. The magic was so strong this time. We won't always find so easy a way to dissipate it."

"Easy?" Abbs asked, staring up at the sky. He lifted his head, then dropped it to the earth again. The village females all walked away from them, the Ma Cho, leaving them lying on the turf as if they were of no importance whatsoever. If he had the strength, he'd...he'd...he'd better leave before he found out *what* he would do. Some mysteries were better not investigated. He rolled over onto his belly and hauled himself to his feet with surprising difficulty. The other men were all scattered nearby like heaps of dirty rags.

"Come on," he said, swaying as he gestured with one arm. He hadn't felt so bad since the time they brewed liquor out of mushrooms. Abbs gathered up those of the tribes who were conscious, and assigned them to carry the ones who weren't. It took four of them to haul the mighty Pex away from the tree where he was resting.

The men boldly slunk out of the village of Hee Kwal. No one attempted to stop them, which Abbs attributed to the reputation of the Ma Cho. And if they told their story first around the pubs in the great cities to the north and east, that reputation would not suffer.

"You forgot the sheep," Delts told Abbs. "We could at least have had the barbecue."

Abbs glanced behind them at the ragged file of warriors. Some of them were walking in a delicate fashion to avoid chafing bruised body parts. Those women did *not* fight fair.

"Bugger the sheep," Abbs said. "No one is in the mood for any kind of Par Tee."

Honi looked down at her knuckles. "Ech! Look at that, will you?" she said, holding out her hand to her friends. "That brute had enough grease on him to light a lamp."

"Filthy," Dahli agreed, shaking her head over the ugly smudges. She offered the edge of her own tunic to her shield-sister and best friend to wipe off the grime, then something occurred to her. "Honi, where is the moss? I really need it now."

"Oh, I dropped it near the birch trees," Honi said, pointing up the hill. "I'll go with you to gather it up. At least now I am certain we won't be disturbed."

~~~~~~~~~~~~~

"Sure, we can reprint 'Alien Radio,'" says Resnick, "but not with *my* name on it."

Oh, the pain! The shame! He loves me—he loves me not! How could he so cavalierly drive a stake between our two hearts, which had formerly beat as one?

"Look, kid," Resnick says. "Look, it's nothing personal. I love the story and, well, you're not totally objectionable either. The thing is, I'm editing this thing, I've already got my name all over it and my own story in it, so I don't want my name on a collaboration, too. What say we drive the bibliographers bananas and print it under your name only? It'll be fun. Just this once. Promise."

Well, what could I say? He asked me so nicely. And the next day he sent me chocolates and roses and a love note that I'll keep forever under my pillow. How could I say no? How could I not forgive him? Just this once.

—*Nick DiChario*

(Editor's note: I never told him he wasn't totally objectionable—but he wrote a hell of a first draft that took only minimal tinkering. —MR.)

Alien Radio

NICK DICHARIO

~~~~~~~~~~~

MUST I USE THIS HEADPHONE? It appears my skull is ill-shaped for such a device. I can just speak into this? Very good. What does that mean? That red light? Oh, are we on? I can go ahead and speak, then? Excellent.

Hello, people of Earth, and good evening. As many of you already know, I have come to your world for the express purpose of studying your race, so that I may offer you the five basic truths of your existence.

But before I begin, I have been asked to deliver this commercial message for a new product called Heaven Scent. Heaven Scent is a liquid chemical bleach used in conjunction with your laundry soaps to whiten whites and brighten colors, and it can be purchased at your local supermarkets, where you will find an introductory rebate offer. The manufacturer claims that the bleach will cause cleaner, fresher-smelling fabrics, and will not be injurious to your garments. They will come out thirty-seven times brighter than the sun, and of course I couldn't say this on the public airwaves if it were not the literal truth. Heaven Scent is the answer to the housewives' and househusbands' prayers. Whoopie.

End of commercial message, the funds of which have been donated to the Home for Terminally Morose *Phlezms* of Indeterminate Gender.

Now, let me begin by saying that you live in terror of your mortality, and while this is a realistic fear, it is also a universally repressed one for all members of your species. You carry on as if your deaths are avoidable, in some way, via your professional or family or religious associations, and therefore, although you can look at your deaths rationally, you cannot *feel* them. Your ultimate fear is repressed.

Although your race has for some reason deemed it necessary to deny yourselves this self-knowledge to proceed with your daily lives, I submit to you the first basic truth of your species: Lurking beneath all your abundant insecurities and depressive states and schizophrenias, is this fear of death that you cannot reconcile. The denial of the death-state is directly responsible for your vast numbers of oppressors and victims, and your wars and injustices against the sanctity of life.

I therefore offer you this solution to the first truth: If you can open your minds and peer into the darkest corners of your hidden neuroses—which every one of you has, without exception—and admit your helplessness in the face of real death, then you will not be such self-destructive animals, creating obscure reasons for your acts of cruelty against self and society, and you will not live in such utter terror of the world that your fear of death makes you unable to live your lives.

Ah, my engineer has indicated that we have our first caller. Hello. *Hello?*

Hello. You are on the air.

Uh...yeah, I have a question for you.

Proceed.

Do you think you could do something about controlling your kids? I mean, we're really glad to have you here visiting our planet and everything, you know, but—

My children? What have they done?

Well, they've kind of built their own little community center down here in our neighborhood—which is okay, you know, they need a comfortable place to hang out and all, but the thing is, they're printing their own money, and that's kind of got the local businesses upset, if you know what I mean.

I have told my children not to meddle in native affairs. If they are in some way harming your economy or threatening your sense of financial stability I shall banish them from the planet's surface.

Well, I don't want you to think we're prejudiced. I mean, that would be a really bad rap to spread across the galaxy.

Fear not, I shall handle it. My engineer has indicated I have another caller. Farewell, kind person. Hello, you are on the air.

Yeah, I'm on, really? No!

Yes.

Cool! I just wanted to say that this used to be a great hemisphere until the Man started bringing it down.

The man? What man?

The Man. You know—like the uniforms, the military, the suits and ties, you know. The government. The Maaaaaaan.

Hmm, no, I am afraid I do not know to what man you are referring, and I fail to see the relevancy of your comment in light of the basic truths of your species. So, farewell, kind person, and thank you for calling. Next caller please.

Hello, Pop? We've been listening to your show down here at the ACC—

The ACC?

The Alien Community Center. We just built it, and we thought one of us should give you a call and explain about the currency.

Yes, perhaps you should.

Well, we're operating in complete conformity with the local government's laws and barter articles, which do not prohibit the establishment of a community currency. Our dollars are of different sizes and designs from the existing tender, and we use our own special ink and a different texture of paper. We've established our own serial-number code and value structure that's a little too complicated for the natives, but our actions are in no way conspiratorial, and developing a currency is something that any local community is free to do within their existing legal system.

Nevertheless, you are upsetting the natives, and I want it stopped immediately.

But, Pop—

No buts! Just do as I say. You are interfering with the message I am trying to deliver to these life forms. Now, I should like to continue with the second basic truth. Mr. Engineer, please disconnect that problem child so I may proceed. Thank you.

Ahem. The second truth deals with sexual relationships, a matter of utmost importance to your race. Other than the obvious physical differences between the male and female of your species, there is a basic psychological truth that both the male and female must accept in order to secure a happy and peaceful coexistence with his or her mate.

The female of your species demands to be loved for the person that she is. A good mate should want "her" and not just "her body." She lives in utter terror that the sexual act will destroy her mate's perception of her inner personality.

The truth your female species must accept is that the male does in fact want only her body, that he is attached to his animal role, a role that thousands of years of evolution cannot and will not and should not obliterate, for it is an essential ingredient in the procreative drive of your race. This is not to say the male is incapable of appreciating a female for who and what she is. I merely wish to point out that the sexual act carries a different meaning for him.

Likewise, the male must accept this truth about himself. Although the "sensitive, caring male" is much in demand in your current culture, and many males, contrary to their natures, are striving to attain this posture to answer the needs of the females and arouse their receptivity, the male should not be anchored in guilt or shame concerning his purely sexual tendencies, for it is the guilt that shrinks his male personality (and we all know what *that* leads to) and threatens to destroy the animal that he is, and indeed must be.

To reconcile the second truth, your species must practice what I call "regression intercourse." You must allow each other to be reduced to nothing more than physical objects during the sexual act, to absolve yourselves of the mind and grasp your primal instincts, for the female is a sexual being as well, although much repressed. You must allow the love and attachment you have for each other to grow out of your natural animal aggressions. Your sex will be happier and healthier and less rooted in the machinations of the mind, and your roles outside the sexual arena should be enhanced as well, since you will not have the insecurities of sexual misinterpretations spilling over into the obligations of your social and professional lives.

Ah, I have been informed I have a caller on Line One. Hello. You are on the air.

I would love you to use my body like an animal. When can we get together?

I believe you have misconstrued the second truth.

Oh, yes, I want to misconstrue you desperately.

Please try not to understand me so fast. I fear that—

Don't be afraid. I know exactly what I'm doing.

I am quite certain that you do, and I suggest you do so immediately, but with a member of your species. Next caller.

Eh, yeah, hi. First off I'd like to say welcome to our planet.

Thank you, kind person.

How do you like the weather here?

As a matter of fact, I can adapt to any kind of weather.

Wow, that's really neat.

Did you have a question concerning the first or second truths of your species?

Well, actually, I was calling to complain about your kids.

My children?

Yeah. They're selling cosmetics. Not that selling cosmetics is a bad thing in and of itself—don't get me wrong, I mean, I don't want to offend you or anything—it's just they've created their own company, and to be honest they can make a better product than we can—you might have guessed I'm in the cosmetics business myself, heh, heh, heh. Anyway, it's not exactly fair competition since you aliens are a lot more intelligent than us, and you've been all over the galaxy—and that kind of free spirit, that daring to explore the universe attitude, well, it really sells in cosmetics because we're youth-oriented, you know. Like, you can make yourself into the kind of person you want to be, or thought you once were, because who you are just won't cut it. Anyway, your kids are taking over a good portion of the market.

I warned them not to interfere. Why won't they listen?

Kids, you know, that's just the way they are. I couldn't imagine having, what?, eighty or ninety of them like you. I can barely handle two. No matter what I tell them they have to challenge me. My son, he's into sports this, sports that. Do you think I could get him to read a book? My daughter is just as bad with her wild music. Dance, dance, dance, that's all she cares about. I keep telling her, what would happen if you were in an accident and lost your legs, God forbid? What would you do with your life? But does she ever think about it? No, she just keeps dancing and saying acid rock is too tame and she's waiting for them to invent base rock.

Fear not, I shall handle my children immediately.

Thanks, I'd appreciate it.

A call awaits me on Line Two. Farewell, good caller. Hello.

Yeah, I'd like to order a large pizza with pepperoni and mushrooms, two tossed salads with feta cheese and no dressing, and a small order of chicken wings.

I'm sorry, but I do believe you have dialed an inappropriate telephone number.

Last time you guys put dressing on the salads, so make sure this time you get it right, okay.

I am sorry to inform you—

Okay, then, Buffalo wings. Boy, you guys are stickers for terminology. And hold the horns, yuk, yuk.

No, no, please hang up your telephone device and dial again, thank you. Next caller, please.

Hello, Pop? We've been listening to your show down here at the ACC—

I am aware of that. Do you have an explanation for the cosmetics?

Well, we were a little bored, and we saw an opportunity to break into the cosmetics industry because, frankly, there's plenty of room for everybody. I'm telling you, there's no top to this market. These people are hungry for new products. We've developed our own line of body spray, perfume creme and lotion, talcum powder, cologne, shampoo and conditioner, we've got foundations, finishers, skin enhancers, eyeliners, glimmersticks, not to mention lip glosses and nail polishes in colors these people have never even seen, like yordishale2.2. Our customers love it! Our signature fragrance is selling out all over the planet. We call it Star Byte, and we're gearing it toward professional females who dream of transcendence (as if there are any who don't). We were thinking of branching out into accessories. Jewelry, for instance, and clothing.

Enough! Put an end to this nonsense immediately!

But, Pop—

You are trying my patience. One more incident and you shall all be confined to the ship for the duration of my stay. Do I make myself clear?

Aw, jeez, Pop....

Mr. Engineer, disconnect that problem child so that I may continue. Thank you.

It is now time for me to reveal the third great truth to your people. I call this the truth of self-imprisonment, and—Excuse me? What about it? Oh, I see.

Dear listeners, I have been asked to endorse yet another product. For those of you who appreciate the rich flavor of a strong beer, and the refreshing flavor of a light beer, Bestend Brewing Company would like to inform you of a new product called On-Tap. On-Tap Beer Tablets can offer you the best of both brews. You may purchase a bottle of one hundred of these tablets, fill a glass with tap water, drop in the tablets, and convert your water to beer, thus making the mixture as dark or as light as you wish. The manufacturers suggest you use no less than two tablets and no more than twelve tablets per average serving.

Now, if I may continue—Pardon? Oh, yes, I must thank them for sponsoring my telecast.

Back to vitally important business. The third basic truth of your species is the truth of self-imprisonment. You are all slaves to your particular cultures. The societal boundaries that you have established are fashioned to encourage *failure*, of all things. To become an accepted member of the fold, you must limit your thoughts and deeds to the status quo. As a result of this, you take your freedom of personality, your freedom of spirit, and stifle it. You crush your individuality. To further complicate this paradox, your enslavement into the group consciousness, your belittling social intercourses and daily routines, works as a shelter. You are safe as a social conformist, and this safety prevents you from reaching the core of your uniqueness.

In order to avoid this breakdown of individual personalities, you must develop a faith in the true self. You must be able to step outside of your boundaries with impunity, so that the despair of self-limitation does not obliterate the natural curiosity and creativity of your species.

Ah, I have a caller.

What are your political associations?

I have none.

Religious beliefs or preferences?

None.

Special interest groups?

No affiliations of any kind.

Have you ever used illegal drugs?

Absolutely not.

Have you ever been arrested for a misdemeanor or a felony?

Don't be ridiculous. What is the purpose behind this line of questioning?

Have you ever cheated on an exam, or your income taxes, or lied to your spouse or significant other?

Definitely not.

Congratulations, you fall into the target market for our new underarm deodorant, called Squeaky Clean, and we would like you to sample our product free of charge for one month, at the end of which we will contact you for your comments and opinions. Would you like to participate?

I don't have any arms!

Hmm.... That might pose a problem.

Next caller!

Yeah, this is the military head of NATO calling, and we have a big problem with your kids. We just discovered they've been building and selling high-tech long-range weaponry and advanced radar equipment to our enemies.

My children? I can't believe they would do such a thing!

Listen, fella, we've got high-speed missiles headed this way that are superior to our defense mechanisms! What are you going to do about it?

My engineer tells me one of my children is on Line Three. I'll straighten this out posthaste.

Hi, Pop, you sound really good on radio. I think the show is coming along nicely.

Do you really think so?

Absolutely. You're a natural.

No, you're just saying that.

Honest! We all think so.

I find radio a comfortable medium, although a bit detached. I would have gone with television, but I was afraid my looks might frighten some of the populace. Now, what about these missles?

Just a crazy misunderstanding, Pop. You've got to believe me. Here's the thing. Although there are international rules and regulations limiting arms sales on this planet, we discovered plenty of precedent for covert transactions. Naturally we assumed this was common practice. All the world leaders have taken part in below-board arms deals. So when we saw how archaic their weapons systems were down here—they haven't even discovered simple quantum-wave explosives yet—we just thought we'd jump into the market. We didn't mean any harm.

Well, maybe you didn't intend to cause any harm, but you've certainly done so. I want your Alien Community Center shut down, and I want all of you to return to the ship.

But, Pop—

No buts! Just do as I say. Is there any way to stop the missiles?

Uh, no, 'fraid not.

What kind of damage are we looking at?

Well, pretty bad.

Please define "pretty bad."

Catastrophic. Cataclysmic. One of those big words that begins with a "C." Unfortunately we sold counter-strike weapons to the west, and from the looks of it, everybody is going to be wiped out.

What about defense systems?

Nobody was interested in those. We had some really good stuff, too.

Curses! I've failed again.

Don't take it personally, Pop, you gave it your best shot, that's the important thing. I'm sure you'll do better next time around. Anyway, we're kind of curious about the fourth truth. What is it?

Thank you for asking. The fourth truth is the truth of "collective destructive realization." Because the beings in question are the only life forms on this planet who are free of instinct, who are capable of conceptualizing their deaths, repressing reality, hiding within social structures and self-limitation, because they fashion their existences around the power of denial, they are subconsciously rooted in self-destruction, and are destined to annihilate themselves unless they can radically restructure their psyches.

Too late for that, I guess.

So it would seem.

Well, to be perfectly honest, we're all kind of bored down here. We're anxious to move on. Where are we going next?

I've had such rotten luck in this galaxy, I thought maybe we'd try M33 in Andromeda next. I just have to give the fifth and final truth, and then we'll leave.

No time, Pop.

But it will tell them how to overcome the fourth truth, live forever, achieve Utopia, rid themselves forever of body odor and halitosis, and become one with the Star Maker.

Pop, you've only got about a minute to get out of there. Can you state it in forty-five seconds?

The fifth truth in forty-five seconds? Well, if I say it very fast....

You're down to forty.

Oh, well, maybe the Adromedans will appreciate it. Ladies and gentlemen, we return you now to your regularly scheduled programming....

"Barry Bonds steps up to the plate, with two men out and a runner on third. He takes his position, hitches up his pants, and shades his eyes...."

"Sure is a bright afternoon, isn't it, Al?"

"Sure is, Ed. Can't remember the last time I saw such a bright sun...."

Long pause.

"Or so many of them?"

~~~~~~~~~~

This story happened to me, in a metaphorical sense.

When I wrote it, I was corresponding with the great Robert Sheckley, having long e-mail conversations with him about what drives creativity and where true genius comes from. We were talking back and forth about how the ego often ruins truth and beauty, which exist naturally in reality without our help. If that had been the only issue floating around in my current conscious mind, I doubt I would have written the story at all, but I was fired up about a multitude of things.

For one thing, I really was reading a book, at the time, by the Dalai Lama about the nature of compassion. I really had just gone shopping in the produce section of Butson's family market. I really had bought some garlic there that didn't have any small cloves, and that seemed to peel itself like the seeds of touch-me-nots when I popped the cloves free of the bulb. And furthermore, I had just spent a day skiing with my uncle and his friends—one of whom was a true Italian chef from New York. He had that thick New Yorker accent, and during rides up on the chair, he described to me, in great and mouth-watering detail, his recipe for making what he called the best chili in the universe.

Things came together that night while I was making supper. I would chop up a vegetable, throw it in the pot, stop and jot down a few lines. I'd pour in some olive oil or add some spices and I'd write a little more. By the time supper was finished, the story was, too. And the meal came out as good as the story did, if I remember right, but print lasts and food has a way of disappearing, especially in close proximity to me. Also, it wasn't chili that I made that night. It was a tofu stir fry. But somehow I got the feeling that "Primordial Tofu" wouldn't have the same ring to it.

I think the humor in this story works better than in

other stories I have written because it grew from roots a little deeper in my mind. I think a lot of humor is kind of disembodied—a series of gags that make you chuckle (or—God help us—groan) but leave you feeling like you've just eaten something insubstantial.

I hope this story fills you like it did me. Of course, what I really hope is that it makes you laugh.

Bon appetit.

—Tom Gerencer

Primordial Chili

TOM GERENCER

~~~~~~~~~

I T WAS THE BEST POT OF CHILI EVER. Really. In the history of this or any other universe.

In the first place, there was magic garlic. Fadrinski didn't know it was magic; he just picked it up one afternoon while snooping through the produce section of Butson's Family Market. But it was magic just the same—magic, self-peeling, all big-cloved garlic from the fields of the fourteenth Bard of Quangarla, a secret society in the midst of the streets of Yalta, so secret, in fact, that the other members didn't even know they were members. But the Bard, who traveled daily to his fields by cab, was well schooled in the ancient art of garlic growing. He was a genius, a master, and in possession of the hallowed Runes of Dunderhans, which, when chanted over with the thirteen sacred philosophies of Rudolf the Curious, imparted to the plants and their pungent roots a flavor so refined and elegant and perfect as to be the very essence of garlic. Anyone eating of this plant would not only experience the taste sensation of a lifetime, but would be (afterward) unpopular in elevators for weeks.

Then, too, there were the tomatoes. Fadrinski got them in the same produce section as the garlic, but, brought into the supermarket that morning on an eighteen wheeler, they had not come from California, as the writing on their box proclaimed, but had fallen through a freak wormhole in space from the dimension of Zanng, where the tomato (or at least, a fruit that grows on many of the worlds there, and which looks, smells, tastes like, and therefore is a tomato) is revered among the seventy-five cultures of the Pakancy, is worshipped, is given lifetimes from the various races and species there, in the form of cultivation and works of art. (In Zanng, for example, the most famous piece of sculpture is not

185

a David or a Perseus on Horseback or an Atlas shouldering the world, but a great big vine-ripened plum tomato on a plate.)

We could go on about the beans, handpicked, not by Juan Valdez, but a monk named Alarcon in a town some sixty miles south of Guadalajara, who had discovered, recently, the meaning of life but decided, somewhat mischievously, not to tell anyone; or the beef—cubed, not ground—the meat of philosopher cows which had realized, at the moment of slaughter, that all life, somehow, was this feeling they could not articulate as love, and so they gave freely and lovingly of themselves, releasing endorphins and antibodies and various subtle healing chemicals into their bloodstreams and therefore into their muscles and meat at the last moment. We could expostulate on the singular nature of the herbs, many of which had been raised by a man in Crete, wildly insane but possessed of the belief that he was here, solely, as a servant of cumin and oregano and basil and pepper, and who raised his plants as one would raise children, and sung to them, day and night, and played lyrical melodies for them on his balalaika until the local police obtained an injunction against him, but by that time the spices had already been harvested and sent on their way.

Or we could think more about the onions, the green peppers, the chives, all of which had come from similarly unprecedented places and pasts, all of which had shown up, at one time or another, in a sauce here, a dish of Chicken Olympia there, making that sauce—that dish—taste exceptionally good, but never, in the history of history itself, had such a panoply—a pantheon—of ingredients come together in one pot.

Was it God that guided his hand, or the Fates, when he diced these ingredients, not knowing, not trying, into the perfect geometrical shapes and sizes that would release their flavors at the most opportune possible microseconds into the mix? Was it magic or luck that caused him, languid and in touch with the inner field of unknowable chaos, to add these ingredients at just the right times (one nanosecond either way and it would have gone wrong) and in just the right proportions? The world may never know. It's like trying to find out how many licks it takes to get to the Tootsie Roll center of a Tootsie Pop, or why public servants are always so condescending. But for some reason all these things came to pass, and connected, and it was chili, and it was good.

Of course, these weren't the only factors. The knife he had used had not been the perfect knife, from a certain standpoint. Simple stainless steel, it was an 87 cent supermarket cheapie that any chef worth his toque would have laughed at and maybe tossed into the trash amongst the compost. But from another angle, it was the perfect knife, because a true, tempered, folded-steel, sharpened Samurai sword, for one thing, would not have fit in the drawer, and for another, the effect of Mars being in Capricorn and the other planets being similarly arranged in a certain form and pattern prescribed by the Druids of old (and in fact this was the very planetary arrangement that had been pointed to by Stonehenge and missed by all the theorizers and archeologists and demented, lovestruck historian architects ever since) would not have acted on a Samurai sword as they acted on this knife, which had lain, overnight, in the one perfect spot on all the Earth where the myriad clockwork gravities could tug gently here, push softly there, and rearrange the otherwise inferiorly interlocked molecules along the edge of the blade.

The cutting board had a similar history. A cheap and mediocre-looking thing, it had been spotted, by Fadrinski, in a garage sale three years ago, labeled with a haggard strip of masking tape, markered with the number 1.00. But it was made of the wood of the one true cross, preserved in the purest mineral oil all these years by an ancient order of nuns and then removed one day, by accident, by another, far less famous carpenter, who had come to do some work on the lavatory. The nuns had been mortified, but the series of coincidences that had led the wood to Fadrinski's kitchen, to be used on this one perfect night, would have met with approval beneath their numerous habits. The Lord, after all, works in mysterious ways.

So Fadrinski diced and chopped and browned and spiced, pouring olive oil from olives pressed by a bored bodhisattva in between visitations, into an old, chintzy-looking Teflon-kote pot which had actually been formed from some metal stolen from Roswell Air Force Base by a journalist in the 1960s, and then hidden and lost and since, now, resurfaced. The metal had come from a sentient spacecraft, and it possessed powers of understanding, which the right conditions would (and did) cause to leach forth into whatever was heated near it.

He drained beans and added tomatoes and he simmered and stirred with a spoon made from wood from a forest blessed by Mohammed. He put in all the ingredients, one by one, at times which, interrelated,

formed an algebraic translation of the meaning of life, and then he went
to his couch and read a book by the fourteenth Dalai Lama on the nature of compassion, and was so engrossed by this book that he let the
chili simmer for four solid hours, giving the flavors a chance not only
to marry, but to settle down and raise little, gorgeous flavor children,
which intermingled and danced. During this time, the pot, releasing its
wisdom, also acted as a parabolic mirror, catching radio and other low-
spectrum light waves from this and other worlds, within which were en-
coded coincidentally co-arriving broadcasts of philosophy and science
and religion and love, and the pot transduced and transferred these signals from space into feelings and flavors, spread deep within the sauce.

This was, at the last, chili that transcended chili, penetrating to the
very core of chili-ness and beyond, into the realm of art. This was art in
the truest interpretation—not the product of an ego, but the product of
God in a nonsecular sense; the bringing together of truth and beauty on
such a level that, were taste not a medium so fleeting, and were this chili
of a volume and amount such that it could be sampled by all the teem-
ing, lucky peoples of the Earth throughout time, it would be deemed,
far and away, the most beautiful piece of work ever produced by mankind, outstripping Bach and Picasso, Da Vinci and Eliot.

Just the aroma that steamed from the surface of this chili was enough
to send Fadrinski, reading his book, into a state of satori and absolute
love, which could be felt, telepathically, by people for miles around.
Young men, forgetting the constraints of political correctness and the
imagined jeers of their friends, were holding doors for old ladies. Spous-
es were making up after fights somehow silly now. People were helping
each other. Pitching in. Caring.

And not only the planets but the Universe aligned, once in its own
long life, and for those hours Copernicus was wrong, and the Earth was
the center, and more specifically, the very crux of the hub was this one
glowing stewpot, and the chili within.

And then it was finished. It was done.

Fadrinski arose, setting aside his book with a gentleness and love
which had not been experienced by a book since the beginning of time.
And he got to his feet, and he went to the stove.

He could understand, now. He could understand everything. All people, all things. He saw them not as separate from himself, but as parts

of a larger whole, and he saw all the times he had been angered by the actions of another, and was able to penetrate to the source of this anger, to the hardships experienced by others just as he himself experienced hardships, until the whole world was one big hardwired circuit of pain, passed from person to person to person, and Fadrinski became a pressure relief valve. His circuit had closed, and he blew this pain off into the stratosphere in the form of complete and total, all-encompassing love.

And he got a spoon out of the drawer beneath the microwave, and slowly, carefully, he let its scoop slide down beneath the surface of the rich, red sauce.

This was a red, too, the likes of which had never been witnessed before. It came from a frequency largely unused, missed, most of the time, to one side or the other, or phased out by the collisions of nearby peaks and troughs of the waves of light.

But here it was pure; even augmented by other frequencies from the spectrum of all possible wavelengths, until this, like and in conjunction with the smell, was a symphony of sense. It washed and played over Fadrinski's features, and it stripped away all heartache, all sorrow, and although he had never been a Mel Gibson, a Kirk Douglas, a Tom Cruise, no woman on the planet, seeing him with that light on his face, would have been able to remember the names of any of these men.

He inhaled the steam, and the chili, its molecules parting to accept the presence of the spoon, lovingly produced more.

And he tasted it.

There are not words to describe such a taste. Delicious? A thrift-shop word, plastic and pale next to the reality of what was happening in the nerves of Fadrinski's tongue. Sumptuous? Mouth-watering? Great? Dry husks of words that could never approach the experience. To say that fireworks were going off in Fadrinski's mouth, and that orchestras of flavor and sense and soul and imagination were playing down his spine, to the tips of his fingers and toes, would be a crude, vaudeville parody of the situation.

This was a religious experience, pure and simple. With that one tiny sip, Fadrinski achieved sainthood.

He stood there for a time, just feeling; not thinking, while the chili digested itself within him and entered his bloodstream. It coursed through his veins, dissolving arterial plaque, boosting his immune system, curing his acne. A slight irregularity in his heartbeat smoothed out, and outgrowths of benign but nonetheless worrisome basal cells (tiny ticking time bombs of a biological nature) acquiesced and let go, giving their energy and substance selflessly back to the good and the preservation of the larger whole.

One sip, and Fadrinski was filled. Was complete. Would not have to eat for weeks. And the thought manifested itself, of its own volition, in his head, of the need to get this chili, in portions however small, to each and every person on Earth.

And that, of course, was the instant when the knock came at the door.

Fadrinski's head turned slowly, in an effortless ballet of biomechanical motion. He did not walk but glided—actually levitated—to the door. He reached out and opened, and it was as though he was simply opening another part of himself, to see a part of himself standing there on his doorstep.

Words were hardly needed, but they were used anyway, and Fadrinski's were, "So. You have come for the chili."

"I have," said the woman on the other side, and Fadrinski, in his all-knowing, all-loving state, knew that he must give it to her; that it was not his chili but belonged to all life everywhere, and that no one in its proximity could steal it or put it to misuse, because such petty, selfish thoughts would be overridden, in the presence of the inimitable foodstuff, by their own better nature.

So he went to the stove and he lifted the pot, bringing it to her and knowing, somehow, that beautiful as she was, she was not a woman at all, but a member of a far older, far wiser race than mankind, which had known all along that this would all happen, and that, if you want to put a fine, exclusory point on things, this one pot of chili had been, since the time the world had congealed out of stardust, Earth's sole (and not unworthy) function.

She took the pot from him as any mother takes her child, and for a time they looked into one another's eyes.

He knew, while he looked, that she was taking this chili, not to be eaten, per se, but both back and forward in time, to be spread to every planet where life would eventually evolve (as the source thereof) and finally, to the singularity, back before time began, where this chili would act as a catalyst for the explosion that started it all—an outpouring, in the purest sense, of energy held back from motion, from action, from life.

"You are," she told him before she left, "one hell of a cook."

Fadrinski nodded, and he shut the door.

He wondered if sometime he ought to make ratatouille.

The story was a gift. Sometimes it happens that way. I was reading a book that featured a talking dog and suddenly felt the urge to write a story with a talking dog in it. But not a four-footed dog, like the one I was reading about.

Into my mind flashed the image of a dog standing on two legs in eighteenth-century pantaloons and lace-cuffed jacket, holding a walking stick in one paw—the sort of picture one might encounter in a Mother Goose book. Which is where the title, the last line of "Old Mother Hubbard," came in. I'd been to Mother Goose's grave in London, so I set the dog down by the Thames. There were no anthropomorphic talking dogs in eighteenth-century London, and so it had to be the future. The first paragraph came to me as easy as that.

Then, because a talking dog needs somebody to talk *with*, I introduced Darger. For contrast to Surplus's flamboyance, I made him serious and colorless. So as to give him a reason to strike up a conversation, I made him a con man. At which point, the two rogues took over.

Usually I know how a story is going to end before I start writing it. But this time, the protagonists hit it off so swiftly that I was left trotting along in their wake, writing furiously and desperately trying to figure out exactly what they were up to. They were, as now seems inevitable, always two jumps ahead of me.

—*Michael Swanwick*

The Dog Said Bow-Wow

MICHAEL SWANWICK

~~~~~~~~~

THE DOG LOOKED LIKE HE had just stepped out of a children's book. There must have been a hundred physical adaptations required to allow him to walk upright. The pelvis, of course, had been entirely reshaped. The feet alone would have needed dozens of changes. He had knees, and knees were tricky.

To say nothing of the neurological enhancements.

But what Darger found himself most fascinated by was the creature's costume. His suit fit him perfectly, with a slit in the back for the tail, and—again—a hundred invisible adaptations that caused it to hang on his body in a way that looked perfectly natural.

"You must have an extraordinary tailor," Darger said.

The dog shifted his cane from one paw to the other, so they could shake, and in the least affected manner imaginable replied, "That is a common observation, sir."

"You're from the States?" It was a safe assumption, given where they stood—on the docks—and that the schooner *Yankee Dreamer* had sailed up the Thames with the morning tide. Darger had seen its bubble sails over the rooftops, like so many rainbows. "Have you found lodgings yet?"

"Indeed I am, and no I have not. If you could recommend a tavern of the cleaner sort?"

"No need for that. I would be only too happy to put you up for a few days in my own rooms." And, lowering his voice, Darger said, "I have a business proposition to put to you."

"Then lead on, sir, and I shall follow you with a right good will."

The dog's name was Sir Blackthorpe Ravenscairn de Plus Precieux, but "Call me Sir Plus," he said with a self-denigrating smile, and "Surplus" he was ever after.

Surplus was, as Darger had at first glance suspected and by conversation confirmed, a bit of a rogue—something more than mischievous and less than a cutthroat. A dog, in fine, after Darger's own heart.

Over drinks in a public house, Darger displayed his box and explained his intentions for it. Surplus warily touched the intricately carved teak housing, and then drew away from it. "You outline an intriguing scheme, Master Darger—"

"Please. Call me Aubrey."

"Aubrey, then. Yet here we have a delicate point. How shall we divide up the…ah, *spoils* of this enterprise? I hesitate to mention this, but many a promising partnership has foundered on precisely such shoals."

Darger unscrewed the salt cellar and poured its contents onto the table. With his dagger, he drew a fine line down the middle of the heap. "I divide—you choose. Or the other way around, if you please. From self-interest, you'll not find a grain's difference between the two."

"Excellent!" cried Surplus and, dropping a pinch of salt in his beer, drank to the bargain.

It was raining when they left for Buckingham Labyrinth. Darger stared out the carriage window at the dreary streets and worn buildings gliding by and sighed. "Poor, weary old London! History is a grinding-wheel that has been applied too many a time to thy face."

"It is also," Surplus reminded him, "to be the making of our fortunes. Raise your eyes to the Labyrinth, sir, with its soaring towers and bright surfaces rising above these shops and flats like a crystal mountain rearing up out of a ramshackle wooden sea, and be comforted."

"That is fine advice," Darger agreed. "But it cannot comfort a lover of cities, nor one of a melancholic turn of mind."

"Pah!" cried Surplus, and said no more until they arrived at their destination.

At the portal into Buckingham, the sergeant-interface strode forward as they stepped down from the carriage. He blinked at the sight of Surplus, but said only, "Papers?"

Surplus presented the man with his passport and the credentials Darger had spent the morning forging, then added with a negligent wave of his paw, "And this is my autistic."

The sergeant-interface glanced once at Darger, and forgot about him completely. Darger had the gift, priceless to one in his profession, of a face so nondescript that once someone looked away, it disappeared from that person's consciousness forever. "This way, sir. The officer of protocol will want to examine these himself."

A dwarf savant was produced to lead them through the outer circle of the Labyrinth. They passed by ladies in bioluminescent gowns and gentlemen with boots and gloves cut from leathers cloned from their own skin. Both women and men were extravagantly bejeweled—for the ostentatious display of wealth was yet again in fashion—and the halls were lushly clad and pillared in marble, porphyry, and jasper. Yet Darger could not help noticing how worn the carpets were, how chipped and sooted the oil lamps. His sharp eye espied the remains of an antique electrical system, and traces as well of telephone lines and fiber optic cables from an age when those technologies were yet workable.

These last he viewed with particular pleasure.

The dwarf savant stopped before a heavy black door carved over with gilt griffins, locomotives, and fleurs-de-lis. "This is a door," he said. "The wood is ebony. Its binomial is *Diospyros ebenum*. It was harvested in Serendip. The gilding is of gold. Gold has an atomic weight of 197.2."

He knocked on the door and opened it.

The officer of protocol was a dark-browed man of imposing mass. He did not stand for them. "I am Lord Coherence-Hamilton, and this"—he indicated the slender, clear-eyed woman who stood beside him—"is my sister, Pamela."

Surplus bowed deeply to the Lady, who dimpled and dipped a slight curtsey in return.

The Protocol Officer quickly scanned the credentials. "Explain these fraudulent papers, sirrah. The Demesne of Western Vermont! Damn me if I have ever heard of such a place."

"Then you have missed much," Surplus said haughtily. "It is true we are a young nation, created only seventy-five years ago during the Partition of New England. But there is much of note to commend our fair land. The glorious beauty of Lake Champlain. The gene-mills of Winooski, that ancient seat of learning the *Universitas Viridis Montis* of Burlington, the Technarchaeological Institute of..." He stopped. "We have much to be proud of, sir, and nothing of which to be ashamed."

The bearlike official glared suspiciously at him, then said, "What brings you to London? Why do you desire an audience with the queen?"

"My mission and destination lie in Russia. However, England being on my itinerary and I a diplomat, I was charged to extend the compliments of my nation to your monarch." Surplus did not quite shrug. "There is no more to it than that. In three days I shall be in France, and you will have forgotten about me completely."

Scornfully, the officer tossed his credentials to the savant, who glanced at and politely returned them to Surplus. The small fellow sat down at a little desk scaled to his own size and swiftly made out a copy. "Your papers will be taken to Whitechapel and examined there. If everything goes well—which I doubt—and there's an opening—not likely—you'll be presented to the queen sometime between a week and ten days hence."

"Ten days! Sir, I am on a very strict schedule!"

"Then you wish to withdraw your petition?"

Surplus hesitated. "I...I shall have to think on't, sir."

Lady Pamela watched coolly as the dwarf savant led them away.

The room they were shown to had massively framed mirrors and oil paintings dark with age upon the walls, and a generous log fire in the hearth. When their small guide had gone, Darger carefully locked and bolted the door. Then he tossed the box onto the bed, and bounced down alongside it. Lying flat on his back, staring up at the ceiling, he said, "The Lady Pamela is a strikingly beautiful woman. I'll be damned if she's not."

Ignoring him, Surplus locked paws behind his back, and proceeded to pace up and down the room. He was full of nervous energy. At last, he expostulated, "This is a deep game you have gotten me into, Darger! Lord Coherence-Hamilton suspects us of all manner of blackguardry."

"Well, and what of that?"

"I repeat myself: We have not even begun our play yet, and he suspects us already! I trust neither him nor his genetically remade dwarf."

"You are in no position to be displaying such vulgar prejudice."

"I am not *bigoted* about the creature, Darger, I *fear* him! Once let suspicion of us into that macroencephalic head of his, and he will worry at it until he has found out our every secret."

"Get a grip on yourself, Surplus! Be a man! We are in this too deep already to back out. Questions would be asked, and investigations made."

"I am anything but a man, thank God," Surplus replied. "Still, you are right. In for a penny, in for a pound. For now, I might as well sleep. Get off the bed. You can have the hearth-rug."

"I! The rug!"

"I am groggy of mornings. Were someone to knock, and I to unthinkingly open the door, it would hardly do to have you found sharing a bed with your master."

The next day, Surplus returned to the Office of Protocol to declare that he was authorized to wait as long as two weeks for an audience with the queen, though not a day more.

"You have received new orders from your government?" Lord Coherence-Hamilton asked suspiciously. "I hardly see how."

"I have searched my conscience, and reflected on certain subtleties of phrasing in my original instructions," Surplus said. "That is all."

He emerged from the office to discover Lady Pamela waiting outside. When she offered to show him the Labyrinth, he agreed happily to her plan. Followed by Darger, they strolled inward, first to witness the changing of the guard in the forecourt vestibule, before the great pillared wall that was the front of Buckingham Palace before it was swallowed up in the expansion of architecture during the mad, glorious years of Utopia. Following which, they proceeded toward the viewer's gallery above the chamber of state.

"I see from your repeated glances that you are interested in my diamonds, 'Sieur Plus Precieux," Lady Pamela said. "Well might you be. They are a family treasure, centuries old and manufactured to order, each stone flawless and perfectly matched. The indentures of a hundred autistics would not buy the like."

Surplus smiled down again at the necklace, draped about her lovely throat and above her perfect breasts. "I assure you, madame, it was not your necklace that held me so enthralled."

She colored delicately, pleased. Lightly, she said, "And that box your man carries with him wherever you go? What is in it?"

"That? A trifle. A gift for the Duke of Muscovy, who is the ultimate object of my journey," Surplus said. "I assure you, it is of no interest whatsoever."

"You were talking to someone last night," Lady Pamela said. "In your room."

"You were listening at my door? I am astonished and flattered."

She blushed. "No, no, my brother...it is his job, you see, surveillance."

"Possibly I was talking in my sleep. I have been told I do that occasionally."

"In accents? My brother said he heard two voices."

Surplus looked away. "In that, he was mistaken."

England's queen was a sight to rival any in that ancient land. She was as large as the lorry of ancient legend, and surrounded by attendants who hurried back and forth, fetching food and advice and carrying away dirty plates and signed legislation. From the gallery, she reminded Darger of a queen bee, but unlike the bee, this queen did not copulate, but remained proudly virgin.

Her name was Gloriana the First, and she was a hundred years old and still growing.

Lord Campbell-Supercollider, a friend of Lady Pamela's met by chance, who had insisted on accompanying them to the gallery, leaned close to Surplus and murmured, "You are impressed, of course, by our queen's magnificence." The warning in his voice was impossible to miss. "Foreigners invariably are."

"I am dazzled," Surplus said.

"Well might you be. For scattered through her majesty's great body are thirty-six brains, connected with thick ropes of ganglia in a hypercube configuration. Her processing capacity is the equal of many of the great computers from Utopian times."

Lady Pamela stifled a yawn. "Darling Rory," she said, touching the Lord Campbell-Supercollider's sleeve. "Duty calls me. Would you be so kind as to show my American friend the way back to the outer circle?"

"Of course, my dear." He and Surplus stood (Darger was, of course, already standing) and paid their compliments. Then, when Lady Pamela was gone and Surplus started to turn toward the exit, "Not that way. Those stairs are for commoners. You and I may leave by the gentlemen's staircase."

The narrow stairs twisted downward beneath clouds of gilt cherubs-and-airships, and debouched into a marble-floored hallway. Surplus and Darger stepped out of the stairway and found their arms abruptly seized by baboons.

There were five baboons all told, with red uniforms and matching choke collars with leashes that gathered in the hand of an ornately mustached officer whose gold piping identified him as a master of apes. The fifth baboon bared his teeth and hissed savagely.

Instantly, the master of apes yanked back on his leash and said, "There, Hercules! There, sirrah! What do you do? What do you say?"

The baboon drew himself up and bowed curtly. "Please come with us," he said with difficulty. The master of apes cleared his throat. Sullenly, the baboon added, "Sir."

"This is outrageous!" Surplus cried. "I am a diplomat, and under international law immune to arrest."

"Ordinarily, sir, this is true," said the master of apes courteously. "However, you have entered the inner circle without her majesty's invitation and are thus subject to stricter standards of security."

"I had no idea these stairs went inward. I was led here by—" Surplus looked about helplessly. Lord Campbell-Supercollider was nowhere to be seen.

So, once again, Surplus and Darger found themselves escorted to the Office of Protocol."The wood is teak. Its binomial is *Tectonia grandis*. Teak is native to Burma, Hind, and Siam. The box is carved elaborately but without refinement." The dwarf savant opened it. "Within the casing is an archaic device for electronic intercommunication. The instrument chip is a gallium-arsenide ceramic. The chip weighs six ounces. The device is a product of the Utopian end-times."

"A modem!" The protocol officer's eyes bugged out. "You dared bring a *modem* into the inner circle and almost into the presence of the queen?" His chair stood and walked around the table. Its six insectile legs looked too slender to carry his great, legless mass. Yet it moved nimbly and well.

"It is harmless, sir. Merely something our technarchaeologists unearthed and thought would amuse the Duke of Muscovy, who is well known for his love of all things antiquarian. It is, apparently, of some cultural or historical significance, though without rereading my instructions, I would be hard pressed to tell you what."

Lord Coherence-Hamilton raised his chair so that he loomed over Surplus, looking dangerous and domineering. "*Here* is the historic significance of your modem: The Utopians filled the world with their computer webs and nets, burying cables and nodes so deeply and plentifully that they shall never be entirely rooted out. They then released into that virtual universe demons and mad gods. These intelligences destroyed Utopia and almost destroyed humanity as well. Only the valiant worldwide destruction of all modes of interface saved us from annihilation.

"Oh, you lackwit! Have you no history? These creatures hate us because our ancestors created them. They are still alive, though confined to their electronic netherworld, and want only a modem to extend themselves into the physical realm. Can you wonder, then, that the penalty for possessing such a device is"— he smiled menacingly—"death?"

"No, sir, it is not. Possession of a *working* modem is a mortal crime. This device is harmless. Ask your savant."

"Well?" the big man growled at his dwarf. "Is it functional?"

"No. It—"

"Silence." Lord Coherence-Hamilton turned back to Surplus. "You are a fortunate cur. You will not be charged with any crimes. However, while you are here, I will keep this filthy device locked away and under my control. Is that understood, Sir Bow-Wow?"

Surplus sighed. "Very well," he said. "It is only for a week, after all."

That night, the Lady Pamela Coherence-Hamilton came by Surplus's room to apologize for the indignity of his arrest, of which, she assured him, she had just now learned. He invited her in. In short order they somehow found themselves kneeling face-to-face on the bed, unbuttoning each other's clothing.

Lady Pamela's breasts had just spilled delightfully from her dress when she drew back, clutching the bodice closed again, and said, "Your man is watching us."

"And what concern is that to us?" Surplus said jovially. "The poor fellow's an autistic. Nothing he sees or hears matters to him. You might as well be embarrassed by the presence of a chair."

"Even were he a wooden carving, I would his eyes were not on me."

"As you wish." Surplus clapped his paws. "Sirrah! Turn around."

Obediently, Darger turned his back. This was his first experience with his friend's astonishing success with women. How many sexual adventuresses, he wondered, might one tumble, if one's form were unique? On reflection, the question answered itself.

Behind him, he heard the Lady Pamela giggle. Then, in a voice low with passion, Surplus said, "No, leave the diamonds on."

With a silent sigh, Darger resigned himself to a long night. Since he was bored and yet could not turn to watch the pair cavorting on the bed without giving himself away, he was perforce required to settle for watching them in the mirror.

They began, of course, by doing it doggy-style.

The next day, Surplus fell sick. Hearing of his indisposition, Lady Pamela sent one of her autistics with a bowl of broth and then followed herself in a surgical mask.

Surplus smiled weakly to see her. "You have no need of that mask," he said. "By my life, I swear that what ails me is not communicable. As you doubtless know, we who have been remade are prone to endocrinological imbalance."

"Is that all?" Lady Pamela spooned some broth into his mouth, then dabbed at a speck of it with a napkin. "Then fix it. You have been very wicked to frighten me over such a trifle."

"Alas," Surplus said sadly, "I am a unique creation, and my table of endocrine balances was lost in an accident at sea. There are copies in Vermont, of course. But by the time even the swiftest schooner can cross the Atlantic twice, I fear me I shall be gone."

"Oh, dearest Surplus!" The Lady caught up his paws in her hands. "Surely there is some measure, however desperate, to be taken?"

"Well…" Surplus turned to the wall in thought. After a very long time, he turned back and said, "I have a confession to make. The modem your brother holds for me? It is functional."

"Sir!" Lady Pamela stood, gathering her skirts, and stepped away from the bed in horror. "Surely not!"

"My darling and delight, you must listen to me." Surplus glanced weakly toward the door, then lowered his voice. "Come close and I shall whisper."

She obeyed.

"In the waning days of Utopia, during the war between men and their electronic creations, scientists and engineers bent their efforts toward the creation of a modem that could be safely employed by humans. One immune from the attack of demons. One that could, indeed, compel their obedience. Perhaps you have heard of this project."

"There are rumors, but... no such device was ever built."

"Say rather that no such device was built *in time*. It had just barely been perfected when the mobs came rampaging through the laboratories, and the Age of the Machine was over. Some few, however, were hidden away before the last technicians were killed. Centuries later, brave researchers at the Technarchaeological Institute of Shelburne recovered six such devices and mastered the art of their use. One device was destroyed in the process. Two are kept in Burlington. The others were given to trusted couriers and sent to the three most powerful allies of the Demesne—one of which is, of course, Russia."

"This is hard to believe," Lady Pamela said wonderingly. "Can such marvels be?"

"Madame, I employed it two nights ago in this very room! Those voices your brother heard? I was speaking with my principals in Vermont. They gave me permission to extend my stay here to a fortnight."

He gazed imploringly at her. "If you were to bring me the device, I could then employ it to save my life."

Lady Coherence-Hamilton resolutely stood. "Fear nothing, then. I swear by my soul, the modem shall be yours tonight."

The room was lit by a single lamp which cast wild shadows whenever anyone moved, as if of illicit spirits at a witch's Sabbath.

It was an eerie sight. Darger, motionless, held the modem in his hands. Lady Pamela, who had a sense of occasion, had changed to a low-cut gown of clinging silks, dark red as human blood. It swirled about her as she hunted through the wainscoting for a jack left unused for centuries. Surplus sat up weakly in bed, eyes half-closed, directing her. It might have been, Darger thought, an allegorical tableau of the human body being directed by its sick animal passions, while the intellect stood by, paralyzed by lack of will.

"There!" Lady Pamela triumphantly straightened, her necklace scattering tiny rainbows in the dim light.

Darger stiffened. He stood perfectly still for the length of three long breaths, then shook and shivered like one undergoing seizure. His eyes rolled back in his head.

In hollow, unworldly tones, he said, "What man calls me up from the vasty deep?" It was a voice totally unlike his own, one harsh and savage and eager for unholy sport. "Who dares risk my wrath?"

"You must convey my words to the autistic's ears," Surplus murmured. "For he is become an integral part of the modem—not merely its operator, but its voice."

"I stand ready," Lady Pamela replied.

"Good girl. Tell it who I am."

"It is Sir Blackthorpe Ravenscairn de Plus Precieux who speaks, and who wishes to talk to . . ." She paused.

"To his most august and socialist honor, the mayor of Burlington."

"His most august and socialist honor," Lady Pamela began. She turned toward the bed and said quizzically, "The mayor of Burlington?"

"'Tis but an official title, much like your brother's, for he who is in fact the spy-master for the Demesne of Western Vermont," Surplus said weakly. "Now repeat to it: I compel thee on threat of dissolution to carry my message. Use those exact words."

Lady Pamela repeated the words into Darger's ear.

He screamed. It was a wild and unholy sound that sent the Lady skittering away from him in a momentary panic. Then, in mid-cry, he ceased.

"Who is this?" Darger said in an entirely new voice, this one human. "You have the voice of a woman. Is one of my agents in trouble?"

"Speak to him now, as you would to any man: forthrightly, directly, and without evasion." Surplus sank his head back on his pillow and closed his eyes.

So (as it seemed to her) the Lady Coherence-Hamilton explained Surplus's plight to his distant master, and from him received both condolences and the needed information to return Surplus's endocrine levels to a functioning harmony. After proper courtesies, then, she thanked the American spy-master and unjacked the modem. Darger returned to passivity.

The leather-cased endocrine kit lay open on a small table by the bed. At Lady Pamela's direction, Darger began applying the proper patches to various places on Surplus's body. It was not long before Surplus opened his eyes.

"Am I to be well?" he asked and, when the Lady nodded, "Then I fear I must be gone in the morning. Your brother has spies everywhere. If he gets the least whiff of what this device can do, he'll want it for himself."

Smiling, Lady Pamela hoisted the box in her hand. "Indeed, who can blame him? With such a toy, great things could be accomplished."

"So he will assuredly think. I pray you, return it to me."

She did not. "This is more than just a communication device, sir," she said. "Though in that mode it is of incalculable value. You have shown that it can enforce obedience on the creatures that dwell in the forgotten nerves of the ancient world. Ergo, they can be compelled to do our calculations for us."

"Indeed, so our technarchaeologists tell us. You must—"

"We have created monstrosities to perform the duties that were once done by machines. But with this, there would be no necessity to do so. We have allowed ourselves to be ruled by an icosahexadexal-brained freak. Now we have no need for Gloriana the Gross, Gloriana the Fat and Grotesque, Gloriana the Maggot Queen."

"Madame!"

"It is time, I believe, that England had a new queen. A human queen."

"Think of my honor!"

Lady Pamela paused in the doorway. "You are a very pretty fellow indeed. But with *this*, I can have the monarchy and keep such a harem as will reduce your memory to that of a passing and trivial fancy."

With a rustle of skirts, she spun away.

"Then I am undone!" Surplus cried, and fainted onto the bed.

Quietly, Darger closed the door. Surplus raised himself from the pillows, began removing the patches from his body, and said, "Now what?"

"Now we get some sleep," Darger said. "Tomorrow will be a busy day."

The master of apes came for them after breakfast, and marched them to their usual destination. By now Darger was beginning to lose track of exactly how many times he had been in the Office of Protocol. They entered to find Lord Coherence-Hamilton in a towering rage, and his sister, calm and knowing, standing in a corner with her arms crossed, watching. Looking at them both now, Darger wondered how he could ever have imagined that the brother outranked his sister.

The modem lay opened on the dwarf-savant's desk. The little fellow leaned over the device, studying it minutely.

Nobody said anything until the master of apes and his baboons had left. Then Lord Coherence-Hamilton roared, "Your modem refuses to work for us!"

"As I told you, sir," Surplus said coolly, "it is inoperative."

"That's a bold-arsed fraud and a goat-buggering lie!" In his wrath, the Lord's chair rose up on its spindly legs so high that his head almost bumped against the ceiling. "I know of your activities"—he nodded toward his sister—"and demand that you show us how this whoreson device works!"

"Never!" Surplus cried stoutly. "I have my honor, sir."

"Your honor, too scrupulously insisted upon, may well lead to your death, sir."

Surplus threw back his head. "Then I die for Vermont!"

At this moment of impasse, Lady Hamilton stepped forward between the two antagonists to restore peace. "I know what might change your mind." With a knowing smile, she raised a hand to her throat and denuded herself of her diamonds. "I saw how you rubbed them against your face the other night. How you licked and fondled them. How ecstatically you took them into your mouth."

She closed his paws about them. "They are yours, sweet 'Sieur Precieux, for a word."

"You would give them up?" Surplus said, as if amazed at the very idea. In fact, the necklace had been his and Darger's target from the moment they'd seen it. The only barrier that now stood between them and the merchants of Amsterdam was the problem of freeing themselves from the Labyrinth before their marks finally realized that the modem was indeed a cheat. And to this end they had the invaluable tool of a thinking man whom all believed to be an autistic, and a plan that would give them almost twenty hours in which to escape.

"Only think, dear Surplus." Lady Pamela stroked his head and then scratched him behind one ear, while he stared down at the precious stones. "Imagine the life of wealth and ease you could lead, the women, the power. It all lies in your hands. All you need do is close them."

Surplus took a deep breath. "Very well," he said. "The secret lies in the condenser, which takes a full day to re-charge. Wait but—"

"Here's the problem," the savant said unexpectedly. He poked at the interior of the modem. "There was a wire loose."

He jacked the device into the wall.

"Oh, dear God," Darger said.

A savage look of raw delight filled the dwarf savant's face, and he seemed to swell before them.

"*I am free!*" he cried in a voice so loud it seemed impossible that it could arise from such a slight source. He shook as if an enormous electrical current were surging through him. The stench of ozone filled the room.

He burst into flames and advanced on the English spy master and her brother.

While all stood aghast and paralyzed, Darger seized Surplus by the collar and hauled him out into the hallway, slamming the door shut as he did.

They had not run twenty paces down the hall when the door to the Office of Protocol exploded outward, sending flaming splinters of wood down the hallway.

Satanic laughter boomed behind them.

Glancing over his shoulder, Darger saw the burning dwarf, now blackened to a cinder, emerge from a room engulfed in flames, capering and dancing. The modem, though disconnected, was now tucked under one arm, as if it were exceedingly valuable to him. His eyes were round and white and lidless. Seeing them, he gave chase.

"Aubrey!" Surplus cried. "We are headed the *wrong way!*"

It was true. They were running deeper into the Labyrinth, toward its heart, rather than outward. But it was impossible to turn back now. They plunged through scattering crowds of nobles and servitors, trailing fire and supernatural terror in their wake.

The scampering grotesque set fire to the carpets with every footfall. A wave of flame tracked him down the hall, incinerating tapestries and wallpaper and wood trim. No matter how they dodged, it ran straight toward them. Clearly, in the programmatic literalness of its kind, the demon from the web had determined that having early seen them, it must early kill them as well.

Darger and Surplus raced through dining rooms and salons, along balconies and down servants' passages. To no avail. Dogged by their hypernatural nemesis, they found themselves running down a passage, straight toward two massive bronze doors, one of which had been left just barely ajar. So fearful were they that they hardly noticed the guards.

"Hold, sirs!"

The mustachioed master of apes stood before the doorway, his baboons straining against their leashes. His eyes widened with recognition. "By gad, it's you!" he cried in astonishment.

"Lemme kill 'em!" one of the baboons cried. "The lousy bastards!" The others growled agreement.

Surplus would have tried to reason with them, but when he started to slow his pace, Darger put a broad hand on his back and shoved. "Dive!" he commanded. So of necessity the dog of rationality had to bow to the man of action. He tobogganed wildly across the polished marble floor between two baboons, straight at the master of apes, and then between his legs.

The man stumbled, dropping the leashes as he did.

The baboons screamed and attacked.

For an instant all five apes were upon Darger, seizing his limbs, snapping at his face and neck. Then the burning dwarf arrived and, finding his target obstructed, seized the nearest baboon. The animal shrieked as its uniform burst into flames.

As one, the other baboons abandoned their original quarry to fight this newcomer who had dared attack one of their own.

In a trice, Darger leaped over the fallen master of apes and was through the door. He and Surplus threw their shoulders against its metal surface and pushed. He had one brief glimpse of the fight, with the baboons aflame and their master's body flying through the air. Then the door slammed shut. Internal bars and bolts, operated by smoothly oiled mechanisms, automatically latched themselves.

For the moment, they were safe.

Surplus slumped against the smooth bronze, and wearily asked, "Where did you *get* that modem?"

"From a dealer of antiquities." Darger wiped his brow with his kerchief. "It was transparently worthless. Whoever would dream it could be repaired?"

Outside, the screaming ceased. There was a very brief silence. Then the creature flung itself against one of the metal doors. It rang with the impact.

A delicate girlish voice wearily said, "What is this noise?"

They turned in surprise and found themselves looking up at the enormous corpus of Queen Gloriana. She lay upon her pallet, swaddled in satin and lace, and abandoned by all, save her valiant (though doomed) guardian apes. A pervasive yeasty smell emanated from her flesh. Within the tremendous folds of chins by the dozens and scores was a small human face. Its mouth moved delicately and asked, "What is trying to get in?"

The door rang again. One of its great hinges gave.

Darger bowed. "I fear, madame, it is your death."

"Indeed?" Blue eyes opened wide and, unexpectedly, Gloriana laughed. "If so, that is excellent good news. I have been praying for death an extremely long time."

"Can any of God's creations truly pray for death and mean it?" asked Darger, who had his philosophical side. "I have known unhappiness myself, yet even so life is precious to me."

"Look at me!" Far up to one side of the body, a tiny arm—though truly no tinier than any woman's arm—waved feebly. "I am not God's creation, but Man's. Who would trade ten minutes of their own life for a century of mine? Who, having mine, would not trade it all for death?"

A second hinge popped. The doors began to shiver. Their metal surfaces radiated heat.

"Darger, we must leave!" Surplus cried. "There is a time for learned conversation, but it is not now."

"Your friend is right," Gloriana said. "There is a small archway hidden behind yon tapestry. Go through it. Place your hand on the left wall and run. If you turn whichever way you must to keep from letting go of the wall, it will lead you outside. You are both rogues, I see, and doubtless deserve punishment, yet I can find nothing in my heart for you but friendship."

"Madame...." Darger began, deeply moved.

"Go! My bridegroom enters."

The door began to fall inward. With a final cry of "Farewell!" from Darger and "Come *on*!" from Surplus, they sped away.

By the time they had found their way outside, all of Buckingham Labyrinth was in flames. The demon, however, did not emerge from the flames, encouraging them to believe that when the modem it carried finally melted down, it had been forced to return to that unholy realm from whence it came.

The sky was red with flames as the sloop set sail for Calais. Leaning against the rail, watching, Surplus shook his head. "What a terrible sight! I cannot help feeling, in part, responsible."

"Come! Come!" Darger said. "This dyspepsia ill becomes you. We are both rich fellows now. The Lady Pamela's diamonds will maintain us lavishly for years to come. As for London, this is far from the first fire it has had to endure. Nor will it be the last. Life is short, and so, while we live, let us be jolly."

"These are strange words for a melancholiac," Surplus said wonderingly.

"In triumph, my mind turns its face to the sun. Dwell not on the past, dear friend, but on the future that lies glittering before us."

"The necklace is worthless," Surplus said. "Now that I have the leisure to examine it, free of the distracting flesh of Lady Pamela, I see that these are not diamonds, but mere imitations." He made to cast the necklace into the Thames.

Before he could, though, Darger snatched away the stones from him and studied them closely. Then he threw back his head and laughed. "The biters bit! Well, it may be paste, but it looks valuable still. We shall find good use for it in Paris."

"We are going to Paris?"

"We are partners, are we not? Remember that antique wisdom that whenever a door closes, another opens. For every city that burns, another beckons. To France, then, and adventure! After which, Italy, the Vatican Empire, Austro-Hungary, perhaps even Russia! Never forget that you have yet to present your credentials to the Duke of Muscovy."

"Very well," Surplus said. "But when we do, *I'll* pick out the modem."

~~~~~~~~~~~~

Please understand this from the get-go: I am not a habitual romance-basher. Though I don't read a lot of capital-R Romance, I do sometimes like the historical romance subgenre.

That said: romance, like science fiction and fantasy, is pure gold for a humorist, especially when you're writing parody. Even non-fans recognize the archetypes and tropes involved; nearly everyone will get the jokes. So what could be easier than doing a romance/fantasy crossover parody?

Sometimes a story idea stands right under the "Wabbit Season" sign while wearing a bull's-eye target. I did it and I'm glad.

—Esther Friesner

Sweet, Savage Sorcerer

ESTHER FRIESNER

~~~~~~~~~~

ARROWS WHIZZED PAST HER AS Narielle drummed slender heels into the heaving sides of her faithful unicorn, Thunderwind. Her bosom rose and fell in perfect cadence with the noble steed's movements as the Black Tower of Burning Doom thrust its massive structure into view. Behind her, the sun was setting in a fiery ball, quenching its flames slowly, achingly, in the moist depths of the Lesser Sea of Northern Alraziah-le-Fethynauri'in-ebu-Korfiamminettash.

Bitterly, Narielle reflected that if her father's men had not stopped to ask directions to the sea, they would never have been caught with their lances down by Lord Eyargh's mercenaries.

Another thick shaft, flying closer than the rest, cut off her meditations and the pointed tip of her left ear. The elfin princess lifted her chin defiantly and raised herself in the stirrups to turn and shout bold yet elegant insults at her pursuers. Then Thunderwind carried her over the threshold of the Black Tower and she was safe . . . for the moment.

Lord Eyargh's mercenaries, cheated of their prey, milled about under the lone window of the Black Tower of Burning Doom and made a collective nuisance of themselves. Narielle leaned out from the unglazed casement and regarded them with haughty disdain. They shot more arrows at her, one of which lodged in the headboard of the large, comfortable bed behind her. Her bold heart stifled the urge to scream her courageous head off. Instead, she seized the handy velvet bell rope on the wall and pulled with firm resolve.

A dark-robed shadow detached itself from the depths of the tower room, strode past the startled elfin princess, paused only to sweep her from her feet in powerfully muscled arms and pitch her onto the large, comfortable bed where she narrowly missed squashing a sleeping cat.

A word of unknown and ecstatic sorcery was spoken out the window. From below, the vile shouts of Lord Eyargh's mercenaries abruptly changed to the peeping of downy baby chicks. The figure at the window smiled with grim amusement. He paused only long enough to release a tethered chicken hawk before turning his attention to his still-rebounding guest.

"Yes?" he said.

"You are the sorcerer of the Black Tower?" Narielle's throat contracted with an emotion she would long deny as anything more than astonishment, dubiety, and the need for a cool drink.

"Does that surprise you?" His voice was low, thrilling, more powerful than any she had ever heard, twisting her ever-more rapidly palpitating heart into a tight knot of unnamable confusion. His azure eyes probed the very depths of her soul with a bold disregard for the empty charade of elfin High Court etiquette. But there was a deep strain of irony in his words, as if his past life contained some unknown secret wound of which no one save himself knew, and whose carefully concealed pain had, if not poisoned, at least tainted the life of one outwardly so strong and unassailable.

"No," she lied. She got off the bed fast.

He laughed; once, shortly. But in that single syllable of supposed merriment, Narielle read many unspoken sorrows. She could not lie to him. He had suffered enough.

"That is...I mean...you're so young."

Now his eyes, bluer than the magic sword Narielle concealed beneath her voluminous velvet skirts sewn with pearls and trimmed with gold lace, narrowed. "I am," he replied. It was a challenge.

The elfin princess was not one to let any man ramp all over her. Hers was a proud spirit. She lifted her chin defiantly and took command of the conversation. "The name of Brandon of the Black Tower has reached my father, Lord Vertig of the Silver Unicorn, king of the elves of the Green Woodlands. Even as we speak, he is besieged in the White Castle of the Golden Arches by his mortal enemy, Lord Eyargh of the Red Sword. By a ruse, I and one hundred fifty of my father's men managed to slip through the enemy lines, dispatched in search of you, hoping to enlist the already legendary aid of your sorcerous powers in our cause."

"I know," he said.

"Do you?" She could not conceal her astonishment.

"I *am* a sorcerer. Perhaps you have heard of crystal balls?" His finely formed yet generous mouth contorted itself into an expression at once fascinating and unreadable. His hand strayed upward to touch her injured extremity. "You've been wounded." A strange catch wrenched all sarcasm from his voice.

Startled as much by the unexpected concern in the young wizard's words as by the almost electrical shock that coursed through her every fiber at this lightest contact of his flesh to her flesh, Narielle replied, "It's nothing."

"Nothing?" Behind his simple repetition of her very word, she thought she detected a new sense of respect for herself as a person in her own right.

His breath burned hot and fierce across the nape of her neck as he murmured a healing spell over her ear. Confusion fluttered in her breast like a caged gryphon. She stepped away from him, saying, "While you waste your magic on what is no more than a scratch, elves perish!"

As she spoke of her people's distress, she could not forbid her eyes from straying the length of the young enchanter's person. Dark, unruly hair fell in a shock of thick, black waves just above his cerulean eyes. When he smiled, the perfect whiteness of his teeth showed in even more startling contrast to his sun-bronzed skin. His nose hinted at past hurts borne with nobility and forbearance. The neck of his necromancer's robe was open, revealing the smooth, enticing expanse of his broad chest. The thin material could not effectively conceal the incredible size, the almost terrifying bulk, the barely thrust and untamed, overwhelming power of his shoulders.

Fortunately, there was a full-length mirror on the wall opposite Narielle, which allowed her the leisure to contemplate her own fiery red hair, emerald green eyes, and lithe, slender, graceful yet self-assured form.

Brandon of the Black Tower chuckled deep in his throat. How did he dare to mock her? She hated him! She would always hate him! Then he spoke: "Such fire. And what will you give me in exchange for my help...my lady?" There was no mistaking the scorn in his voice. She hated him still more wildly, yet more passionately! "Gold?" She couldn't stand him!

Narielle's reply was as cold and formal as wounded pride and the narrowly repressed desire to slap the sorcerer's grinning face could make it: "No."

"No?" His craggy eyebrows rose.

"On my honor as a highborn elfin princess and virgin. My father's men carried the gold for your fee. When Lord Eyargh's men attacked my father's men the chest fell over a cliff into the sea, and the men of Vargas Sands made off with it."

"So you have no chest." Now he no longer smiled. "You speak much of men, my lady... for one who calls herself a virgin."

She would kick him in the shins and tell her noble father on him! "Do you doubt the evidence of your eyes, my lord Brandon? I rode into your tower on a unicorn."

"It is well known by the lowest village idiot that elfin women can fake their unicorns." The ancient pain rose ever nearer to the surface of the young sorcerer's emotions and threatened to pierce through. In that instant, with a lurch of her own heart, Narielle understood the long-past but never forgotten betrayal that had embittered Brandon's proud soul. Why had she done it? What wouldn't Narielle give to get her hands on the little point-eared bitch and teach her some manners?

Compassion for Brandon welled up in Narielle's bosom, inflating it nicely. It was only her own fierce, overweening, foolish pride that prevented her from taking him into her arms at once and soothing away all his past hurts as if he were no more than a little boy, or a wrongfully whipped puppy. Yet even as she snapped harsh words at him, her heart swelled with the dreadful ache of longing to cuddle him.

"Then perhaps you had better hire a consulting village idiot!" She tossed her glorious mane of hair, her nostrils flaring, and pawed the ground with grand bravado. "Even he would be able to tell you that the virtue of the ladies of the royal house of Lord Vertig of the Silver Unicorn of the White Castle of the Golden Arches of the Green Woodlands is one that we protect with steel!" So saying, she drew the full, awe-inspiring length of the impossibly hard enchanted blade from the clinging embrace of the soft scabbard beneath her skirts. With a wild, untrammeled exultation to feel her hand close around the imposing diameter of that wondrous hilt once more, Narielle realized just how deeply she loved her sword.

Brandon looked mildly amused. He made a gesture whose mystic significance was known to few wizards. Narielle watched with mounting horror as her blade shuddered, then drooped like sunstruck celery. The enchanter took it from her nerveless hand and flung it across the room where it bounced off the large, comfortable bed and scared the cat.

"You have no gold, yet you would have my services," he said. "Very well, you shall have them. And in exchange, I shall have—"

"What?" The elfin princess's bosom lifted defiantly.

"—you."

With a hoarse ejaculation he crushed her to his chest. She felt his wizardhood pressing against her thigh and could not tell whether the emotions also now rising within her were so much fear as hesitantly joyous anticipation of what was to come. Roughly, he tore aside her golden lace, stripping the lush green velvet from her heaving shoulders in one masterful motion. Pearls popped and caromed off everything in sight. The cat yelped and leaped off the large, comfortable bed.

After he returned from burying the unicorn, he knelt like the meanest supplicant beside the pile of new-mown hay which had housed so much recent passion. "Can you ever forgive me...Narielle?"

Her eyes brimmed with the ebbing tide of complete fulfillment and a tender fondness for the repentant sorcerer. "Forgive you, Brandon? For making a *real* elf of me? Oh, you are more magician than any of those wand-waving charlatans!" Playfully, he plucked fragrant straws from her tousled hair and threw them at the cat who was back on the large, comfortable, convenient, unromantic, deliberately overlooked bed.

"Forgive me for doubting you, my love. And about the unicorn—"

She laughed the rich, full-throated laugh of newly, sweetly acquired wisdom. "Thunderwind was a loyal beast, but in his heart he understood that this day would come. I think he was glad it came quickly and painlessly."

But Brandon was not assuaged. Unaccustomed anguish filled his sapphire eyes. With a harsh sob he buried his face between the soft, welcoming curves of her two hands and implored her pardon for ever having doubted her. "It is you who are the enchanter, Narielle!" he gasped. "You have taken a blind, headstrong fool and made a man of him!"

"Did I? Good. Now, about Daddy...."

~~~~~~~

Brandon of the Black Tower raised his large yet sensitive hands to a sky no less blue than his eyes and turned Lord Vertig's foes into frogs. The siege was lifted, although the transformed Lord Eyargh hung around the moat defiantly. He was finally routed when Lord Vertig dispatched a contingent of net-wielding victualers to scoop up those of the enemy they could catch. That night there was great feasting and rejoicing in the White Castle of the Golden Arches.

Laughing, Narielle attempted to force another deep-fried nugget between her beloved's lips.

"What *is* that?" he asked, returning her joyous laughter a hundred-fold.

"Batrachian bits," she replied, smearing sweet-and-sour nectar down the front of his chest on purpose for future reference. "Try them; they're delicious."

"Not half so delicious as you," he murmured, and as the undeniable surge of their mutual attraction and respect mounted inexorably, he dragged her beneath the banqueting table and they missed dessert.

This story arose out of boredom. Mild, low-level boredom, at least.

My wife, Susan Casper, is a were-creature of a sort, although there's nothing supernatural about her, nor are her transformations tied to the cycles of the moon. Every few years, though, she will suddenly transform into a rabid baseball fan, particularly into a fierce and dedicated Phillies fan, and, during baseball season, she will insist on watching every televised game, so that we'll spend night after night sitting in front of the television, watching tiny phosphor-dot men hit the ball (or, more often than not, not hit the ball) and scurry around the bases. Then, just as suddenly as it came on, the fever is gone (usually after the Phillies have irreversibly blown what appeared to be another promising season), and she will pay no attention to baseball for several more years.

Now, I like baseball well enough. Truth be told, I like it a good deal more as a spectator sport than I like any other team sport; I'd much rather watch a baseball game, for instance, if I have to watch something sport-like, than a football game or a basketball game or a hockey game.

But I'm not as dedicated a fan as Susan is when the fit is upon her, and as the season unfolds, and game after game flickers by, I find myself, in the late innings of lackluster games where the players appear to be saying smugly to themselves, "What do I care? I get paid millions of dollars a year!", getting a bit, well, distracted. Okay, bored. I find my mind wandering, and since the game is in front of my eyes, my mind starts playing with it, thinking up more interesting things that could be happening than what actually is happening on the field.

"The Hanging Curve" was the result of one such evening's TV viewing. A few years ago, during another of Susan's transformations, I wrote my other baseball story, "The Mayan Variation," although since the Phils were in the process of blowing a particularly promising season that year, I invented a scenario where the entire losing team is ritually sacrificed at the end of the game, which seemed, at the time, only fitting and proper.

So, if I'd been a bigger sports fan, someone who really got riveted into the game no matter how slow it was, I'd never have written these stories, and the history of Western Civilization would not have been changed in any significant way whatsoever.

—Gardner Dozois

The Hanging Curve

GARDNER DOZOIS

I T WAS A COOL OCTOBER NIGHT in Philadelphia, with a wet wind coming off the river that occasionally shifted to bring in the yeasty spoiled-beer smell of the nearby refineries. Independence Stadium, the relatively new South Philly stadium that had been built to replace the old Veteran's Stadium, which still stood deserted a mile or so away, was filled to capacity, and then some, with people standing in the aisles. It was the last game of a hard-fought and bitterly contested World Series between the New York Yankees and the Philadelphia Phillies, 3–2 in favor of the Phillies, the Yankees at bat with two outs in the top of the ninth inning, and a man on third base. Eduardo Rivera was at bat for the Yankees against pitcher Karl Holzman, the Yankees' best slugger against the Phillies' best stopper, and Holzman had run a full count on Rivera, 3–2. Everything depended on the next pitch.

Holzman went into his slow, deliberate windup. Everybody in the stadium was leaning forward, everybody was holding their breath. Though there were almost ten thousand people in the stands, nobody was making a sound. Even the TV announcers were tense and silent. Hey, there it is! The *pitch*—

Some pundits later said that what was about to happen happened *because* the game was so tight, because so much was riding on the next pitch—that it was the psychic energy of the thousands of fans in the stands, the millions more in the viewing audience at home, every eye and every mind focused on that particular moment. That what happened was *caused* by the tension and the ever-tightening suspense felt by millions of people hanging on the outcome of that particular pitch....

And yet, in the more than a century and a half that people had been playing professional baseball, there had been many games as important as this

223

one, many contests as closely fought, many situations as tense or tenser, with as much or more passion invested in the outcome—and yet what happened that night had never happened before, in any other game.

Holzman pitched. The ball left his hand, streaked toward the plate. . . .

And then it froze.

The ball just *stopped*, inches from the plate, and hung there, motionless, in midair.

After a second of stunned surprise, Rivera stepped forward and took a mighty hack at the motionless ball. He broke his bat on it, sending splinters flying high in the air. But the ball itself didn't move.

The catcher sat back on his butt with a thump, then, after a second, began to scoot backward, away from the plate. He was either praying or cursing in Spanish, perhaps both. Hurriedly, he crossed himself.

The home-base umpire, Kellenburger, had been struck dumb with astonishment for a moment, but now he raised his hands to call time. He took his mask off and came a few steps closer to lean forward and peer at the ball, where it hung impossibly in midair.

The umpire was the first to actually touch the ball. Gingerly, he poked it with his finger, an act either very brave or very foolish, considering the circumstances. "It felt like a baseball," he later said, letting himself in for a great deal of comic ridicule by late-night talk-show hosts, but it really wasn't that dumb a remark, again considering the circumstances. It certainly wasn't *acting* like a baseball.

He tried to scoop the ball out of the air. It wouldn't budge. When he took his hand away, there it still was, the ball, hanging motionless in the air, a few feet above home plate.

The fans in the stadium had been shocked into stunned silence for a few heartbeats. But now a buzzing whisper of reaction began to swell, soon growing into a waterfall roar. No one understood what had happened. But *something* had happened to stop the game at the most critical possible moment, and nobody liked it. Fistfights were already beginning to break out in the outfield bleachers.

Rivera had stepped forward to help Kellenburger tug at the ball, trying to muscle it down. They couldn't move it. Holzman, as puzzled as everyone else, walked in to see what in the world was going on. Managers flew out of the dugouts, ready to protest *something*, although they weren't quite sure *what*. The rest of the umpires trotted in to take a look. Soon home plate was surrounded by almost everybody who was down on the ballfield, both dugouts emptying, all shouting, arguing, making suggestions, jostling to get a close look at the ball, which still hung serenely in midair.

Within minutes, fights were breaking out on the field as well. The stadium cops already had their hands full trying to quell disturbances in the seats, where a full-fledged riot was brewing. They couldn't handle it. The fans began tearing up the seats, trampling each other in panicked or angry surges, pouring out on to the field to join in fistfights with the players. The city cops had to be called in, then more cops, then the riot squad, who set about forcibly closing the stadium, chasing the outraged fans out with tear gas and rubber bullets. Dozens of people were injured, some moderately seriously, but, by some other miracle, none were killed. Dozens of people were arrested, including some of the players and the manager of the Yankees. The stadium was seriously trashed. By the time the umpires got around to officially calling the game, it had become clear a long time before that World Series or no World Series, no game was going to be played in Independence Stadium that night, or, considering the damage that had been done to the bleachers, probably for many nights to come.

Finally, the last ambulance left, and the remaining players and grounds crew and assorted team personnel were herded out, still complaining and arguing. After a hurried conference between the police and the owners, the gates were locked behind them.

The ball still hung there, not moving. In the empty stadium, gleaming white under the klieg lights, it somehow looked even more uncanny than it had with people swarming around it. Two cops were left behind to keep an eye on it, but the sight spooked them, and they stayed as far away from it as they could without leaving the infield, checking it every few minutes as the long night crept slowly past. But the ball didn't seem to be going anywhere.

Most of the riot had been covered live across the nation, of course, television cameras continuing to roll as fans and players beat each other bloody, while the sportscasters provided hysterical commentary (and barricaded the doors of the press room). Reporters from local stations had been there within twenty minutes, but nobody knew quite how to handle the event that had sparked the riot in the first place; most ignored it, while others treated it as a Silly Season item. The reporters were back the next morning, though, some of them, anyway, as the owners and the grounds crew, more cops, the Commissioner of Baseball and some Concerned City Hall Big-wigs went back into the stadium. In spite of the bright, grainy, mundane light of morning, which is supposed to chase all fancies away and dissolve all troubling fantasms, the ball was still frozen there in midair, motionless, exactly the same way it had been the night before. It looked even spook-ier, though, more bewilderingly inexplicable, under the ordinary light of day than it had looked under the garish artificial lighting the night before. This was no trick of the eyes, no confusion of light and shadow. Although it *couldn't* be, the goddamn thing was *there*.

The grounds-crew did everything that they could think of to get the ball to move, including tying a rope around it and having a dozen hefty men yank and heave and strain at it, their feet scrambling for purchase, as if they were playing tug-of-war with Mighty Joe Young and losing, but they could no more move the ball than Kellenburger had been able to the night before.

It was becoming clear that it might be a long time before another game could be played in Independence Stadium.

After two days of heated debate in the highest baseball circles, Yankee Stadium was borrowed to restage the final out of the series. Thousands of fans in the stadium (who had paid heretofore unheard-of prices for tickets) and millions of television viewers watched breathlessly as Hol-zman went into his wind-up and delivered the ball to the plate at a re-spectable ninety-five miles per hour. But nothing happened except that Rivera took a big swing at the ball and missed. No miracle. The ball thumped solidly into the catcher's mitt (who'd had to be threatened with heavy sanctions to get him to play, and who had a crucifix, a St. Christopher's medal, *and* an evil-eye-warding set of horns hung around his neck). Kellenburger, the home-plate umpire, pumped his fist and roared "You're out!" in a decisive, no-nonsense tone. And that was that. The Philadelphia Phillies had won the World Series.

The fans tore up the seats. Parts of New York City burned. The riots were still going on the following afternoon, as were riots in Philadelphia and (for no particular reason anyone could see; perhaps they were sym-pathy riots) in Cincinnati.

After another emergency session, the commissioner announced that entire last game would be replayed, in the interests of fairness. This time, the Yankees won, 7–5.

After more rioting, the commissioner evoked special executive powers that no one was quite sure he had, and declared that the Series was a draw. This satisfied nobody, but eventually fans stopped burning bits of various cities down, and the situation quieted.

The bizarre result went into the record books, and baseball tried to put the whole thing behind it.

In the larger world outside the insular universe of baseball, things weren't quite that simple.

Dozens of newspapers across the country had independently—and perhaps inevitably—come up with the headline HANGING CURVE BALL!!!, screamed across the front page in the largest type they could muster. A novelty song of the same name was in stores within four days of the Event, and available for download on some Internet sites in two. Nobody knows for sure how long it took for the first Miracle Ball joke to appear, but they were certainly circulating widely by as early as the following morning, when the strange non-ending of the World Series was the hot topic of discussion in most of the workplaces and homes in America (and, indeed, around the world), even those homes where baseball had rarely—if ever—been discussed before.

Media hysteria about the Miracle Ball continued to build throughout the circus of replaying the World Series; outside of sports circles, where the talk tended to be centered around the dolorous affect all this was having on baseball, the focus was on the Miracle itself, and what it might—or might not—signify. Hundreds of conspiracy-oriented Internet sites, of various degrees of lunacy, appeared almost overnight. Apocalyptic religious cults sprung up almost as fast as wacko Internet sites. The Miracle was widely taken as a Sign that the Last Days were at hand, as nearly anything out of the ordinary had been, from an earthquake to Jesus' face on a taco, for the last thousand years. Within days, some people in California had sold their houses and all their worldly possessions and had begun walking barefoot toward Philadelphia.

After the Gates-of-Armageddon-are-gaping-wide theory, the second most popular theory, and the one with the most Internet sites devoted to it, was that Aliens had done it—although as nobody ever came up with an even remotely convincing reason *why* aliens would want to do this, that theory tended to run out of gas early, and never was as popular as the Apocalypse Now/Sign From The Lord theory. The respectable press tended to ridicule both of these theories (as well as the Sinister Government Conspiracy theory, a dark horse, but popular in places like Montana and Utah)—still, it was hard for even the most determined skeptic to deny that *something* was going on that no one could even begin to explain, something that defied the laws of physics as we thought we knew them, and more than one scientist, press-ganged into appearing on late-night talk shows or other Talking Head venues, burbled that if we could learn to understand the strange cosmic forces, whatever they were, that were making the Ball act as it was acting, whole new sciences would open up, and Mankind's technological expertise could be advanced a thousand years.

Up until this point, the government had been ignoring the whole thing, obviously not taking it seriously, but now, perhaps jolted into action by watching scientists on *The Tonight Show* enthuse about the wondrous new technologies that might be there for the taking, they made up for lost time (and gave a boost to the Sinister Government Conspiracy theory) by swooping down and seizing Independence Stadium, excluding all civilians from the property.

The city and the owners protested, then threatened to sue, but the feds smacked them with Eminent Domain and stood pat (eventually they would be placated by the offer to build a new stadium elsewhere in the city, at government expense; since you certainly couldn't play a game in the Independence Stadium anyway, with *that* thing hanging in the air, the owners were not really all that hard to convince). Hordes of scientists and spooks from various alphabet-soup agencies swarmed over the playing field. A ring of soldiers surrounded the stadium day and night, military helicopters hovered constantly overhead to keep other helicopters with prying television cameras away, and when it occurred to somebody that this wouldn't be enough to frustrate spy satellites or high-flying spy planes, a huge tent enclosure was raised over the entire infield, hiding the Ball from sight.

Months went by, then years. No news about the Miracle Baseball was coming out of Independence Stadium, although by now a tent city had been raised in the surrounding parking lots to house the influx of government-employed scientists, who were kept in strict isolation. Occasionally, a fuss would be made in the media or a motion would be raised in Congress in protest of such stringent secrecy, but the government was keeping the lid down tight, in spite of wildfire rumors that scientists were conferring with UFO Aliens in there, or had opened a dimensional gateway to another universe.

The cultists, who had been refused admittance to Independence Stadium to venerate the Ball, when they'd arrived with blistered and bleeding feet from California several months after the Event, erected a tent city of their own across the street from the government's tent city, and could be seen keeping vigil day and night in all weathers, as if they expected God to pop his head out of the stadium to say hello at any moment, and didn't want to miss it. (They eventually filed suit against the government for interfering with their freedom to worship by refusing them access to the Ball, and the suit dragged through the courts for years, with no conclusive results.)

The lack of information coming out of Independence Stadium did nothing to discourage media speculation, of course. In fact, it was like pouring gasoline on a fire, and for several years it was difficult to turn on a television set at any time of the day or night without finding *somebody* saying *something* about the Miracle Ball, even if it was only on the PBS channels. Most of the players and officials who were down on the field When It Happened became minor media celebrities, as did the rounds of all the talk-shows. Rivera, the batter who'd been at the plate that night, refused to talk about it, seeming bitter and angry about the whole thing—the joke was that Rivera was pissed because God had been scared to pitch to him—but Holzman, the pitcher, showed an unexpected philosophical bent—pitchers were all head-cases anyway, baseball fans told each other—and was a fixture on the talk-show circuit for years, long after he'd retired from the game. "I'm not sure it proves the existence of God," he said one night. "You'd think that God would have better things to do. But it sure shows that there are forces at work in the universe we don't understand." Later, on another talk show, discussing the theory that heavenly intervention had kept his team from winning the Series, Holzman famously said, "I don't know, maybe God *is* a Yankees fan—but if He hates the Phillies all that much, wouldn't it have been a lot easier just to let Rivera get a *hit*?"

In the second year after the Event, a book called *Schrödinger's Baseball*, written by a young Harvard physicist, postulated the theory that those watching the game in the stadium that night had been so evenly split between Yankees fans wanting Rivera to get a hit and Phillies fans wanting him to strike out, the balance so exquisitely perfect between the two opposing pools of observers, that the quantum wave function had been unable to "decide" which way to collapse, and so had just frozen permanently into an indeterminate state, not resolving itself into *either* outcome. This was immediately derided as errant nonsense by other scientists, but the book became an international bestseller of epic proportions, staying at the top of the lists for twenty months, and, although it had no plot at all, was later optioned for a (never actually made) Big Budget movie for a hefty seven-figure advance.

Eventually, more than four years later, after an election where public dislike of the Secret of Independence Stadium had played a decisive role, a new administration took charge and belatedly declared an Open Door policy, welcoming in civilian scientists, even those from other nations, and, of course, the media.

As soon became clear, they had little to lose. Nothing had changed in almost half a decade. The Ball still hung there in midair. Nothing could move it. Nothing could affect it. The government scientists had tried taking core samples, but no drill bit would bite. They'd tried dragging it away with tractor-hauled nets and with immense magnetic fields, and neither the brute-force nor the high-tech approach had worked. They'd measured it and the surrounding space and the space above and below it with every instrument anybody could think of, and discovered nothing. They'd hit it with high-intensity laser beams, they'd tried crisping it with plasma and with flame-throwers, they'd shot hugely powerful bolts of electricity into it. Nothing had worked.

They'd learned nothing from the Ball, in spite of years of intensive, round-the-clock observation with every possible instrumentation, in spite of hundreds of millions of dollars spent, in spite of dozens of scientists working themselves into nervous exhaustion, mental breakdowns, and emotional collapse. No alien secrets. No heretofore unexpected forces of nature (none that they'd learned to identify and control, anyway). The Ball was just *there*. Who knew why? Or how?

More years of intensive investigation by scientists from around the world followed, but eventually, as years stretched into decades, even the scientists began to lose interest. Most ordinary people had lost interest long before, when the Miracle Ball resolutely refused to do anything else remarkable, or even moderately nonboring.

Baseball the sport did its best to pretend the whole thing had never happened. Game attendance had soared for a while, as people waited for the same thing to happen again, then, when it didn't, declined disastrously, falling to record lows. Many major-league franchises went out of business (although, oddly, sandlot and minor-league games were as popular as ever), and those who were lucky enough to survive did their best to see that the Ball was rarely mentioned in the sports pages.

Other seasons went into the record books, none tainted by the miraculous.

Forty more years went by.

Frederick Kellenberger had not been a young man even when he officiated at home plate during the Event. Now he was fabulously old, many decades into his retirement, and had chosen to spend the remaining few years of his life living in a crumbling old brownstone building in what remained of a South Philadelphia neighborhood, a few blocks from Independence Stadium. In the last few years, almost against his will, since he had spent decades resolutely trying to put the whole business behind him, he had become fascinated with the Event, with the Ball—in a mellow, nonobsessive kind of way, since he was of a calm, phlegmatic, even contemplative, temperament. He didn't expect to solve any mysteries, where so many others had failed. Still, he had nothing better to do with the residue of his life, and as almost everybody else who had been involved with the Event was dead by now, or else tucked away in nursing homes, it seemed appropriate somehow that someone who had been there from the start should keep an eye on the Ball.

He spent the long, sleepless nights of extreme old age on his newly acquired (only twenty years old) hobby of studying the letters and journals of the Knights of St. John of 12th Century Rhodes, a hobby that appealed to him in part just because it was so out of character for a retired baseball umpire, and an area in which, to everyone's surprise—including his own—he had become an internationally recognized authority. Days, he would pick up a lightweight cloth folding chair, and hobble the few blocks to Independence Stadium, moving very, very slowly, like an ancient tortoise hitching itself along a beach in the Galapagos Islands. Hurry wasn't needed, even if he'd been capable of it. This neighborhood had been nearly deserted for years. There was no traffic, rarely anybody around. The slowly rising Atlantic lapped against the base of the immense Jersey Dike a few blocks to the east, and most of the buildings here were abandoned, boarded up, falling down. Weeds grew through cracks in the middle of the street. For decades now, the city had been gradually, painfully, ponderously shifting itself to higher ground to the west, as had all the other cities of the slowly foundering East Coast, and few people were left in this neighborhood except squatters, refugees from Camden and Atlantic City who could afford nothing better, and a few stubborn South Philly Italians almost as old as he was, who'd been born here and were refusing to leave. No one paid any attention to an old man inching his way down the street. No one bothered him. It was oddly peaceful.

Independence Stadium itself was half-ruined, falling down, nearly abandoned. The tent cities were long gone. There was a towheaded, lazily smiling young boy with an old and probably nonfunctional assault rifle who was supposed to keep people out of the Stadium, but Kallenburger bribed him with a few small coins every few days, and he always winked and looked the other way. There were supposed to be cameras continuously running, focused on the Ball, part of an ongoing study funded by the University of Denver, recording everything just in case something ever happened, but the equipment had broken down long since, and nobody had seemed to notice, or care. The young guard never entered the stadium, so, once inside, Kallenburger had the place pretty much to himself.

Inside, Kallenburger would set up his folding chair behind the faded outline of home plate, right where he used to stand to call the games, sit down in the dappled sunlight (the tent enclosing the infield had long since fallen down, leaving only a few metal girders and a few scraps of fabric that flapped lazily in the wind), and watch the Ball, which still hung motionless in the air, just as it had for almost fifty years now. He didn't expect to see anything, other than what had always been there to be seen. It was quiet inside the abandoned stadium, though, and peaceful. Bees buzzed by his ears, and birds flew in and out of the stadium, squabbling under the eaves, making their nests in amongst the broken seats, occasionally launching into liquid song. The air was thick with the rich smells of morning glory and honeysuckle, which twined up around the ruined bleachers. Wildflowers had sprung up everywhere, and occasionally the tall grass in the outfield would rustle as some small unseen creature scurried through it. Kallenburger watched the Ball, his mind comfortably blank. Sometimes—more often than not, truth be told—he dozed and nodded in the honeyed sunlight.

As chance would have it, he happened to be awake and watching when the Ball moved at last.

Without warning, the Ball suddenly shot forward across the plate, just as if Holzman had thrown it only a second before, rather than nearly a half a century in the past. With no catcher there to intercept it, it shot past home plate, hit the back wall, bounced high in the air, fell back to earth, bounced again, rolled away, and disappeared into the tall weeds near what had once been the dugout.

After a moment of silent surprise, Kallenburger rose stiffly to his feet. Ponderously, he shuffled forward, bent over as much as he could, tilted his head creakingly this way and that, remembering the direction of the ball as it shot over the faded ghost of home plate, analyzing, judging angles. At last, slowly, he smiled.

"Strike!" he said, with satisfaction. "I *knew* it would be. You're *out*."

Then, without a backward look, without even a glance at where the famous Ball lay swallowed in the weeds, he picked up his folding chair, hoisted it to his shoulder, went out of the ruins of Independence Stadium, and, moving very slowly, shuffled home along the cracked and deserted street through the warm, bright, velvet air of spring.

One of the more dismaying aspects of life is its sense of transience. Everything is temporary, everything goes away. The seventeen-year-old girls we remember so fondly become grandmothers. Console radios and drive-in movies disappear. And we ourselves are ultimately headed out of town. It's why the finale of *Planet of the Apes* is so moving, why all those post-apocalyptic novels continue to hold our interest.

The Colossus has vanished out of Rhodes, and the Hanging Gardens are gone. We read regularly of the ongoing deterioration of the Parthenon, the Coliseum, and the Sphinx. All but two of Homer's books are lost, and most of the works of Sophocles. But it's hard not to believe that something, somewhere, survives. Something hangs on. If so, what more likely than those objects handled by, or associated with, the divine?

—*Jack McDevitt*

Deus Tex

JACK MCDEVITT

~~~~~~~~~~

THE BUILDING WAS DARK, except for a table lamp in the living room and a ruddy glow on the third floor. The upstairs light didn't give us any concern because a lot of people leave a second light on somewhere when they go out.

I looked around at the railroad tracks and warehouses and freight terminals and wondered why anybody would want to live down here. But Armin Rankowski had.

At least he had until he walked in front of a truck. That had happened the previous evening. Hatch had seen the story, and had read that there were no known survivors. That meant nobody home until the county got its act together.

The telephone book listed his home address as 511 S. Eddy in Pemberton, a small industrial town just south of Houston. We found a partially refitted warehouse at the address. It was three stories high, with new siding and a freshly painted front entrance, and plants and curtains in the windows.

The ambiance was by no means luxurious, but it was of a higher order than we'd expected. "Definitely worthwhile," Toxie said.

I mean, somebody lives alone, he dies, his place is an easy hit. We moved to the rear of the building, out of sight of the street. Hatch measured the window, levered it open, and poked his head in. "I think we're okay," he whispered. He threw a leg over the sill. Like the rest of him, it was big and meaty.

Toxie was little and sharp-nosed and rat-quick. He was good to have along because he scared easy and you knew he wasn't going to let you take any chances. You might think excessive caution is not a good idea, but in our line of work, it is a virtue of the first order. He went next and I followed.

I should point out here that it's always a rewarding moment to encounter a house of modest appearance and discover that the occupants have done well. We had entered the dining room, which was furnished with leather chairs and a nicely executed hand-carved table that would look good in my den. Two impressionist oils hung on the walls, and we found another one out in the hallway. They looked like originals, which presented a problem because they're awkward to carry and you can't be sure what they're worth, if anything. I've taken a couple of classes in contemporary art, in order to upgrade my professional skills, but they tend to deal exclusively with the big names whose stuff hangs in museums.

"How about this?" said Toxie happily, surveying the furnishings. "We need a van."

Hatch was big and easygoing. He was career-oriented in every sense of the term, and he took pride in the fact that neither he nor anyone accompanying him on an operation had ever been charged, let alone jailed. He was at an age when most people are starting to think about retirement, and in fact he talked about it a lot. He'd invested his money and I knew he could turn off the lights any time he wanted. But Hatch could never be satisfied with sitting on a front porch. "Gentlemen," he said, maintaining the monotone he always used when he was working, "I believe we have just met the mortgage payment."

We moved through the first floor. There was enough light coming in from the street to allow us to work. The house was electronically well-equipped. TV, stereo, blender, microwave, everything was state of the art. Rankowski had owned a substantial supply of electronics. In addition, there was good silverware and a set of Dauvier crystal bookends, a top-of-the-line Miranda camera, and a Pavilion notebook. We found a tin box stashed in a cabinet in the dining room, under some folded tablecloths. It contained about three hundred cash, some cheap jewelry, a pair of diamond cuff links, and a bundle of thousand dollar bonds. Toxie and I carried black utility bags. We put the cuff links and the cash into the bags and left the rest.

I knew Hatch was trying to decide about the van. There weren't many cops in this neighborhood, but anybody doing major removal at this hour would be fairly visible. "Maybe," I said, "we should just take what we can carry and come back in the morning for the rest."

"No." Hatch's eyes narrowed while he thought about it. "The county will be in here tomorrow. We'll take what we can carry tonight and that'll be it."

"Whatever you say, boss," said Toxie.

"Wait a minute," I complained. "We're going to have to leave some nice stuff."

Hatch's eyes caught mine. "Carry it or forget it."

There was an elevator in the rear. We got in and punched the button for the second floor. It lurched, whined, moved up, and shuddered to a halt. The doors creaked open. Long shelves loaded with books lined the place. We took a chance and used our flashlights.

A dozen sheets of paneling lay against one wall. The area was half done. A newly installed bathroom still smelled of fresh-cut lumber.

I wandered through the rows of books. "Might be some first editions," I said.

Hatch shook his head. "If there are, it'll take too much time to find them."

I didn't see any mysteries. In fact, most of the books were in foreign languages. Greek. Arabic. German. Some I didn't recognize. There were a couple of English titles: *Olympian Nights*, which I figured was about sports. And *The Coming of Apollo*, which I figured to be a history of the moon program.

Cardboard cartons were stacked along the far side. "You want to open these?" asked Toxie, cutting a hole in one. "It looks like Christmas stuff."

Hatch waved it away. We had never, in our careers, found anything of value in a storeroom.

At the front, we opened a pair of double doors and looked out on a wide staircase. The woodwork had been recently varnished and it glittered in the moonlight.

We walked up to the third floor. Top of the building. Pushed our way in through another set of double doors.

We were now above the level of the streetlights, which threw fragmented illumination against the ceiling. Two dim electric candles, mounted on either wall toward the rear, almost seemed to add to the darkness.

We turned on our flashlights, and Toxie let go with an expletive. We were in a large single room, like the one below. But this was filled with rows of display cases. "It's a goddamn store," he said.

We kept our lights down, so they couldn't be seen outside. Hatch approached the nearest case, rapped his knuckles on it, looked into it, and shook his head. "Now isn't that the damndest thing?" he said.

I walked up next to him and looked in. The case came about hip high. Inside, laid on a cushion that looked like satin, was a *seashell*. A *conch*.

The case was fitted with a lamp. I turned it on and it highlighted the shell. Hatch extinguished his flashlight. "What's so special about this thing?" demanded Toxie.

I broke the lock, lifted the top, and reached in, expecting to discover that it was maybe jade. But it *was* only a shell. We looked at one another and we were all thinking the same thing, that this Rankowski had been a nut.

The next display held a white flute, also on a cushion. But this time it made a little sense. The flute was made of ivory, and would go for a nice piece of change. Hatch picked it up, checked to make sure he hadn't set off an alarm somewhere, and handed it to Toxie. Toxie put it in the bag.

We moved on and found a gold sundisk, about the general size and shape of a CD, except that a chain was attached. Toxie took out his loupe, screwed it into his eye, and checked it. "Might be," he said. "Far as I can tell, it looks real."

Into the bag.

He was beaming. "Boys," he said, "I think we've hit the jackpot."

Next up was a bushel basket made from balsa wood. Yet there it lay in a gleaming case, illuminated as if Jesus himself had carried it. Hatch shook his head. "I don't know what to make of it," he said. "It's like treasures and trash."

"This place," said Toxie, "is starting to spook me." Hatch and I traded grins because it doesn't take much to spook Toxie. We found a coiled chain, maybe twelve feet long, made of dark blue and green fabric. There was a winecup engraved with laurel and people engraved on it who looked like Romans. And a quiver filled with silver arrows. We even found a bellows. I mean, who today has any use for a bellows?

And there was a mallet that was nothing more than a shaved rock tied to an oversized handle with leather thongs. It didn't look like something you'd have wanted to get hit with, but it wasn't worth five bucks.

We saw something against the wall, covered by a tarpaulin. In fact, two somethings. The front one was a little bigger than Hatch; the other reached almost to the ceiling. We pulled the tarp off the small one, and Toxie made a funny sound in his throat. We were looking at a silver harp. Maybe eight feet high. Too big for anybody to use it, except maybe an NBA center. The crown was engraved with a winged woman. Hatch took a deep breath, grinned, and plunked the strings. Making any kind of unnecessary noise on the job was out of character for him, and moreover he couldn't carry a tune in a bucket. But it almost sounded good. Hatch rarely looked happy. This time, he was enjoying himself until he became aware that Toxie and I were staring at him.

We had trouble lifting the other tarp and decided to come back to it later. We spread out through the room. Toxie found a water sprinkler that resembled a pine cone. Hatch called us over to look at a trident that was set in a case mounted on the wall. It was battered, about fourteen feet long, made of iron. "What the hell," asked Hatch, "would anybody want with that?" We broke the case open and pulled it out. It weighed a ton.

We found a golden war helmet with wings.

We found an enormous shield with multiple figures drawn on it.

We hadn't brought enough bags.

Eventually we went back to the remaining tarp. It gave us a battle but we finally pulled it down. At first I thought it was covering a small yellow truck.

But when Hatch turned his flashlight on it, I caught my breath. The thing was a *chariot*. Except that it wasn't because it was too big. The wheels were almost as high as Hatch's head, and the rim of the car was only inches below the ceiling. It looked like gold, golden wheels and axles, golden shafts and rods, a golden platform for the driver protected by a blazing golden chassis.

We all stood and stared.

Toxie produced a knife and gouged out a piece. "Looks real," he said. "Gold all the way down."

"You sure?"

"Yeah. This ain't plate."

"It can't be." Hatch stood back and stared up. "Look at the size of this thing."

Toxie grinned and laid his cheek against the bright metal in a clear display of affection. "There must be a couple of tons of it," he whispered, awestruck. "But how the hell are we going to get it out of here?"

Hatch looked from the chariot to the elevator. To the stairway. No chance. Not in a thousand years.

"Even if we did get it downstairs," I said, "there's no door big enough."

"We're missing something," said Hatch. "How'd they get it in here?"

I looked at the ceiling.

"Bingo," said Hatch.

Two freight doors opened out onto the roof. "That's how they did it," he said. "They must have brought it in on a chopper. You believe that?"

"Hell of a big chopper," said Toxie.

I couldn't figure it out. Why would anybody want a golden chariot up here?

I looked out the window. The sky was hard and clear but washed out by the glare of Houston's lights. "The guy must have been a collector," said Hatch.

I've seen collectors before. Burgled some of the best in Texas. But nothing like this guy.

A sixteen-wheeler crossed Eddy Street and started up the ramp onto the interstate.

I looked back at the chariot and the harp. And the display cases. Wooden baskets and golden helmets and stone mallets and fabric chains. "What does he collect? What *is* this stuff?"

While we were thinking about it, Toxie found still more gold. It was in the form of a shaft that looked like something you might fly a flag from. One end was rounded, about the size of a softball. An eagle perched on it. It was about sixteen feet long, and when he tried to move it from its case, he poked the back end into the display with the flute, and almost brained Hatch with the eagle.

"That won't fit in the elevator either." Hatch pointed at me. "Cash," he said, "we'll need to take it down the staircase." He produced a screwdriver and a wrench, knelt down beside the chariot, and started trying to remove one of the wheels.

There were two cases left. One held a silver staff with two snakes wrapped around it. The thing you always see in drug stores. The other had a pair of sandals and an odd-looking silver hat shaped a bit like a soldier's helmet. The sandals and the hat were equipped with little ornamental wings.

None of it looked worth anything and I was about to move on when the windows lit up, and we heard the not-too-distant roar of thunder. Odd. Only moments ago, the night had been clear. Toxie was still holding the golden shaft.

"That must be heavy. Why don't you put it down?"

His eyes met mine; they were bright with an emotion I couldn't figure. "It feels funny," he said.

"What do you mean?"

As big as it was, he was balancing it pretty well, grasping it just below the eagle. It rested almost lightly in his grip. "Don't know," he said. But his eyes were luminous and he seemed happier than usual.

"Let's get it downstairs." I reached toward it, expecting to help him. But at that moment lightning ripped across the sky, throwing the room into relief, and thunder shook the building. A sudden wind beat against the windows. Rain began to fall.

Hatch was too busy to look up. He gave the chariot hub a good crack with his wrench and the wheel came off. The axle banged down and he grinned, grabbed the wheel, and rolled it onto the elevator.

"Damn," laughed Toxie. "I feel like king of the world." He held the staff toward the window.

"Hey," I said. "Be careful."

The sky was full of lightning.

Toxie paid no attention to me.

I backed away. I'd never seen a storm come up that quickly before. The rain hammered against the skylight and the windows. A lightning bolt exploded over the roof.

"I think you should put it down," I said.

He wasn't listening.

Hatch seemed not to notice. He was starting to work on the other wheel.

Toxie held up a thumb, straight up, everything under control, and smiled like a man holding four aces. Then, without warning, he rammed the staff through the glass and seemed to challenge the storm.

The wind howled and beat against the side of the building. Hatch looked up and saw the danger and shouted for him to stop. But Toxie stayed with it, alternately jabbing at the rain and jerking the staff away. My imagination kicked in: The storm rolled and subsided and surged as if he were orchestrating it. Thunder danced across the rooftops.

Rain poured in and lightning fell all around us. Toxie stood in the middle of it, cautious, prudent, cagey, take-no-chances Toxie, drenched, wearing that godawful grin, his face illuminated with flashing light, conducting thunderbolts.

It is the vision of him that I will take to my grave. That was how it was just before blue-white light caught the rod, danced its length, connected Toxie to the eagle, and held him, held them both. The window exploded, and Toxie still laughed, laughed over the roar of the storm. Then he was gone, and I was listening to the steady beat of the rain. What remained looked like an oversized charred sausage, steam pouring off blackened meat. The curtains were on fire and so was the carpet and a couple of cabinets. The golden shaft, still bright, still the color of the sun despite everything, lay where it had fallen.

Hatch let go the axle and staggered to his feet and backed away with a desperate look. He ripped one of the curtains down and tried to beat out the fire but it was spreading too fast.

"Let's go," I said, heading for the elevator. "The place is going to burn down."

He tried a few more swings, gave up, and grabbed the Viking war helmet and the sundisk. "I can't believe this is happening," he gasped.

The fire spread fast. I kept my eyes off the place where Toxie had been. Later I felt sorry for him but at the moment it was hard to be too sympathetic to a guy who kept waving a metal pole at an electrical storm. The truth is, I couldn't get my mind off all the gold that we were about to lose.

I grabbed our two bags and threw them on the elevator and punched the button for the first floor. Nothing happened. I looked at the power indicator lamp. It was off. The electric candles were also out. "We'll have to use the stairs," I said.

We rolled the wheel back out onto the floor, but it was slowing us up too much. "Let it go," I told him.

"Are you crazy, Cash?" He was almost in tears. "Do you have any idea what this thing is worth?" At that moment the staff with the snakes caught his eye. But we had our hands full.

We navigated among the burning cases. At one point the wheel fell over and smashed the bellows. Hatch kicked the bellows out of the way and we righted the wheel again. By the time we got to the double doors, the rear of the building was an inferno.

"It'll be easy to get it downstairs," he said, trying to laugh. He leaned it against the wall while I rattled first one doorknob and then the other.

"What's the matter *now*?" he demanded.

"It must have locked behind us."

Sweat was pouring into his eyes. "I'd like to kill this guy Rankowski." He threw his shoulder against the doors and bounced off. We tried it together, while I thought what would happen to us if the doors came open. But they didn't. They had a little bit of give, and that was all. Smoke was becoming a problem, and I suspected we would smother before we burned.

"Wait a minute." I went back and retrieved the staff with the snakes. I jammed it between the doors and tried to lever them open. Hatch put his weight behind mine, but it wasn't working. I had never seen Hatch scared before. His eyes were wide with terror and I wasn't feeling so good myself. "We need something more," he grunted. He ran back into the roiling clouds and returned with the hammer. This was the big mallet with the flat rock attached to its business end.

He waved me out of the way, and I had this bad feeling and bolted for the far end of the room. He wound up with both hands, took careful aim and swung it in a long arc.

Monitors as far away as Los Angeles picked up the shock wave. CNN reported a Richter scale reading of 5.7. The epicenter was pinpointed as being just outside Pemberton. That was almost right. I suspect, if the sensors had been a little more precise, they would have baffled the watch officers by putting it on the third floor at 511 S. Eddy.

The lights went out. Permanently, as it happened, for Hatch. They never found him, and he was declared simply missing. But I know what really happened because I heard the explosion and anyhow I knew he would not have gone off without a word and left his wife and kids and his many friends.

I woke up on a table with a sheet over my face. What brought me around, apparently, was the cops trying to pry the staff with the snakes loose from my fingers. They told me later I had a death grip on it.

They also told me my heart had been stopped for two hours. I'd been dead when brought in, dead when found. Shows you what cops know.

The newspapers never reported any of the strange stuff that turned up on that third floor. I guess the cops kept it for themselves.

Next time I saw the silver staff, it was in evidence at my trial. I don't know what happened to it after that. In a pre-sentencing statement to the court, I suggested they take it down to the Briarson Memorial Hospital and hang it in the emergency room. The judge thought I was trying to make him look silly and gave me eighteen years.

Which meant, of course, that I was out by Christmas.

~~~~~~~~~~~~~

As a Southern high mountain man, born and bred, I like thinking about the clash of our culture against that of high-tech, even a high-tech alien. Would a good ole boy win out against an interstellar flim-flam artist? Dang right we would! Us mountain folk often get underestimated, mostly with hilarious results for them what don't know no better.

I wrote this story almost twenty-five years ago. In the magazine, it says that I was thirty-four, single, read avidly, worked ungodly hours, wrote whenever possible, and had been known to scratch fleas and chase cars. Little of that has changed, except I am no longer single. As to other qualifications, I listed then that I drove a Volvo. That remains true, and I'm delighted to still be thirty-four.

— Ralph Roberts

The Flim-Flam Alien

RALPH ROBERTS

~~~~~~~~~~~~~

EMMYLOU GOFORTH SLAPPED A BEER down in front of Billy Bumpus. She waited impatiently, one hand on hip, while Billy fumbled out his electronic funds transfer card and passed it over. Willie Nelson's great-grandson was wailing a soulful country ballad on the bar's tiny holostage. Billy couldn't recall the good ol' boy's name at the moment. But he was sure 'nuff toe-tapping good.

"Thank ya, sweetheart," he said when she returned the card, his eyes roving over her lush figure as he raised the foaming stein to his mouth. "What da ya say me and you—"

"Shut yo' pie trap, Billy Bumpus," Emmylou responded. "If you was the last man on three planets, I'd become a nun."

"Bull. You ain't even Catholic," was Billy's good-natured rejoinder.

As Emmylou moved down the bar to another customer, Billy rotated on his stool and surveyed the action in Goforth's Goodtime Bar. There weren't none, he quickly concluded. A few solitary drinkers sat here and there, nursing their Yellow Ribbon beers and enjoying the bar's cool relief from the blazing Southern sun outside. Emmylou had come back up opposite where Billy leaned his elbows on the genuine imitation-wood bar.

"Billy," she said quietly, tilting her delightful blonde head toward the door, "here comes that dirty old Ferd Harris. Yo' throw that drunk out if he starts making trouble. Hear?"

"Heck, Emmylou. Ol' Ferd's all right. I'll buy him a beer."

He stood up and waved at the old boy. "Over here, hoss. Been wanting ta talk with you, son. Let me treat yo' to a free beer."

Ferd grinned, his wrinkled old face looking to crack even in the dim light of Emmylou's place. He shambled over and sunk onto the stool next to Billy Bumpus. He was clenching and unclenching his gnarled hands. Over and over. Like it was no trouble. Must be having a good day with his danged rheumatize, Billy noted.

"Why thankee, Billy-boy," he said in his quavering old voice. "Believe I will purely accept yore most kind offer."

And he snatched up the beer Emmylou placed before him, draining half of it in one of his few graceful or quick moves.

"Hiya, Emmylou, yo' purty little thang."

"Listen, Ferd. I don't want no hassle from yo' to...."

Her voice trailed off funny-like and her admonition ended up in a sweet-sad smile that enhanced her already considerable beauty. Billy shook his head in bafflement. Emmylou looked downright friendly. Usually she wouldn't give ol' Ferdie a second glance.

"Hey, Emmylou," he started.

"Clam up, Billy Bumpus," she said in a distracted manner and sashayed off to serve up beer to some of the boys what had run dry down the bar. Ferd grinned again like he knew somethin' or the other and took another sip of his brew.

"Be seventy-five next month, Billy-boy," he said proudly.

"Oh...huh?" Billy said absently. He was still trying to figure just what in the cotton-picking heck had gotten into Emmylou. She just purely didn't like Ferd at all up to now. Plain didn't make sense. Besides, he always ignored Ferd's divulging of his age. The ol' fellow was gonna be seventy-five the very next month for twelve months a year, every single year since Billy had known the old geezer. Sure did get him a bunch of free beers from strangers passing through but he had done passed that mark a good long time ago.

"Listen here, Billy Bumpus," Ferd said, while leaning over confidential-like so's they couldn't be heard. Which was kinda silly seeing there weren't anybody within twenty feet. "I done met me up with a real, honest-to-goodness alien. Me and that old boy sure 'nuff done us some trading, too." Ferdie's time and drink-ravaged face took on a sly, triumphant look. He was still opening and closing his hand; the one not holding his Yellow Ribbon beer, that is.

Billy felt sudden concern for his friend. "They ain't no aliens in Howard County. Just what did this here creature look like, Ferdie?"

Ferdie blinked bloodshot eyes at Billy's disbelief. "Why, he looked just like me and you, son. Said he's from a mighty far piece away, though. Done forget how he named it."

Shaking his head, Billy sighed. Did appear that Ferd Harris had done been taken in by a no-good, low-down flim-flam man a passing through Howard County.

"Ferdie," he said sadly. "Now, you watch holovision more than 'bout anybody in this here town. You know them NASA boys done only discovered two other intelligent races. So's either your alien woulda been like a great big ol' purple snake with tentacles growing outa his head like them Varrexians or he's gonna be like one o' them little green blobs they found out Vega way. He ain't gonna look like me an' you unless he's some damn yankee flim-flammer. Mark my words."

Old Ferd Harris had a disgusted expression on his face, it being at Billy not at what it was Billy was a saying.

"You gotta be stupid, Billy-old-boy. I was a flim-flamming con artist before your pappy was even a born. This here fellow was a true enough visitor from another world. You hear me, boy?"

"Yeah, yeah," Billy said resignedly. "What'd you give him and what'd you get."

"Well, it cost me a purty penny, I tell you. But I done got me three wishes." Old Ferdie grinned big like.

Billy Bumpus shook his head in disgust. But afore he could say anything, Emmylou had set two more tall, frosted mugs of Yellow Ribbon beer in front of them.

"On the house," she muttered as though it hurt. Billy was startled, to say the least. Emmylou flat didn't give drinks on the house. What the ever-loving heck had gotten into her? Everybody was acting purely weird today.

"Ferdie just got hisself flim-flammed," Billy told Emmylou.

Emmylou seemed to be coming back to her senses. She was looking kinda regretful-like at the two free beers. A frown crossed her face.

"Ferdie, you old fool. You know better than to . . ." But all of a sudden, a misty expression came to her face and she just smiled at old Ferdie again and drifted off down the bar.

"Migawd," said Billy Bumpus. "Is this here world coming to an end?"

He shrugged and turned on Ferd once more. "All right. Lay it out.

What'd you give up? You ain't got nothin' worth a dang but your medals from the Persian Wars and that used holovision I fixed up for ya."

"Them's what I had ta give," said Ferd. He did have the grace to look ashamed at trading off the holovision.

Billy gave a sigh and took a healthy swig of his beer. Why'd free beer always taste so cotton-pickin' good? "What three wishes?" he asked resignedly.

Ferd clunked down his beer mug and held up both hands, opening and closing them several times for Billy's benefit. "He give me some little pills that done cured my rheumatize."

Billy grimaced. "Ferd, there must be twenty or thirty medicines available down at the drugstore that'll do the same thing. What was the second one?"

He shook his head at his friend's gullibility. Not only was old Ferdie not playing with a full deck, so to speak, but he had done lost several cards.

"Did, too, cure my rheumatize," Ferd asserted. "Second thing now is he give me the power to turn copper into gold. Now, that is gonna be mighty handy seeing as how gold is a selling for four thousand an ounce these here days."

"Have you tried that?" Billy asked patiently.

"Well, no. Ain't found no hunk o' copper to hand just yet. Copper being pretty rare these days, ya know."

"Yeah, pert' nigh the same price as gold, Ferd." Billy Bumpus reached into his pocket and pulled out a copper penny. "This here's my lucky piece. Don't see many of these anymore. Go ahead and change it to gold."

He tossed it to the bar in front of Ferd and it rattled to a halt. The old man picked up the coin, held it just before his face, crossed his eyes, and visibly concentrated. Billy could see that the little copper disc was being mighty obstinate; it remained a steady though corroded reddish-brown.

"Don't seem to be a working," Ferd commented unnecessarily.

"Course not. You been flim-flammed, son!" Billy plucked his penny from Ferdie's twisted old fingers and returned it to his pocket. "What was the third wish you asked for?"

Ferd looked somewhat disconcerted. "The first one worked," he muttered, "but not the second?" Then his confidence seemed to return. "But ah do reckon the third will."

"I done told you how the scudder pulled off the first trick," growled Billy Bumpus. "He just laid some prescription pill on you. So far, yo' sure ain't got yore money's worth."

Ferd shoved himself to his feet. "Well, I reckon I better test ol' number three."

He shuffled down along the bar to where Emmylou Goforth was polishing up some plastic beer mugs. He beckoned her close and she leaned over the bar while Ferdie whispered something in her ear. Billy watched in amusement. Any minute now ol' Emmylou was a gonna cut loose. She didn't tolerate no hanky a panking in her bar. Specially not when she was the target of it.

But Billy's mouth dropped plumb wide-open in surprise 'cause Emmylou took off her apron, come right around the bar, and put her arm around ol' Ferdie's waist. That purely got everybody else's attention too. The bar fell silent except for the good ol' heel-stomping music coming from the holostage. Billy just couldn't understand it, what with Emmylou gazing down at the top of Ferd's white-haired old head with the kind of adoring look that every hot-blooded good ol' boy in Howard County had dreamed of at one time or another.

They started for the door and passed Billy on the way. Ol' Ferdie Harris winked slyly at him, while opening and closing his hand easily; the one that weren't already getting a little fresh with Emmylou and her a liking it as plain as day could be.

"Two outa three ain't bad, hoss," he said, his voice definitely sounding younger and stronger.

"Close up for me tonight, Billy Bumpus," Emmylou added demurely.

Kristine Kathryn Rusch isn't well known for her humor writing; Kristine Grayson is. Kristine Grayson is Kristine Kathryn Rusch's romance byline—and all five books by Grayson are humorous paranormal romances. (The most recent is *Absolutely Captivated* from Zebra Books.)

Rusch has only written a handful of humorous short stories—and only mailed a smaller handful. "Present" is her all-time favorite of the funny short stories—and if you'll notice, the byline should probably be Kristine Grayson instead of Kristine Kathryn Rusch. Yes, there's SF. Yes, it's short fiction (and Grayson doesn't write short fiction). But at heart, "Present" is a romance. A humorous paranormal one. (In romance, paranormal is anything that isn't realistic—and if you're going to argue that romance fiction isn't realistic, well then—never mind.)

—Kristine Kathryn Rusch

Present

KRISTINE KATHRYN RUSCH

M ASON EVERS SAT ON THE EDGE OF THE BED, expecting another failure. He hadn't even taken off his tie.

Roxy had made her intentions clear. She had rolled up the television screen, turned down the bedroom lights and changed the wall colors to a light, but sexy red. She had put satin sheets on the bed, and turned down the coverlet. On the bedside table, she'd placed a magnum of champagne and the crystal goblets they'd gotten for their last wedding anniversary. Right now, she was in the bathroom, preparing her entrance.

He wished he hadn't called out her name as he walked into the bedroom, heard her husky response as she asked him to wait. He'd followed the trail of clothing she'd left like breadcrumbs from the front door, his stomach churning as he picked up each piece—the silk blouse, the bra, the stockings, the panties.

Part of him worried for her—this littering of clothes had never happened before—and part of him worried for him. Not that he was afraid he'd find her with someone else. Roxy was nothing if not loyal. But he really didn't want to go in that bedroom, not with her expectations up, especially if they'd been up all day.

He sighed and flopped backward on the bed. It was his thirtieth birthday. Thirty years old, and a complete and total failure.

During his lunch appointment, his shrink had tried to convince him otherwise. His job, linking hospital operating rooms with each other for virtual surgery, was going very well. He didn't have to travel as much as he used to, and people had become quite accepting of the technology. The virtual operation—having the surgeon in one location and the patient in another—was no longer the wave of the future. It was the here and now, and he'd helped to bring that about.

But it didn't satisfy him.

He had good friends, a strong family, and an eleven-year-old marriage, which he was convinced would end in the next year. His shrink believed otherwise, but Mason knew that sooner or later, Roxy would get tired of him and his problems.

The bathroom door opened and Roxy swept into the room. She was wearing a diaphanous nightgown, so thin that it barely qualified as clothing, and it revealed every inch of her body. Her breasts were fuller than they had been when he first touched them in the backseat of his parents' car all those years ago, but her waist was still thin, her stomach still flat, and her legs as perfect as they ever were.

A wave of desire ran through him and he willed it away. *The mind can control everything*, the shrink had told him. Only Mason's mind didn't seem to control anything.

He closed his eyes, but the desire didn't fade. Amazing that the girl who had attracted him when they were both sixteen still attracted him now. That was, the shrink said, part of the problem. Mason's attraction to her had formed during his sexual development, and his response was a young man's response.

Control was what he needed. Not the drugs he'd tried (which left him fuzzy and uninterested), not the various tantric techniques the sex clinic had tried to teach, not even the weird virtual devices his company made as a sideline.

He had control in every other area of his life. The doctors said there was nothing physically wrong with him. He would eventually outgrow this, or so they assured him. Or he could learn to outthink it.

Yeah. Right.

"Mason." Roxy sat beside him on the bed. "Sit up, honey. I have a present for you."

He didn't want to sit up. He didn't want to move. He squeezed his eyes even tighter.

"Mason." The bed moved as she lay down beside him. She knew better than to touch him so soon. "Please, honey."

"Rox," he said. "I don't think this'll be such a good present this year."

"It's not what you think."

"Rox, I'm not in the mood."

She shifted her weight slightly, rolling closer to him. He could feel her warmth. "You are in the mood. I can tell."

He was always in the mood around her—at least, physically. But not mentally. Not now. "I don't want to struggle, not on this birthday. Turning thirty's difficult enough without being reminded about my inadequacies."

"Trust me, Mase," she said. "I have a little something that's going to make this birthday a whole lot of fun."

Something rattled above him. He opened his eyes as a bell went off, saw Roxy holding a square box the size of a grapefruit, wrapped in white paper and tied with a gold ribbon.

Only Roxy wasn't smiling. "Damn," she said. "How the hell did I do that? This wasn't exactly how I—"

The bathroom door opened and Roxy swept into the room. She was wearing a diaphanous nightgown, so thin that it barely qualified as clothing. He found himself staring at her and got so aroused that he was dizzy.

"Son of a bitch." Roxy was staring at the small white box in her hand. "I did not plan things this way."

She strode toward the bed and sat beside him. He couldn't help himself. He reached for her.

She slapped his hand away. "If we don't do this right, you're gonna hate this. Damn."

He was still dizzy and confused, his hand stinging from her slap. Still, he reached for the single ribbon tied loosely around her neck. The ribbon held the nightgown in place. So much for control. All pretext of control had disappeared when she came out of the bathroom, looking just like he had imagined she would when he had stretched out on the bed and closed his eyes.

Never before had his wife so matched one of his fantasies. It was incredibly erotic.

She pushed his hand away.

"Mason," she snapped. "You have to concentrate."

"I don't concentrate well at moments like this," he said, loosening his tie. He didn't think he could get this aroused anymore. He thought he had analyzed the entire problem to death, that only his body responded—much more quickly than he wanted it too. His mind had been teaching him to avoid all sexual situations.

He leaned in to kiss her, and she shook that small gold-ribboned package at him.

"Mason," she said. "You have to help me with this."

A bell went off.

She rolled her eyes. "I can't believe I did it again."

"What?" he asked, feeling slightly irritated. He'd have to tell her that he'd been fantasizing about her a moment before she walked through the door.

"Well," she said. "You see—"

The bathroom door opened and Roxy swept into the room. She was wearing a diaphanous nightgown, so thin that it barely qualified as clothing, and for some reason he was still lying on his back. He remembered loosening his tie, but it was tight around his neck.

"Oh, this is going to get old real quick," Roxy said.

Mason sat up. He wasn't aroused at all. He was a little dizzy, though. But she did look beautiful, the way that gown held just enough of her in shadow so that he had to imagine the rest.

She leaned against the bathroom door. "Mason, we have to talk."

"You're not dressed for talking," he said, distracted in spite of himself.

"I hadn't planned on talking," she said. "But things have gotten out of control."

"Not yet." He stood up and walked toward her. He took the box out of her hand and kissed her. He'd been wanting to do that since—

He pulled away and frowned at her. "What the hell is going on here?"

She raised her eyebrows and gave him her impatient look. "That's what I've been trying to tell you. We've got a problem."

He liked the way she was pressed up against him. The material of her gown was so thin that he could feel her warmth through it.

The arousal was back. But how could it be back if it hadn't been there in the first place?

Was he drunk? He glanced at the champagne. Nope. The bottle was still closed.

"Mason," she said, putting her hands between them. "Give me that box."

He had forgotten he was holding it. "What is it?"

"Don't shake it," she said, taking it from him as if it were going to break at any moment. She slipped away from him, and pulled the box open. "This is going all wrong."

"Oh, no, babe," he said. "It's weird, but I'm kinda enjoying it."

She frowned at him, and tipped the open box toward him. "Look in here."

He sighed. Anything to please his wife. He peered inside the box. Inside, he saw a gold egg-shaped device. It looked like a Faberge Egg, only without the elaborate scrollwork.

"What is it?"

"A time machine." She sounded panicked.

"A what?" he asked.

"It's not functioning right." She ran a hand through her hair. "I must have set it off when I waved the package at you. I didn't mean to start it for a while. After all, I figured we had—"

The bathroom door opened and Roxy swept into the room. She was wearing a diaphanous nightgown and even though he'd seen it three times before, the look of her bathed in light, half her body in shadow, turned him on.

Mason sat up. "This has happened before."

"Of course it has." She leaned against the door and set the package down. The box was closed. "That's the beauty of the thing."

"What thing?" He wanted to touch her, but he didn't get off the bed. Although he did take off his tie.

"Haven't you been reading up on this?"

"No," he said.

"Time travel is impossible."

"Huh?" he asked. "You just said that was a time machine. Not to mention we've been going through the same five minutes for maybe twenty minutes now."

She sighed. "What I mean is, they found out that time travel like in the movies is impossible. You can only go back about five minutes, and then you loop for a while, and then time goes on. This is a novelty item, An expensive novelty item, but a novelty item all the same."

He frowned at her. "Then why did you get it?"

"Think, Mason," she said. "We clocked you at six minutes. If I turned this machine on at the right time, we'd get fifty minutes of lovemaking without yoga or breathing exercises."

He stared at her, his mouth open. "But I'm six minutes on a good day."

She grinned. "I know. But with this thing, you go back in time. Your body resets."

He felt a little overwhelmed. And he was still having trouble concentrating. His wife, after all, was naked under that see-through gown.

He made himself focus. "But—"

The bathroom door opened and Roxy banged into the room. This time she didn't even try to be sexy as she slammed the door behind her. She set the box down.

"But what?" she asked, sounding very annoyed.

He was a bit disconcerted too, lying on his back, his damned tie too tight—again. But he wasn't aroused. He wouldn't be aroused until he really looked at her.

Which he did. He couldn't help himself. She was so beautiful. How lucky was he to have such a beautiful wife?

"But what?" she asked again, using that tone she always used when she was about to get angry.

But? What had he been about to say? Oh, yeah. "But your body would reset too."

She nodded, her mouth a thin line. "That's why I wanted to time this perfectly. But I screwed it up. I had the machine set so that all I had to do was touch it at the exact right moment, and apparently I made it too touchy. And now we're in the middle of this thing, and *I don't know how to shut it off.*"

He recognized that tone of frustration. He loosened his tie and got up. "Give me the machine."

"It's also reset," she said. "One wrong shake and it'll go off again."

"Was that the bell I heard?" he asked.

"Yes," she said.

"So it's running twice."

"Yes," she said.

"Two loops?"

"Yes," she said.

"What does that mean?" he asked.

"I don't know," she said.

He picked up the box very carefully and tugged at the bow. It came loose in his fingers. He could see his wife's hip over the edge of the box. Her skin looked peach, thanks to the effect of the gown. He loved that curve there, the way it—

The bathroom door slammed open. Roxy tugged the lid off the box and handed it to Mason. She was close enough to touch, and he did, running his hand along her arm.

She pulled away. "Let's solve this first."

He sighed and peered in the box. "Instructions?"

"Against the side." She caught his hand. "Better let me. My fingers are smaller."

She removed a slip of paper and handed it to him. The instructions were calligraphed on the page, making it hard to read. A novelty item. A curiosity. Not meant to be used so much as admired.

He squinted, read, and frowned.

"What?" she asked, sitting next to him.

"There are ten loops," he said, "every time you try this thing. Ten loops and no way to shut it off."

She put a hand against her forehead and closed her eyes. He remembered that posture from college. It happened whenever she got stumped by a math problem.

The posture also made her left breast rise slightly. He stared at it.

"Okay," she said. "I hit it twice. So does that mean we're going to have twenty loops or twelve?"

"Twelve?" His concentration was fading. He had to touch her.

"The ten from the first time, and then the ten from the second, which started in the second loop—I mean, the first real loop, so nine would be overlapping."

He took the box out of her hand and set it on the floor. He made certain his movements were deliberate so that he didn't make the machine go off again.

"I have no idea," he said as he—

The bathroom door slammed open and Roxy stomped out. "Did it say in those damn instructions why I go back to the bathroom and not the bed? I shook the box at you on the bed."

She was getting very angry. Her color had risen, making her skin flush from her cheeks all the way down to her chest.

Mason stood and took off his tie in a single movement. "It said something about a two-minute delay."

She let out an exasperated sigh. "I have to stop skimming instructions."

He was already across the room. He took the box out of her hand, reached around her, and set the box inside the bathroom where neither of them could kick it.

"What are you doing?" she asked.

He untied the ribbon holding her gown together, and pulled her against him. He was aroused, but his body was a little bit behind him for the very first time in his life.

"You were wrong, you know." He kissed her. She tasted very good.

"Wrong?" she asked against his mouth.

He nodded. "I don't reset."

She pulled away ever so slightly. "Oh, honey, I'm sorry. I thought—"

He caught her mouth, silenced her with his own, letting the kiss linger. She—

The bathroom door slammed open and Roxy ran out, untying her gown, letting it fall off of her. She must have set the box down before she came out because it wasn't in her hands as she dove onto the bed.

"We have to get this timing down," she said, reaching for his tie.

"See?" He smiled at her.

"What?"

"You don't reset either."

She shook her head at him. "I'm afraid I did."

"Your body resets," he said softly, "but not your mind. And the mind, the shrinks tell me, is all that matters."

"Oh," she said and then her eyebrows went up as she understood. "Oh."

He leaned forward and kissed her like he hadn't kissed her since they were dating. For once, he had time.

"I figure," he said after a moment, "that we have at least five more loops, if we don't waste them. And maybe as many as thirteen."

"Thirteen?" Her eyes sparkled.

"Maybe."

Then she frowned. "But we have to take off our clothes every time."

"Just mine," he said, grinning. This was the best birthday present she had ever given him. "Just mine."

I would love to have written an introduction for this story that illuminated the techniques of writing humor or helped to define that elusive quality that makes us laugh.

Unfortunately, the most insightful utterance that can be added is a warning: Humor is hard work. It involves creating something that is not only funny to you, but that will amuse others. You really do have to step out of your head. There are many kinds of humor, as well. Since my best scenes tend to involve explosions, mayhem, and the like, writing a light piece for the anthology *Don't Forget Your Spacesuit, Dear* was a stretch. Perhaps the easiest type of humor to write successfully, because it goes where others have gone before, is parody.

"Your Death of Colds" began as a parody. But, like all good stories, it got out of hand. Rather than a classy parody of Ingmar Bergman's well-known scene of playing chess on the beach against Death, this story moved quickly into being closer to some hilarious scenes in the movie *Bill and Ted's Bogus Journey* and went on from there. Hope you enjoy it.

—Bill Fawcett

You'll Catch Your Death of Colds

BILL FAWCETT

~~~~~~~~~~

IT WAS MY DREAM AND I was confused. At least I think it was my dream. Strange, though: I normally dream in color and this was all black and white like an art film from Europe. And if it was my dream, why was I terrified?

The terror, I understood, had something to do with the cowled black shape sitting across the gaming table from me. The figure stood about my height and was wearing a hooded robe like some monks wear that hid all of its body. The robe itself was hard to focus on, the folds just didn't look quite right. I had a good idea who it was in the robe and didn't like what that meant. Worse yet, I'd come in halfway through the feature, and I'll bet there was no cartoon.

"So, Herr Professor, as we say," the figure was saying, "isn't sleep just 'the little death'? What better time for me to appear?"

Oh, great, I'm dreaming I'm in a remake of an Ingmar Bergman movie and I've got the accent wrong. The voice itself was raspy, like a distant radio broadcast obscured by so much static you had to concentrate to understand what was being said. I was definitely going to have to talk to my subconscious about continuity.

The beach was covered with, of course, light gray sand, and the distant cliffs were darkening shades of gray in the fading gray light of the sunset. Though I had the feeling it was almost always sunset on this beach. Brighter gray gulls hovered in the distance, adding ambience to the surge of a metallic gray sea against the pale gray—oops, said that already—sand. You get the idea.

The only breaks in the monotony were a mostly blue game board on the table between us and the tan picnic basket my mother had packed me a lunch in. I'd been fighting a cold all week and it had just won. I'd

269

been too miserable to eat. At this point I paid little attention to the cold game itself, rather assuming it was chess, like in the movie.

Mostly, I was relieved that there was some color in this bizarre fabrication of my sleeping mind. Except my last memory was not of sleeping, but of driving home after the semester had ended. The cold hadn't made me any more pleasant, and grading fifty-three freshman world history exams in two days hadn't helped my disposition. Facing the prospect of rubbing my nose even more raw on the hundred-mile drive to my folks', I'd taken a few of those cold pills that promise instant relief.

Still, I had been in an optimistic mood. I don't know who had been more excited that the summer break had now begun, I or the students. I wonder if they ever suspect how much the teachers look forward to the long breaks. Or that those breaks probably go far in preventing high mortality rates resulting from crazed teachers taking out their frustrations with rifles only the NRA could love. After all, we aren't even paid as much as most postal workers.

The picnic basket was open and I could see the thermos and two tuna sandwiches it contained. There was a lot of sand in the basket as well, though I'm not sure how it got there as there was no wind, and it was, well, deathly still. I was irrationally glad the sandwiches were in those little bags which seal tight and was perturbed to notice the seals were gray and not the advertised green.

I brought my gaze back to Death and decided to look him in the eye. It was my dream, after all. This proved difficult, as there was no face, just a darkness under his gray hood that seemed a lot deeper than there was room for. He took this as a signal to continue talking.

"So, now that your time may be near, I have taken the opportunity to have this conversation with you. There are certain risks involved, but those have to be endured."

I didn't like that "my time was near" bit. I'd read somewhere that certain African tribes teach their children to control and even direct their dreams. This seemed a good time to give it a try.

"You are no longer Death," I announced, startling a few nearby gulls, gray ones, into flight. "Now you are Miss May. And let's try to bring a little color into this dream," I added, as an afterthought.

I then worked very hard picturing the rather abundantly formed image I'd just seen in the center of the most recent *Playboy* magazine. It was hard to tell since I couldn't see any face, but from the angle he cocked his cowl at, I suspect Death was a bit confused. Unfortunately, even as I concentrated with all of my mental willpower he remained Death, which I found to be both disappointing and more than a bit frightening.

Then Death laughed. It was an unpleasant sound. But I guess it was supposed to be. His laugh included equal parts of the rustling leaves under an enemy's foot, a hyena's howl, the cracking of bones, and distant echoes of mortality. As he laughed his shoulders shook and I discovered that I was suddenly afraid that his hood would fall back. It seemed that as the situation began to seem more real, without getting any less surreal, I was less anxious to look Death in the face.

"Sorry about the laugh. I don't get much practice. Are you again under the illusion that this is a dream?" Death asked.

After the, umm, haunting laugh I was surprised at how gentle and concerned Death sounded. We were both standing beside folding chairs that bore a painful resemblance to those on which I had endured countless band concerts. I sat down. Did I mention that the chairs were gray? But then it was the exact same lifeless gray color as the ones at the college were painted. Considering their low comfort level, my mind tried to slip away into a conspiracy theory about death, boredom, and high school assemblies. Then I was distracted by Death assuming the seat across from me.

"Don't tell me I've made another temporal slip?" Death asked in almost conversational tones.

"I think so," I stammered. "What am I doing here?"

"Why, we're gaming for your life." Death seemed surprised at my question. "I told you so before we started this game several turns ago."

"Started?" I sputtered out, looking at the game board for the first time. "Gaming for my life?"

Death shrugged and began speaking in flat, well, *dead* tones, as if he had told this story one time too many already.

"First the time slip. You've been here for a while. Though there were no words in your language that will allow me to describe what or where *here* is. The problem is as a lesser Death I don't get this level of socializing very often and the mechanism I brought you here with isn't very stable to start with. It's hard adjusting to modern philosophical states. I'm only a minor Death, after all."

"Minor Death?" I managed to question as the import of what he was saying sunk in. I was gaming for my life and he was only a minor Death? There was a slight pause, as if Death wasn't sure he wanted to answer. Then he spoke in slightly hushed tones.

"To serve so many people, there are really thousands of deaths. How else could we greet each new soul? But with so many of us, the organizational responsibility for making sure each gets to the right place when needed is horrendous. The solution was borrowed from the ancient Babylonians, or maybe the Chicago School Board, a totally hierarchical bureaucracy that only sort of works. On top is the chief and each of us is on a level below. The fewer souls you greet, the lower your status. I'm near the bottom."

"The chief?" I asked, seemingly limited to two-word questions. Then I looked around. If this was a minor Death, I wasn't too anxious to meet the Top Cowl.

"He never takes an interest in individual cases, or rarely so. I believe he only personally greets those who have really attracted his attention: Attila, Genghis Khan, Stalin, most Democratic U.S. Presidents. No chance he'd deign to notice the efforts of someone as unimportant as me."

"Unimportant?" Great, now I was down to one-word replies. This situation was getting out of control. In fact, it had never been in control. But I needed information.

"Yeah, unimportant. I mean, hey, I had my day. There was a time when thirty thousand died from the flu one year in London alone. But then came all those drugs and everyone became aware of it and I was relegated to a much smaller office with no window. Why, the nearest bathroom is three floors down."

I wondered what the view out such a window might be, and then decided to stick to my own problem. I had better learn all I could, quick. "The flu?" I was back up to two-word questions and determined to try for three the next time.

"Why," Death explained, "I'm that Death of Colds everyone is warned about catching."

"Catching?" Damn, one word. "Why catching?" I added quickly to bring up the count.

"Always sounded strange to me," Death of Colds answered, while tilting his head in thought, and actually sniffled as if he had sinus problems as well. "You don't catch me; *I* catch *you*...permanently."

I decided I had asked enough semiliterate questions. It was time I got some idea what was going on here. Or maybe found out what I feared was happening wasn't the case. "So if you are the Death of Colds, what am I doing here? No one dies from a cold anymore."

"And don't I know it!" Death of Colds moaned, and no one can moan like Death, even if it did end in a cough. "But there's some hope. You're the first soul in a new program I'm trying to get made permanent. Instead of just the paltry few souls of those who actually die from a cold, I'm trying to get them to expand my territory to include all of those who die from the secondary effects."

"Like their wives killing them for being such big babies?"

"No, *that* type of thing already has a really big staff working overtime," Death corrected me. "What I'm trying to claim are those like you who take some cold medicine and ignore the warning label."

"Like me?" It was only two words again, but I didn't care.

"Yeah, like you. Those who forget the part about not driving or using heavy machinery...you drove. In this case, you fell asleep, drove directly off a bridge and onto a garbage scow. Your former students will be most amused."

"And all this is just to greet me?" I gestured around me. It seemed a bit much, the gray beach and all. "No wonder you need such a large staff."

"Actually this is something special. It was the idea of the traffic types. They rather resented what they consider my poaching." He shrugged and the robe rustled ominously.

"So, what's special?" I asked hopefully. The concept that I might already be dead was just sinking in and panic rising in proportion.

"Something they learned from a Swede over in the Korean mini-division of Auto Related Fatalities. We Deaths approve of a car that gives us an even chance. You and I were to meet like this, and you are to be given a fair chance to stop me from taking your soul."

"A *fair* chance. *What* chance?" The words came pouring out as adrenaline surged and bile rose. "A fair chance to stop you? *How*? With what? Who? Huh?" I just sort of ran down and sat there hyperventilating.

Death of Colds waited until my breathing slowed and then tried to calm me with a friendly hand on my shoulder. Unfortunately the clasp of bare bones with incredible strength is painful, and not at all soothing. I winced and pulled away, almost knocking over the table between us.

"Sorry about us. Death grip and all that, you know," he apologized. "Forgot my own strength. It's amazing you mortals last as long as you do, so frail and all."

Death waited while I forced myself to be calm. A chance to stop Death, he said I had a chance. I wasn't dead yet. That would mean I'd go on living. If I could figure it out.

"This is your game," I said. "It isn't fair. Help me."

Death thought for a moment. "I may give you one hint on how to stop me. It's traditional and part of the deal. Then you can figure it out on your own, or not. One hint, that's all," Death explained and I waited.

"What is it?"

"*You got it from her,*" Death of Colds announced in even, studied tones. Then I realized that as Death gave me the hint I no longer got shivers along my spine. Either I was getting used to his voice or it was becoming even more normal and humanlike. I stared at him blankly. After a few moments of thought, nothing came to mind.

"Got what? Who gave me something?" I demanded as forcefully as panic might encourage. Death of Colds raised his arms in mock protection. Having experienced his strength he had to know I was no real threat on a physical level. "How can I beat Death?" I asked, beginning to lose hope.

I would swear that even without a face Death of Colds was smiling. With a grand gesture he pointed to the board between us. It took a moment for me to focus. Winning the game, of course, like that man in the chess game in that foreign flick. Or was that how he beat Death? I wish I'd stayed awake for the ending.

For the first time I paid real attention to the game itself. I mean, when you are sitting across from Death Incarnate, even a minor Death Incarnate, it sort of grabs all of your attention. It was apparent the game was already in progress and, assuming Death had chosen black, it appeared he had just captured all four parts of Australia for the two-point Risk.

"Risk!" I blurted out, overwhelmed. "I'm playing Risk with Death for my life on a beach in the middle of nowhere!"

"On a *gray* beach in the middle of nowhere," Death corrected me.

"We had been playing Risk when time twitched. I'm black and you're red. It's your turn."

So we played. I had always been good at it in life, but here Death had a psychological advantage. I tried to ignore it. The next turn went okay: I took Kamchatka from Alaska, but lost Greenland from Iceland. I couldn't believe he tried to take my England, with four armies on it, from Iceland with only six. His play seemed a bit erratic. There was no way he could unite Europe this early in a game. I was contemplating where to place my next five armies when Death of Colds interrupted.

"You are aware that when this game is over, so is our *other* game?"

"Huh, okay," I responded brilliantly, suspecting he was trying to distract me. I managed to take Brazil and only Venezuela stood between me and South America's three-army bonus. I was worried Death would load Venezuela up, but he went for England again instead. This time he won, but I was beginning to suspect Death hadn't reckoned with those lost semesters in college I spent in the dorm lounge. I had virtually majored in Risk and pinochle.

Death had great dice the next turn and I was lucky to get a card. Another turn like this and I'd be spending all my armies building up the Ukraine to prevent his taking all of Europe. Maybe it wasn't going to be a walkover. I started worrying about the cold medicine and the car accident. Then I remembered the hint he'd given me to save my life. It must have been something important. "You got it from her." Now I needed to figure out who the "her" was.

We were playing a war game. Maybe "she" was a general. Joan of Arc? I glanced at Western Europe on the map. A rectangular black marker sat on it. The young lass from Orleans really hadn't been much of a strategist. She was more concerned about morale than military planning. Maybe the hint was not to lose hope. Naw, too obscure. It had to be someone important. Real important. Maybe the feminists were right. If God was either a He or a She, maybe that was the answer. That worked in some other movie, something about the devil and Daniel Quayle or something.

I tried praying. It was hard to remember the words I hadn't used since childhood, but after Death of Colds plunked down the first Risk and managed to drive all the way to Central America I got inspired.

I prayed through three turns. Things had not gone well. He was getting too close to actually completing Europe and I was fighting to hold on to South America. After a few lucky rolls I managed to hold the Urals and even knock him out of Southern Europe. But meanwhile Death had been slowly pushing up from his Australian position and was threatening to break out in a big way.

"Prayer is often a good idea," Death informed me after a pair of very bad dice rolls. "But He, She, or It never interferes with our mission. I suspect in some indirect way we're under contract there as well."

Damn the feminists, three turns wasted and the wrong "her." I racked my brains. Who could it be? Hillary? Couldn't be. Maggie? Gave me what? What advice have I gotten from a woman? Then I had an inspiration.

"Mind if I put on a sweater?" I asked casually. Though I had no idea where I'd get one. If this was the answer I'd find one. Death had promised it would be a fair contest.

"Don't need one, won't help, and haven't you noticed that your sinuses aren't even clogged anymore?" Death said as he rolled a four and five to knock me out of Mongolia and gain another card. "Never cold here. Never warm either. Besides, it won't help. That's a different cliché."

"What?" I suspect I was beginning to sound panicky.

"Never mind. A sweater won't help."

The game continued. I rallied with a Risk and took most of North America, but lost all my gains when Death of Colds cashed in his next one. It was proving to be a tough game and I was slowly being eliminated . . . in every sense of the word. "You wouldn't want to tell me who the her in the hint was?" I probed without much hope as we battled over the Middle East.

"The most important woman in your life," Death answered cryptically.

Excluding several movie stars and models I'd spent a lot of time thinking about and never met, this left me with just a few candidates. There was Jackie Duocean, my first love, a short, skinny girl with braces. I tried to imagine what wisdom spouting from her metal-filled mouth might help me win the game. Nothing seemed to help, though the fond memories calmed me a bit.

Sarah Neiburger had sure taught me a lot about people and feelings while we lived together, but her most frequent advice was for me to brush my teeth before trying to kiss her. Then there was Mrs. Felker, the principal of the first school I had taught at. Mostly she told me to keep the class in order. Old-school type in every sense of the word but good. If she'd been less of a pain, I'd never have gone back for my doctorate and ended up teaching at the college level. Most of what I learned from her was how to avoid meetings that might get me in trouble. Too late this time.

As I rolled to invade Central America for the sixth time I narrowed the "her" down to one woman: my mother. The attack failed and I was one cannon short of a Risk. Death, seeing his advantage, poured a handful of armies onto North Africa and grabbed for the dice. It looked like he was going to get his office window. Except for Egypt all I had left was South America and the Urals. I could see the end of the game was near, and with it, my end. It seemed to ridiculous to be real. Maybe it was a dream. I was beginning to really hope so.

"Time to wake up," I sallied as Brazil was overwhelmed.

"This is not a dream, not even a nightmare," Death corrected me. I couldn't think of anything to say.

I tried rolling the dice very slowly, offering more prayers to a variety of gods, even sneaking a piece onto Argentina. None of it did me any good. When the turn ended I had three pieces left in play and not enough cards to cash in. My defeat was inevitable. So what had Mom told me that would save me at this point? The game was lost. Not to cheat? I should have cheated earlier. Be a good sport? Great, I'll congratulate Death of Colds as I die. Sweaters were out already. To say thank you? Clean underwear? I *had* clean briefs on and it was doing me no good. What had Mom said that would save me from the Death of Colds? Then I understood. I had the right woman, but the wrong idea. Not what she *said*, but what she had given me. The lunch? It had to be. Why else would it be here on the beach? This was to be a fair contest. That meant the means to win was available. Unless Death had a taste for tuna, that only left the soup. The soup!

Of course! The chicken soup!

With a smooth motion I reached down and grabbed my lunch. The thermos opened easily. I could smell the spicy-sweet aroma of the broth. Death had stopped and jumped away from the game, knocking the board over and spilling little black wooden blocks everywhere. Suddenly I understood. The game had been a ruse, a way to distract me and set a time limit. I'd had the means at hand to regain my life all the time.

Exuberantly I filled a cap with golden soup chock full of chunks of chicken and thick noodles. Then I hesitated. Should I splatter the Death of Colds with it? Visions of Dorothy melting the wicked witch came to mind. I drew back my hand.

"Did your mother teach you to spill your soup?" Death asked, almost too casually.

I hesitated. I wondered if it was a trap. What Mom had said was to eat my soup, it would help me with any cold, maybe even the Death of Colds. Keeping my eyes on the cowled image, I raised my cup and took a sip.

With a shrug, the ominous black figure began to fade.

"You have found the one thing I am totally helpless against. The secret mothers have known for millennia." The raspy voice sighed. "I guess taking it easy won't be that bad. Car wrecks are so messy. Enjoy the rest of your life. It's now rescheduled to be a long one...." I could barely hear the last words as Death and the gray beach faded out together.

I awoke with a start and raised my head to see the edge of the bridge over the top of the steering wheel. It was approaching much too quickly. Reflex took over and I slammed on the brakes and spun the wheel. I wasn't really awake until the car had already skidded to a halt. Then I remembered. What a dream. I'd woken up just in time to save my life. Funny, my sinuses weren't full anymore. The deep whistle of a garbage barge that was just passing under the bridge echoed along the river fifty yards below.

Just in time to save my life....

Thanks, Mom.

This story was written after I received an invitation into a DAW Books anthology, *Villains Victorious*, published in 2001. I didn't want to write a downbeat story, or one in which evil triumphed, particularly not after 9/11. But what could be worse than a traditional villain? Bureaucracy, of course! And so the idea of a usurping ruler being overwhelmed by memos was born!

—*Josepha Sherman*

The Usurper Memos

JOSEPHA SHERMAN

~~~~~~~~

> To: The most foul and villainous usurper who dares name himself Regis I.

Know that your sins have been found out, and that vengeance will be both swift and—

~~~~~~~~

> To: Kregar, Captain of the Royal Guard
> From: Regis I, Ruler of All Tavara
> Re: The attached scrap of parchment

Captain Kregar, what is the meaning of this? I found the attached in my council room. My council room, Kregar! Look into this, and bring me the letter writer without delay. We shall have no more of this nonsense! We both know I am the right and just ruler of Tavara, as I have been since the late Etyk, false and self-styled king, met with his unfortunate accident.

~~~~~~~~

> To: His Most Puissant and Merciful Majesty, King Regis I, Ruler of all Tavara, Son of the Sun, Master of Destinies
> From: Jertic Kei, Overseer of Qet
> Delivered Via: Royal Carrier Pigeon #415
> Re: Wheat Production in the Province of Qet

Know ye, oh most powerful ruler, the harvest has not been, mmm, quite as bountiful as it was in the Year of the Purple Dragon. While this is not an agreeable situation, the committee does not predict any true difficulties. However, I feel it only prudent to advise Your Most Puissant Majesty that there have been some grumblings among the peasantry to the effect that—dare I write it?—this decrease is the land's own protest over the late king's untimely death.

~~~~~~

To: Jertic Kei, Overseer of Qet
From: His Majesty, King Regis I, etc. etc.
Delivered Via: Royal Carrier Pigeon # 416
Re: Wheat Production, etc. etc.

Define "not quite as bountiful."

The peasants are always grumbling.

And I do not need to remind you again that Etyk is only to be named the false or self-styled ruler, never "the late king." Nor is there to be any more mention by you or anyone else of "untimely death." He never should have been foolish enough to go walking on the ramparts alone, the stones were slippery, and it was surely the gods who punish all foolishness.

~~~~~~

To: The Hunter of Heads
From: Regis I
Delivered Via: Unofficial Carrier Pigeon

Interesting offer. Most. But you tell me why I should consider it. I have a kingdom to rule!

~~~~~~

To: His Most Wondrous Majesty, Hammer of the Foe
From: General Whesten Gar
Delivered Via: Royal Carrier Pigeon # 551
Re: Victory!

Rejoice! We have this day won our battle with the false Pretender with only minimal damage to our troops. The Pretender has been taken alive, as you commanded. Your Majesty, what are we to do with him?

To: General Whesten Gar
From: Regis I
Delivered Via: Royal Carrier Pigeon # 552
Re: Victory!

Define "minimal damage." One man lost? One troop? How many, eh?

As to the traitor—what do you *think* you are to do with him? Bring him to me! And this time, I want him, or at least his head, undamaged. No more rumors of live Pretenders to the throne!

~~~~~~~

To: His Most Puissant and Powerful Majesty, Regis I, Lord of Tavara
From: Chamberlain Pitatalan
Re: Overdue Notice

Your Majesty, I beg forgiveness for such an interruption of the Most Royal's time. But has it, perchance, and pray forgive the assumption, slipped Your Majesty's mind that the pay due to the workers restoring the Northern Wall is now three months overdue?

~~~~~~~

To: Chamberlain Pitatalan
From: His Majesty, Regis I
Re: Overdue Notice

Why, in the name of all the deities, are you bothering me about this? Contact the Chancellor of the Exchequer!

~~~~~~~

To: His Most Puissant and Powerful Majesty, Regis I, Lord of Tavara
From: Chamberlain Pitatalan
Re: Overdue Notice

I humble myself before Your Majesty, and I would not dream of contradicting Your Majesty, but I must remind Your Majesty that right now, there *is* no Chancellor of the Exchequer. Your Majesty had him executed last month for the treason of challenging Your Majesty's economic reforms.

~~~~~

To: Chamberlain Pitatalan
From: Regis I
Re: Overdue Notice

Sarcasm, I need not remind you, does not become you.

~~~~~

To: His Most Puissant and Generous Majesty, Regis I,
Ruler of Tavara
From: Secretary Ekata
Re: Protocol

If it please His Majesty, the royal signature is required in triplicate on the enclosed documents, not merely in duplicate. And to complete the legality, the royal seal must be affixed to each copy.

~~~~~

To: Goldsmith Gearth
From: Regis I

Dammit, I need a royal seal! Haven't you finished the copy *yet*?

~~~~~

To: His Majesty Regis I
From: Goldsmith Gearth

Surely His Majesty understands that such sensitive matters take time? And surely His Majesty understands that had he retrieved the seal from the former ruler's body, there would be no need for a counterfeit?

~~~~~

To: Goldsmith Gearth
From: Regis I

Surely I understand that you're going to be joining your predecessor in that newly reheating batch of molten lead if the seal isn't on my desk by tomorrow.

To: His Most Glorious Majesty by the Will of the Highest Ones, Regis I
From: High Priest Tatuiat
Delivered Via: Sacred Carrier Pigeon
Re: Rites of the Seventh Moon

Majesty, the Rites of the Seventh Moon are fast approaching, and yet the Temple has still to receive the standard donation of gold. I need not remind you that your late predecessor was most prompt in his donations.

To: High Priest Tatuiat
From: His Puissant and Merciless Majesty, Regis I
Re: Rites of the Seventh Moon
Delivered Via: Royal Carrier Pigeon # 467

While I appreciate that the palms of the gods must, as the saying goes, have their divine palms greased, may I remind you that mentions of the late Etyk, false and self-styled king, are not appreciated? It would be most unfortunate should even so exalted an individual as yourself meet with an unfortunate accident.

The donation will be made. Through the proper channels. Kindly contact the Chancellor of the Exchequer.

To: Chamberlain Pitatalan
From: Regis I

Round up the standard lot of bureaucratic idiots. Find one who can add two and two without adding four to his own pockets, and tell him he's now the Chancellor of the Exchequer Pro Tem.

To: The foul usurper who dares call himself a king, the self-styled and false Regis I

Beware! The forces of justice and liberty have not forgotten your sins, oh most villainous of usurpers! You will pay for your many crimes of murder!

To: Kregar, Captain of the Royal Guard
From: Regis I

All right, Kregar, enough is enough. I don't know what you've been doing, and I don't much care, but put an end to this nonsense here and now, or I'll put an end to you!

Have a pleasant day.

To: The Hunter of Heads
From: Regis I
Delivered Via: Unofficial Carrier Pigeon

Yes, yes, I know the deal is still open. I'll get back to you.

To: His Most Puissant and Merciful Majesty, King Regis I, Ruler of all Tavara, Son of the Sun, Master of Destinies
From: Jertic Kei, Overseer of Qet
Delivered Via: Royal Carrier Pigeon # 443
Re: Distribution

Behold, three weeks have passed without another word from the royal presence. I regret to inform you that the peasants are now flatly refusing to pay their taxes. Your Majesty, they claim that the poor harvest is to blame. And the rumors concerning the, ah, reason behind that poor harvest continue to spread. I fear that these rumors cannot easily be blocked.

To: Jertic Kei, Overseer of Qet
From: Regis I
Delivered Via: Royal Carrier Pigeon # 446
Re: Distribution

You do well to fear. So do the peasants. Enough pampering of the idiots! If they fail to give up their taxes, see that they give up their ears. Keep me advised of your progress.

To: His Most Puissant and Powerful Majesty, Regis I, Lord of Tavara
From: Secretary Ekata
Re: Protocol

I understand the pressures on Your Majesty, truly, but I respectfully wish to remind you that while the papers have been most satisfactorily signed in triplicate, they still do lack the royal seal.

To: Goldsmith Gearth
From: Regis I

Where the hell is my seal?

To: His Majesty Regis I
From: Warrik, First Undersmith
Re: Goldsmith Gearth

Your correspondence, Majesty, has been forwarded to my desk. I fear I must inform you that Gearth has disappeared from the palace, leaving behind only a note saying, "I'm getting the lead out—or out of the lead."

Please advise.

To: The Hunter of Heads
From: Regis I
Delivered Via: Unofficial Carrier Pigeon

All right, all right, I'm considering your deal.

To: General Whesten Gar
From: Regis I
Delivered Via: Royal Carrier Pigeon # 543
Re: Victory!

Where is the Pretender? And where, for that matter, are you?

To: His Most Wondrous Majesty, Hammer of the Foe
From: General Whesten Gar
Delivered Via: Royal Carrier Pigeon # 544
Re: Victory!

I regret to tell you that the Pretender is dead. He managed to escape briefly—that's what took us so long, tracking him down. And in the skirmish, well, one of the men got a little overenthusiastic.

To: General Whesten Gar
From: Regis I
Delivered Via: Royal Carrier Pigeon # 552
Re: Victory!

His head! Did you bring me his head?

To: His Most Wondrous Majesty, Hammer of the Foe
From: General Whesten Gar
Delivered Via: Royal Carrier Pigeon # 544
Re: Victory!

Rejoice! I am even now sending you under separate cover the head you requested, Majesty—the head of the soldier who so foolishly slew the Pretender!

To: His Majesty, Regis I
From: Chamberlain Pitatalan

Sire, surely you would not have some uneducated man as Chancellor of the Exchequer?

We must have time to study each candidate, and test his—*or her*—qualifica—

To: His Most Glorious Majesty by the Will of the Highest Ones, Regis l
From: High Priest Tatuiat
Delivered Via: Sacred Carrier Pigeon
Re: Rites of the Seventh Moon

I have, as you so advised, sought to consult with the Chancellor of the Exchequer—only to be told that there is, as of now, no longer such an individual. Is it true that so high-placed an official was dispatched without the customary religious rites? Kindly advise—and remember, oh Mighty Majesty, that the gods watch—

To: His Most Puissant and Merciful Majesty, King Regis I, Ruler of all Tavara, Son of the Sun, Master of Destinies
From: Matati, Second Overseer of Qet
Delivered Via: Royal Carrier Pigeon # 445
Re: Distribution

Alas, Majesty, Jertic Kei is no longer with us. The peasants are besieging the gates even now, and I don't know how much longer we can—

To: His Most Puissant and Powerful Majesty, Regis I, Lord of Tavara
From: Secretary Ekata
Re: Protocol

I would not dream of lecturing Your Majesty, but I fear I must inform you that the supposed "royal" seal imprinted on the documents is clearly not the official version. It will become necessary for each document to be completed anew, in triplicate, and properly signed and sealed, with, of course, the official seal—

To: Regis I, Ruler of All Tavara
From: Kregar, Captain of the Royal Guard

We got him! We got the idiot who was sending those rotten messages to you! A more formal report is attached, in triplicate—but we got him!

To: The tyrant who styles himself Regi—

To: The Hunter of Heads
From: Regis I
Delivered Via: Hell, Who Cares?

Deal!

To: The Entire Cursed Bureaucracy of Tavara
From: Regis I
Re: The HELL with "Re's!"

All right, you idiots—*I quit!*

That's right. I, Regis I, Ruler of Tavara, quit! Rather than be nudged and prodded and nibbled to death by you and your cursed memorandums, I hereby resign my royal office. Period.

But you haven't won. You're not rid of me. Oh no. I have just taken a new position as Chief Executing Officer of Avian Transit and Transmission. That's right, you bloody bureaucrats—from now on, *I* control your carrier pigeons. There you have it: *I* control what memorandums you send, and where, and when.

In short: I win!

And may I but conclude in traditional fashion:

Bwahahahahahah!

~~~~~~~~~~~~~~~~~

There's funny, and then there's funny.

Humor can range from slapstick through whimsy and on down (or up) to satire. I have stayed at the satiric end of the landscape, never writing anything that could be called belly-guffawing, knee-slapping humorous. In fact, my writing has been characterized as "grim." I don't know why this is; I'm not a grim person. Ask Mike Resnick. Go ahead, I dare you.

Nor do I usually know where my stories come from, but this one is an exception. The TV show *Sixty Minutes* aired a segment about an AIDS patient who was struggling to gain the acknowledgment that his tissue donations had contributed to the manufacture of one of the major drugs used for AIDS. I simply extended the concept farther. Satire does that—pushes real-world situations as far as they will go, including unpleasant real-world situations.

Ask Jonathan Swift. Go ahead, I dare you.

—Nancy Kress

Patent Infringement

NANCY KRESS

~~~~~~~~

PRESS RELEASE

Kegelman-Ballston Corporation is proud to announce the first public release of its new drug, Halitex, which cures Ulbarton's Flu completely after one ten-pill course of the treatment. Ulbarton's Flu, as the public knows all too well, now afflicts upward of thirty million Americans, with the number growing daily as the highly contagious flu spreads. Halitex "flu-proofs" the body by inserting genes tailored to confer immunity to this persistent and debilitating scourge, whose symptoms include coughing, muscle aches, and fatigue. Because the virus remains in the body even after symptoms disappear, Ulbarton's Flu can recur in a given patient at any time. Halitex renders each recurrence ineffectual by "flu-proofing" the body.

The General Accounting Office estimates that Ulbarton's Flu, the virus of which was first identified by Dr. Timothy Ulbarton, has cost four billion dollars already this calendar year in medical costs and lost work time. Halitex, two years in development by Kegelman-Ballston, is expected to be in high demand throughout the nation.

New York Post
KC Zaps Ulbarton's Flu
New Drug Does U's Flu 4 U

~~~~~~

Jonathan Meese
538 Pleasant Lane
Aspen Hill, MD 20906

Dear Mr. Kegelman and Mr. Ballston,

I read in the newspaper that your company, Kegelman-Ballston, has recently released a drug, Halitex, that provides immunity against Ulbarton's Flu by gene therapy. I believe that the genes used in developing this drug are mine. Two years ago, on May 5, I visited my GP to explain that I had been exposed to Ulbarton's Flu a lot (the entire accounting department of The Pet Supply Catalogue Store, where I work, developed the flu. Also my wife, three children, and mother-in-law. Plus, I believe my dog had it, although the vet disputes this). However, despite all this exposure, I did not develop Ulbarton's.

My GP directed me to your research facility along I-270, saying he "thought he heard they were trying to develop a med." I went there, and samples of my blood and bodily tissues were taken. The researcher said I would hear from you if the samples were ever used for anything, but I never did. Will you please check your records to verify my participation in this new medicine, and tell me what share of the profits are due me.

Thank you for your consideration.

Sincerely,

Jon Meese
Jonathan J. Meese

From the Desk of Robert Ballston
Kegelman-Ballston Corporation

To: Martin Blake, Legal
Re: attached letter

Marty—
Is he a nut? Is this a problem?

Bob

~~~~~~~~

Internal Memo

To: *Robert Ballston*
From: *Martin Blake*
Re: gene-line Claimant Jonathan J. Meese

Bob—
I checked with Records in Research and yes, unfortunately this guy donated the tissue samples from which the gene line was developed that led to Halitex. Even more unfortunately, Meese's visit occurred just before we instituted the comprehensive waiver for all donors. However, I don't think Meese has any legal ground here. Court precedents have upheld corporate right to patent genes used in drug development. Also, the guy doesn't sound very sophisticated (his dog?). He doesn't even know Kegelman's been dead for ten years. Apparently Meese has not yet employed a lawyer. I can make a small nuisance settlement if you like, but I'd rather avoid setting a corporate precedent for these people. I'd rather send him a stiff letter that will scare the bejesus out of the greedy little twerp.
   Please advise.

Marty

From the Desk of Robert Ballston
Kegelman-Ballston Corporation

To: Martin Blake, Legal
Re: J. Meese

Do it.

Bob

~~~~~~~~

Martin Blake, Attorney at Law
Chief Legal Counsel, Kegelman-Ballston

Dear Mr. Meese:
Your letter regarding the patented Kegelman-Ballston drug Halitex has been referred to me. Please be advised that you have no legal rights in Halitex; see attached list of case precedents. If you persist in any such claims, Kegelman-Ballston will consider it harassment and take appropriate steps, including possible prosecution.

Sincerely,

Martin Blake
Martin Blake

~~~~~~~~

Jonathan Meese
538 Pleasant Lane
Aspen Hill, MD 20906

Dear Mr. Blake,
But they're my genes!! This can't be right. I'm consulting a lawyer, and you can expect to hear from her shortly.

Jon Meese
Jonathan Meese

Catherine Owen, Attorney at Law

Dear Mr. Blake,

I now represent Jonathan J. Meese in his concern that Kegelman-Ballston has developed a pharmaceutical, Halitex, based on gene therapy which uses Mr. Meese's genes as its basis. We feel it only reasonable that this drug, which will potentially earn Kegelman-Ballston millions if not billions of dollars, acknowledge financially Mr. Meese's considerable contribution. We are therefore willing to consider a settlement and are available to discuss this with you at your earliest convenience.

Sincerely,

Catherine Owen

Catherine Owen

From the Desk of Robert Ballston
Hegelman-Ballston Corporation

To: Martin Blake, Legal
Re: J. Meese

Marty—

Damn it, if there's one thing that really chews my balls it's this sort of undercover sabotage by the second-rate. I played golf with Sam Fortescue on Saturday, and he opened my eyes (you remember Sam; he's at the agency we're using to benchmark our competition). Sam speculates that this Meese bastard is really being used by Irwin-Lacey to set us up. You know that bastard Carl Irwin has had his own Ulbarton's drug in development, and he's sore as hell because we beat him to the market. Ten to one he's paying off this Meese patsy.

We can't allow it. Don't settle. Let him sue.

Bob

Internal Memo

To: Robert Ballston
From: Martin Blake
Re: gene-line Claimant Jonathan J. Meese

Bob—

I've got a better idea. *We* sue *him*, on the grounds he's walking around with our patented genetic immunity to Ulbarton's. No one except consumers of Halitex have this immunity, so Meese must have acquired it illegally, possibly on the black market. We gain several advantages with this suit: we eliminate Meese's complaint, we send a clear message to other rivals who may be attempting patent infringement, and we gain a publicity circus to both publicize Halitex (not that it needs it) and, more important, make the public aware of the dangers of black-market substitutes for Halitex, such as Meese obtained.

Incidentally, I checked again with Records over at Research. They have no documentation of any visit from a Jonathan J. Meese on any date whatsoever.

Marty

From the Desk of Robert Ballston
Kegelman-Ballston Corporation

To: Martin Blake, Legal
Re: J. Meese

Marty—

Brilliant! Do it. Can we get a sympathetic judge? One who understands business? Maybe O'Connor can help.

Bob

New York Times
Halitex Black Market Case to Begin Today

This morning the circuit court of Manhattan County is scheduled to begin hearing the case of Kegelman-Ballston v. Meese. This case, heavily publicized during recent months, is expected to set important precedents in the controversial areas of gene patents and patent infringement of biological properties. Protestors from the group FOR US: CANCEL KID-NAPPED-GENE ULBARTON PATIENTS, which is often referred to by its initials, have been in place on the court steps since last night. The case is being heard by Judge Latham P. Farmington III, a Republican who is widely perceived as sympathetic to the concerns of big business.

This case began when Jonathan J. Meese, an accountant with The Pet Supply Catalogue Store....

Catherine Owen, Attorney at Law

Dear Mr. Blake,
Just a reminder that Jon Meese and I are still open to a settlement.

Sincerely,

Catherine Owen

Martin Blake, Attorney at Law
Chief Legal Counsel, Kegelman-Ballston Corporation

Cathy—

Don't they teach you at that law school you went to (I never can remember the name) that you don't settle when you're sure to win?
You're a nice girl; better luck next time.

Martin Blake

New York Times

MEESE CONVICTED

PLAINTIFF GUILTY OF "HARBORING" DISEASE-FIGHTING GENES
WITHOUT COMPENSATING KEGELMAN-BALLSTON

From the Desk of Robert Ballston
Kegelman-Ballston Corporation

To: Martin Blake, Legal
Re: Kegelman-Ballston v. Meese

Marty—

I always said you were a genius! My God, the free publicity we got out of this thing, not to mention the future edge.... How about a victory celebration this weekend? Are you and Elaine free to fly to Aruba on the Lear, Friday night?

Bob

New York Times

BLUE GENES FOR DRUG THIEF

JONATHAN J. MEESE SENTENCED TO SIX MONTHS FOR PATENT INFRINGEMENT

From the Desk of Robert Ballston
Kegelman-Ballston Corporation

To: Martin Blake, Legal
Re: Halitex

Marty! I just had a brilliant idea I want to run by you. We got Meese, but now that he's at Ossining the publicity has died down. Well, my daughter read this squib the other day in some science magazine, how the Ulbarton's virus has in it some of the genes that Research combined with Meese's to create Halitex. I didn't understand all the egghead science, but apparently Halitex used some of the flu genes to build its immune properties. And we own the patent on Halitex. As I see it, that means Dr. Ulbarton was working with *our* genes when he identified Ulbarton's flu and published his work. Now, if we could go after Ulbarton in court, the publicity would be tremendous, as well as strengthening our proprietorship position.

And the publicity, Marty! The publicity!

This little piece of silliness is the "cyberpunk" segment of a comedy I've been poking at for years, trying out every style of humor or satire I can think of. Set *very* loosely in (and making fun of) my own Uplift Universe, the larger work is entitled *Gorilla My Dreams*, or at least it is for now. This section tried to do something that a few people claimed to call impossible: mix cyberpunk with space opera. And why not? Hey, comedy may not pay well and it may be a lot harder, but we'd be sorry creatures without a sense of fun.

—David Brin

Ickies in Mirrorshades

DAVID BRIN

~~~~~~~~~~~~~~~

A RIGEL-86 RIP-SORTER FROM NUDAR NUCLEONICS, buffed to a finish that drank light—it felt like looking at a blank TV with your own blind spot. At the bottom of a dark cave. At night.

A palomino countershaded Galactronics time-frame distorter. Puppy leather trim.

An unregistered ninety-terawatt zeitgeist adjuster with the ident plate filed off and the word-glyph, *know thyself very much*, acid-etched in its angry place.

Dett knew what would happen if he was caught with these things, especially in the act. Not that he had much choice. The Tinics had offered him his implants back.

Purple scar tissue still throbbed, feeling to the touch like rippled organic ice. Glass-hard. Ever painful, like a lecture on semiotics. And it made shopping in the stylish precincts of Shinjukumaegashira Mall especially difficult, since mauve was completely out this year.

Dett *really* wanted those implants back. Even if it meant giving the insectoids a strategic advantage in their war of domination.

So, like a vacuumflit, shadow-kayaking inside the radar penumbra of some death-dusty meteoroids, Dett glissanded up the wake of a Calumnic Star Obliterator, third class, until he was close enough to eyeball the rivets holding down the aft sanitary hatch. *Might as well leave a welcome mat out*, he thought contemptuously. *Please wipe your feet.*

The zeitgeist adjustor couldn't be used at full power, but a narrow beam negotiated with the hatch for a little while before persuading the rivets to call themselves vapor and depart without protest. Of course a laser could have done the same job quicker.

A laser would have lacked style.

307

Dettt dragged off the plate, heaving it away with all four scaly arms, and then crawled inside, hauling a frayed denim satchel after him. The waste channel's inner surface was overgrown with a riot of desperately proliferating structures, sharply angled pseudo–life forms flowing and commingling, their interlocking integuments rising entwined toward a liquid-lined core that aimed like a corkscrew at the ship's collective, corporate heart. A cloaca stink flowed through osmotic pores in Dettt's vac armor, pre-humus dank, sweetly fetid. The Calumnics ate well.

He crept toward an inverse horizon, like a spiral umbilicus, squeezing through a tight oval orifice and emerging at last into a room lit by UV glare bulbs and decorated with stained Aldeberan tile. *Penrose patterns*, he noted while vibro-vapping thick gobbets of organic detritus off his spandex cutoffs. There were just two things Dettt approved of about the Calumnics.

One: their taste in geometric recursion imagery.

Two: their pastry.

This trip wouldn't offer much chance to sample the latter.

The former he was absolutely counting on.

Elegant tile designs continued outside the lavatory, where Dettt flourished the illegal distorter, making passing crew members turn away from him without a glance. Of the fifteen patron-level species, the twenty client-class races, and two hundred types of AI mobiles one might find aboard a warship of the Calumnic Alliance, only three varieties stood much chance of seeing through his disguise. Before one of them came along, Dettt had to find a jack.

He hopped aboard a moving slidewalk. Speed quickly made the walls blur, tiles merging and mating in a frenzied, dizzying sensation of headlong movement. Entropically induced colors.

Dettt rubbed his mouth with the back of his upper right hand, feeling the rasp of a six-year growth of stubble and wishing he had a drink. Whipping around corners, the slider suddenly appeared to drive straight toward a solid bulkhead! "Yowp," he grunted, and focused hard on *not blowing it*. Not like that night when old French Curve had needed him, but he had been too plastered, too scared, too self-absorbed to care....

Brace for it!

The wall came on.

Dettt's body mimicked memory, seeming to flow through several meters of solid metal the way regret penetrates a drunken stupor. Narrow-eyed, he concentrated to pick the moment—the *right* moment—and stepped off the slideway into the next narrow passage.

He found himself in a fluted corridor marked by pebbly texture, circumferenced by pale neon every few meters. A sign loomed over a nearby door—the emblem for ACCOUNTING: RECEIVABLES/PAY-ABLES—his destination for the Tinic job. Five minutes inside, futzing inter-empire title records, and the insectoids who had hired him would officially *own* this fleet. In the middle of a battle against the Calumnics, the Tines could simply serve a writ and take over, without firing another shot! Tough on the poor Calumnics...and too bad about the Earth...the whole galaxy for that matter...but Dettt would have his implants again.

Not yet, though. Something else, first. Dettt wasn't just doing all this for himself. There was Pansy to think about.

Pansy. All decked in black polycarbon leather-laminate. Nanothin, self-guiding needles projecting from her fingernails, tongue, and eye-lashes, like self-aware follicles, deadly, but oh so arousing.

Pansy. Freelance ronin deconstructionalist for the toughest unit of mercenary lit profs in the entire west spiral arm. Optic implants blood-shot from watching soaps and grading term papers.

Pansy. Now she wanted out. White picket fence. Curlers in the hair. Little ones in jackboots. Her one chance. Help me, Dettt.

He searched further down the hall—now coarse-grained, like oat-meal left to collect flies and then dry in the sun—searching til he found a door of fine Aldeberan teak with a delicate inlay of carbonaceous clois-soné. Overhead, he found at last the rayed spiral glyph he was looking for. The Great Galactic Library. It had branches on all ships, but only a few were big enough to handle the transaction he needed to perform.

There was a guard, of course. An avian soldier, like an armored Earth-ling ostrich. Its sidearm clicked. Dettt went into zen-solipsist mode, moving like a blur, like a de-synced projection hologram, or HBO on a set with only basic cable. The Nudar flashed. Coming back into focus, he stepped over a large, ovoid egg to enter the chamber.

And there it stood. Upon a pedestal of purified spun amine crystals rested a beige cube, misty amid a swirling, heartless chill.

The Omega. The yoni. The nexus-sexus.

If this cyber-trick worked, Dettt knew he'd become a legend. More important, he'd be reviewed in all sorts of non-genre publications, and be told by countless ignoramuses how great he was for inventing tropes he had actually copied straight out of Raymond Chandler novels, with a little pseudomodernist glitter.

Dettt approached the Library unit, plug in hand. Seconds later he was jacked in, weaving past security algorithms, slithering by software portcullises, dodging metaphorical guardians dressed in pinstripes, hurling knuckleballs. He knew he was getting close when feathered serpents pounding bongos tried sprinkling him with ersatz chicken blood while waving restraining orders. Dancing a Fibonacci Series across a field of psychic mines brought him at last before a gate, seemingly made of iron-ivory, inlaid with synthetic, arsenic-doped rubies.

The cyber-voice of the *Library* itself crashed through his head. All in caps, yet.

SO, IT IS FRENCHIE'S YOUNG APPRENTICE, BACK FOR MORE. WHY HAVE YOU COME? WHAT IS IT YOU WISH?

Dettt's real body felt dry-mouth, saline, as he recognized the master persona called Autumn Reticence.

Swallow the sandy dread, he thought.

Now. *Will* the words. Do it, Dettt. Speak!

Um, sir, it's my girlfriend. She asked me to....

YES?

By touch, Dettt rummaged through his bag, drawing forth several giga-mega-tera-bytes of data spool, which he inserted into the Library's front panel. Night Drop.

She forgot all about these. Didn't know they were overdue. Will you forgive her?

Half a second. A long pause for a being as mighty as this. Clearly, there were ramifications.

Finally—

YES. FORGIVEN.

Dettt felt a great pressure unknot. *That's done, then. Now to get on with the Tinic job. Transfer title. Change the balance of power in several galaxies....*

He prepared to withdraw, only to find himself held fast. Paralyzed.

NEVERTHELESS, THERE REMAINS THE MATTER...OF THE FINE.

But that's all been arranged! Query her bank. She said she'd leave funds—

INDEED? I HAVE ALREADY INQUIRED. HER ACCOUNT WAS CLOSED YESTERDAY.

Time felt like a helical string of semirefined drug capsules, ratcheting, tightening around Dett's autonomic nervous system, clamping him like some hapless gerbil to a running wheel.

NOW, SHALL WE DISCUSS THE PERIOD OF YOUR SERVICE?

Dett tried to scream. The Calumnics were preferable, by far. But they would never hear sounds that he could not utter.

Lost. Used.

Worse yet, caught in a clichéd plot gimmick!

All because he had been fool enough to love.

I have great affection for "Ligdan and the Young Pretender," which was the first comic story I ever wrote, and very possibly the first story of any kind that I ever sold, though curiously enough it was far from the first story published.

It was bought for a Jerry Pournelle anthology, but oddly enough, the anthology appeared in print without it. After the editor bought the story, the publisher pulled the story on the grounds that it lacked realism—unlike, for example, all those stories about the Soviet Union conquering the world that the same publisher was producing by the truckload.

Some years later, Jerry Pournelle, who has always been a strong supporter of new writers, put the story in another anthology over which he had rather more control, and for this I owe him my thanks.

As I look at the story now for the first time in decades, I see that it's a prototype for all the comic stories that followed. I never noticed it till now, but I seem to have an affinity for cross-cultural humor. "Ligdan" draws its energy from the juxtaposition of Mongols, Scots, and the supernatural. A later story, "Broadway Johnny," involves the supernatural again, and features a Chinese narrator who tries to live the life of a 1920s jazz-baby hepcat. A more recent story, "The Tang Dynasty Underwater Pyramid," is set in Asia yet again and involves a superheated combination of Aymara Indian spies, biotechnology, hopping Chinese vampires, and extreme water ballet. And my series of novels featuring Drake Maijstral draws much of its humor from the repeated failures of the main character to live up to strict moral standards that aliens have imposed on humanity.

One may fairly say that "Ligdan and the Young Pretender" is the story that started it all.

If only it were as realistic as all those Soviets-Conquer-the-World stories.

—*Walter Jon Williams*

Ligdan and the Young Pretender

WALTER JON WILLIAMS

~~~~~~~~~~~

WE HAD JUST SPENT SIX whole months making the Hypsipyle System safe for Standard Oil of Ohio and now the war was over, the Tandies having been forced into concessions. We had pulled back to Nova Caledonia awaiting transport to our homes in Agaratu, where we would be demobbed, and where the *Daily Star*, no doubt, would return me to my pointless and depressing job of chasing down advertisers.

After spending many weeks playing Beau Geste in a lonesome, godforsaken wilderness, our delight was palpable when we discovered that we were sharing a barrack compound with the Highland Light Infantry. Not because they were Highlanders, mind, but because it was an all-woman battalion, from the white-haired lantern-jawed colonel to the puff-cheeked pipe sergeant.

Our delight, I suspect, was somewhat lessened by our first leave, when we were at last free to fraternize with the apple-cheeked Caledonian lassies. Apple-cheeked they proved to be—also clog-footed, hoarse-voiced, brawny-armed, and drunk as only veterans of their first three-day pass can be.

I remember watching in fascinated horror at the scene in the Braigh Mhàr pub, after the Kilties decided to dance the Highland Reel. Agaratans tend as a rule to be short, bandy-legged, wiry, and Mongolian, and to see those great-bosomed brawny red-haired women, skirts flying, all screeching like the damned as they flung our terrified lads from one pair to another, while half the battalion pipers perched on the bar to provide a heathen wailing accompaniment—well, if Dante had seen it after his journey through Hell, he would have keeled right over in shock, I assure you.

315

I was lucky; I was fortified behind a majestic oaken bar table, with my arm around Lance Corporal Sandy MacDonald. Sandy was petite, for this company anyway, which meant she was about my size. She was raven-haired and lovely, with a pert nose and a peaches-and-cream complexion that was set off with breathtaking beauty by her black jacket and the dab of white lace at her throat. Under her green bonnet her blue eyes sparkled with amusement and delight at the horrible scene spread before us; I therefore concluded that she was a hardened warrior, used to the dismal sight of many a battlefield, and not susceptible to my usual run of impressive war stories, all of which are lies anyway.

My arm was around this lovely prize not because I was the greatest Don Juan in my regiment, but rather because we had met twice earlier in the week standing sentry, which duty consisted of sitting in the duty hut, drinking coffee, and staring at a succession of monitors hoping to have our boredom relieved by the sight of a saboteur. We had talked, I of my various careers before my conscription, she of her interrupted university career. We discovered that we shared an interest in nineteenth-century English literature, the works of Thackeray in particular. She had also been fascinated to discover that I had actually been to Scotland, several years before, having got a grant to go to Terra to write my dissertation. I had actually spent most of my time in London, but had got to Scotland on a holiday after I'd decided to throw my dissertation to the winds. My committee chairman was a great Bulwer-Lytton man, you see, and had more or less forced me to follow in his footsteps. The great liberation had come when I realized that I hated Bulwer-Lytton *and* my committee chairman, and I was damned if I'd spend the rest of my career with either one. So much for academics.

Sandy, it turned out, didn't like Bulwer-Lytton, either—which is not an unusual response, by the way. She also wanted me to describe Scotland to her, comparing it with Nova Caledonia. I didn't want to tell her that Nova Caledonia is a ghastly awful place resembling a strip-mined ash heap, and so I'd said that, barring the heather, they looked enough alike.

"If it were spring, Dan," she said, "ye could see the heather. We imported it, o' course, but it isnae in bloom noo."

"I'd like to see that," I said. So she'd said she could show me pictures, and in the end we'd agreed to meet at the Braign Mhàr. We had each brought a friend; one on the other end of the bench was Communications Specialist Ghantemur—he was an exception to the usual run of Agaratans, being the Chingiz Khan type: six feet four, red-haired, and, with the exercise he'd been getting from humping his communications pack all over the Great Hypsipyle Antediluvian Desert, a solid block of muscle. He was making shameless advances toward Lucy Macdonough, a heavy-weapons specialist, who showed every sign of inviting same. Both being brawny red-haired giants, Sandy and I had figured they would get along, and we were right—as I watched, Ghantemur began a lazy, deliberate exploitation of Lucy's sporran, while she swallowed her single malt in one gulp, waved her hand dismissively, and said, "G'wan, ye bluidy awfu' heathen, ye."

I looked up from the grinning pair as something jostled the table, sending half my beer in a brown tidal wave out of the pint glass. As I mopped myself, I saw the interrupted was Corporal Galdan, who had been flung against the table by his companion, a Q.M.C. corporal with the forearms of a blast furnace operator. I caught a glimpse of mingled terror and appeal in Galdan's eyes in the mute half-second or so before his guffawing partner seized him and whirled him back into the dance. "Poor bastard," thought I. "Well. Better him than me."

As Galdan was dragged back into the reel a G'nartan ghost appeared in the middle of the room, its three soulful eyes widened, its mouth opened in a dismal shriek—a shriek made completely inaudible by the pipers wailing away at the bar. The ghost, apparently offended, drew its shroud about itself indignantly and prepared to give vent to another banshee moan, but just at that moment the Q.M.C. corporal, who had polished her technique, no doubt, flinging the caber in the games, hurled Corporal Galdan clean through the G'nartan and into the arms of another red-faced bawling Kiltie. The G'nartan gave the entire room a look of indignant majesty and left, walking straight through the wall behind the bar.

"Ye look, Dan," said Sandy MacDonald, "as if ye havnae seen a gheistie before."

"I've never seen one this close," I said. "I did see that one through the monitor, remember, the other night."

"Aye. Ye get used to 'em after awha'." She looked up and then quailed for a moment under my protective arm as one of my company—I think it was Private Toton, but I'm not sure—came thundering backward into the table, then was snatched back into the reel before he could so much as moan for mercy. Then she looked up at me.

"'Tis a wee bit noisy here, Dan," she said, leaning close to my ear in order to be heard over the howling of the pipes. "Dinnae ye want to find a place a leetle more quiet? I've a nice place a wee drive frae here—it's closed down till I'm demobbed, but I think I could make ye some tea."

Anything seemed better than continuing to watch the decimation of my battalion at the hands of the Picts while having my eardrums blasted out by the demented godforsaken pipe band, and having a quiet, deserted house in which to enfold a willing Sandy MacDonald in my arms without having an entire battalion of her comrades on hand to defend outraged virtue seemed too good to be true. I nodded hastily and gulped the remains of my beer. Sandy reached over to bash Ghantemur on the shoulder and mime that he and Lucy were to precede us, and he gave her a nod and Lucy a coarse grin.

It was lucky Ghantemur and Lucy left first; I doubt Sandy and I could have made our way through that close-packed reeling mob without our comrades forming a battering ram before us. And then at last we were out in the cool Caledonian night, with the unspeakable moan of the pipes muted by the door. There was a light rain coming down, and so I pulled my cap out of my back pocket and put it on my head while Sandy used her bleeper to call for a cab. When it arrived, I settled down with her in the backseat, and she coded in her destination and put the bleeper back into her sporran.

"I'm so glad the traditionalists lost on this one," she said with a smile, patting the sporran again.

"On the bleeper?" I asked.

"Nay, th' sporran!" she said. "It used tae be tha' only Highland men wore the kilt an' sporran, while women wore the pleated tartan skirt. When the female battalions began tae to be recruited, we were given trews tae wear—but some o' the officers wanted kilts for dress parade, and got 'em. But there wasnae a sporran, that bein' for men only, and so we had these great bluidy shoulder bags weighin' us doon. Finally there was almost a mutiny, all the women insistin' on bein' allowed tae wear the sporran and the kilt at all time—an' thank the guid Goad we won." She sniffed. "Can ye imagine us haulin' those damn' manky shoulder bags aroun' the flamin' desert? It don't bear thinkin' about."

"I'm glad you won," I said. "I think you look lovely in kilts. That dark green suits you very well."

"I thank ye, Dan," she said, smiling. "Annaway, tha's how we got our nickname o' Kilties. It's also the name of a Highland spirit, sort o' like a wee elf, alwa' making mischief." She pursed her lips doubtfully. "I dinnae ken whether I like all the implications o' that, but it's better than bein' called what the men are called. Jocks, that is."

There was a guffaw from the front seat, where Ghantemur had apparently made a scandalous suggestion to Lucy, which she seemed all for implementing right there and then. I looked forward and saw that the taxi had taken us well outside of Glasgow, and that the terrain around us was a kind of desolate hillocky moor, with little circular outcrops like pimples. It was the kind of horribly unlovely country for which Nova Caledonia is famous, and which resulted in most of it being settled by disgruntled Scottish nationalists in the first place—all the civilized nations, you see, having already claimed all the garden spots. I half expected the Hound of the Baskervilles to jump up on top of one of the hills and slaver at the moon. Had there been a moon, of course: Nova Caledonia lacks even that.

"Where are we heading?" I demanded. "I didn't realize you had a place in the country."

"I'm taking ye tae see some gheisties," she said, with a sweet smile that let me know instantly I'd been had. "Ye said ye havenae seen the like before."

I looked at her for a moment and wondered what kind of horrific surprise she was going to hand me. We don't find the idea of spirits congenial on Agaratu, not that there are any, mind...but when a man expects to spend the evening snuggling in some cozy little cottage with the most lovely woman on Nova Caledonia, and then discovers she intends to spend the night stirring up the long-dead residents of the planet, it's enough to make him sit up and think.

"Ah—that won't be necessary," I said. "I'll leave all that table-tapping stuff to the scientists."

Because, you see, the phenomenon of spirit manifestation on Nova Caledonia *had* been a topic of scientific research, not that they'd ever managed to discover anything that wasn't already apparent to the layman. Call it a ghost or call it a "self-generating plasma field, origin unknown, endowed with the sentient personality and appearance of a predeceased being," it's all one. I'd even read some of the reports, trying to lay the phenomenon on to a unique pattern of cosmic rays, a peculiarly unbalanced magnetic field, or miniature black holes hidden somewhere at the planet's core, and great nonsense they all were. The truth is, no one understands it, and no one has a clue.

But it was undeniable that there were a *lot* of ghosts on Nova Caledonia. For whatever reason they came into existence, there were virtual swarms of them. By far the vast majority of the ghosts were G'nartans, the previous civilized inhabitants of the place. They were shaped something like squared-off refuse containers with an arm and leg at each corner, three platter eyes, a doleful mouth, and various other sensory apparatus scattered promiscuously about their anatomy. Perhaps intimidated by the inexpressible bleakness of their planet, they'd huddled in small, isolated communities. They'd developed technology but didn't, apparently, do much with it. And eventually, after the first Earth ship landed, they'd all died of chicken pox, or some other silly Earth disease.

The crew of the first Earth ship also died, presumably of the G'nartan equivalent of the common cold. Who could have suspected that two species so dissimilar would have been susceptible to the same bugs? At any rate, by the time the second Earth ship landed, the G'nartans were gone. The explorers found a bare, arid, ugly planet, mostly grassy and with no native vegetation taller than my shoulder, a few mildly interesting aboriginal dwelling places, and no animal life whatever. Barring, of course, the ghosts.

It was lucky that the G'nartans never really existed in large numbers, because otherwise the planet would have been absolutely swarming with the things. As it was, there seemed to have been only a small chance that any given G'nartan would return from the dead, but over a couple million years of inhabitation all those numbers added up. Fortunately the G'nartan ghosts seemed to confine themselves principally to their own areas.

The odd thing was that whatever strange local conditions that led to the appearance of the G'nartan ghosts led to the production of the human variety as well. It must have been a shock to the inhabitants of that second Earth vessel, as they approached the still, dead hulk of their predecessor with fear, trepidation, and all the vacuum suits they could find, to discover three or four human spirits inhabiting the place, doing all the usual useless spiritlike things—moving objects, walking through solid walls, clanking chains, uttering doleful wails—nothing with any point to it, just the usual asinine spirit behavior.

Everyone saw them, not just a few sensitives. Cameras took their pictures. Instruments detected their emanations. And all the mediums in the civilized galaxy failed to put a single one of them to rest. They were here to stay.

Now that the Hiberians had been inhabiting the planet for over a century, all the living inhabitants stood a reasonable chance of having their long-deceased Great-Uncle Angus appear suddenly over their breakfast table to utter a moan of Celtic drear—quite enough to put a man off his porridge, I'd imagine. Still, I suppose one gets used to these things; but even so I'd hate to visit Nova Caledonia in a few hundred years, when the spirits begin to outnumber the living.

All this aside, ghost hunting was not my intended sport of the evening. "Say, Sandy," I said. "We don't need to go bothering the spirits, you know. Let 'em rest in peace—they've lived hard lives, they probably deserve it."

"Oh, it isnae a *bother*, Dan," said Sandy, a twinkle in her eye. Oh, well, thinks I to myself, I might as well steer myself to acquaint myself with Dear Dead Papa, or whoever it is she's setting me up to meet. Ligdan has never yet quailed before man or beast—not more than once or twice, anyway—let it not be said he shrank before the host of Hades.

And then, through the clear window of the taxi, I saw Sandy's home drawing near and sat up in amazement. Black-toothed battlements rearing up on a desolate crag, looming over the surrounding moor like a vast and malevolent condor...a sight to gladden the heart of any hunchbacked bellringer. "What in hell is *that*?" I gasped, or something like it.

"Ach, noo," Sandy shrugged. "It's ma family's little place, Castle Beinnean. It was brocht here frae Scotland a hundred year ago, stone by stone, and set oop on yon mount—the MacDonalds couldnae live wi'oot it, ye see. It disnae belong tae me, but the family lets me use it—I'm the only one who likes the place, see."

The place grew worse as we approached; it was the most monstrous pile of ungainly stonework I'd ever seen, all crags and towers and black foreboding, bringing thoughts of rack and wheel and thumbscrew... Otranto would have been right at home. Even Ghantemur, who hadn't so much as turned a hair when we discovered that the Tandies' voracious sand toads were only angered by our sonic guns instead of killed, though our weapons worked well enough on their riders—even Ghantemur sat up with a horrified gasp once the place finally caught his attention. We were right up to the gate by then, and Sandy opened the door and nonchalantly straightened her kilt.

I stepped out of the taxi and stood looking up at the appalling place while Sandy operated the lock. It was the first, and I hope the last, glimpse I've ever had of a palm-lock keyed to open a portcullis. The great iron-shod wooden fangs rose, the inner gate opened, and then as I followed Sandy inside, a great shuddering, burbling shriek rose up from the courtyard, enough to send a ripple of cold up my spine. Ghantemur's eyes were as wide as platters. "Ligdan...." he said softly, and then another shriek rose up from the interior of the castle. I'm sure he would have bolted had not Lucy kept a firm grip on his arm.

Well, I wasn't about to admit to being shaken by that bloodcurdling wail, so I just straightened my shoulders, frowned a bit as if I'd just heard an exhibition of bad manners, and strode on in. There in the castle courtyard was a ghost—a G'nartan, by the way—wailing away as if Torquemada had just turned the screws. It was looking right at us as we walked in, and he showed every sign of recognizing us for what we were, for he promptly sent up a series of wails that was louder than the first, as if whatever was distressing him was our fault. Which, come to that, it probably was.

Sandy just marched past him as if he weren't there, so I took my cue from her and followed, only nodding to the little transparent fellow as we passed, a little how-d'ye-do. It seemed only the polite thing.

We passed a miniature little chapel set in one corner of the courtyard, apparently as an afterthought, and then Sandy keyed the lock on the largest pile of masonry, obviously the keep, and we stepped into a short flagstone foyer, lined with about what I'd expected, namely family portraits, old flags, weapons, suits of armor, and other complicated iron objects of uncertain purpose that must have kept the robot housekeeping staff busy with their dusting. Sandy led us through a number of passages and alcoves to a pleasant snug little room, leather chairs and couches, dark old paintings, and a huge fireplace which lit itself at her verbal command. She turned to me and grinned.

"It's got all the comforts of home, does it nae?" she asked. "Make yersel' at home, an' I'll fetch ourselves some tea. Unless ye'd like somethin' a wee bit stronger?"

"I'll take tea, thanks," I said, my voice half drowned by another call from Old Yowler in the courtyard. Sobriety, I thought, might be in order; one never knew that the late Hilda MacDonald, currently a whiz at telekinetics, might decide to avenge some ancient grudge against my race and animate one of those suits of armor to my intense pain and displeasure. Lucy asked for a single malt once more, evidently being on a firm footing with the MacDonald shades, and Ghantemur, a bit white about the eyes, called for the same.

Sandy was gone for a few minutes; Lucy and Ghantemur settled onto the couch to begin again where they'd left off in the cab, and I stuck my hands in my pockets and looked out the ancient leaded windows past the chapel and into the courtyard, where the G'nartan was still serenading. Beyond him there was movement on the battlements, and I caught a brief sight of an unearthly figure all in armor, pacing along above the barbican, the starlight shining on his plume.... "Who's the ghost of Hamlet's father?" I asked as Sandy returned with a tray holding a teapot, cups, and a dusty bottle of malt whiskey, the latter of which Ghantemur seized with all the delight of Galahad reaching for the Grail.

"Who?" Sandy asked. She narrowed her eyes as she peered out the window. "Och, that'll be the man in armor," she said. "We're not sure who he was. We think he may be Sir David MacDhòmhnuill, who returned frae Flodden Field only to be poisoned by his faithless wife. But we arnae sure—he keeps his visor doon, an' disnae say a word."

I turned toward Sandy. She'd taken off her bonnet, jacket, and jabot, and looked lovelier than I'd ever seen her—but the distracting sight of her only slowed my thinking for a few moments.

"But it couldn't be Sir David, could it?" I asked. "I mean, his ghost would be back on earth...." My words trailed off as the G'nartan let go another wail, but it wasn't the howling outside that sent a cold realization trickling up my neck. Sandy paused, tray in hand, her eyes expectant as she awaited my revelation. "Wait a minute," I said. "D'you mean to say that—that the castle ghosts—that they all came with the castle when it was moved?"

"That's a fly man, tha' Ligdan," Lucy called from the sofa, and then turned to grin at me. "You're verra good. They usually take longer tae realize."

"Congratulations, Dan," Sandy said, beaming. "Aye, it's true. All the Beinnean gheisties came wi' us." She set the tray down, patting the teapot in its cozy. "I'll let ye to steep awha'," she said to the teapot, and then turned back to me.

"They all came," she said. "But we didnae ken just how many there were. The manifestations are stronger on this planet, ye know. We thought the castle had only three or four ghosts, but now we know we have *dozens*! That one on the battlements, for example—he hadnae been seen, before. And then there's Sir Thomas MacDonald. He'd just been a puir lonely legend, slammin' doors and settin' chairs tae rockin' by themselves, throwin' books down frae shelves in his temper. Now tha' he's on Nova Caledonia, ev'raone can see him, and he's a perfect gentleman."

"I thank ye, Sandy dear," said a new voice. I turned to discover a slender man in a white-powdered wig, dressed in an eighteenth-century coat and waistcoat over his kilt. Only the fact that I could see the flames through his dark red MacDonald tartan gave him away. He was middle-aged, with a shrewd face and genteel air. He gave me a brief bow. "Sir Thomas MacDonald, at yer service," he said.

"Corporal Ligdan, at yours," I said, and bowed back—allow me to recommend a career of reading nineteenth-century historical romances to give a courtly polish to your manners, by the way. He smiled as if pleased to see me, then turned to Ghantemur, who looked as if he were wishing to be back among the sand toads.

"An' whom do I have the pleasure of addressin'?" he asked.

"This is Ghantemur, Uncle Tom," Lucy said with a grin; apparently they were old friends. "Here's to yer health?" She downed her glass of malt. Sir Thomas looked longingly at the bottle for a long moment, then glanced up with a scowl as the G'nartan uttered another yowl.

"You G'nartan's a-greetin' again!" he barked. "Ev'ra fortnight for fivescore year—I wish he'd give't a rest!"

"After all, it's his planet," Sandy said sympathetically, then looked at me and brightened. "I think the tea's ready. D'ye take twa lumps or just th' one?"

"None," I said. "And just a wee drop—just a little milk, thanks." The local dialect was beginning to seize control of my speech centers. I took tea from Sandy, thanked her, and took a sip. I glanced at Sir Thomas, then looked at Sandy.

"Are you—ah, has he—have the scientists found an explanation for your Uncle Thomas yet?" I asked. "A ghost that holds conversations, I mean—that isn't in the literature, I suppose." It was growing difficult to talk about Sir Thomas as a specimen, with him looking on, and I sensed he was growing impatient. I blundered on. "I mean—perhaps they can—they can cure his condition, or something, if you see what I mean."

Sandy pursed her lips in anticipation of reply, but was cut short by a blast from Sir Thomas. "Corporal Ligdan," he snapped, "I'll ha' ye know tha' on my death I swore a michty oath tha' I wouldnae rest in peace until the glorious House o' Stuart were restort to the throne o'Scotland! An' I have *kept* tha' oath, sire, through five centuries, like the Highland gentleman tha' I was in life!"

"Besides, Dan," Sandy said, giving an affectionate glance at her remote ancestor, "the family wouldnae have scientists pokin' and proddin' at Sir Thomas as if he were some freak o' nature. He's a proper Scottish gheistie, an' we wouldnae ha' him disturbed. He can walk our ancestral halls as long as he likes."

"Tha's my lass, Sandy!" Sir Thomas beamed. I took another sip of my tea, beginning to understand why the family MacDonald had vacated their ancestral home, leaving it to the likes of Sandy and Sir Thomas— it was one thing to look up genealogical charts of one's ancestors and wonder what they might have been like, and quite another to have to watch them demonstrate every day what a lot of contumacious, arrogant old bores they all really were. And Sir Thomas seemed tame compared with what I knew of my own ancestors, who seemed to have spent most of their time drinking, cutting one another's throats, and occasionally mounting up to ride off and have another whack at the Great Wall—no thanks, I thought, let the dead stay dead, for all I care.

"Sir Thomas, I beg your pardon," I said. "But I wonder about your oath, now—the House of Stuart, if the memory serves, is extinct. And so for that matter are your enemies, the House of Hanover. I'm afraid, Sir Thomas, you're condemned to walk the halls of Castle Beinnean for a very long time."

Sir Thomas drew himself up, and I suspect the fire in his eye was not a reflection the blaze behind him. "Tha's as may be, Corporal Ligdan. But the word o' a Highland gentleman is intended tae stand forever! Besides, it may not be as long as a' that . . ." He softened for a moment, looked as if he were about to continue, but then he gave his head a shake. "Ye'll pardon me, ladies an' gentlemen," he said, "but maintainin' my form at its present level of materialization is a wee bit wearyin'. An' I just want-ed tae welcome our Sandy back frae the wars—ye'll have tae tell me all aboot it, dear, next time we meet!" He gave a gentlemanly smile to us and dematerialized. I heard a little choking sound from Ghantemur and then the sound of malt whiskey being gulped at great speed.

Sandy looked at me with an indulgent smile. "He's a wee bit fanat-ic on the subject o' Charlie Stuart, but ye cannae blame him," she said. "After Culloden he had tae flee tae France, but they caught him in Scot-land later, in '49, tryin' tae get back in tae collect his rents. They hanged him in front o' his tenants." She nodded toward the window. "Right oot there, in the castle courtyard. Where yon four-legged beastie was how-lin' not a few minutes ago."

"Oh," I said. "Sorry."

"Tha's all right, Dan. It wasnae ye who did it," Sandy said. She frowned, still looking down at the courtyard. "We're lucky his wife is-nae hauntin' the place, too. She married a Whig afterward, an' a Camp-bell tae boot." She sipped her tea and looked at me doubtfully. "Still, 'twas she who reconciled us tae the House of Hanover, so her son by Sir Thomas could inherit. She did as she thought best, puir creature, but I'm glad I dinnae have t'hear her an' Uncle Tom refightin' the '45 ev'ra day in the parlor."

"Lord, yes," I said, only now becoming aware of some of the impli-cations of having the former owners cluttering up one's castle. It would be bad enough if they didn't like one another, but what if they didn't like *you*? My mind quailed before a vision of books, furniture, weapons, and household implements tearing themselves loose and flying against me while the room echoed with barbaric Highland wails, and I vowed my manners would be at their best whenever I encountered another of Sandy's ancestors.

"Uncle Tom's made a friend, thank Goad," Sandy went on. "Margaret, Lady Macleod—who is actually his great-aunt, though they never met in life. She's verra nice, almost as guid at materialization as Uncle Tom, an' with a talent for telekinesis. They're great friends, th' auld dears, an' o' course he's made a great Jacobite oot o' her, the Macleods havin' been a wee bit infirm on the subject." She smiled affectionately. "They play duets together in the music room, him on his pipes and she at the harpsichord. It's a pleasant way to spend eternity, isnae?"

I sipped my tea and said it seemed a very nice way, indeed. Sandy beamed, and took me by the hand.

"Would ye like tae see the battlements, Dan?" she asked. "The view is verra lovely, wi' the stars an' all."

I looked at her lovely face and smiled. "Of course," I said. "I'd love it." I put down my teacup and squeezed her hand. She turned to Lucy and Ghantemur.

"Wi' ye be comin' along wi' us, then?" she asked.

Ghantemur still looked as if he'd been whanged across the skull with a skillet, but Lucy waved a hand and shouted, "Nay, we'll stay here an' enjoy the fire. Ah've seen the bluidy battlements annaway."

Sandy led me to a steep oaken stairway that went up to the roof of the keep. She released the lock from the inside and led me up into the air.

I had been half expecting another ghostly uncle, but saw only a flagged square with a flagpole standing bare against the sky. Its halliards rattled in the brisk northern wind that tugged at Sandy's hair. The sky had cleared, with only a few low clouds skidding away on the northern horizon, and the stars were out in all their rare beauty, burning in the heavens like a river of diamonds. Sandy walked across the stones and leaned out through a crenellation, smiling into the wind.

"I love this place, truly," she said. "It isnae much tae look at, all bare and drear, but when all's said and done, it's home." I leaned on the nearest merlon and gazed at her, knowing what she meant: a place doesn't have to be beautiful to be home, but just the cradle of one's memories, a place that one can look at when far away, say in a sand-bound post in Hypsipyle, and remember an earlier happiness. So it had been with me and Agaratu, a place of harsher contrasts than this; so, no doubt, had it been for Sandy and Castle Beinnean. She looked over her shoulder at me and smiled wistfully. "It does look like the real Scotland, hey?" she asked again.

"Like parts of it. Scotland tends to be greener."

"Och, well," she said, turning back to look over the moor. "I like it well enough as it is."

"That's what matters, then," I said. I waited a few moments while she drank her fill of the place, the darkling moor beneath the star-spattered sky, and then she sighed and turned back to me, her eyes dreamy. "Hey," I said. "I was wondering about Charlie Stuart."

"Wha' aboot him?"

"What's this fascination with the man?" I demanded. "I've read enough books about his time, and about the Jacobites, and I've seen the memorials to him all over the Highlands, but by everyone's account he was a fool and an ingrate—he didn't give the Highlanders a single word of thanks for all they did for him, after all they'd suffered."

She frowned and cocked her head to one side. "Weel, I was brocht up wi' a Jacobite tradition, so ye'll have to forgive a wee family bias," she said. "But when all's said and done, I cannae understand it, either. I think it may have tae do more wi' Charles as King than Charles as man, if ye see wha' I'm drivin' at. Scarce enna one would fight for Charlie Stuart the man, but tae them he was King Charles, an' they owed him their loyalty for that reason, just as the tenants owed loyalty tae their lairds. An' their sufferings just confirmed them in their loyalty; with Sackville and the bluidy Campbells in power in the Highlands, it just showed the clans their enemies were villains all along." She smiled. "An' there's always a great romance in a lost cause, is there nae?"

Personally I thought that the comforts of romance were scarce compensation for burned cottages, confiscated cattle, and all those bodies lying cold on Culloden field, but I didn't say it. I just nodded and smiled and hugged Sandy as called for. "Welcome home, Lance Corporal Mac-Donald," I said, and kissed her.

"You're a fly man, Ligdan," she said, and took me by the hand to lead me to the stair. We passed the crenellations overlooking the courtyard as we walked, and then Sandy looked down, hesitated, and then came to a stop.

"Look ye there, noo," she said, nodding. "What in blazes d'ye suppose is goin' on in the chapel?"

I peered through the battlements and saw ghosts below, four of them drifting toward the chapel. One was Sir Thomas, in full tartan fig, broadsword and all, walking arm-in-arm with a lady in early eighteenth-century dress; he carried a set of bagpipes in the crook of his free arm. There was another less distinct personality, still in the dark red MacDonald tartan, but wearing the breastplate and helmet of Mary Stuart's time, just disappearing into the chapel door; and walking from the keep below us to the chapel was a tall strapping dark-haired woman in a pleated tartan skirt with a sash and a glengarry bonnet, complete with the tails and the red and white dicing, perched on the side of her head.

"Tha's my grandmother!" Sandy gasped. "She hasnae ever materialized ootside the drawing room before!"

I could see, glowing softly through the stained-glass windows of the chapel, a strange, subtle, shifting light, as of moving will-o'-the-wisps; it was a stirring, eerie sight, that light, and I could feel a whisper of warning crawling up my spine. Sandy, feeling it too, looked at me, her eyes wide. "We've got tae get doon there, Dan," she said. "There's somethin' verra wrong!"

My mind urged me to let the dead walk in peace, but something in me felt an eldritch pull drawing me to the chapel, a pull with something of the same urgency a person feels when reading a good fright novel, that keeps him turning the pages even though he's scared out of his wits. Besides, it was clear that Sandy was alarmed, so I nodded swift agreement and followed her down the stair, out of the keep, and across the courtyard to the chapel. The same strange, shifting light glowed out the wide-flung iron-bound doors, and I could feel my heart beating faster as I approached. I swallowed my fear and stepped up onto the threshold.

I'll never forget the sight. The pews of the little chapel were filled with a congregation of spirits, all moving, all flickering transparencies in various degrees of substantiality, an eerie multitude dressed in every kind of clothing from a blue, scowling Pict in his breechclout to a stern leather-clad trooper in his lobster-tail burgonet. The shades were all astir, moving, flickering, as if a sheet of thick translucent glass had been dropped between us. I could see the dim shade of a clergyman standing in the pulpit; I could see Sir Thomas's companion of a moment before stooping in the aisle to talk to a little fair-haired girl; and near a side chapel stood Sir Thomas, frowning, in grim conversation with a pair of armored pikemen. Above them ten centuries of battle flags waved solemnly in some unfelt wind, and I realized with a shiver that all here—the chapel, the flags, the castle itself, everything but Sandy and me—belonged more to these shades than to us. It was all from their time, not mine, and I wondered with what grim ferocity they would dispute its possession.

The sight was so awesome, so unearthly, that I stopped dead in my tracks and stood rooted to the spot. Sandy stopped dead, too, though I think in her case it was more from amazement. "Ah niver knew!" she gasped, looking left and right and back again. "Where'd they all come frae? There must be four dozen!"

That outburst turned their heads, and I felt in the silence all the ponderous weight of those long-dead eyes as they fell upon me, looking across the gap of centuries.... The hairs rose on my neck. "Uncle Thomas!" Sandy snapped. "Wha's goin' on here?"

Sir Thomas MacDonald looked worried for a moment, then he gathered himself, smiled, and walked toward us, his footfalls silent. "Sandy dear," he said, "'tis a solemn moment, a solemn moment. Our plans are fulfilled at last." He leaned close to her, his voice a breathless rush, as if a long-delayed joy was upon him. "We ha' our king, Sandy!" he said. "Our king is come a' last!"

Sandy gasped and took a step back. "Name o' Goad," she said, stunned. "What ha' ye been up tae?"

"We ha' raised the banner o' the Stuarts," Sir Thomas proclaimed. "The royal remains o' the prince lie yonder, brocht hither tha' his spirit may return tae us!"

"Name o' Goad," Sandy said again, her eyes turning to the little side chapel where Sir Thomas had been standing, and where we now saw a long, narrow packing crate, just the size to encompass a tall coffin. I received a sensation of other eyes, spirit eyes, turning as well, the dead looking on the coffin with silent, dreadful anticipation and hope. Sandy seemed struck dumb, and she raised a hand to her forehead as if to somehow clear it, but then she gathered herself together and walked toward the side chapel with slow steps. Sir Thomas, this thin face contorted with fanatic rapture, followed in her footsteps—and somehow I followed, too, moving my leaden feet in slow reluctance. Sandy stopped dead at the arched entrance to the chapel; she paused, took a breath, and reached out a wondering hand to touch the crate.

"Has he come?" she asked finally, in a tone of strange wonderment.

"Weel, noo," Sir Thomas said, and for a second there was hesitation in his manner. "Not yet. But ye cannae expect a prince o' the blood royal tae just leap right out o' a packin' crate like a joompin' jack, noo, can ye? He must be welcomed among us wi' all proper ceremony."

Sandy turned to the transparent shade of her ancestor. I could see her recovering slowly from her astonishment, her intelligence returning to her eyes. Look out, I thought, here comes the storm; and sure enough she flashed clear anger.

"Ye've stolen the prince's tomb from Rome!" she cried.

"Weel. Aye, we did," Sir Thomas said. It may have been an illusion in that ghostly light, but I thought I saw the shadow of a blush stealing across Sir Thomas's cheek. He looked at Sandy sharply, his face showing stubborn resolve. "We spirits all agreed," he said, "that we needed a king. Tae rule amongst us, an' resolve disputes betwixt us all."

"Ye could resolve disputes amongst ye," Sandy said, her eyes flashing blue fire, "by leavin' each other alone, did ye evair think o' that? An' wha's yer bluidy king goin' tae think when he's asked tae judge disputes over who's goin' tae haunt the parlor at a given hour, which is all that ye fight about anyway, for Goad's sake? An' why Charlie Stuart? Whynae Robert the Bruce, or James the Fourth, or even bluidy Macbeth—why the hell must it be Charlie Stuart?"

Sir Thomas looked a bit uncomfortable, but he held his head high with undiminished pride. "There was a wee bit o' discussion, but once I told these others aboot Prince Charlie's virtues"—there was a smugness in his tone that, I could tell, was driving Sandy into a fury—"weel, it was almost unanimous, in the end. Yon Pict held out for someone called Goieidh. Besides," he added, "the MacDonalds alwa' were divided on the subject o' the Bruce, and it was easier for us tae get tae the tomb in Rome than tae those others."

"For *ye* tae get tae the tomb!" Sandy shrieked, and for a moment I knew what it must be like to face an entire battalion of Kilties, with the pipes wailing away and all of them screaming for blood. No doubt Sir Thomas was somewhat fortified by the knowledge that he was already dead, but still he seemed to shrink before the force of her words. "For *ye*!" she cried. "Ye cannae leave the planet, and ye know it! Ye cannae even carry the blasted create! Ye had tae hire it done, and wha' I want tae know is *who paid for it*, ye blasphemous shilpit schemer, ye?" She wheeled, singling out the tall woman in the glengarry cap, her grandmother. "How could ye do it?" she demanded. "I would ha' thought ye'd have had more sense!"

The woman shrugged and glanced away. "Ah guess Ahm' gust a romantic a' heart, dear," she said, but Sandy was not mollified.

"*Romantic!*" she bellowed. "*Romantic!* How much did this *romantic* excursion cost, I want tae know!"

"Calm yersel', Sandy dear," said a low female voice. "Wha's done is done." Sandy whirled to face the newcomer, her face like thunder and her fists bunched. Margaret, Lady Macleod—or so I assumed—had moved from her place to stand by Sandy. She was a willowy, gentle-seeming lady, in a gown of heavy green silk with an ermine collar, her auburn hair curled into ringlets to frame an intelligent, sympathetic face.

"I *know* wha's *done!*" Sandy roared in a voice that Ahab might have used to carry past the royal yard in a force-ten gale. "Wha' I cannae seem tae find oot is who paid for it!"

"If ye'll calm yersel', lass, I'll explain it tae ye," Sir Thomas said, trying nervously to pat her on the arm—his hand went right through her, and she glared at him for trying. He pulled his hands back. "It only required a wee sum o' money frae oot o' the reserve kept frae the oopkeep o' the castle."

"An' how did ye get yer hands on it?" Sandy demanded, her nose only an inch from Sir Thomas's chin. He blinked and drew back. "The same way ye would yersel', child," Lady Maclead said softly. "We accessed to the bank account through one of the terminals in the castle."

"We used the bonds, none o' the ready money," Sir Thomas explained. "Caldeonian twenty-year bonds at eighteen an' one-quarter percent redeemable at five an' one-half percent...."

"Ye cashed my *bonds?*" Sandy shrieked.

"Nay, o' course not! D'ye take me for a fool?" Sir Thomas was indignant. "I borrowed on 'em, at a verra reasonable rate o' interest, eight and three-quarters percent. The payments can be spread oot over twelve year, an' taken frae the revenues laid aside for the castle oopkeep."

Sandy listened to this, quietly nodding, chin in hand. I could see that her initial rage had passed, to be replaced by a cold, merciless calculation. "How," she said, her voice calmer now, "could ye use the terminals wit'oot knowin' the codes?"

Sir Thomas looked away, unable to meet her eyes, his cheek twitching. "Weel...." he began, but could go no further. It was Lady Macleod who had to say it for him.

"Ye understan', dear, that we shades, because we can move verra quietly an' sometimes we're nae seen because we're nae fully materialized...."

"Ye stole 'em," Sandy said. "Ye lookt over my shoulder when I was doin' the accounts an' ye stole my access codes. An' then ye waited till I was off in the army, an' then Margaret here used her telekinetic ability to operate the terminal. Ye puisny leetle thieves," she said sadly, shaking her head. "Ye sorry wretched bluidy lyin' thieves!"

Sir Thomas, his head turned away, seemed to shrink into himself at the accusation, parts of him fading away altogether. He seemed too mortified to speak.

"Sandy, dear," said Lady Macleod, her sympathetic eyes looking at Sandy gently, "it's been many centuries since Sir Thomas here had a king. And it's so *important* tae him. I'm afraid the rest o' us were just carried awa' by his enthusiasm." She looked at Sandy with sorrow. "We really should ha' told ye, Sandy. I'm sorry tha' we didnae."

"Tae steal a bluidy coffin," Sandy said, shaking her head. She glared up at Sir Thomas. "D'ye realize the chance any Nova Caledonian has o' becomin' a ghost? Only twelve percent, d'ye know that?"

"I ha' read the stateestics," Sir Thomas said, his voice choked. "I felt it wa' worth...."

"And of the thousands o' people who lived an' died in Castle Beinnean on Earth, only three or four became shades on Earth, aye?" Sandy went on, remorselessly. "An maybe twa—" She looked around the chapel, at all the flickering shadows that were watching the debate in all their utter graveyard silence. "Three or four dozen," she amended, "became apparent once the castle was moved here, is that nae true?"

"Aye," Sir Thomas conceded. But then he looked up. "But there's a better probability for the Celts. I've heard we carry a gene o' witchcraft and so on...."

Sandy just shook her head, and Sir Thomas's voice faded. It was a pretty lame point at that, I thought; and besides, even if the Celts carried a gene for witchery, it hadn't done them much good whenever the Saxons had decided to throw their weight around.

"So tha's perhaps two or three percent at the most, correct?" Sandy asked. "An' therefore ye have decided, wi'oot consultin' any of yer livin' kin, tae put our family in debt for twelve year, hopin' that yer precious Charlie Stuart is one o' the two percent who can manifest themselves."

Sir Thomas, even considering he'd been dead for five centuries, looked thoroughly miserable. He turned away, his head hanging down, and Lady Macleod walked over to him, looking at him with concerned attention. "Bluidy hell," Sandy said, her anger fading. "Could ye nae have asked me?"

Lady Macleod looked at Sandy, her face full of concern. "We're all sorry, Sandy," she said. "But cannae ye understand how badly he wants his king? He's been so long wi'oot him."

I can still see Sandy standing there, a small, dark form in her kilt, the shifting, eerie light of the assembled spirits flickering off her features, and standing by her the sorrowing figure of an eighteenth-century gentleman bereft of the king he worshipped, with Lady Macleod looking at him, sorry for him in his misery. "I'm verra sorry, Sandy," he said.

"No, ye're nae, ye lyin' wee boy," she said, cocking her head, her lips curled into a wry, affectionate smile; and then she stepped forward to try to hug her old Uncle Tom, and promptly won every heart in the place, mine included. She turned to me.

"Weel, Dan," she said, "we may as well see wha' we boucht oursel'. I think yon crate is beyond the ability of any o' the gheisties, here, so wha' d'ye say tae havin' a whack at it?"

"Happy to," I said. There was movement among the shades in the pews, the lights flickering as they shifted in their excitement. A claw hammer and chisel floated up into my hands from the top of the crate where they'd been sitting, and I said, "Thank you," to whoever had moved them. I set to work. It was a sturdy crate, and several sweaty minutes passed before I had the crate knocked to pieces and the pieces stowed away. What was within proved disappointing; it was a plain lead inner coffin that had obviously been ripped from the embrace of some grander memorial. I stood back, hammer and chisel still in hand, and waited. Sandy stood in the wide chapel door, looking dubiously at the dark coffin; Sir Thomas and Lady Macleod flanked her; and I could sense the shades gathering behind, waiting for the appearance of their promised king.

Minutes passed, and nothing happened. I could feel a wave of aching disappointment welling out from the congregation, and then I saw Sandy shake her head. "Maybe," I said, "it'll help if we can open the coffin and, ah, liberate the remains."

"Nay," Sandy said. "He should a' come, if he were comin'."

Sir Thomas seemed too stricken to speak; he had wilted into himself, despairing agony in his eyes. "I'm so sorry, Tommy," Lady Macleod said slowly. "I knew how much ye wanted it tae happen."

And then, with slow dignity, Prince Charles Edward Stuart, the Young Pretender, rose from the dead, first coming through the coffin lid to a sitting position, then rising awesomely to his full height. Sandy took a step back, thunderstruck. With slow astonishment, Sir Thomas went down on one knee in hushed reverence, and the rest of the spirits followed suit, their faces upturned, in blazing hope, to view Bonnie Prince Charlie as he rose.

He was a couple inches over six feet and handsome in an imperturbable way that can either reflect great strength of character or great density of mind—from what I'd heard of him, I'd suspect the latter. His eyes were blue, and he wore a white-powdered wig with side-curls. I had expected him to be dressed in the Highland tartan and homespun coats of his followers, but his clothes were of silk and cut to a continental pattern—knee breeches in garish yellow and green, lots of gold lace around the buttonholes of his coat, lace billowing at throat and wrist. He carried a long walking stick in his hand, and his speech, when it came, was purest Saxon upper crust.

"We are pleased," he said, "to have awwived at last. We are wegwetful that this has not happened sooner."

In other words, I thought, what took you so long? And please note there was not a word of thanks, either.

Bonnie Prince Charlie looked down his long nose at Sir Thomas. "We wecognize you, Sir Thomas MacDonald," he said. "Pway pwesent us to our subjects."

Sir Thomas, that proud, stiff-necked Highland laird, was gazing up at his king with the cringing, abject adoration of a basset hound for his master. Scraping like any serf, he stepped forward and said, "If it please Your Highness, may I present my living descendant, Sandra MacDonald." Sandy, looking up at the Young Pretender as if she had half a mind to tweak him by the nose to see if he was real, stepped forward and curtsied—which is not an easy motion in a kilt, by the way. The other

ghostly presences came forward to bow and back away, Sir Thomas giving their names where he knew them—some of the more obscure ones
he simply referred to as "Your Highness's loyal subject"—and last of all
he introduced me. I bowed civilly, but Prince Charles took no more notice of me than he would of any laborer, which is to say none.

"Is this all?" asked Charles Edward Stuart when all had come before
him. "Vewy well." He looked up at the chapel, at the dusty flags hung
on high, at the brass memorial plates screwed into the walls. "Will we
be staying here for the pwesent?" he asked, as if he didn't much relish
the idea. "Sir Thomas, I would be obliged if you would escort us to our
place of wesidence."

"O' course, Your Highness," Sir Thomas said, still bowing and scraping, and then he straightened and turned to his shades, his eyes shining
with Gaelic exultation. "Let us pipe the Prince to his bower!" he proclaimed. "God save the King!"

"God save the King!" they all echoed, the first sound most of them
had made; the words rang echoing from the walls of the small chapel,
filling the air with wild joy—and then drums crashed out from somewhere in the mob, and the pipes began to drone the most stirring of
the Highland marches, "Hey, Johnnie Cope, are ye waukin' yet?" the
wild and barbaric battle hymn commemorating the day the Highland
broadswords chopped up General Cope's redcoats at Prestonpans, one
of Charlie Stuart's better days...I put down my hammer and chisel and
went to stand near Sandy at the chapel doors as the procession surged
past, all the ghostly flickering spirits from all the ages since being a
Highlander had begun to mean something, all the old mountain folk
with the blaze of battle in their eye as they walked behind their king.
What did it matter that he was a fool or an ass? He was theirs, their old
king come back to his rightful place among them, and they were mad
with the joy of it. Even the old armored figure from above the gate was
there, his visor up to reveal a craggy old face with a white mustache, his
mouth open to cry, "*Vive le roi!*" Sandy pursed her lips.

"Ach, me," she said. "It disnae Sir David after all—he's some sort of
Frenchman." She shook her head. "I'll nae ever get it sortit oot. I've nae
seen half this lot before."

And then she shivered, and I took her hand, knowing how she felt.
We were alone, the two of us, among the long procession of the dead,

the half-seen, flickering figures who marched to the weird and savage call of the pipes, moving in their ghostly armor and twilight tartans, waving their fans and old pikes and ancient dim banners. We watched as they poured into the keep and the old tower's windows began to flash with strange, shifting light, and the courtyard echo to the sounds of ghostly revelry. We stood hand in hand and listened to the wild celebrations of the dead, and we could see those shadows marching on behind their dim piper, going on through the centuries, growing in numbers, eventually submerging the living beneath their roistering swarm, triumphing over death itself as they piped, and sang, and marched, obedient servants to their long-dead, newfound king.

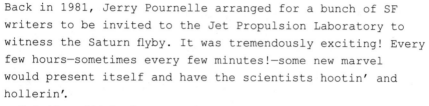

Back in 1981, Jerry Pournelle arranged for a bunch of SF writers to be invited to the Jet Propulsion Laboratory to witness the Saturn flyby. It was tremendously exciting! Every few hours—sometimes every few minutes!—some new marvel would present itself and have the scientists hootin' and hollerin'.

But they didn't have any beer.

So whenever there was a lull in the data, Jerry and I would wander down the road to where he'd parked his jeep with its big cooler of iced beer. We'd sit in the shade with long-necked Budweisers and talk of science and science fiction.

Star Wars had just come out, and I told Jerry how much I admired the scene with a bar full of aliens. Jerry was not so impressed. "Every science fiction writer has written the aliens-in-a-bar scene a dozen times," he said.

Well, not every one. Not me, for instance. So I did.

—Joe Haldeman

A !Tangled Web

JOE HALDEMAN

~~~~~~~~~

YOUR SPACEPORT BARS FALL INTO TWO DISTINCT GROUPS: the ones for the baggage and the ones for the crew. I was baggage, this trip, but didn't feel like paying the prices that people who space for fun can afford. The Facility Directory listed under "Food and Drink" four establishments: the Hartford Club (inevitably), the Silver Slipper Lounge, Antoine's, and Slim Joan's Bar & Grill.

I went to a currency exchange booth first, assuming that Slim Joan was no better at arithmetic than most bartenders, and cashed in a hundredth share of Hartford stock. Then I took the drop lift down to the bottom level. That the bar's door was right at the drop-lift exit would be a dead giveaway even if its name had been the Bell, Book, and Candle. Baggage don't generally like to fall ten stories, no matter how slowly.

It smelled right, stir-fry and stale beer, and the low lighting suggested economy rather than atmosphere. Slim Joan turned out to be about a hundred thousand grams of transvestite. Well, I hadn't come for the scenery.

The clientele seemed evenly mixed between humans and others, most of the aliens being !tang, since this was Morocho III. I've got nothing against the company of aliens, but if I was going to spend all next week wrapping my jaws around !tangish, I preferred to mix my drinking with some human tongue.

"Speak English?" I asked Slim Joan.

"Some," he/she/it growled. "You would drink something?" I'd never heard a Russian-Brooklyn accent before. I ordered a double saki, cold, in Russian, and took it to an empty booth.

One of the advantages of being a Hartford interpreter is that you can order a drink in a hundred different languages and dialects. Saves money; they figure if you can speak the lingo you can count your change.

I was freelancing this trip, though, working for a real-estate cartel that wanted to screw the !tang out of a few thousand square kilometers of useless seashore property. It wouldn't stay useless, of course.

Morocho III is a real garden of a planet, but most people never see it. The tachyon nexus is down by Morocho I, which we in the trade refer to as "Armpit," and not many people take the local hop out to III (Armpit's the stopover on the Earth-Sammler run). Starlodge, Limited, was hoping to change that situation.

I couldn't help eavesdropping on the !tangs behind me. (I'm not a snoop; it's a side effect of the hypnotic-induction learning process). One of them was leaving for Earth today, and the other was full of useless advice. "He"—they have seven singular pronoun classes, depending on the individual's age and estrous condition—was telling "her" never to make any reference to human body odor, no matter how vile it may be. He should also have told her not to breathe on anyone. One of the by-products of their metabolism is butyl nitrite, which smells like well-aged socks and makes humans get all faint and cross-eyed.

I've worked with !tangs a few times before, and they're some of my favorite people. Very serious, very honest, and their logic is closer to human logic than most. But they *are* strange-looking. Imagine a perambulating haystack with an elephant's trunk protruding. They have two arms under the pile of yellow hair, but it's impolite to take them out in public unless one is engaged in physical work. They do have sex in public, constantly, but it takes a zoologist with a magnifying glass to tell when.

He wanted her to bring back some Kentucky bourbon and Swiss chocolate. Their metabolisms part company with ours over protein and fats, but they love our carbohydrates and alcohol. The alcohol has a psychedelic effect on them, and sugar leaves them plastered.

A human walked in and stood blinking in the half-light. I recognized him and shrank back into the booth. Too late.

He strode over and stuck out his hand. "Dick Navarro!"

"Hello, Pete." I shook his hand once. "What brings you here? Hartford business?" Pete was also an interpreter.

—Oh, no, he said in Arabic. —Only journeying.

—Knock it off, I said in Serbo-Croatian. —Isn't your native language English? I added in Greek.

"Sure it is. Yours?"

"English or Spanish. Have a seat."

I smacked my lips twice at Slim Joan, and she came over with a menu. "To be eating you want?"

"Nyet," he said. "Vodka." I told her I'd take another.

"So what are you doing here?" Pete asked.

"Business."

"Hartford?"

"Nope."

"Secret."

"That's right." Actually, they hadn't said anything about its being secret. But I knew Peter Lafitte. He wasn't just passing through.

We both sat silently for a minute, listening to the !tangs. We had to smile when he explained to her how to decide which public bathroom to use when. This was important to humans, he said. Slim Joan came with the drinks and Pete paid for both, a bad sign.

"How did that Spica business finally turn out?" he asked.

"Badly." Lafitte and I worked together on a partition-of-rights hearing on Spica IV, with the Confederación actually bucking Hartford over an alien-rights problem. "I couldn't get the humans to understand that the minerals had souls, and I couldn't get the natives to believe that refining the minerals didn't affect their spiritual status. It came to a show of force, and the natives backed down. I wouldn't like to be there in twenty years, though."

"Yeah. I was glad to be recalled. Arcturus all over."

"That's what I tried to tell them." Arcturus wasn't a regular stop anymore, not since a ship landed and found every human artistically dismembered. "You're just sightseeing?"

"This has always been one of my favorite planets."

"Nothing to do."

"Not for you city boys. The fishing is great, though."

Ah ha. "Ocean fishing?"

"Best in the Confederación."

"I might give it a try. Where do you get a boat?"

He smiled and looked directly at me. "Little coastal village, Pa'an!al."

Smack in the middle of the tribal territory I'd be dickering for. I dutifully repeated the information into my ring.

I changed the subject and we talked about nothing for a while. Then I excused myself, saying I was time-lagging and had to get some sleep. Which was true enough, since the shuttle had stayed on Armpit time, and I was eight hours out of phase with III. But I bounced straight to the Hartford courier's office.

The courier on duty was Estelle Dorring, whom I knew slightly. I cut short the pleasantries. "How long to get a message to Earth?"

She studied the clocks on the wall. "You're out of luck if you want it hand-carried. I'm not going to Armpit tomorrow. Two days on the shuttle and I'll miss the Earth run by half a day.

"If broadcast is all right, you can beam to Armpit and the courier there will take it on the Twosday run. That leaves in seventy-two minutes. Call it nineteen minutes' beam time. You know what you want to say?"

"Yeah. Set it up." I sat down at the customers' console.

STARLODGE LIMITED
642 EASTRIVER
NEW YORK, NEW YORK 10099-27654
ATTENTION: PATRICE DUVAL

YOU MAY HAVE SOME COMPETITION HERE. NOTHING OPEN YET BUT A GUY WE CALL PETER RABBIT IS ON THE SCENE. CHECK INTERPRETERS GUILD AND SEE WHO'S PAYING PETER LAFITTE. CHANGE TERMS OF SALE? PLEASE SEND REPLY NEXT SAMMLER RUN—RICARDO NAVARRO/rm 2048/MOROCHO HILTON

I wasn't sure what good the information would do me, unless they also found out how much he was offering and authorized me to outbid him. At any rate, I wouldn't hear for three days, earliest. Sleep.

Morocho III—its real name is !ka'al—rides a slow sweeping orbit around Morocho A, the brighter of the two suns that make up the Morocho system (Morocho A is a close double star itself, but its white dwarf companion hugs so close that it's lost in the glare). At this time of day, Morocho B was visible low in the sky, a hard blue diamond too bright to stare at, and A was right overhead, a bloated golden ball. On the sandy beach below us the flyer cast two shadows, dark blue and faint yellow, which raced to come together as we landed.

Pa'an!al is a fishing village thousands of years old, on a natural harbor formed where a broad jungle river flows into the sea. Here on the beach were only a few pole huts with thatched roofs, where the fishers who worked the surf and shallow pools lived. Pa'an!al proper was behind a high stone wall, which protected it on one side from the occasional hurricane and on the other from the interesting fauna of the jungle.

I paid off my driver and told him to come back at second sundown. I took a deep breath and mounted the steps. There was an open-cage Otis elevator beside the stairs, but people didn't use it, only fish.

The !tang are compulsive about geometry. This wall was a precise 1:2 rectangle, and the stairs mounted from one corner to the opposite in a satisfying Euclidian 30 degrees. A guardrail would have spoiled the harmony. The stairs were just wide enough for two !tang to pass, and the rise of each step was a good half meter. By the time I got to the top I was both tired and slightly terrified.

A spacefaring man shouldn't be afraid of heights, and I'm not, so long as I'm in a vehicle. But when I attained the top of the wall and looked down the equally long and perilous flight of stairs to ground level, I almost swooned. Why couldn't they simply have left a door in the wall?

I sat there for a minute and looked down at the small city. The geometric regularity *was* pleasing. Each building was either a cube or a stack of cubes, and the rock from which the city was built had been carefully sorted, so that each building was a uniform shade. They went from white marble through sandy yellow and salmon to pearly gray and obsidian. The streets were a regular matrix of red brick. I walked down, hugging the wall.

At the bottom of the steps a !tang sat on a low bench, watching the nonexistent traffic. —Greetings, I clicked and snorted at him. —It is certainly a pleasant day.

—Not everywhere, he grunted and wheezed back. An unusually direct response.

—Are you waiting for me?

—Who can say? I am waiting. His trunk made a philosophical circle in the air. —If you had not come, who knows for what I would have been waiting?

—Well, that's true. He made a circle in the other direction, which I think meant What else? I stood there for a moment while he looked at me or the ground or the sky. You could never tell.

—I hope this isn't a rude question, he said. —Will you forgive me if this is a rude question?

—I certainly will try.

—Is your name !ica'o *va!o?

That was admirably close. —It certainly is.

—You could follow me. He got up. —Or enjoy the pleasant day.

I followed him closely down the narrow street. If he got in a crowd I'd lose him for sure. I couldn't tell an estrus-four female from a neuter, not having sonar (they tell each other apart by sensing body cavities, very romantic).

We went through the center of town, where the well and the market square were. A dozen !tang bargained over food, craft items, or abstractions. They were the most mercantile race on the planet, although they had sidestepped the idea of money in favor of labor equivalence: for those two ugly fish I will trade you an original sonnet about your daughter and three vile limericks for your next affinity-group meeting. Four limericks, tops.

We went into a large white building that might have been City Hall. It was evidently guarded, at least symbolically, since two !tang stood by the door with their arms exposed.

It was a single large room similar to a Terran mosque, with a regular pattern of square columns holding up the ceiling. The columns supported shelves in neat squares, up to about two meters; on the shelves were neat stacks of accordion-style books. Although the ceiling had inset squares of glass that gave adequate light, there was a strong smell of burnt fish oil, which meant the building was used at night. (We had introduced them to electricity, but they used it only for heavy machinery and toys.)

The !tang led me to the farthest corner, where a large haystack was bent over a book, scribbling. They had to read or write with their heads a few centimeters from the book, since their light-eyes were only good for close-work.

—It has happened as you foretold, Uncle. Not too amazing a prophecy, as I'd sent a messenger over yesterday.

Uncle waved his nose in my direction. —Are you the same one who came in four days ago?

—No. I have never been to this place. I am Ricardo Navarro, from the Starlodge tribe.

—I grovel in embarrassment. Truly it is difficult to tell one human from another. To my poor eyes you look exactly like Peter Lafitte.

(Peter Rabbit is bald and ugly, with terrible ears. I have long curly hair with only a trace of gray, and women have called me attractive.)— Please do not be embarrassed. This is often true when different peoples meet. Did my brother say what tribe he represented?

—I die. O my hair falls out and my flesh rots and my bones are cracked by the hungry ta!a'an. He drops me behind him all around the forest and nothing will grow where his excrement from my marrow falls. As the years pass the forest dies from the poison of my remains. The soil wash-es to the sea and poisons the fish, and all die. O the embarrassment.

—He didn't say?

—He did but said not to tell you.

That was that. —Did he by some chance say he was interested in the small morsel of land I mentioned to you by courier long ago?

—No, he was not interested in the land.

—Can you tell me what he was interested in?

—He was interested in *buying* the land.

Verbs. —May I ask a potentially embarrassing question?

He exposed his arms. —We are businessmen.

—What were the terms of his offer?

—I die. I breathe in and breathe in and cannot exhale. I explode all over my friends. They forget my name and pretend it is dung. They wash off in the square and the well becomes polluted. All die. O the em-barrassment.

—He said not to tell me?

—That's right.

—Did you agree to sell him the land?

—That is a difficult question to answer.

—Let me rephrase the question: is it possible you might sell the land to my tribe?

—It is possible, if you offer better terms. But only possible, in any case.

—This is embarrassing. I, uh, die and, um, the last breath from my

lungs is a terrible acid. It melts the seaward wall of the city and a hurricane comes and washes it away. All die. O the embarrassment.

—You're much better at it than he was.

—Thank you. But may I ask you to amplify the possibility?

—Certainly. Land is not a fish or an elevator. Land is something that
keeps you from falling all the way down. It gives the sea a shore and
makes the air stop. Do you understand?

—So far. Please continue.

—Land is time, but not in a mercantile sense. I can say "In return for
the time it takes me to decide which one of you is the guilty party, you
must give me so-and-so." But how can I say "In return for the land I
am standing on you must give me this-and-that?" Nobody can step off
the time, you see, but I can step off the land, and then what is it? Does
it even exist? In a mercantile sense? These questions and corollaries to
them have been occupying some of our finest minds ever since your
courier came long ago.

—May I make a suggestion?

—Please do. Anything might help.

—Why not just sell it to the tribe that offers the most?

—No, you don't see. Forgive me, you Terrans are very simpleminded
people, for all your marvelous Otis elevators and starships (this does
not embarrass me to say because it is meant to help you understand
yourself; if you were !tang you would have to pay for it). You see, there
are three mercantile classes. Things and services may be of no worth, of
measurable worth, or of infinite worth. Land has never been classified
before, and it may belong in any of the categories.

—But Uncle! The Lafitte and I have offered to buy the land. Surely
that eliminates the first class.

—O you poor Terran. I would hate to see you try to buy a fish. You
must think of all the implications.

—I die. I, uh, have a terrible fever in my head and it gets hotter and
hotter until my head is a fire, a forge, a star. I set the world on fire and
everybody dies. O the embarrassment. What implications?

—Here is the simplest. If the land has finite value, when at best all
it does is keep things from falling all the way down, how much is air
worth? Air is necessary for life, and it makes fires burn. If you pay for
land do you think we should let you have air for free?

—An interesting point, I said, thinking fast and !tangly. —But you have answered it yourself. Since air is necessary for life, it is of infinite value, and not one breath can be paid for with all the riches of the universe.

—O poor one, how can you have gotten through life without losing your feet? Air would be of infinite worth thus only if *life* were of infinite worth, and even so little as I know of your rich and glorious history proves conclusively that you place very little value on life. Other people's lives, at any rate. Sad to say, our own history contains a similarly bonehungry period.

—Neither are we that way now, Uncle.

—I die. My brain turns to maggots....

I talked with Uncle for an hour or so but got nothing out of it but a sore soft palate. When I got back to the hotel there was a message from Peter Lafitte, asking whether I would like to join him at Antoine's for dinner. No, I would not *like* to, but under the circumstances it seemed prudent. I had to rent a formal tunic from the bellbot.

Antoine's has all the *joie de vivre* of a frozen halibut, which puts it on par with every other French restaurant off Earth. We started with an artichoke vinaigrette that should have been left to rot in the hydroponics tank. Then a filet of "beef" from some local animal that I doubt was even warm-blooded. All this served by a waiter who was a Canadian with a fake Parisian accent.

But we also had a bottle of phony Pouilly-Fuissé followed by a bottle of ersatz Burgundy followed by a bottle of synthetic Château-d'Yquem. Then they cleared the table and set a bottle of brandy between us, and the real duel began. Short duel, it turned out.

"So how long is your vacation going to last?" I made a gesture that was admirably economical. "Not long at these prices."

"Well, there's always Slim Joan's." He poured himself a little brandy and me a lot. "How about yourself?"

"Ran into a snag," I said. "Have to wait until I hear from Earth."

"They're not easy to work with, are they?"

"Terrans? I'm one myself."

"The !tang, I mean." He stared into his glass and swirled the liquor. "Terrans as well, though. Could I set to you a hypothetical proposition?"

"My favorite kind," I said. The brandy stung my throat.

"Suppose you were a peaceable sort of fellow."

"I am." Slightly fuzzy, but peaceable.

"And you were on a planet to make some agreement with the natives."

I nodded seriously.

"Billions of bux involved. Trillions."

"That would really be something," I said.

"Yeah. Now further suppose that there's another Terran on this planet who, uh, is seeking to make the same sort of agreement."

"Must happen all the time."

"For trillions, Dick? Trillions?"

"Hyp'thetical trillions." Bad brandy, but strong.

"Now the people who are employing you are ab-solute-ly ruthless."

"*Ma!ryso'ta*," I said, the !tang word for "bonehungry." Close to it, anyway.

"That's right." He was starting to blur. More wine than I'd thought. "Stop at nothing. Now how would you go about warning the other Terran?"

My fingers were icy cold and the sensation was crawling toward my elbows. My chin slipped off my hand and my head was so heavy I could hardly hold it up. I stared at the two fuzzy images across the table. "Peter." The words came out slowly, and then not at all: "You aren't drinking...."

"Terrible brandy, isn't it." My vision went away, although it felt as if my eyes were still open. I heard my chin hit the table.

"Waiter?" I heard the man come over and make sympathetic noises. "My friend has had a little too much to drink. Would you help me get him to the bellbot?" I couldn't even feel them pick me up. "I'll take this brandy. He might want some in the morning." Jolly.

I finally lapsed into unconsciousness while we were waiting for the elevator, the bellbot lecturing me about temperance. I woke up the next afternoon on the cold tile floor of my suite's bathroom. I felt like I had been taken apart by an expert surgeon and reassembled by an amateur mechanic. I looked at the tile for a long time. Then I sat for a while and studied the interesting blotches of color floating between my eyes and my brain. When I thought I could survive it, I stood up and took four Hangaways.

I sat and started counting. Hangaways hit you like a pile driver. At eighty the adrenaline shock came. Tunnel vision and millions of tiny needles being pushed out through your skin. Rivers of sweat. Cathedral bells tolling, your head the clapper. Then the dry heaves and it was over.

I staggered to the phone and ordered some clear soup and a couple of cold beers. Then I stood in the shower and contemplated suicide. By the time the soup came I was contemplating homicide.

The soup stayed down and by the second beer I was feeling almost human. Neanderthal, anyhow. I made some inquiries. Lafitte had checked out. No shuttle had left, so he was either still on the planet or he had his own ship, which was possible if he was working for the outfit I suspected he was working for. I invoked the holy name of Hartford, trying to find out to whom his expenses had been billed. Cash.

I tried to order my thoughts. If I reported Lafitte's action to the Guild he would be disbarred. Either he didn't care, because They were paying him enough to retire in luxury—for which I knew he had a taste—or he actually thought I was not going to get off the planet alive. I discarded the dramatic second notion. Last night he could have more easily killed me than warned me. Or had he actually *tried* to kill me, the talk just being insurance in case I didn't ingest a fatal dose? I had no idea what the poison could have been. That sort of knowledge isn't relevant to my line of work.

I suppose the thoroughly rational thing would have been to sit tight and let him have the deal. The fortunes of Starlodge were infinitely less important to me than my skin. He could probably offer more than I could, anyhow.

The phone chimed. I thumbed the vision button and a tiny haystack materialized over the end table.

—Greetings. How is the weather?

—Indoors, it's fine. Are you Uncle?

—Not now. Inside the Council Building I am Uncle.

—I see. Can I perform some worthless service for you?

—For yourself, perhaps.

—Pray continue.

—Our Council is meeting with Lafitte this evening, with the hope of resolving this question about the mercantile nature of land. I would be embarrassed if you did not come too. The meeting will be at *ala'ang in the Council Building.

—I would not cause embarrassment. But could it possibly be postponed?

He exposed his arms. —We are meeting.

He disappeared and I spent a few minutes translating *ala'ang into human time. The !tang divide their day into a complicated series of varying time intervals depending on the position of the suns and state of appetite and estrous condition. Came to a little before ten o'clock, plenty of time.

I could report Lafitte, and probably should, but decided I'd be safer not doing so, retaining the threat of exposure for use as a weapon. I wrote a brief description of the situation—and felt a twinge of fear on writing the word "Syndicate"—and sealed it in an envelope. I wrote the address of the Hartford Translators' Guild across the seal and bounced up to the courier's office.

Estelle Dorring stared at me when I walked into the office. "Ricardo! You look like a corpse warmed over!"

"Rough night," I said. "Touch of food poisoning."

"I never eat that Tang stuff."

"Good policy." I set the envelope in front of her. "I'm not sure whether to send this or not. If I don't come get it before the next shuttle, take it to Armpit and give it to the next Earth courier."

She nodded slowly and read the address. "Why so mysterious?"

"Just a matter of Guild ethics. I wanted to write it down while it was still fresh. Uh...." I'd never seen a truly penetrating stare before. "But I might have more information tonight that would invalidate it."

"If you say so, Ricardo." She slipped the envelope into a drawer. I backed out, mumbling something inane.

Down to Slim Joan's for a sandwich of stir-fried vegetables in Syrian bread. Slightly rancid and too much curry, but I didn't dare go to the Council meeting on an empty stomach; !tang sonar would scan it and they would make a symbolic offer of bread, which wouldn't be refused. Estelle was partly right about "Tang" food: one bite of the bread contained enough mescaline to make you see interesting things for hours. I'd had enough of that for a while.

I toyed with the idea of taking a weapon. There was a rental service in the pharmacy, to accommodate the occasional sporting type, and I could pick up a laser or a tranquilizer there. But there would be no way to conceal it from the !tang sonar. Besides, Lafitte wasn't the kind of person who would employ direct violence.

But if it actually were the Syndicate behind Lafitte, they might well have sent more than one person here; they certainly could afford it. A hitter. But then why would Lafitte set up the elaborate poisoning scheme? Why not simply arrange an accident?

My feet were taking me toward the pharmacy. Wait. Be realistic. You haven't fired a gun in twenty years. Even then, you couldn't hit the ground with a rock. If it came to a burnout, you'd be the one who got crisped. Better to leave their options open.

I decided to compromise. There was a large clasp knife in my bag; that would at least help me psychologically. I went back up to my room.

I thumbed the lock and realized that the cube I'd heard playing was my own. The door slid open and there was Lafitte, lounging on my sofa, watching an old movie.

"Dick. You're looking well."

"How the hell did you get in here?"

He held up his thumb and ripped a piece of plastic off the fleshy part. "We have our resources." He sat up straight. "I hear you're taking a flyer out to Pa'an!al. Shall we divide the cost?"

There was a bottle of wine in a bucket of ice at his feet. "I suppose you charged this to my room." I turned off the cube.

He shrugged. "You poked me for dinner last night, *mon frère*. Passing out like that."

I raised the glass to my lips, flinched, and set it down untouched. "Speaking of resources, what was in that brandy? And who are these resourceful friends?"

"The wine's all right. You seemed agitated; I gave you a calmative."

"A *horse* calmative! Is it the Syndicate?"

He waved that away. "The Syndicate's a myth. You—"

"Don't take me for an idiot. I've been doing this for almost as long as you have." Every ten years or so there was a fresh debunking. But the money and bodies kept piling up.

"You have indeed." He concentrated on picking at a hangnail. "How much is Starlodge willing to pay?"

I tried not to react. "How much is the Syndicate?"

"If the Syndicate existed," he said carefully, "and if it were they who had retained me, don't you think I would try to use that fact to frighten you away?"

"Maybe not directly...last night, you said 'desperate men.'"

"I was drunk." No, not Peter Rabbit, not on a couple of bottles of wine. I just looked at him. "All right," he said, "I was told to use any measures short of violence—"

"Poisoning isn't violence?"

"Tranquilizing, not poisoning. You couldn't have died." He poured himself some wine. "Top yours off?"

"I've become a solitary drinker."

He poured the contents of my glass into his. "I might be able to save you some trouble, if you'll only tell me what terms—"

"A case of Jack Daniel's and all they can eat at Slim Joan's."

"That might do it," he said unsmilingly, "but I can offer fifteen hundred shares of Hartford."

That was $150 million, half again what I'd been authorized. "Just paper to them."

"Or a million cases of booze, if that's they way they want it." He checked his watch. "Isn't our flyer waiting?"

I supposed it would be best to have him along, to keep an eye on him. "The one who closes the deal pays for the trip?"

"All right."

On the hour-long flyer ride I considered various permutations of what I could offer, My memory had been jammed with the wholesale prices of various kinds of machinery, booze, candy, and so forth, along with their mass and volume, so I could add in the shipping costs from Earth to Armpit to Morocho III. Lafitte surely had similar knowledge; I could only hope that his figure of 1500 shares was a bluff.

(I had good incentive to bargain well. Starlodge would give me a bonus of up to ten percent of the difference between a thousand shares and whatever the settlement came to. If I brought it in at 900, I'd be a millionaire.)

We were turning inland; the walls of the city made a pink rectangle against the towering jungle. I tapped the pilot on the shoulder. "Can you land inside the city?"

"Not unless you want to jump from the top of a building. I can set you on the wall, though." I nodded.

"Can't take the climb, Dick? Getting old?"

"No need to waste steps." The flyer was a little wider than the wall, and it teetered as we stepped out. I tried to look just at my feet.

"Beautiful up here," Lafitte said. "Look at that sunset." Half the large sun's disk was visible on the jungle horizon, a deeper red than Earth's sun ever shone. The bloody light stained the surf behind us purple. It was already dark in the city below; the smell of rancid fish oil burning drifted up to us.

Lafitte managed to get the inside lane of the staircase. I tried to keep my eyes on him and the wall as we negotiated the high steps.

"Believe me," he said (a phrase guaranteed to inspire trust), "it would make both our jobs easier if I could tell you who I'm representing. But I really am sworn to secrecy."

An oblique threat deserves an oblique answer. "You know I can put you in deep trouble with the Standards Committee. Poisoning a Guild brother."

"Your word against mine. And the bellbot's, the headwaiter's, the wine steward's . . . you did have quite a bit to drink."

"A couple of bottles of wine won't knock me out."

"Your capacity is well known. I don't think you want a hearing investigating it, though, not at your age. Two years till retirement?"

"Twenty months."

"I was rounding off," he said. "Yes, I did check. I wondered whether you might be in the same position as I am. My retirement's less than two months away; this is my last big-money job. So you must understand my enthusiasm."

I didn't answer. He wasn't called Rabbit for lack of "enthusiasm."

As we neared the bottom, he said, "Suppose you weren't to oppose me too vigorously. Suppose I could bring in the contract at a great deal less than—"

"Don't be insulting."

In the dim light from the torches sputtering below, I couldn't read his expression. "Ten percent of my commission wouldn't be insulting."

I stopped short. He climbed another step. "I can't believe even *you*—"

"*Verdad.* Just joking." He laughed unconvincingly. "Everyone knows how starchy you are, Dick. I know better than most." I'd fined him several times during the years I was head of the Standards Committee.

We walked automatically through the maze of streets, our guides evidently having taken identical routes. Both of us had eidetic memories, of course, that being a minimum prerequisite for the job of an interpreter. I was thinking furiously. If I couldn't outbargain the Rabbit I'd have to somehow finesse him. Was there anything I knew about the !tang value system that he didn't? Assuming that this council would decide that land was something that could be bought and sold.

I did have a couple of interesting proposals in my portfolio, that I'd written up during the two-week trip from Earth. I wondered whether Lafitte had seen them. The lock didn't appear to have been tampered with, and it was the old-fashioned magnetic key type. You can pick it but it won't close afterward.

We turned a corner and there was the Council Building at the end of the street, impressive in the flickering light, its upper reaches lost in darkness. Lafitte put his hand on my arm, stopping. "I've got a proposition."

"Not interested."

"Hear me out, now; this is straight. I'm empowered to take you on as a limited partner."

"How generous. I don't think Starlodge would like it."

"What I *mean* is Starlodge. You hold their power of attorney, don't you?"

"Unlimited, on this planet. But don't waste your breath; we get an exclusive or nothing at all." Actually, the possibility had never been discussed. They couldn't have known I was going into a competitive bidding situation. If they had, they certainly wouldn't have sent me here slow freight. For an extra fifty shares I could have gone first class and been here a week before Peter Rabbit; could have sewn up the thing and been headed home before he got to the Armpit.

Starlodge had a knack for picking places that were about to become popular—along with impressive media power, to make sure they did—and on dozens of worlds they did have literally exclusive rights to tourism. Hartford might own a spaceport hotel, but it wasn't really competition, and they were usually glad to hand it over to Starlodge anyhow. Hartford, with its ironclad lock on the tachyon drive, had no need to diversify.

There was no doubt in my mind that this was the pattern Starlodge had in mind for Morocho III. It was a perfect setup, the beach being a geologic anomaly: there wasn't another spot for a hotel within two thousand kilometers of the spaceport. Just bleak mountaintops sprouting occasionally out of jungles full of large and hungry animals. But maybe I could lead the Rabbit on. I leaned up against a post that supported a guttering torch. "At any rate, I certainly couldn't consider entering into an agreement without knowing who you represent."

He looked at me stone-faced for a second. "Outfit called A. W. Stoner Industries."

I laughed out loud. "Real name, I mean." I'd never heard of Stoner, and I do keep in touch.

"That's the name I know them by."

"No concern not listed in *Standard, Poor and Tueme* could come up with nine figures for extraterrestrial real-estate speculation. No legitimate concern, I mean."

"There you go again," he said mildly. "I believe they're a coalition of smaller firms."

"I don't. Let's go."

Back in my luggage I had a nasal spray that deadened the sense of smell. Before we even got inside, I knew I should have used it.

The air was gray with fish-oil smoke, and there were more than a hundred !tang sitting in neat rows. I once was treated to a "fish kill" in Texas, where a sudden ecological disaster had resulted in windrows of rotting fish piled up on the beach. This was like walking along that beach using an old sock for a muffler. By Lafitte's expression, he was also unprepared. We both walked forward with slightly green cheerfulness.

A !tang in the middle of the first row stood up and approached us. —Uncle? I ventured, and he waved his snout in affirmation.

—We have come to an interim decision, he said.

—Interim? Lafitte said. —Were my terms unacceptable?

—I die. My footprints are cursed. I walk around the village not knowing that all who cross where I have been will stay in estrous zero, and bear no young. Eventually, all die. O the embarrassment. We want to hear the terms of Navarro's tribe. Then perhaps a final decision may be made.

This was frighteningly direct. I'd tried for an hour to tell him our terms before, but he'd kept changing the subject.

—May I hear the terms of Lafitte's tribe? I asked.

—Certainly. Would Lafitte like to state them, or should I?

—Proceed, Uncle, Lafitte said, and then, in Spanish, —Remember the possibility of a partnership. If we get to haggling....

I stopped listening to the Rabbit as Uncle began a long litany of groans, creaks, pops, and whistles. I kept a running total of wholesale prices and shipping costs. Bourbon, rum, brandy, gin. Candy bars, raw sugar, honey, pastries. Nets, computers, garbage compactors, water-purifying plant, hunting weapons. When he stopped, I had a total of only H620.

—Your offer, Navarro? Could it include these things as a subset?

I had to be careful. Lafitte was probably lying about the 1500, but I didn't want to push him so hard he'd be able to go over a thousand on the next round. And I didn't want to bring out my big guns until the very end.

—I can offer these things and three times the specified quantity of rum—(the largest distillery on Earth was a subsidiary of Starlodge)—and furthermore free you from the rigors of the winter harvest, with twenty-six fully programmed mechanical farm laborers. (The winters here were not even cool by Earth standards, but something about the season made the local animals restless enough to occasionally jump over the walls that normally protected farmland.)

—These mechanical workers would not be good to eat? For the animals?

—No, and they would be very hard for the animals even to damage.

There was a lot of whispered conversation. Uncle conferred with the !tang at the front of each row, then returned.

—I die. Before I die my body turns hair-side-in. People come from everywhere to see the insides of themselves. But the sight makes them lose the will, and all die. O the embarrassment. The rum is welcome, but we cannot accept the mechanical workers. When the beast eats someone he sleeps, and can be killed, and eaten in turn. If he does not eat he will search, and in searching destroy crops. This we know to be true.

—Then allow me to triple the quantities of gin, bourbon, and brandy. I will add two tons each of vermouth and hydrochloric acid, for flavoring. (That came to about H710.)

—This is gratefully accepted. Does your tribe, Lafitte, care to include these as a subset of your final offer?

—Final offer, Uncle?

—Two legs, two arms, two eyes, two mouths, two offers.

—I die, Lafitte said. —When they bury me, the ground caves in. It swallows up the city and all die, O the embarrassment. Look, Uncle, that's the market law for material objects. You can't move land around; its ownership is an abstraction.

Uncle exposed one arm—the Council tittered—and reached down and thumped the floor twice. —The land is solid, therefore material. You can move it around with your machines; I myself saw you do this in my youth, when the spaceport was built. The market law applies.

Lafitte smiled slowly. —Then the Navarro's tribe can no longer bid. He's had two.

Uncle turned toward the Council and gestured toward Rabbit, and said, —Is he standing on feet? And they cracked and snuffled at the joke. To Lafitte, he said, —The Navarro's offer was rejected, and he made a substitution. Yours was not rejected. Do you care to make his amended offer a subset of yours?

—If mine is rejected, can I amend it?

This brought an even louder reaction. —Poor one, Uncle said. —No feet, no hands. That would be a third offer. You must see that.

—All right. Lafitte began pacing. He said he would start with my amended offer and add the following things. The list was very long. It started with a hydroelectric generator and proceeded with objects of less and less value until he got down to individual bottles of exotic liqueurs. By then I realized he was giving me a message: he was coming down as closely as he could to exactly a thousand shares of Hartford. So we both had the same limit. When he finished he looked right at me and raised his eyebrows.

Victory is sweet. If the Rabbit had bothered to spend a day or two in the market, watching transactions, he wouldn't have tried to defeat me by arithmetic; he wouldn't have tried by accretion to force me into partnership.

Uncle looked at me and bared his arms for a split second. —Your tribe, Navarro? Would you include this offer as a subset to your final offer?

What Rabbit apparently didn't know was that this bargaining by pairs of offers was a formalism: if I did simply add to his last offer, the haggling would start over again, with each of us allowed another pair. I unlocked my briefcase and took out two documents.

—No. I merely wish to add two inducements to my own previous offer (sounds of approval and expectation).

Lafitte stared, his expression unreadable.

—These contracts are in Spanish. Can you read them, Uncle?

—No, but there are two of us who can.

—I know how you like to travel. (I handed him one of the documents.) —This allows each of five hundred !tang a week's vacation on the planet of its choice, any planet where Starlodge has facilities.

"What?" Lafitte said, in English. "How the hell can you do that?"

"Deadheading," I said.

One of the Council abruptly rose. "Pardon me," he said in a weird parody of English. "We have to be dead to take this vacation? That seems of little value."

I was somewhat startled at that, in view of the other inducement I was going to offer. I told him it was an English term that had nothing to do with heads or death. —Most of the Hartford vessels that leave this planet are nearly empty. It is no great material loss to Hartford to take along nonpaying guests, so long as they do not displace regular passengers. And Hartford will ultimately benefit from an increase in tourism to !ka'al, so they were quite willing to make this agreement with my tribe.

—The market value of this could be quite high, Uncle said.

—As much as five or six hundred shares, I said, —depending on how distant each trip is.

—Very well. And what is your other inducement?

—I won't say. (I had to grin.) —It is a gift.

The Council chattered and tweeted in approval. Some even exposed their arms momentarily in a semi-obscene gesture of fellowship. "What kind of game are you playing?" Peter Rabbit said.

"They like surprises and riddles." I made a polite sound requesting attention and said, —There is one thing I will tell you about this gift: It belongs to all three mercantile classes. It is of no value, of finite value, and infinite value, all at once, and to all people.

—When considered as being of finite value, Uncle said, —how much is it worth in terms of Hartford stock?

—Exactly one hundred shares.

He rustled pleasantly at that and went to confer with the others.

"You're pretty clever, Dick," Rabbit said. "What, they don't get to find out what the last thing is unless they accept?"

"That's right. It's done all the time; I was rather surprised that you didn't do it."

He shook his head. "I've only negotiated with !tang off-planet. They've always been pretty conventional."

I didn't ask him about all the fishing he had supposedly done here. Uncle came back and stood in front of us.

—There is unanimity. The land will go to Navarro's tribe. Now what is the secret inducement, please? How can it be every class at once, to all people?

I paused to parse out the description in !tangish. —Uncle, do you know of the Earth corporation, or tribe, Immortality Unlimited?

—No.

Lafitte made a strange noise. I went on. —This Immortality Unlimited provides a useful service to humans who are apprehensive about death. They offer the possibility of revival. A person who avails himself of this service is frozen solid as soon as possible after death. The tribe promises to keep the body frozen until such time as science discovers a way to revive it.

—The service is expensive. You pay the tribe one full share of Hartford stock. They invest it, and take for themselves one tenth of the income, which is their profit. A small amount is used to keep the body frozen. If and when revival is possible, the person is thawed, and cured of whatever was killing him, and he will be comparatively wealthy.

—This has never been done with nonhumans before, but there is nothing forbidding it. Therefore I purchased a hundred "spaces" for !tang; I leave it to you to decide which hundred will benefit.

—You see, this is of no material value to any living person, because you must die to take advantage of it. However, it is also of finite worth, since each space costs one share of Hartford. It is also of infinite worth, because it offers life beyond death.

The entire Council applauded, a sound like a horde of locusts descending. Peter Rabbit made the noise for attention, and then he made it again, impolitely loud.

—This is all very interesting, and I do congratulate the Navarro for his cleverness. However, the bidding is not over.

There was a low, nervous whirring. "Better apologize first, Rabbit," I whispered.

He bulled ahead. —Let me introduce a new mercantile class: negative value.

"Rabbit, don't—"

—This is an object or service that one does *not* want to have. I will offer not to give it to you if you accept my terms rather than the Navarro's.

—Many kilometers up the river there is a drum full of a very powerful poison. If I touch the button that opens it, all of the fish in the river, and for a great distance out into the sea, will die. You will have to move or. . . . He trailed off.

One by one, single arms snaked out, each holding a long sharp knife.

"Poison again, Rabbit? You're getting predictable in your old age."

"Dick," he said hoarsely, "they're completely nonviolent. Aren't they?"

"Except in matters of trade." Uncle was the last one to produce a knife. They moved toward us very slowly. "Unless you do something fast, I think you're about to lose your feet."

"My God! I thought that was just an expression."

"I think you better start apologizing. Tell them it was a joke."

—I die! he shouted, and they stopped advancing. —I, um . . .

—You play a joke on your friends and it backfires, I said in Greek.

Rapidly: —I play a joke on my good friends and it backfires. I, uh. . . . "Christ, Dick, help me."

"Just tell the truth and embroider it a little. They know about negative value, but it's an obscenity."

—I was employed by . . . a tribe that did not understand mercantilism. They asked me, of all things, to introduce the terms of negative value into a trivial transaction. My friends know I must be joking and they laugh. They laugh so much they forget to eat. All die. O the embarrassment.

Uncle made a complicated pass with his knife and it disappeared into his haybale fur. All the other knives remained in evidence, and the !tang moved into a circle around us.

—This machine in your pocket, Uncle said, —it is part of the joke?

Lafitte pulled out a small gray box. —It is. Do you want it?

—Put it on the floor. The fun would be complete if you stayed here while the Navarro took one of your marvelous floaters up the river. How far would he have to go to find the rest of the joke?

—About twelve kilometers. On an island in midstream.

Uncle turned to me and exposed his arms briefly. —Would you help us with our fun?

The air outside was sweet and pure. I decided to wait a few hours, for light.

That was some years ago, but I still remember vividly going into the Council Building the next day. Uncle had divined that Peter Rabbit was getting hungry, and they'd filled him up with !tang bread. When I came in, he was amusing them with impersonations of various Earth vegetables. The effect on his metabolism was not permanent, but when he left Morocho III he was still having mild attacks of cabbageness.

By the time I retired from Hartford, Starlodge had finished its hotel and sports facility on the beach. I was the natural choice to manage it, of course, and though I was wealthy enough not to need employment, I took the job with enthusiasm.

I even tried to hire Lafitte as an assistant—people who can handle !tang are rare—but he had dropped out of sight. Instead, I found a young husband-and-wife team who have so much energy that I hardly have to work at all.

I'm not crazy enough to go out in the woods, hunting. But I do spend a bit of time fishing off the dock, usually with Uncle, who has also retired. Together we're doing a book that I think will help our two cultures understand one another. The human version is called *Hard Bargain*.

~~~~~~~~~~~~~~~~

One day, Marty Greenberg asked me to contribute a story to
After The King, which would feature Tolkienesque fantasy
stories. Ordinarily I would have politely declined, as I'm
one of the few people on Earth who isn't especially fond of
Tolkien—but it was the highest-paying fantastic anthology in
history (up to that time, anyway), so of course I consented.
And wondered what the hell to do next.

Well, Tolkien and his serial imitators loved cute,
undersized, mildly human critters, so I supposed I'd have to
do something with that. It just so happens that my wife was
watching a tape of Disney's *Fantasia* that evening, and when
I passed through the room where it was playing on the TV
set, it was at the part that showed the sugar plum fairies
skating across the ice. I took one look and decided that
I might as well write about them as any other undersized
creatures—but they were so damned *cute* I was afraid I
might go into insulin shock. And then I thought, rather
perversely: "Why do I have to make them sweet and innocent?
This is an *assignment*; he *can't* turn it down."

So in the end I combined a little Tolkien and a little
Disney into a story that is, for better or worse, uniquely
Resnick. *Somebody* must like what I did with it; a decade
later I'm still selling it all over the world and cashing
checks on the original every six months.

—*Mike Resnick*

Revolt of the Sugar Plum Fairies

MIKE RESNICK

A RTHUR CRUMM DIDN'T BELIEVE IN LEPRECHAUNS.

He didn't believe in centaurs, either.

He also didn't believe in ghosts or goblins or gorgons or anything else beginning with a G. Oh, and you can add H to the list; he didn't believe in harpies or hobbits, either.

In fact, you could write an awfully thick book about the things he didn't believe in. You'd have had to leave out only one item: the one about the Sugar Plum Fairies.

Them, he believed in.

Of course, he had no choice. He had a basement full of them.

They were various shades of blue, none of them more than eighteen inches tall, and possessed of high, squeaky voices that would have driven his cats berserk if he had owned any cats. Their eyes were large and round, rather like they had been drawn by someone who specialized in painting children on black velvet, and their noses were small and pug, and each of them had a little pot belly, and they were dressed as if they were about to be presented to Queen Elizabeth. They looked cloyingly cute, and they made Mickey Mouse sound like a baritone—but they had murder on their minds.

They had been in Arthur's basement for less than an hour, but already he had managed to differentiate them, which was harder than you might think with a bunch of tiny blue fairies. There was Bluebell, who struck Arthur as the campus radical of the bunch. There was Indigo, with his Spanish accent, and old Silverthorne, the arch-conservative, and Purpletone, the politician, and Inkspot, who spoke jive like he had been born to it. Royal Blue seemed to be their leader, and there was also St. Looie Blues, standing off by himself playing a mournful if tiny saxophone.

367

"Well, I still don't understand how you guys got here," Arthur was saying.

Now, most men are not really inclined to sit on their basement stairs and converse with a bunch of Sugar Plum Fairies, but Arthur was a pragmatist. Their presence meant one of two things: either he was quite mad, or his house was infested with fairies. And since he didn't feel quite mad, he decided to assume that the latter was the case.

"I keep telling you: We came here by interdimensional quadrature," snapped Bluebell. "Open your ears, fathead!"

"That's no way to speak to our host," said Purpletone placatingly.

"Host, *schmost!*" snapped Bluebell. "If he was our host, he'd set us free. He's our captor."

"*I* didn't capture you," noted Arthur mildly. "I came down here and found you all stuck to the floor."

"That's because some of the Pepsi you stored leaked all over the floor," said Bluebell. "What kind of fiend stores defective pop bottles in his basement, anyway?"

"You could at least have carpeted the place," added Silverthorne. "It's not only sticky, it's *cold*."

"Now set us free so we can take our grim and terrible vengeance," continued Bluebell.

"On *me*?" asked Arthur.

"You are an insignificant spear carrier in the pageant of our lives," said Royal Blue. "We have a higher calling."

"Right, man," chimed in Inkspot. "You let us free, maybe we don't mess you up, you dig?"

"It seems to me that if I *don't* let you free you won't mess me up, either," said Arthur.

"You see?" said Indigo furiously. "I tole you and I tole you: you can't trust Gringos!"

"If you don't like Gringos, why did you choose *my* basement?" asked Arthur.

"Well, uh, we didn't exactly *choose* it," said Royal Blue uneasily.

"Then how did you get here?"

"By interdimensional quadrature, dummy!" said Bluebell, who finally succeeded in removing his feet from his shoes, only to have them stick onto the floor right next to the empty shoes.

"So you keep saying," answered Arthur. "But it doesn't mean anything to me."

"So it's *my* fault that you're a scientific illiterate?" demanded Bluebell, grabbing his left foot and giving it a mighty tug to no avail.

"Try explaining it another way," suggested Arthur, as Bluebell made another unsuccessful attempt to move his feet.

"Let *me* try," said Silverthorne. He turned his head so that he was facing Arthur. "We activated the McLennon/Whittaker Space-Time Displacement Theorem, but we didn't take the Helmhiser Variables or the Kobernykov Uncertainty Principle into account." He paused. "There. Does that help?"

"Not very much," admitted Arthur.

"What difference does it make?" said Royal Blue. "We're here, and that's all that matters."

"I'm still not clear why you're here at all," persisted Arthur.

"It's a matter of racial pride," answered Royal Blue with some dignity.

Arthur scratched his head. "You're proud of being stuck to the floor of my basement?"

"No, of course not," said old Silverthorne irritably. "We're here to defend our honor."

"How?"

"We've mapped out a campaign of pillage and destruction and vengeance," explained Royal Blue. "The entire world will tremble before us. Strong men will swoon, women and children will hide behind locked doors, even animals will scurry to get out of our path."

"A bunch of Sugar Plum Fairies who can't even get their feet unstuck from the floor?" said Arthur with a chuckle.

"Don't underestimate us," said Bluebell in his falsetto voice. "We Sugar Plum Fairies are tough dudes. We are capable of terrorizing entire communities." He grimaced. "Or we would be, if we could just get our feet free."

"And the seven of you are the advance guard?"

"What advance guard? We're the entire invasion force."

"An invasion force of just seven Sugar Plum Fairies?" repeated Arthur.

"Didn't you ever see *The Magnificent Seven*?" asked Royal Blue. "Yul

Brynner didn't need more than seven gunslingers to tame that Mexican town."

"And Toshiro Mifune only needed seven swordsmen in *The Seven Samurai*," chimed in Bluebell.

"Seven is obviously a mystical number of great spiritual power," said Purpletone.

"Besides, no one else would come," added Silverthorne.

"Has anyone thought to point out that you're neither seven swordsmen nor seven gunfighters?" asked Arthur. "You happen to be seven undersized, pot-bellied, and totally helpless fairies."

"Hey, baby," said Inkspot. "We may be small, but we're wiry."

"Yeah," added Indigo. "We sleet some throats, watch some feelthy videos, and then we go home."

"If we can figure out how to get there," added Silverthorne.

"We tried invading the world *your* way and look where it got us," said Bluebell irritably. "On the way home, we'll take the second star to the right."

"Thass an old wives' tale," protested Purpletone.

"Yeah?" shot back Bluebell. "How would *you* do it?"

"Simple. You close your eyes, click your heels together three times and say 'There's no place like home'," answered Purpletone. "Any fool knows that."

"Who are you calling a fool?" demanded Bluebell.

"Uh...I don't want to intrude on your argument," put in Arthur, "but I have a feeling that both of you are the victims of false doctrine."

"Okay, wise guy!" squeaked Bluebell. "How would *you* do it?"

Arthur shrugged. "I haven't the foggiest notion where you came from."

"From Sugar Plum Fairyland, of course! How dumb can you be?"

"Oh, I can be pretty dumb at times," conceded Arthur. "But I've never been dumb enough to get stuck to the floor of a basement in a strange world with no knowledge of how to get home."

"All right," admitted Bluebell grudgingly. "So we got a little problem here. Don't make a federal case out of it."

"Be sure and tell me when you have a *big* problem," said Arthur. "The mind boggles."

"You stop making fun of us, Gringo," said Indigo, "or we're gonna add you to the list."

"The list of people you plan to kill?"

"You got it, hombre."

"Just out of curiosity, how long *is* this list?" asked Arthur.

"Well," said Royal Blue, "so far, at a rough count, an estimate, so to speak, it comes to three."

"Who are they?" asked Arthur curiously.

"Number One on our hit list is Walt Disney," said Royal Blue firmly.

"And the other two?"

"That choreographer—what was his name—oh, yeah: Balanchine. And the Russian composer, Tchaikovsky."

"What did they ever do to you?" asked Arthur.

"They made us laughingstocks," said Bluebell. "Disney made us cute and cuddly in *Fantasia,* and Balanchine had us dancing on our tippy-toes in *The Nutcracker.* How are we expected to discipline our kids with an image like that? Our women giggle at us when they should be swooning. Our children talk back to us. Our enemies pay absolutely no attention when we lay siege to their cities." The little fairy paused for breath. "We *warned* that Russkie what would happen if he didn't change it to the '*March* of the Sugar Plum Fairies.' Now we're going to make him pay!"

"I don't know how to lay this on you," said Arthur, "but all three of them are dead."

St. Looie Blues immediately began playing a jazz version of "Happy Days Are Here Again" on his saxophone.

"Stop that!" squeaked Bluebell furiously.

"Whassa matter, man?" asked St. Looie Blues.

"This is nothing to celebrate! We've been robbed of our just and terrible vengeance!"

"If they were all the size of this here dude," said St. Looie Blues, indicating Arthur, "you wasn't gonna be able to do much more than bite each of 'em on the great toe, anyway." He went back to playing his instrument.

"Well, what are we going to do?" asked Bluebell in a plaintive whine. "We can't have come all this way for nothing!"

"Maybe we could kill each of their firstborn sons," suggested Purple-tone. "It's got a nice religious flavor to it."

"Maybe we should just go home," said Royal Blue.

"Never!" said Bluebell. "They still perform the ballet, they still listen to the symphony, they still show the movie!"

"In 70-millimeter, these days," added Arthur helpfully.

"But how can we stop them?" asked Royal Blue.

"I suppose we'll have to kill every musician and dancer on this world, and destroy all the prints of the movie," said Silverthorne.

"Right!" said Bluebell. "Let's go!"

Nobody moved.

"Arthur, old friend," said Purpletone. "I wonder if we could appeal to you, as one of the potential survivors of our forthcoming bloody war of conquest, to get us unstuck."

Arthur sighed. "I don't think so."

"Why not?" asked Royal Blue. "We've told you everything you want to know, and *you're* not on our hit list."

"It would be murder."

"Definitions change when you're in a state of war," responded Purpletone. "We don't consider ourselves to be murderers."

Arthur shook his head. "You don't understand. *They* would murder *you*."

"Preposterous!" squeaked Bluebell.

"Ridiculous," added Silverthorne.

"Do you have any weapons?" asked Arthur.

"No," admitted Bluebell. "But we've got a lot of gumption. We fear absolutely nothing."

"Well, that's not entirely true," said Purpletone after a moment's consideration. "Personally, I'm scared to death of banshees, moat monsters, and high cholesterol levels."

"*I'm* terrified of heights," added Royal Blue. "And I don't like the dark very much, either."

Soon all of the Sugar Plum Fairies were making long lists of things that frightened them.

"Well, some of us are hardly afraid of anything, with certain exceptions," amended Bluebell weakly. "And the rest can be bold and daring under rigidly defined conditions."

"If I were you, I'd pack it in and go home," said Arthur.

"We can't!" said Bluebell. "Even if we knew how to get there, we can't face our people and tell them that our mission was a failure, that we never even got out of your basement."

"I know you've got our best interests at heart, Arthur," added Silverthorne. "But we've got our pride."

"So now," concluded Royal Blue, "if you'll just help free us, we'll be on our way, leaving a modest trail of death and destruction in our wake."

Arthur shook his head. "You're going about it all wrong."

"What do *you* know about cataclysmic wars of revenge?" demanded Bluebell.

"Nothing," admitted Arthur.

"Well, then."

"But I *do* know that killing a bunch of people, even if you had the power to do it, wouldn't keep *Fantasia* from getting re-released every couple of years."

"That's what *you* say," replied Bluebell with more conviction than he felt.

"That's what I *know*," said Arthur. He paused. "Look, I don't know why I should want to help you, except that you're cute as buttons" —all seven of them growled high falsetto growls at this— "and I don't think I really believe in you anyway. But if it was *me* planning this operation," he continued, "I'd break into the Disney distribution computer and recall all the copies of *Fantasia*. I mean, it beats the hell out of going to every theater in the world looking for a handful of prints."

"That's a *great* idea!" said Royal Blue enthusiastically. "Men, isn't that a great idea? Simply marvelous!" He paused for a moment. "By the way, Arthur, what's a computer?"

Arthur explained it to them.

"That's all very well and good," said Silverthorne when Arthur had finished, "but how does it prevent the ballet from ever being performed?"

"I would imagine that Balanchine's notes—the play-by-play, so to speak—have been computerized by now," answered Arthur. "Just find the proper computer and wipe them out."

"And Tchaikovsky's music?"

Arthur shrugged. "That's a little more difficult."

"Well, two out of three ain't bad," said Inkspot. "You're an okay guy, Arthur, for someone what ain't even blue."

"Yeah, Gringo," added Indigo. "My sombrero's off to you. Or it would be, if I could find a sombrero in my size."

"Okay, Arthur," said Royal Blue. "We're primed to go. Just set us free and point us in the right direction."

"We're a long way from California," said Arthur as he began freeing each fairy in turn. "How do you plan to get there?"

"The same way we got here," answered Silverthorne.

"In which case you'll probably end up in Buenos Aires," said Arthur.

"A telling point," agreed Purpletone.

"We could fly," suggested Silverthorne.

"Great idea!" said Purpletone enthusiastically. Then he paused and frowned. "*Can* we fly?"

"I dunno, man," said Inkspot, flapping his arms. "If we can, I sure don't remember how."

"I'm afraid of heights anyway," said Royal Blue. "We'll have to find another way."

"Maybe we could reduce our bodies to their composite protons and electrons and speed there through the telephone lines,"suggested Bluebell.

"You first," said Purpletone.

"Me?" said Bluebell.

"Why not? It's your idea, isn't it?"

"Well, I thought of it, so it's only fair that someone else should test it out," said Bluebell petulantly.

"Maybe we could hitchhike," suggested Indigo.

"What do you think, Arthur?" said Royal Blue. He looked around the basement. "Hey, where did Arthur go?"

"If he's reporting us to the authorities, I'm gonna give him such a kick on the shin . . ." said Bluebell.

Suddenly Arthur appeared at the head of the stairs with a large box in his hands.

"I got tired of listening to you squabble," he said, carrying the box down to the basement.

"What's that for?" asked Royal Blue, nervously pointing to the box.

"Get in," said Arthur, starting to pry them loose from the floor.

"All of us?"

Arthur nodded.

"Why?"

"I'm shipping you to the Disney corporate offices," answered Arthur. "Once you're there, you're on your own."

"Great!" cried Royal Blue. "Now we can wreak havoc amongst our enemies and redeem the honor of our race."

"Or at least get a couple of gigs at Disneyland," added St. Looie Blues.

It was two weeks later that Arthur Crumm returned home from work, a bag of groceries in his arms, and found the seven Sugar Plum Fairies perched on various pieces of furniture in his living room.

Bluebell was wearing sunglasses and a set of gold chains. Indigo was smoking a cigar that was at least as long as he was. Silverthorne had a small diamond tiepin pierced through his left ear. St. Looie Blues had traded in his saxophone for a tiny music synthesizer. The others also displayed telltale signs of their recent excursion to the West Coast.

"How the hell did you get in here?" said Arthur.

"United Parcel got us to the front door," answered Royal Blue. "We took care of the rest. I hope you don't mind."

"I suppose not," said Arthur, setting down his bag. "You're look-ing...ah...well."

"We're *doing* well," said Royal Blue. "And we owe it all to you, Arthur."

"So you really managed to stop distribution of *Fantasia*?"

"Oh, *that*," said Bluebell with a contemptuous shrug. "We found out that we were meant for better things."

"Oh? I thought your goal was to destroy every last print of the film."

"That was before we learned to work their computer," answered Blue-bell. "Arthur, do you know how much money that film makes year in and year out?"

"Lots," guessed Arthur.

"'Lots' is an understatement," said Royal Blue. "The damned thing's a gold mine, Arthur—and there's a new generation of moviegoers every couple of years."

"Okay, so you didn't destroy the prints," said Arthur. "What *did* you do?"

"We bought a controlling interest in Disney!" said Bluebell proudly.

"You did *what*?"

"Disney," repeated Bluebell. "We own it now. We're going to be man-ufacturing Sugar Plum Fairy dolls, Sugar Plum Fairy T-shirts, Sugar Plum Fairy breakfast cereals...."

"Carnage and pillage are all very well in their place," explained Pur-pletone. "But *marketing*, Arthur—that's where the *real* power lies!"

"How did you manage to afford it?" asked Arthur curiously.

"We're not very good at dimensional quadrature," explained Royal Blue, "but we found that we have a real knack for computers. We simply manipulated the stock market—buying the New York City Ballet and all the rights to Balanchine's notes in the process—and when we had enough money, we sold Xerox short, took a straddle on Polaroid, and bought Disney on margin." He looked incredibly pleased with of himself. "Nothing to it."

"And what about Tchaikovsky?"

"We can't stop people from listening," replied Bluebell, "but we now own a piece of every major recording company in America, England, and the Soviet Union. We'll have the distribution channels tied up in another three weeks' time." He paused. "Computers are *fun!*"

"So are you going back to Sugar Plum Fairyland now?" asked Arthur.

"Certainly not!" said Royal Blue. "Anyone can be a Sugar Plum Fairy. It takes a certain innate skill and nobility to be a successful corporate raider, to properly interpret price-earnings ratios and find hidden assets, to strike at just the proper moment and bring your enemy to his financial knees."

"I suppose it does."

"Especially when you're handicapped the way we are," continued Royal Blue. "We can't very well address corporate meetings, we can't use a telephone that's more than twenty inches above the floor, we can only travel in UPS packages...."

"We don't even have a mailing address," added Purpletone.

"The biggest problem, though," said Bluebell, "is that none of us has a social security number or a taxpayer ID. That means that the Internal Revenue Service will try to impound all our assets at the end of the fiscal year."

"To say nothing of what the SEC will do," put in Silverthorne mournfully.

"You don't say," mused Arthur.

"We do say," replied Bluebell. "In fact, we just did."

"Then perhaps you'll be amenable to a suggestion...."

Three days later Arthur Crumm & Associates bought a seat on the New York Stock Exchange, and they added a seat on the Nasdaq within a month.

To this day nobody knows very much about them, except that they're a small, closely held investment company, they turn a truly remarkable annual profit, and they recently expanded into Sugar Plum Fairy theme parks and motion picture production. In fact, it's rumored that they've signed Sylvester Stallone, Arnold Schwarzenegger, and Madonna to star in *Fantasia II*.

How did I come to write this? Esther Friesner, bless
her heart, needed a story for *Chicks 'N Chained Males*.
That's one of the more, um, evocative titles for a fantasy
anthology anybody ever came up with. Since the basic theme
was already perverted, I figured perverting a Greek myth to
meet it probably wouldn't send me to heck in a hobgoblin, or
whatever the saying is.

—*Harry Turtledove*

Myth Manners' Guide to Greek Missology #1: Andromeda and Perseus

HARRY TURTLEDOVE

~~~~~~~~~

A NDROMEDA WAS FEELING THE STRAIN. "Why *me*?" she demanded. She'd figured Zeus wanted something from her when he invited her up to good old Mount Olympus for the weekend, but she'd thought it would be something else. She'd been ready to play along, too—how did you go about saying no to the king of the gods? You didn't, not unless you were looking for a role in a tragedy. But...this?

"Why you?" Zeus eyed her as if he'd had something else in mind, too. But then he looked over at Hera, his wife, and got back to the business at hand. "Because you're the right man—uh, the right person—for the job."

"Yeah, right," Andromeda said. "Don't you think you'd do better having a man go out and fight the Gorgons? Isn't that what men are for?—fighting, I mean." She knew what else men were for, but she didn't want to mention that to Zeus, not with Hera listening.

And Hera *was* listening. She said, "Men are useless—for fighting the Gorgons, I mean." She sounded as if she meant a lot of other things, too. She was looking straight at Zeus.

No matter how she sounded, the king of the gods dipped his head in agreement. "My wife's right." By the sour look on his face, that sentence didn't pass his lips every eternity. "The three Gorgons are fearsome foes. Whenever a man spies Cindy, Claudia, or Tyra, be it only for an instant, he turns to stone."

381

"*Part* of him turns to stone, anyway," Hera said acidly.

"And, so, you not being a man, you being a woman..." Zeus went on.

"Wait a minute. Wait just a linen-picking minute," Andromeda broke in. "You're not a man, either, or not exactly a man. You're a god. Why don't you go and take care of these Gorgons with the funny names your own self?"

Zeus coughed, then brightened. "Well, my dear, since you put it that way, maybe I ought to—"

"Not on your immortal life, Bubba," Hera said. "You lay a hand on those hussies and you're mythology."

"You see how it is," Zeus said to Andromeda. "My wife doesn't understand me at all."

Getting in the middle of an argument between god and goddess didn't strike Andromeda as Phi Beta Kappa—or any other three letters of the Greek alphabet, either. Telling Zeus to find himself another boy—or girl—wouldn't be the brightest thing since Phoebus Apollo, either. With a sigh, she said, "Okay. You've got me." Zeus's eyes lit up. Hera planted an elbow in his divine ribs. Hastily, Andromeda went on, "Now what do I have to do?"

"Here you are, my dear." From behind his gold-and-ivory throne, Zeus produced a sword belt. He was about to buckle it on Andromeda— and probably let his fingers do a little extra walking while he was taking care of that—when Hera let out a sudden sharp cough. Sulkily, the king of the gods handed Andromeda the belt and let her put it on herself.

From behind her throne, Hera pulled out a brightly polished shield. "Here," she said. "You may find this more useful against Cindy, Claudia, and Tyra than any blade. Phallic symbols, for some reason or other, don't much frighten them."

"Hey, sometimes a sword is just a sword," Zeus protested.

"And sometimes it's *not*, Mr. Swan, Mr. Shower-of-Gold, Mr. Bull— plenty of bull for all the girls from here to Nineveh, and I'm damned Tyred of it," Hera said. Zeus fumed. Hera turned back to Andromeda. "If you look in the shield, you'll get some idea of what I mean."

"Is it safe?" Andromeda asked. As Zeus had, Hera dipped her head. Her divine husband was still sulking, and didn't answer one way or the other. Andromeda cautiously looked. "I can see myself!" she exclaimed—not a claim she was likely to be able to make after washing earthenware plates, no matter the well from which the house slaves brought back the dishwashing liquid. A moment later, her hands flew to her hair. "Eeuw! I'm not so sure I want to."

"It isn't you, dearie—it's the magic in the shield," Hera said, not unkindly. "If you really looked like that, loverboy here wouldn't be interested in feeling your pain... or anything else he could get his hands on." She gave Zeus a cold and speculative stare. "At least, I don't *think* he would. He's not always fussy."

A thunderbolt appeared in Zeus's right hand. He tossed it up and down, hefting it and eyeing Hera. "Some of them—most of them, even—keep their mouths shut except when I want them to be open," he said meaningfully.

Hera stood up to her full height, which was whatever she chose to make it. Andromeda didn't quite come up to the goddess' dimpled knee. "Well, I'd better be going," she said hastily. If Zeus and Hera started at it hammer and tongs, they might not even notice charbroiling a more or less innocent mortal bystander by mistake.

Just finding Cindy, Claudia, and Tyra didn't prove easy. Minor gods and goddesses weren't allowed to set up shop on Olympus; they lowered surreal-estate values. Andromeda had to go through almost all of Midas's Golden Pages before getting so much as a clue about where she ought to be looking.

Even then, she was puzzled. "Why on earth—or off it, for that matter—would they hang around with a no-account Roman goddess?" she asked.

"What, you think I hear everything?" Midas's long, hairy, donkeyish ears twitched. "And why should I give a Phryg if I do hear things?" His ears twitched again, this time, Andromeda judged, in contempt. "You know about the Greek goddess of victory, don't you?"

"Oh, everybody knows about *her*." Andromeda sounded scornful, too. Since the Greeks had pretty much stopped winning victories, the goddess formerly in charge of them had gone into the running-shoe business, presumably to mitigate the agony of defeat on de feet. Nike had done a gangbanger business, too, till wing-footed Hermes hit her with a copyright-infringement suit that showed every sign of being as eternal as the gods.

"So there you are, then," Midas said. "I don't know what Victoria's secret is, and I don't give a darn."

"That's my shortstop," Andromeda said absently, and let out a long, heartfelt sigh. "I'll just have to go and find out for myself, won't I?"

Thinking of Hermes and his winged sandals gave her an idea. Back to the high-rent district of Mount Olympus she went. The god raised his eyebrows. He had a winged cap, too, one that fluttered off his head in surprise. "You want *my* shoes?" he said.

"I can't very well walk across the Adriatic," Andromeda said.

"No, that's a different myth altogether," Hermes agreed.

"And then up to Rome, to see if the gods are in," Andromeda went on.

"They won't be, not when the mercury rises," Hermes said, "They'll be out in the country, or else at the beach. Pompeii is very pretty this time of year."

"Such a *lovely* view of the volcano," Andromeda murmured. She cast Hermes a melting look. "May I *please* borrow your sandals?"

"Oh, all right," he said crossly. "The story would bog down if I told you no at this point."

"You'd better not be reading ahead," Andromeda warned him. Hermes just snickered. Gods had more powers than mortals, and that was all there was to it. When Andromeda put on the winged sandals and hopped into the air, she stayed up. "Gotta be the shoes," she said.

"Oh, it is," Hermes assured her. "Have fun in Italy."

As she started to fly away, Andromeda called back, "Do you know what Victoria's secret is?"

The god dipped his head to show he did. "Good camera angles," he replied.

Good camera angles. A quiet hostel. A nice view of the beach. And, dammit, a lovely view of the volcano, too. Vesuvius *was* picturesque. And so were Cindy, Claudia, and Tyra, dressed in lacy, colorful, overpriced wisps of not very much. As soon as Andromeda set eyes on them, she started hoping the mountain would blow up and bury those three in lava. Molten lava. Red-hot molten lava. The rest of Pompeii? So what? Herculaneum? So what? Naples, up the coast? Who needed it, really?

But Vesuvius stayed quiet. Of course it did. Hephaestus or Vulcan or whatever name he checked into motels with locally was probably up at the top of the spectacular cone, peering down, leering down, at some other spectacular cones. "Men," Andromeda muttered. No wonder they'd given her this job. And they wouldn't thank her for it once she did it, either.

As Andromeda flew down toward the Gorgons with the spectacularly un-Hellenic names, Victoria flew up to meet her, saying, "Whoever you are, go away. We're just about to shoot."

Shooting struck Andromeda as altogether too good for them. "Some victory you're the goddess of," she sneered, "unless you mean the one in *Lysistrata*."

"You're just jealous because you can't cut the liquamen, sweetheart," Victoria retorted.

Andromeda smiled a hemlock-filled smile. "Doesn't matter whether I am or not," she answered. "I'm on assignment from Zeus and Hera, so you can go take a flying leap at Selene."

"Uppity mortal! You can't talk to me like that." Victoria drew back a suddenly very brawny right arm for a haymaker that would have knocked the feathers right off of Hermes' sandals.

"Oh, yes, I can," Andromeda said, and held up the shield Hera had given her.

She didn't know whether it could have done a decent job of stopping the goddess' fist. That didn't matter. Victoria took one brief look at her reflection and cried, "*Vae! Malae comae! Vae!*" She fled so fast, she might have gone into business with her Greek cousin Nike.

A grim smile on her face, Andromeda descended on Cindy, Claudia, and Tyra. They were lined up on the beach like three tenpins—*except not so heavy in the bottom*, Andromeda thought resentfully. Had they been lined up any better, she'd have bet she could've looked into the left ear of the one on the left and seen out the right ear of the one on the right.

They turned on her in unison when she alighted on the sand. "Ooh, I like those sandals," one of them crooned fiercely. "Gucci? Louis Vuitton?"

"No, Hermes'," Andromeda answered. She fought panic as they advanced on her, swaying with menace—or something.

"I wonder what she's doing here," one of the Gorgons said. She waved at the gorgeous scenery, of which she and her comrades were the most gorgeous parts. "I mean, she's so plain."

"Mousy," agreed another.

"Nondescript. Utterly nondescript," said the third, proving she did have room in her head for a three-syllable word: two of them, even.

And the words flayed like fire. Cindy, Claudia, and Tyra weren't even contemptuous. It was as if Andromeda didn't rate contempt. That was their power; just by existing, they made everyone around them feel inadequate. *Zeus wanted me*, Andromeda thought, trying to stay strong. But what did that prove? Zeus wanted anything that moved, and, if it didn't move, he'd give it an experimental shake.

Andromeda felt like curling up on the beach and dying right there. If she put the shield up over her, maybe it would keep her from hearing any more of the Gorgons' cruel words. The shield...!

With a fierce cry of her own, Andromeda held it up to them. Instead of continuing their sinuous advance, they fell back with cries of horror. Peering down over the edge of the shield, Andromeda got a quick glimpse of their reflections. The shield had given her and Victoria bad hair. It was far more pitiless to Cindy, Claudia, and Tyra, perhaps because they had further to fall from the heights of *haute couture*. Whatever the reason, the three Gorgons' hair might as well have turned to snakes once the shield had its way with them.

"Plain," Andromeda murmured. "Mousy. Nondescript. Utterly nondescript."

How the Gorgons howled! They fell to their knees in the sand and bowed their heads, trying to drive out those images of imperfection.

Still holding the shield on high, Andromeda drew her sword. She could have taken their heads at a stroke, but something stayed her hand. It wasn't quite mercy: more the reflection that they'd probably already given a good deal of head to get where they were.

Roughly, she said, "Stay away from Olympus from now on, if you know what's good for you. You ever come near there again, worse'll be waiting for you." She didn't know if that was true, but it would be if Hera could make it so.

"But where shall we go?" one of them asked in a small, broken voice. "What shall we do?"

"Try *Sports Illustrated*," Andromeda suggested, "though gods only know what sport you'd be illustrating."

"Been there," one said. Andromeda had no idea which was which, and didn't care to find out. The other two chorused, "Done that."

"Find something else, then," Andromeda said impatiently. "I don't care what, as long as it's not in Zeus' back yard." *And mine*, she thought. Thinking that, she started to turn the terrible shield on them again and added, "Or else."

Cindy, Claudia, and Tyra cringed. If they weren't convinced now, they never would be, Andromeda judged. She jumped into the air and flew off. That way, she didn't have to look at them anymore, didn't have to be reminded that they didn't really look the way Hera's shield made them seem to. Plain. Mousy. Nondescript. Utterly nondescript. Her hand went to the hilt of the sword. *Maybe I should have done a little slaughtering after all.* But she kept flying.

She took the scenic route home—after all, when would she be able to talk Hermes out of his sandals again? She saw Scylla and Charybdis, there by the toe of the Italian boot, and they were as horrible as advertised. She flew over the Pyramids of Egypt. Next door, the Sphinx tried his riddle on her. "Oh, everybody knows *that* one," Andromeda said, and listened to him gnash his stone teeth.

She admired the lighthouse at Alexandria. It would be very impressive when they got around to building it—and when there was an Alexandria. Then she started north across the wine-dark sea toward Greece.

When she got to the coast near Argos, she saw a naked man chained to the rocks just above the waves. He was a lot more interesting than anything else she'd seen for a while—and the closer she got, the more interesting he looked. By the time she was hovering a few feet in front of him, he looked mighty damn fine indeed, you betcha. "I know it's the obvious question," she said, "but what are you doing here?"

"Waiting to be eaten," he answered.

"Listen, garbagemouth, has it occurred to you that if I slap you silly, you can't do thing one about it?" Andromeda said indignantly. "Has it?"

"No, by a sea serpent," he explained.

"Oh. Well, no accounting for taste, I suppose," she said, thinking of

Pasiphaë and the bull. Then she realized he meant it literally. "How did that happen?" Another obvious question. "And who are you, anyway?"

"I'm Perseus," he said. "My grandfather, Acrisius, is King of Argos. There's a prophecy that if my mother had a son, he'd end up killing Gramps. So Mom was grounded for life, but Zeus visited her in a shower of gold, and here I am."

"And on display, too," Andromeda remarked. Zeus had been catching Hades from Hera ever since, too—Andromeda remembered the snide *Mr. Shower-of-Gold*. But that was neither here nor there, and Perseus was definitely here. "The sea serpent will take your granddad off the hook for doing you in?"

"You got it," Perseus agreed.

"Ah...what about the chains? Doesn't he think those might have something to do with him?"

Perseus shrugged. Andromeda admired pecs and abs. The chains clanked. "He's not *real* long on ethics, Acrisius isn't."

"If you get loose, you'll do your best to make the prophecy come true?" Andromeda asked.

Another shrug. More clanks. More admiration from Andromeda. Perseus said, "Well, I've sure got a motive now, and I didn't before. But I'm not in a hurry about it. Omens have a way of working out, you know? I mean, would you be here to set me free if I weren't fated to do Gramps in one of these years?"

"I'm not here to set you free," Andromeda said. "I just stopped by for a minute to enjoy the scenery, and—"

Perseus pointed. He didn't do it very well—he was chained, after all—but he managed. "Excuse me for interrupting," he said, "but the sea serpent's coming."

Andromeda whirled in the air. "Eep!" she said. Perseus hadn't been wrong. The monster was huge. It was fast. It was hideous. It was wet (which made sense, it being a sea serpent). It had an alarmingly big mouth full of a frighteningly large number of terrifyingly sharp teeth. Andromeda could have rearranged those adverbs any which way and they still would have added up to the same thing. Trouble. Big trouble.

She could also have flown away. She glanced back at Perseus and shook her head. That would have been a waste of a great natural resource. And, no matter what Hera had to say about it, Zeus wouldn't be overjoyed if she left his bastard son out for sea-serpent fast food.

She drew her sword—Zeus' sword—and flew toward the monster. One way or another, this story was going to get some blood in it. Or maybe not. She held up Hera's mirrored shield, right in the sea serpent's face. It might figure it was having a bad scales day and go away.

But no such luck. Maybe the shield didn't work because the sea serpent had no hair. Maybe the serpent had already maxed out its ugly account. Or maybe it was too stupid to notice anything had changed. Andromeda shook her head again. If Cindy, Claudia, and Tyra had noticed, the sea serpent would have to.

No help for it. Sometimes, as Zeus had said, a sword was just a sword. Andromeda swung this one. It turned out to cut sea serpent a lot better than her very best kitchen knife cut roast goose. Chunk after reptilian chunk fell away from the main mass of the monster. The Aegean turned red. The sea serpent really might have been dumber than the Gorgons, because it took a very long time to realize it was dead. Eventually, though, enough of the head end was missing that it forgot to go on living and sank beneath the waves. If the sharks and the dolphins didn't have a food fight with the scraps, they missed a hell of a chance.

Chlamys soaked with seawater and sea-serpent gore, Andromeda flew back toward Perseus. "I would applaud," he said, "but under the circumstances . . ." He rattled his chains to show what he meant. "That was very exciting."

Andromeda looked him over. He meant it literally. She could tell. She giggled. Greek statues always underestimated things. Quite a bit, here. She giggled again. Sometimes a sword wasn't just a sword.

She looked up toward the top of the rocks. Nobody was watching; maybe Acrisius's conscience, however vestigial, bothered him too much for that. She could do whatever she pleased. Perseus couldn't do anything about it, that was plain enough. Andromeda giggled once more. She flew a little lower and a lot closer.

Perseus gasped. Andromeda pulled back a bit and glanced up at him, eyes full of mischief. "You said you were here to be eaten," she pointed out.

"By a *sea serpent!*"

"If you don't think this is more fun. . . ." Her shrug was petulant. But, when you got down to the bottom of things, what Perseus thought didn't matter a bit. She went back to what she'd been doing. After a little while, she decided to do something else. She hiked up the clammy chlamys and did it. Though she hadn't suspected it till now, there were times when the general draftiness of Greek clothes and lack of an underwear department at the Athens K-Mart came in kind of handy. Up against the side of a cliff, winged sandals didn't hurt, either. A good time was had by all.

Afterward, still panting, Perseus said, "Now that you've ravished me, you realize you'll have to marry me."

Andromeda stretched languorously. A *very* good time had been had by all, or at least by her. She wished for a cigarette, and wished even more she knew what one was. "That can probably be arranged," she purred.

"First, though, you'll have to get me off," Perseus said.

She squawked. "Listen, mister, if I didn't just take care of that—"

"No, off this cliff," he said.

"Oh." Andromeda dipped her head in agreement. "Well, that can probably be arranged, too." She drew the sword again and swung it. It sheared through the metal that imprisoned Perseus like a divine sword cutting cheap bronze chains. After four strokes—considerably fewer than he'd been good for—he fell forward and down. They caught each other in midair. Hermes' sandals were strong enough to carry two. Andromeda had figured they would be. She and Perseus rose together.

After topping the rocks, they flew north toward Argos. Perseus said, "Can I borrow your sword for a minute?"

"Why?" Andromeda looked at him sidelong. "I like the one you come equipped with."

"It won't cut through the manacles on my ankles and wrists," Perseus said.

"Hmm. I suppose not. Sure, go ahead."

Divine swords had a lot going for them. This one neatly removed the manacles without removing the hands and feet they'd been binding. Thinking about all the times she'd sliced herself carving wild boar— those visiting Gauls could really put it away—Andromeda wished she owned cutlery like that.

Perseus said, "Can you steer a little more to the left?"

"Sure," Andromeda said, and did. "How come?"

"That's Acrisius's palace down there." Perseus pointed. "Who knows? Maybe I can make a prophecy come true." He dropped the manacles and the lengths of chain attached to them, one after another. He and Andromeda both watched them fall.

"I can't tell," Andromeda said at last.

"Neither can I." Perseus made the best of things: "If I did nail the old geezer, Matt Drudge'll have it online before we get to Olympus."

The wedding was the event of the eon. Andromeda's mother and father, Cepheus and Cassiopeia, flew up from their Ethiopian home in their private Constellation. Acrisius's cranium apparently remained undented, but nobody sent him an invitation. Danaë, Perseus's mother, did come. She and Hera spent the first part of the weekend snubbing each other.

Zeus dishonored two maids of honor, and, once in his cups, seemed convinced every cupbearer was named Ganymede. After he got into the second maid of honor, he also got into a screaming row with Hera. A couple of thunderbolts flew, but the wedding pavilion, though scorched, survived.

Hera and Danaë went off in a corner, had a good cry together, and were the best of friends from then on out. A little later, Zeus sidled up to Andromeda and asked in an anxious voice, "What is this *First Wives' Club* my wife keeps talking about? Do you suppose it is as powerful as my sword?"

"Which one, your Godship, sir?" she returned; she was in her cups, too. Zeus didn't answer, but went off with stormy, and even rather rainy, brow. Before long, he and Hera were screaming at each other again.

And then Andromeda and Perseus were off for their wedding night at the Mount Olympus Holiday Inn. In her cups or not, Andromeda didn't like the way the limo driver handled the horses. Perseus patted her knee. "Don't worry, sweetie," he said. "Phaëthon hasn't burned rubber, or anything else, for quite a while now."

She might have argued more, but Perseus's hand, instead of stopping at the knee, kept wandering north. And, with all the gods in the wedding party following the limo, odds were somebody could bring her back to life even if she did get killed.

Ambrosia—Dom Perignon ambrosia, no less—waited on ice in the honeymoon suite. The bed was as big as Boeotia, as soft as the sea-foam that spawned Aphrodite. Out in the hallway, the gods and demigods and mortals with pull who'd been at the wedding made a deityawful racket, waiting for the moment of truth.

They didn't have to wait very long. Perseus was standing at attention even when he lay down on that inviting bed. Wearing nothing but a smile, Andromeda got down beside him. At the appropriate time, she let out a squeal, pretending to be a maiden. Everybody in the hallway let out a cheer, pretending to believe her.

After the honeymoon, things went pretty well. Perseus landed an editorial job at *Argosy*. Andromeda spent a while on the talk-show circuit: Loves Fated to Happen were hot that millennium. They bought themselves a little house. It was Greek Colonial architecture, right out of Grant Xylum, and they furnished it to match.

When Andromeda sat down on the four-poster bed one night, she heard a peculiar sound, not one it usually made. "What's that?" she asked Perseus.

"What's what?" he said, elaborately casual.

"That noise. Like—metal?"

"Oh. That." Elaborately casual, all right—too elaborately casual. Perseus's face wore an odd smile, half sheepish, half . . . something else. "It's probably these." He lifted up his pillow.

"Chains!" Andromeda exclaimed. "Haven't you had enough of chains?"

"Well—sort of." Perseus sounded sheepish, too, sheepish and . . . something else. An eager something else. "But it was so much fun that first time, I, I . . . thought we might try it again."

"*Did* you?" Andromeda rubbed her chin. You don't find out everything right away about the person you marry, especially if it's a whirlwind courtship. Gods knew she hadn't expected *this*. Still . . . "Why not?" she said at last. "Just don't invite that damn sea serpent."

And a good time was had by all.

I have no idea if "The Soul Selects Her Own Society, etc." is my funniest story. Writers are notoriously bad about judging their own works. (Mark Twain thought *Tom Sawyer* was his best book. It's not.) But "The Soul Selects..." certainly has the longest title of all my stories, and it has footnotes, which I think fiction should have more of. It was also the most fun to write.[1]

I was asked to write the story for a collection commemorating the hundredth anniversary of H. G. Wells's *The War of the Worlds*. The idea for the book was that the Martians had not only landed in England, but at various places all over the globe, where the invasion was chronicled by famous people.[2] When they asked me to participate, they said, "We thought you might like to be Laura Ingalls Wilder."

I said, "Laura Ingalls Wilder! Laura Ingalls Wilder! I am *appalled* that you would even *think* of me in connection with Laura Ingalls Wilder!" and they said okay, okay, I didn't have to be Laura Ingalls Wilder, I could use anybody I wanted, but it had to be a woman[3] and she had to be alive in 1896, the year of the Martian invasion.

(Actually, the *real* Martian invasion was in 1937. Orson Welles reported it. But after the Laura Ingalls Wilder outburst, I thought it best not to make any more comments. Because writing a story about the War of the Worlds did sound like fun. See footnote 1.)

---

[1] I use the word "fun" in its comparative sense. Most of the time writing for me is like poking myself in the eye with a sharp stick.*

    *Or watching reality TV.**

        **Notice how I am using footnotes.

[2] Jules Verne in Paris, Mark Twain on the Mississippi, etc.

[3] They were short on women.*

    *Wasn't that another invasion story, *Mars Needs Women*?

So I started thinking of women authors I actually liked—
Louisa May Alcott (dead), Jane Austen (also dead), Helen
Fielding (the author of *Bridget Jones's Diary*—not born yet).
For a little while I thought Dorothy Parker (born 1893) might
work, but she would only have been three years old, and even
though I'm sure she was a precocious child, she would hardly
have known the word "horticulture"[4] yet, and thus probably
was not up to taking on the Martians.[5]

That left Emily Dickinson, who was also, unfortunately,
dead,[6] but after a little thought, that didn't really seem
all that much of a handicap. As you shall see. . . .

—Connie Willis

---

[4] As in, "You can lead a horticulture, but you can't make her think."

[5] Although I could be wrong. Look at the way she took on Clare Boothe Luce that time when Clare stepped back to let Dorothy go through the door first. "Age before beauty," Clare said. "Pearls before swine," Dorothy said and swept through the door.

[6] And didn't have nearly as good an epitaph as Dorothy's.*

   *"Excuse my dust."

The Soul Selects
Her Own Society:
Invasion and Repulsion
A Chronological Representation of Two of
Emily Dickinson's Poems: A Wellsian Perspective

CONNIE WILLIS

~~~~~~~~~

UNTIL RECENTLY IT WAS THOUGHT that Emily Dickinson's poetic output ended in 1886, the year she died. Poems 186B and 272?, however, suggest that not only did she write poems at a later date, but that she was involved in the "great and terrible events"[7] of 1897.

The poems in question originally came to light in 1991,[8] while Nathan Fleece was working on his doctorate. Fleece, who found the poems[9] under a hedge in the Dickinsons' backyard, classified the poems as belonging to Dickinson's Early or Only Slightly Eccentric Period, but a recent examination of the works[10] has yielded up an entirely different interpre-

---

[7] For a full account, see H. G. Wells, *The War of the Worlds*, Oxford University Press, 1898.

[8] The details of the discovery are recounted in *Desperation and Discovery: The Unusual Number of Lost Manuscripts Located by Doctoral Candidates*, by J. Marple, Reading Railway Press, 1993.

[9] Actually a poem and a poem fragment consisting of a four-line stanza and a single word fragment* from the middle of the second stanza.

    *Or word. See later on in this paper.

[10] While I was working on *my* dissertation.

tation of the circumstances under which the poems were written. The sheets of paper on which the poems were written are charred around the edges, and that of number 272? has a large round hole burnt in it. Martha Hodge-Banks claims that said charring and hole were caused by "a pathetic attempt to age the paper and forgetting to watch the oven,"[11] but the large number of dashes makes it clear they were written by Dickinson, as well as the fact that the poems are almost totally indecipherable. Dickinson's unreadable handwriting has been authenticated by any number of scholars, including Elmo Spencer in *Emily Dickinson: Handwriting or Heiroglyphics?*, and M. P. Cursive, who wrote, "Her a's look like c's, her e's look like 2's, and the whole thing looks like chicken scratches."[12]

The charring seemed to indicate either that the poems had been written while smoking[13] or in the midst of some catastrophe, and I began examining the text for clues.

Fleece had deciphered Number 272? as beginning, "I never saw a friend—/I never saw a moom—," which made no sense at all,[14] and on closer examination I saw that the stanza actually read:

"I never saw a fiend—
I never saw a bomb—
And yet of both of them I dreamed—
While in the—dreamless tomb—"

A much more authentic translation, particularly in regard to the rhyme scheme. "Moom" and "tomb" actually rhyme, which is something Dickinson hardly ever did, preferring near-rhymes such as "mat/gate," "tune/sun" and "balm/hermaphrodite."

The second stanza was more difficult, as it occupied the area of the

---

[11] Dr. Banks's assertion that "the paper was manufactured in 1990 and the ink was from a Flair tip pen," is merely airy speculation.*

    *See "Carbon Dating Doesn't Prove Anything," by Jeremiah Habakkuk, in *Creation Science for Fun and Profit*, Golden Slippers Press, 1974.

[12] The pathetic nature of her handwriting is also addressed in *Impetus to Reform: Emily Dickinson's Effect on the Palmer Method*, and in "Depth, Dolts and Teeth: An Alternate Translation of Emily Dickinson's Death Poems," in which it is argued that Number 712 actually begins, "Because I could not stoop for darts," and recounts an arthritic evening at the local pub.

[13] Dickinson is not known to have smoked, except during her Late or Downright Peculiar Period.

[14] Of course, neither does, "How pomp surpassing ermine." Or, "A dew sufficed itself."

round hole, and the only readable portion was a group of four letters farther down that read, "ulla."[15]

This was assumed by Fleece to be part of a longer word such as "bullary" (a convocation of popes),[16] or possibly "dullard" or "hullabaloo."[17]

I, however, immediately recognized "ulla" as the word H. G. Wells had reported hearing the dying Martians utter, a sound he described as "a sobbing alternation of two notes[18]...a desolating cry."

"Ulla" was a clear reference to the 1897 invasion by the Martians, previously thought to have been confined to England, Missouri, and the University of Paris.[19] The poem fragment, along with 186B, clearly indicated that the Martians had landed in Amherst and that they had met Emily Dickinson.

At first glance, this seems an improbable scenario due to both the Martians' and Emily Dickinson's dispositions. Dickinson was a recluse who didn't meet anybody, preferring to hide upstairs when neighbors came to call and to float notes down on them.[20] Various theories have been advanced for her self-imposed hermitude, including Bright's Disease, an unhappy love affair, eye trouble, and bad skin. T. L. Mensa suggests the simpler theory that all the rest of the Amherstonians were morons.[21]

None of these explanations would have made it likely that she would like Martians any better than Amherstates, and there is the added difficulty that, having died in 1886, she would also have been badly decomposed.

The Martians present additional difficulties. The opposite of recluses, they were in the habit of arriving noisily, attracting reporters, and blasting at everybody in the vicinity. There is no record of their having landed in Amherst, though several inhabitants mention unusually loud thunderstorms in their diaries,[22] and Louisa May Alcott, in nearby

---

[15] Or possibly "ciee." Or "vole."

[16] Unlikely considering her Calvinist upbringing.

[17] Or the Australian city, Ulladulla. Dickinson's poems are full of references to Australia. W. G. Mathilda has theorized from this that "the great love of Dickinson's life was neither Higginson nor Judge Lord, but Mel Gibson." See *Emily Dickinson: The Billabong Connection*, by C. Dundee, Outback Press, 1985.

[18] See Rod McKuen.

[19] Where Jules Verne was working on *his* doctorate.

[20] The notes contained charming, often enigmatic sentiments such as, "Which shall it be—Geraniums or Tulips?" and "Go away—and Shut the door When—you Leave."

[21] See *Halfwits and Imbeciles: Poetic Evidence of Emily Dickinson's Opinion of Her Neighbors*.

[22] Virtually everyone in Amherst kept a diary, containing entries such as "Always knew she'd turn out to be a great poet," and "Full moon last night. Caught a glimpse of her out in her garden planting peas. Completely deranged."

Concord, wrote in her journal, "Wakened suddenly last night by a loud noise to the west. Couldn't get back to sleep for worrying. Should have had Jo marry Laurie. To Do: Write sequel in which Amy dies. Serve her right for burning manuscript."

There is also indirect evidence for the landing. Amherst, frequently confused with Lakehurst, was obviously the inspiration for Orson Welles's setting the radio version of "War of the Worlds" in New Jersey.[23] In addition, a number of the tombstones in West Cemetery are tilted at an angle, and, in some cases, have been knocked down, making it clear that the Martians landed not only in Amherst, but in West Cemetery, very near Dickinson's grave.

Wells describes the impact of the shell[24] as producing "a blinding glare of vivid green light" followed by "such a concussion as I have never heard before or since." He reports that the surrounding dirt "splashed," creating a deep pit and exposing drainpipes and house foundation. Such an impact in West Cemetery would have uprooted the surrounding coffins and broken them open, and the resultant light and noise clearly would have been enough to "wake the dead," including the slumbering Dickinson.

That she was thus awakened, and that she considered the event an invasion of her privacy is made clear in the longer poem, Number 186B, of which the first stanza reads:

"I scarce was settled in the grave—
When came—unwelcome guests—
Who pounded on my coffin lid—
Intruders—in the dust—"[25]

Why the "unwelcome guests" did not hurt her,[26] in light of their usual behavior, and how she was able to vanquish them are less apparent, and we must turn to H. G. Wells's account of the Martians for answers.

---

[23] The inability of people to tell Orson Welles and H. G. Wells apart lends credence to Dickinson's opinion of humanity. (See Footnote 15.)

[24] Not the one at the beginning of the story, which everybody knows about, the one that practically landed on him in the middle of the book which everybody missed because they'd already turned off the radio and were out running up and down the streets screaming, "The end is here! The Martians are coming!"*

    * Thus proving Emily was right in her assessment of the populace.

[25] See "Sound, Fury, and Frogs: Emily Dickinson's Seminal Influence on William Faulkner," by W. Snopes, Yoknapatawpha Press, 1955.

[26] She was, of course, already dead, which meant the damage they could inflict was probably minimal.

On landing, Wells tells us, the Martians were completely helpless due to Earth's greater gravity, and remained so until they were able to build their fighting machines. During this period they would have posed no threat to Dickinson except that of company.[27]

Secondly, they were basically big heads. Wells describes them as having eyes, a beak, some tentacles, and "a single large tympanic drum" at the back of the head which functioned as an ear. Wells theorized that the Martians were "descended from beings not unlike outselves, by a gradual development of brain and hands...at the expense of the body." He concluded that, without the body's vulnerability and senses, the brain would become "selfish and cruel" and take up mathematics,[28] but Dickinson's effect on them suggests that the overenhanced development of their neocortexes had turned them instead into poets.

The fact that they picked off people with their heat rays, sucked human blood, and spewed poisonous black smoke over entire counties would seem to contraindicate poetic sensibility, but look how poets act. Take Shelley, for instance, who went off and left his first wife to drown herself in the Serpentine so he could marry a woman who wrote monster movies. Or Byron. The only people who had a kind word to say about him were his dogs.[29] Take Robert Frost.[30]

The Martians' identity as poets is corroborated by the fact that they landed seven shells in Great Britain, three in the Lake District[31] and none at all in Liverpool. It may have determined their decision to land in Amherst.

But they had reckoned without Dickinson's determination and literary technique, as Number 186B makes clear.[32] Stanza Two reads:

"I wrote a letter—to the fiends—
And bade them all be—gone—

---

[27] Which she considered a considerable threat. "If the butcher boy should come now, I would jump into the flour barrel,"* she wrote in 1873.

    * If she was in the habit of doing this, it may account for her always appearing in white.

[28] Particularly nonlinear differential equations.

[29] See "Lord Byron's Don Juan: The Mastiff as Muse" by C. Harold.

[30] He didn't like people either. See "Mending Wall," *The Complete Works*, Random House. Frost preferred barbed wire fences with spikes on top to walls.

[31] See "Semiotic Subterfuge in Wordsworth's 'I Wandered Lonely as a Cloud': A Dialectic Approach," by N. Compos Mentis, Postmodern Press, 1984.

[32] Sort of.

In simple words—writ plain and clear—
'I vant to be alone.'"

"Writ plain and clear" is obviously an exaggeration, but it is manifest
that Dickinson wrote a note and delivered it to the Martians, as the next
line makes even more evident:

"They (indecipherable)[33] it with an awed dismay—"

Dickinson may have read it aloud or floated the note down to them
in their landing pit in her usual fashion, or she may have unscrewed the
shell and tossed it in, like a hand grenade.

Whatever the method of delivery, however, the result was "awed dismay" and then retreat, as the next line indicates:

"They—promptly took—their leave—"

It has been argued that Dickinson would have had no access to writing implements in the graveyard, but this fails to take into consideration
the Victorian lifestyle. Dickinson's burial attire was a white dress, and all
Victorian dresses had pockets.[34]

During the funeral Emily's sister Lavinia placed two heliotropes in
her sister's hand, whispering that they were for her to take to the Lord.
She may also have slipped a pencil and some Post-its into the coffin, or
Dickinson, in the habit of writing and distributing notes, may simply
have planned ahead.[35]

In addition, grave poems[36] are a well-known part of literary tradition.
Dante Gabriel Rossetti, in the throes of grief after the death of his beloved Elizabeth Siddell, entwined poems in her auburn hair as she lay
in her coffin.[37]

However the writing implements came to be there, Dickinson obvi-

---

[33] The word is either "read" or "heard" or possibly "pacemaker."

[34] Also pleats, tucks, ruching, flounces, frills, ruffles, and passementerie.*
    *See "Pockets as Political Statement: The Role of Clothing in Early Victorian Feminism," by
E. and C. Pankhurst, Angry Women's Press, 1978.

[35] A good writer is never without pencil and paper.*
    *Or laptop.

[36] See "Posthumous Poems" in *Literary Theories that Don't Hold Water* by H. Houdini.

[37] Two years later, no longer quite so grief-stricken and thinking of all that lovely money, he dug
her up and got them back.*

ously made prompt and effective use of them. She scribbled down several stanzas and sent them to the Martians, who were so distressed at them that they decided to abort their mission and return to Mars.

The exact cause of this deadly effect has been much debated, with several theories being advanced. Wells was convinced that microbes killed the Martians who landed in England, who had no defense against Earth's bacteria, but such bacteria would have taken several weeks to infect the Martians, and it was obviously Dickinson's poems which caused them to leave, not dysentery.

Spencer suggests that her illegible handwriting led the Martians to misread her message and take it as some sort of ultimatum. A. Huyfen argues that the advanced Martians, being good at punctuation, were appalled by her profligate use of dashes and random capitalizing of letters. S. W. Lubbock proposes the theory that they were unnerved by the fact that all of her poems can be sung to the tune of "The Yellow Rose of Texas."[38]

It seems obvious, however, that the most logical theory is that the Martians were wounded to the heart by Dickinson's use of near-rhymes, which all advanced civilizations rightly abhor. Number 186B contains two particularly egregious examples: "gone/alone" and "guests/dust," and the burnt hole in 272? may indicate something even worse.

The near-rhyme theory is corroborated by H. G. Wells's account of the damage done to London, a city in which Tennyson ruled supreme, and by an account of a near landing in Ong, Nebraska, recorded by Muriel Addleson:

> "We were having our weekly meeting of the Ong Ladies Literary Society when there was a dreadful noise outside, a rushing sound, like something falling off the Grange Hall. Henrietta Muddie was reading Emily Dickinson's "I Taste a Liquor Never Brewed" out loud, and we all raced to the window but couldn't see anything except a lot of dust,[39] so Henrietta started reading again and there was a big whoosh, and a big round metal thing like a cigar[40] rose straight up in the air and disappeared."

---

[38] Try it. No, really. "Be-e-e-cause I could not stop for Death, He kindly stopped for me-e-e." See?*

   *Not all of Dickinson's poems can be sung to "The Yellow Rose of Texas." ** Numbers 2, 18, and 1411 can be sung to "The Itsy-Bitsy Spider."

     **Could her choice of tunes be a coded reference to the unfortunate Martian landing in Texas? See "Night of the Cooters" by Howard Waldrop, p. 37.

[39] Normal to Ong, Nebraska.

[40] See Freud.

It is significant that the poem in question is Number 214, which rhymes "pearl"[41] and "alcohol."[42]

Dickinson saved Amherst from Martian invasion and then, as she says in the final two lines of 186B, "rearranged" her "grassy bed—/And Turned—and went To sleep." She does not explain how the poems got from the cemetery to the hedge, and we may never know for sure,[43] as we may never know whether she was being indomitably brave or merely crabby.

What we do know is that these poems, along with a number of her other poems,[44] document a heretofore unguessed-at Martian invasion. Poems 186B and 272?, therefore, should be reassigned to the Very Late or Deconstructionist Period, not only to give them their proper place as Dickinson's last and most significant poems, but also so that the full symbolism intended by Dickinson can be seen in their titles. The properly placed poems will be Numbers 1775 and 1776, respectively, a clear Dickinsian reference to the Fourth of July,[45] and to the second Independence Day she brought about by banishing[46] the Martians from Amherst.

NOTE: *It is unfortunate that Wells didn't know about the deadly effect of near-rhymes. He could have grabbed a copy of the Poems, taken it to the landing pit, read a few choice lines of "The Bustle in a House," and saved everybody a lot of trouble.*

---

[41] Sort of.

[42] The near-rhyme theory also explains why Dickinson responded with such fierceness when Thomas Wentworth Higgenson changed "pearl" to "jewel." She knew, as he could not, that the fate of the world might someday rest on her inability to rhyme.

[43] For an intriguing possibility, see, "The Literary Litterbug: Emily Dickinson's Note-Dropping as a Response to Thoreau's Environmentalism," P. Walden, *Transcendentalist Review*, 1990.

[44] Number 187's "awful rivet" is clearly a reference to the Martian cylinder. Number 258's "There's a certain slant of light" echoes Wells's "blinding glare of green light," and its "affliction/Sent us of the air" obviously refers to the landing. Such allusions indicate that as many as fifty-five* of the poems were written at a later date than originally supposed, that and the entire chronology and numbering system of the poems needs to be considered.

 *Significantly enough, the age Emily Dickinson was when she died.

[45] A holiday Dickinson did not celebrate because of its social nature, although she was spotted in 1881 lighting a cherry bomb on Mabel Dodd's porch and running away.*

 *Which may be why the Martian landing attracted so little attention. The Amherstodes may have assumed it was Em up to her old tricks again.

[46] There is compelling evidence that the Martians, thwarted in New England, went to Long Island. This theory will be the subject of my next paper,* "The Green Light at the End of Daisy's Dock: Evidence of Martian Invasion in F. Scott Fitzgerald's *The Great Gatsby*."

 * I'm up for tenure.

I've decided to stick with "Cordle." It may or may not be my
funniest. That's a judgment call I don't care to make. But,
on rereading it, I still find it funny. And it brings back
the golden days of my youth when I wrote it.

I was in Ibiza at that time, living one of my marriages
that didn't work out. I fantasized myself into the role of
Cordle, and I invented a magical means for me to change my
ways, my temperament, my way of doing things. The original
Cordle was based on me. The changed Cordle, under the
influence of the magical drug, was who I wanted to be.

In the story, Cordle had a choice of behaviors after the
drug. In real life, it doesn't seem to work that way. Not
for me, anyhow. Maybe it did for Richard Alpert, who became
Ram Dass on LSD, or for Freud, who perhaps became Freud on
cocaine. In real life, we are given no choice as to the
contours of our personalities. And maybe that's the best
way. Otherwise, a lot of us might become the bad Mr. Hyde
permanently, instead of the good Dr. Jekyll.

— *Robert Sheckley*

Cordle to Onion to Carrot

ROBERT SHECKLEY

SURELY, YOU REMEMBER THE BULLY who kicked sand on the 97-pound-weakling? Well, that puny man's problem has never been solved, despite Charles Atlas's claims to the contrary. A genuine bully *likes* to kick sand on people; for him, simply, there is gut-deep satisfaction in a put-down. It wouldn't matter if you weighed 240 pounds—all of it rock-hard muscle and steely sinew—and were as wise as Solomon or as witty as Voltaire; you'd still end up with the sand of an insult in your eyes, and probably you wouldn't do anything about it.

That was how Howard Cordle viewed the situation. He was a pleasant man who was forever being pushed around by Fuller Bush men, fund solicitors, head waiters, and other imposing figures of authority. Cordle hated it. He suffered in silence the countless numbers of manic-aggressives who shoved their way to the heads of lines, took taxis he had hailed first, and sneeringly steered away girls to whom he was talking at parties.

What made it worse was that these people seemed to welcome provocation, to go looking for it, all for the sake of causing discomfort to others.

Cordle couldn't understand why this should be, until one midsummer's day, he was driving through the northern regions of Spain while stoned out of his mind, the god Thoth-Hermes granted him original enlightenment by murmuring, "Uh, look, I groove with the problem, baby, but dig, we gotta put carrots in or it ain't no stew."

"*Carrots?*" said Cordle, struggling for illumination.

"I'm talking about those types who get you uptight," Thoth-Hermes explained. "They *gotta* act that way, baby, on account of they're carrots, and that's how carrots are."

405

"If they are carrots," Cordle said, feeling his way, "then I—"

"You, of course, are a little pearly white onion."

"Yes! My God, yes!" Cordle cried, dazzled by the blinding light of satori.

"And, naturally, you and all the other pearly white onions think that carrots are just bad news, merely some kind of misshapen orangey onion; whereas the carrots look at you and rap about *freaky round white carrots, wow!* I mean, you're just too much for each other, whereas, in actuality—"

"Yes, go on!" cried Cordle.

"In actuality," Thoth-Hermes declared, "*everything's got a place in The Stew!*"

"Of course! I see, I see, I see!"

"And *that* means that everybody who exists is necessary, and you *must* have long hateful orange carrots if you're also going to have nice pleasant decent white onions, or vice versa, because without all the ingredients, it isn't a Stew, which is to say, life, it becomes, uh, let me see...."

"A soup!" cried ecstatic Cordle.

"You're coming in five by five," chanted Thoth-Hermes. "Lay down the word, deacon, and let the people know the divine formula...."

"A *soup!*" said Cordle. "Yes, I see it now—creamy, pure-white onion soup is our dream of heaven, whereas fiery orange carrot broth is our notion of hell. It fits, it all fits together!"

"Om mandipadme hum," intoned Thoth-Hermes.

"But where do the green peas go? What about the *meat*, for God's sake?"

"Don't pick at the metaphor," Thoth-Hermes advised him, "it leaves a nasty scab. Stick with the carrots and onions. And, here, let me offer you a drink—a house specialty."

"But the spices, where do you put the *spices*?" Cordle demanded, taking a long swig of burgundy-colored liquid from a rusted canteen.

"Baby, you're asking questions that can be revealed only to a thirteenth-degree Mason with piles, wearing sandals. Sorry about that. Just remember that everything goes into The Stew."

"Into The Stew," Cordle repeated, smacking his lips.

"And, especially, stick with the carrots and onions; you were really grooving there."

"Carrots and onions," Cordle repeated.

"That's your trip," Thoth-Hermes said. "Hey, we've gotten to Coruna; you can let me out anywhere around here."

Cordle pulled his rented car off the road. Thoth-Hermes took his knapsack from the backseat and got out.

"Thanks for the lift, baby."

"My pleasure. Thank *you* for the wine. What kind did you say it was?"

"*Vino de casa* mixed with a mere smidgen of old Dr. Hammerfinger's essence of instant powdered Power-Pack brand acid. Brewed by gnurrs in the secret laboratory of UCLA in preparation for the big all-Europe turn-on."

"Whatever it was, it surely *was*," Cordle said deeply. "Pure elixir to me. You could sell neckties to antelopes with this stuff; you could change the world from an oblate spheroid into a truncated trapezoid.... What did I say?"

"Never mind, it's all part of your trip. Maybe you better lie down for a while, huh?"

"Where gods command, mere mortals must obey," Cordle said iambically. He lay down on the front seat of the car. Thoth-Hermes bent over him, his beard burnished gold, his head wreathed in plane trees.

"You okay?"

"Never better in my life."

"Want me to stand by?"

"Unnecessary. You have helped me beyond potentiality."

"Glad to hear it, baby, you're making a fine sound. You really are okay? Well, then, ta."

Thoth-Hermes marched off into the sunset. Cordle closed his eyes and solved various problems that had perplexed the greatest philosophers of all ages. He was mildly surprised at how simple complexity was.

At last he went to sleep. He awoke some six hours later. He had forgotten most of his brilliant insights, the lucid solutions. It was inconceivable: How can one misplace the keys of the universe? But he had, and there seemed no hope of reclaiming them. Paradise was lost for good.

He did remember about the onions and carrots, though, and he remembered The Stew. It was not the sort of insight he might have chosen if he'd had any choice; but this was what had come to him, and he did not reject it. Cordle knew, perhaps instinctively, that in the insight game, you take whatever you can get.

The next day, he reached Santander in a driving rain. He decided to write amusing letters to all his friends, perhaps even try his hand at a travel sketch. That required a typewriter. The *conserje* at his hotel directed him to a store that rented typewriters. He went there and found a clerk who spoke perfect English.

"Do you rent typewriters by the day?" Cordle asked.

"Why not?" the clerk replied. He had oily black hair and a thin aristocratic nose.

"How much for that one?" Cordle asked, indicating a thirty-year-old Erika portable.

"Seventy pesetas a day, which is to say, one dollar. Usually."

"Isn't this usually?"

"Certainly not, since you are a foreigner in transit. For you, one hundred and eighty pesetas a day."

"All right," Cordle said, reaching for his wallet. "I'd like to have it for two days."

"I shall also require your passport and a deposit of fifty dollars."

Cordle attempted a mild joke. "Hey, I just want to type on it, not marry it."

The clerk shrugged.

"Look, the *conserje* has my passport at the hotel. How about taking my driver's license instead?"

"Certainly not. I must hold your passport, in case you decide to default."

"But why do you need my passport *and* the deposit?" Cordle asked, feeling bullied and ill at ease. "I mean, look, the machine's not worth twenty dollars."

"You are an expert, perhaps, in the Spanish market value of used German typewriters?"

"No, but—"

"Then permit me, sir, to conduct my business as I see fit. I will also need to know the use to which you plan to put the machine."

"The *use?*"

"Of course, the use."

It was one of these preposterous foreign situations that can happen to anyone. The clerk's request was incomprehensible and his manner was insulting. Cordle was about to give a curt little nod, turn on his heel, and walk out.

Then he remembered about the onions and the carrots. He saw The Stew. And suddenly, it occurred to Cordle that he could be whatever vegetable he wanted to be.

He turned to the clerk. He smiled winningly. He said, "You wish to know what use I will make of the typewriter?"

"Exactly."

"Well," Cordle said, "quite frankly, I had planned to stuff it up my nose."

The clerk gaped at him.

"It's quite a successful method of smuggling," Cordle went on. "I was also planning to give you a stolen passport and counterfeit pesetas. Once I got into Italy, I would have sold the typewriter for ten thousand dollars. Milan is undergoing a typewriter famine, you know; they're desperate, they'll buy anything."

"Sir," the clerk said, "you choose to be disagreeable."

"Nasty is the word you were looking for. I've changed my mind about the typewriter. But let me compliment you on your command of English."

"I have studied assiduously," the clerk admitted, with a hint of pride.

"That is evident. And, despite a certain weakness in the Rs, you succeed in sounding like a Venetian gondolier with a cleft palate. My best wishes to your esteemed family. I leave you now to pick your pimples in peace."

Reviewing the scene later, Cordle decided that he had performed quite well in his maiden performance as a carrot. True, his closing lines had been a little forced and overintellectualized. But the undertone of viciousness had been convincing.

Most important was the simple resounding fact that he had done it. And now, in the quiet of his hotel room, instead of churning his guts in a frenzy of self-loathing, he had the tranquilizing knowledge of having put someone else in that position.

He had done it! Just like that, he had transformed himself from onion into carrot!

But was his position ethically defensible? Presumably, the clerk could not help being detestable; he was a product of his own genetic and social environment, a victim of his conditioning; he was naturally rather than intentionally hateful—

Cordle stopped himself. He saw that he was engaged in typical onionish thinking, which was an inability to conceive of carrots except as an aberration from oniondom.

But now he knew that both onions *and* carrots had to exist; otherwise, there would be no Stew.

And he also knew that a man was free and could choose whatever vegetable he wanted to be. He could even live as an amusing little green pea, or a gruff, forceful clove of garlic (though perhaps that was scratching at the metaphor). In any event, a man could take his pick between carrothood and oniondom.

There is much to think about here, Cordle thought. But he never got around to thinking about it. Instead, he went sightseeing, despite the rain, and then continued his travels.

The next incident occurred in Nice, in a cozy little restaurant on the Avenue des Diables Bleus, with red-checkered tablecloths and incomprehensible menus written in longhand with purple ink. There were four waiters, one of whom looked like Jean-Paul Belmondo, down to the cigarette drooping from his long lower lip. The others looked like run-of-the-mill muggers. There were several Scandinavian customers quietly eating a *cassoulet*, one old Frenchman in a beret, and three homely English girls.

Belmondo sauntered over. Cordle, who spoke a clear though idiomatic French, asked for the ten-franc menu he had seen hanging in the window.

The waiter gave him the sort of look one reserves for pretentious beggars. "Ah, that is all finished for today," he said, and handed Cordle a thirty-franc menu.

In his previous incarnation, Cordle would have bit down on the bul-

let and ordered. Or possibly he would have risen, trembling with out-
rage, and left the restaurant, blundering into a chair on the way.

But now—

"Perhaps you did not understand me," Cordle said. "It is a matter of
French law that you must serve from all of the fixed-price menus that
you show in the window."

"*M'sieu* is a lawyer?" The waiter inquired, his hands perched inso-
lently on his hips.

"No. *M'sieu* is a troublemaker," Cordle said, giving what he considered to be fair warning.

"Then *m'sieu* must make what trouble he desires," the waiter said. His
eyes were slits.

"Okay," Cordle said. And just then, fortuitously, an elderly couple came
into the restaurant. The man wore a double-breasted slate-blue suit with
a half-inch white pin stripe. The woman wore a flowered organdy dress.
Cordle called to them, "Excuse me, are you folks English?"

A bit startled, the man inclined his head in the barest intimation of
a nod.

"Then I would advise you not to eat here. I am a health inspector for
UNESCO. The chef has apparently not washed his hands since D-Day.
We haven't made a definitive test for typhoid yet, but we have our suspi-
cions. As soon as my assistant arrives with the litmus paper...."

A deathly hush had fallen over the restaurant.

"I suppose a boiled egg would be safe enough," Cordle said.

The elderly man probably didn't believe him. But it didn't matter,
Cordle was obviously trouble.

"Come, Mildred," he said, and they hurried out.

"There goes sixty francs plus five percent tip," Cordle said, coolly.

"Leave here at once!" the waiter snarled.

"I like it here," said Cordle, folding his arms. "I like the *ambience*, the
sense of intimacy—"

"You are not permitted to stay without eating."

"I shall eat. From the ten-franc menu."

The waiters looked at one another, nodded in unison, and began to
advance in a threatening phalanx. Cordle called to the other diners, "I
ask you to bear witness! These men are going to attack me, four against
one, contrary to French law and universal human ethics, simply be-

cause I want to order from the ten-franc menu, which they have falsely advertised."

It was a long speech, but this was clearly the time for grandiloquence. Cordle repeated it in English.

The English girls gasped. The old Frenchman went on eating his soup. The Scandinavians nodded grimly and began to take off their jackets.

The waiters held another conference. The one who looked like Belmondo said, "*M'sieu*, you are forcing us to call the police."

"That will save me the trouble," Cordle said, "of calling them myself."

"Surely, *m'sieu* does not wish to spend his holiday in court?"

"That is how *m'sieu* spends most of his holidays," Cordle said.

The waiters conferred again. Then Belmondo stalked over with the thirty-franc menu. "The cost of the *prix fixe* will be ten francs, since evidently that is all *m'sieu* can afford."

Cordle let that pass. "Bring me onion soup, green salad, and the *boeuf bourguinon*."

The waiter went to put in the order. While he was waiting, Cordle sang "Waltzing Matilda" in a moderately loud voice. He suspected it might speed up the service. He got his food by the time he reached "You'll never catch me alive, said he" for the second time. Cordle pulled the tureen of stew toward him and lifted a spoon.

It was a breathless moment. Not one diner had left the restaurant. And Cordle was prepared. He leaned forward, soupspoon in shoveling position, and sniffed delicately. A hush fell over the room.

"It lacks a certain something," Cordle said aloud. Frowning, he poured the onion soup into the *boeuf bourguinon*. He sniffed, shook his head and added a half loaf of bread, in slices. He sniffed again and added the salad and the contents of a saltcellar.

Cordle pursed his lips. "No," he said, "it simply will not do."

He overturned the entire contents of the tureen onto the table. It was an act comparable, perhaps, to throwing gentian violet on the *Mona Lisa*. All of France and most of western Switzerland went into a state of shock.

Unhurriedly, but keeping the frozen waiters under surveillance, Cordle rose and dropped ten francs into the mess. He walked to the door, turned and said, "My compliments to the chef, who might better be employed as a cement mixer. And this, *mon vieux*, is for you."

He threw his crumpled linen napkin onto the floor.

As the matador, after a fine series of passes, turns his back contemptuously on the bull and strolls away, so went Cordle. For some unknown reason, the waiters did not rush out after him, shoot him dead, and hang his corpse from the nearest lamppost. So Cordle walked for ten or fifteen blocks, taking rights and lefts at random. He came to the Promenade de Anglais and sat down on a bench. He was trembling and his shirt was drenched with perspiration.

"But I did it," he said. "I did it! I was unspeakably vile and I got away with it!"

Now he really knew why carrots acted that way. Dear God in heaven, what joy, what delectable bliss!

Cordle then reverted to his mild-mannered self, smoothly and without regrets. He stayed that way until his second day in Rome.

He was in his rented car. He and seven other drivers were lined up at a traffic light on the Corso Vittorio Emanuele II. There were perhaps twenty cars behind them. All of the drivers were revving their engines, hunched over their steering wheels with slitted eyes, dreaming of Le Mans. All except Cordle, who was drinking in the cyclopean architecture of downtown Rome.

The checkered flag came down! The drivers floored their accelerators, trying to spin the wheels of their underpowered Fiats, wearing out their clutches and their nerves, but doing so with éclat and *brio*. All except Cordle, who seemed to be the only man in Rome who didn't have to win a race or keep an appointment.

Without undue haste or particular delay, Cordle depressed the clutch and engaged the gear. Already he had lost nearly two seconds—unthinkable at Monza or Monte Carlo.

The driver behind him blew his horn frantically.

Cordle smiled to himself, a secret, ugly expression. He put the gearshift into neutral, engaged the hand brake and stepped out of his car. He ambled over to the hornblower, who had turned a pasty white and was fumbling under his seat, hoping to find a tire iron.

"Yes?" said Cordle, in French, "is something wrong?"

"No, no, nothing," the driver replied in French—his first mistake. "I merely wanted you to go, to move."

"But I was just doing that," Cordle pointed out.

"Well, then! It is all right!"

"No, it is not all right," Cordle told him. "I think I deserve a better explanation of why you blew your horn at me."

The hornblower—a Milanese businessman on holiday with his wife and four children—rashly replied, "My dear sir, you were slow, you were delaying us all."

"*Slow*?" said Cordle. "You blew your horn two seconds after the light changed. Do you call two seconds slow?"

"It was much longer than that," the man riposted feebly.

Traffic was now backed up as far south as Naples. A crowd of ten thousand had gathered. *Carabinieri* units in Viterbo and Genoa had been called into a state of alert.

"That is untrue," Cordle said. "I have witnesses." He gestured at the crowd, which gestured back. "I shall call my witnesses before the courts. You must know that you broke the law by blowing your horn within the city limits of Rome in what was clearly not an emergency."

The Milanese businessman looked at the crowd, now swollen to perhaps fifty thousand. Dear God, he thought, if only the Goths would descend again and exterminate these leering Romans! If only the ground would open up and swallow this insane Frenchman! If only he, Giancarlo Morelli, had a dull spoon with which to open up the veins of his wrist!

Jets from the Sixth Fleet thundered overhead, hoping to avert the long-expected *coup d'etat*.

The Milanese businessman's own wife was shouting abuse at him: Tonight he would cut out her faithless heart and mail it back to her mother.

What was there to do? In Milan, he would have had this Frenchmen's head on a platter. But this was Rome, a southern city, an unpredictable and dangerous place. And legalistically, he was possibly in the wrong, which left him at a further disadvantage in the argument.

"Very well," he said. "The blowing of the horn was perhaps truly unnecessary, despite the provocation."

"I insist on a genuine apology," insisted Cordle.

There was a thundering sound to the east: Thousands of Soviet tanks were moving into battle formation across the plains of Hungary, ready to resist the long-expected NATO thrust into Transylvania. The water supply was cut off in Foggia, Brindisi, Bari. The Swiss closed their frontiers and stood ready to dynamite the passes.

"All right, I apologize!" the Milanese businessman screamed. "I am sorry I provoked you and even sorrier that I was born! Again, I apologize! Now will you go away and let me have a heart attack in peace?"

"I accept your apology," Cordle said. "No hard feelings, eh?" He strolled back to his car, humming "Blow the Man Down," and drove away as millions cheered.

War was once again averted by a hairbreadth.

Cordle drove to the Arch of Titus, parked his car and—to the sound of a thousand trumpets—passed through it. He deserved this triumph as well as any Caesar.

God, he gloated, I was *loathsome*!

In England, Cordle stepped on a young lady's toe just inside the Traitor's Gate of the Tower of London. This should have served as an intimation of something. The young lady was named Mavis. She came from Short Hills, New Jersey, and she had long straight dark hair. She was slender, pretty, intelligent, energetic, and she had a sense of humor. She had minor faults, as well, but they play no part in this story. She let Cordle buy her a cup of coffee. They were together constantly for the rest of the week.

"I think I am infatuated," Cordle said to himself on the seventh day. He realized at once that he had made a slight understatement. He was violently and hopelessly in love.

But what did Mavis feel? She seemed not unfond of him. It was even possible that she might, conceivably, reciprocate.

At that moment, Cordle had a flash of prescience. He realized that one week ago, he had stepped on the toe of his future wife and mother of his two children, both of whom would be brought up in a split-level house with inflatable furniture in Summit, New Jersey, or possibly Millburn.

This may sound unattractive and provincial when stated baldly; but it was desirable to Cordle, who had no pretensions to cosmopolitanism. After all, not all of use can live at Cap Ferrat. Strangely enough, not all of us even want to.

That day, Cordle and Mavis went to the Marshall Gordon Residence in Belgravia to see the Byzantine miniatures. Mavis had a passion for Byzantine miniatures that seemed harmless enough at the time. The collection was private, but Mavis had secured invitations through a local Avis manager, who was trying very hard, indeed.

They came to the Gordon Residence, an awesome Regency building in Huddlestone Mews. They rang. A butler in full evening dress answered the door. They showed the invitations. The butler's glance and lifted eyebrow showed that they were carrying second-class invitations of the sort given to importunate art poseurs on seventeen-day all-expense economy flights, rather than the engraved first-class invitations given to Picasso, Jackie Onassis, Sugar Ray Robinson, Normal Mailer, Charles Goren, and other movers and shakers of the world.

The butler said, "Oh, yes...." Two words that spoke black volumes. His face twitched, he looked like a man who has received an unexpected visit from Tamerlane and a regiment of his Golden Horde.

"The miniatures," Cordle reminded him.

"Yes, of course.... But I am afraid, sir, that no one is allowed into the Gordon Residence without a coat and necktie."

It was an oppressive August day. Cordle was wearing a sport shirt. He said, "Did I hear you correctly? Coat and necktie?"

The butler said, "That is the rule, sir."

Mavis asked, "Couldn't you make an exception this once?"

The butler shook his head. "We really must stick by the rules, miss. Otherwise . . ." He left the fear of vulgarity unsaid, but it hung in the air like a chrome-plated fart.

"Of course," Cordle said, pleasantly. "Otherwise. So it's a coat and tie, is it? I think we can arrange that."

Mavis put a hand on his arm and said, "Howard, let's go. We can come back some other time."

"Nonsense, my dear. If I may borrow your coat...."

He lifted the white raincoat from her shoulders and put it on, ripping a seam. "There we go, mate!" he said briskly to the butler. "That should do it, *n'est ce pas?*"

"I think *not*," the butler said, in a voice bleak enough to wither artichokes. "In any event, there is the matter of the necktie."

Cordle had been waiting for that. He whipped out his sweaty handkerchief and knotted it around his neck.

"Suiting you?" he leered, in an imitation of Peter Lorre as Mr. Moto, which only he appreciated.

"Howard! Let's go!"

Cordle waited, smiling steadily at the butler, who was sweating for the first time in living memory.

"I'm afraid, sir, that is not—"

"Not what?"

"Not precisely what was meant by coat and tie."

"Are you trying to tell me," Cordle said in a loud, unpleasant voice, "that you are an arbiter of men's clothing as well as a door opener?"

"Of course not! But this impromptu attire—"

"What has 'impromptu' got to do with it? Are people supposed to prepare three days in advance just to pass your inspection?"

"You are wearing a woman's waterproof and a soiled handkerchief," the butler stated stiffly. "I think there is no more to say."

He began to close the door. Cordle said, "You do that, sweetheart, and I'll have you up for slander and defamation of character. Those are serious charges, buddy, and I've got witnesses."

Aside from Mavis, Cordle had collected a small, diffident but interested crowd.

"This is becoming entirely too ridiculous," the butler said, temporizing, the door half closed.

"You'll find a stretch at Wormwood Scrubs even more ridiculous," Cordle told him. "I intend to persecute—I mean prosecute."

"*Howard!*" cried Mavis.

He shook off her hand and fixed the butler with a piercing glance. He said, "I am Mexican, though perhaps my excellent grasp of English has deceived you. In my country, a man would cut his own throat before letting such an insult pass unavenged. A woman's coat, you say? *Hombre*, when I wear a coat, it becomes a *man's* coat. Or do you imply that I am a *maricon*, a—how do you say it?—homosexual?"

The crowd—becoming less modest—growled approval. Nobody except a lord loves a butler.

"I meant no such implication," the butler said weakly.

"Then it is a man's coat?"

"Just as you wish, sir."

"Unsatisfactory! The innuendo still exists. I go now to find an officer of the law."

"Wait, let's not be hasty," the butler said. His face was bloodless and his hands were shaking. "Your coat is a man's coat, sir."

"And what about my necktie?"

The butler made a final attempt at stopping Zapata and his blood-crazed peons.

"Well, sir, a handkerchief is demonstrably—"

"What I wear around my neck," Cordle said coldly, "becomes what it is intended to be. If I wore a piece of figured silk around my throat, would you call it ladies' underwear? Linen is a suitable material for a tie, *verdad*? Function defines terminology, don't you agree? If I ride to work on a cow, no one says that I am mounted on a steak. Or do you detect a flaw in my argument?"

"I'm afraid that I don't fully understand it...."

"Then how can you presume to stand in judgment over it?"

The crowd, which had been growing restless, now murmured approval.

"Sir," cried the wretched butler, "I beg of you...."

"Otherwise," Cordle said with satisfaction, "I have a coat, a necktie, and an invitation. Perhaps you would be good enough to show us the Byzantine miniatures?"

The butler opened wide the door to Pancho Villa and his tattered hordes. The last bastion of civilization had been captured in less than an hour. Wolves howled along the banks of the Thames, Morelos's barefoot army stabled its horses in the British Museum, and Europe's long night had begun.

Cordle and Mavis viewed the collection in silence. They didn't exchange a word until they were alone and strolling through Regent's Park.

"Look, Mavis," Cordle began.

"No, you look," she said. "You were horrible! You were unbelievable! You were—I can't find a word rotten enough for what you were! I never dreamed that you were one of those sadistic bastards who get their kicks out of humiliating people!"

"But, Mavis, you heard what he said to me, you heard the way—"

"He was a stupid, bigoted old man," Mavis said. "I thought you were not."

"But he said—"

"It doesn't matter. The fact is, you were enjoying yourself!"

"Well, yes, maybe you're right," Cordle said. "Look, I can explain."

"Not to me you can't. Ever. Please stay away from me, Howard. Permanently. I mean that."

The future mother of his two children began to walk away, out of his life. Cordle hurried after her.

"Mavis!"

"I'll call a cop, Howard, so help me, I will! Just let me alone!"

"Mavis, I love you!"

She must have heard him, but she kept on walking. She was a sweet and beautiful girl and definitely, unchangeably, an onion.

Cordle was never able to explain to Mavis about The Stew and about the necessity for experiencing behavior before condemning it. Moments of mystical illumination are seldom explicable. He *was* able to make her believe that he had undergone a brief psychotic episode, unique and un-precedented and—with her—never to be repeated.

They are married now, have one girl and one boy, live in a split-level house in Plainfield, New Jersey, and are quite content. Cordle is visibly pushed around by Fuller Brush men, fund solicitors, head waiters, and other imposing figures of authority. But there is a difference.

Cordle makes a point of taking regularly scheduled, solitary vaca-tions. Last year, he made a small name for himself in Honolulu. This year, he is going to Buenos Aires.

$\mathscr{C}ontributors$

Harry Harrison was born in 1925 and was drafted into the army on his eighteenth birthday. His experiences during World War II left him with a hatred of all things military, demonstrated in his satirical novel *Bill, the Galactic Hero*. Many of his early stories appeared in John W. Campbell's *Astounding*, often reflecting his interest in environmental issues and nonviolent resolutions to conflict. His best-known creations are *The Stainless Steel Rat*, and *Make Room! Make Room!* on which the film *Soylent Green* was based. More recent works include bestselling alternate world trilogies *West of Eden* and *Stars and Stripes Forever!*

William Tenn has been professionally writing science fiction since 1945 and has appeared in many anthologies as well as Best-of-the-Year collections. He is Professor Emeritus of English and comparative literature at The Pennsylvania State University and was granted Author Emeritus status by the Science Fiction Writers of America in 1999. He has thirteen books to his credit, most recently *Immodest Proposals*, *Here Comes Civilization*, and *Dancing Naked,* published by NESFA Press. He was guest of honor at the science fiction Worldcon 2004 in Boston.

Jane Yolen, often called "the Hans Christian Andersen of America," is the author of almost 300 books. They range from rhymed picture books and baby board books, through middle-grade fiction, poetry collections, nonfiction, novels, and story collections for young adults and adults. Her books and stories have won an assortment of awards— two Nebulas, a World Fantasy Award, a Caldecott, the Golden Kite Award, three Mythopoeic awards, two Christopher Medals, a nomination for the National Book Award and the Jewish Book Award, among others. She is also the winner (for body of work) of the Kerlan Award and the Catholic Library's Regina Medal. Five colleges and universities have given her honorary doctorates. If you need to know more about her, visit her Web site at www.janeyolen.com.

Howard Waldrop works mainly in short fiction and won both a Nebula and a World Fantasy Award for his short story "The Ugly Chickens." He has been nominated for eight other Nebulas and seven Hugos, in addition to various other awards. In addition to writing short fiction, he reviews films for Locusmag.com with Lawrence Person and enjoys fishing. He currently lives in Austin, Texas.

Barry Malzberg sold his first science fiction story ("We're Coming Through the Windows," Galaxy 8/67) in 1966. Previously the Shubert Foundation Playwriting Fellow at Syracuse University, he went on to sell more than fifty novels and 400 short stories in many genres. He is, however, best known as a science fiction writer. *Beyond Apollo* (Random House 1972) was the first winner of the John W. Campbell Memorial Award for best science fiction novel of the year. *In the Stone House*, a summary short story collection, was published in 2000, and *Engines of the Night* (1982), a collection of essays about science fiction, will be reissued (with added new material) in 2007.

Laura Resnick is the author of the comedic Manhattan Magic fantasy series, the first two books of which are *Disappearing Nightly* and *Doppelgangster*. She is also the author of a traditional epic fantasy series for Tor, which includes *In Legend Born*, *The White Dragon*, and *The Destroyer Goddess*. You can find her on the Web at www.LauraResnick.com.

David Gerrold is the author of science fiction classics *The Man Who Folded Himself* and *When HARLIE Was One* (both nominated for Hugo and Nebula awards), and the immensely popular Star Wolf and Chtorr series. He is also the author of "The Trouble with Tribbles," identified by Paramount as the most popular *Star Trek* episode of all time. David Gerrold can be found at www.gerrold.com.

Spider Robinson was born six years before color TV, over three days (they had to handle him in sections). His parents moved often, but he always found them again. He became a writer after folksinging was outlawed in 1972, somehow producing thirty-three books so far. His latest novel, *Variable Star* (Tor Books), is a collaboration begun fifty years ago by the late grandmaster Robert A. Heinlein. He and choreographer Jeanne Robinson live on an island near Vancouver, British Columbia, where they raise and exhibit prize hopes.

Robert Silverberg has been writing science fiction for more than fifty years. Among his best-known books are *Dying Inside*, *The Book of Skulls*, and *Lord Valentine's Castle*. He has won five Hugos and five Nebulas, and in 2004 was designated a Grand Master by the Science Fiction Writers of America.

James Patrick Kelly has written novels, short stories, essays, reviews, poetry, plays, and planetarium shows. His books include *Burn* (2005), *Strange But Not A Stranger* (2002), and *Think Like A Dinosaur* (1997). His fiction has been translated into sixteen languages. He has won the World Science Fiction Society's Hugo Award twice. He writes a column on the Internet for *Asimov's Science Fiction* magazine and is on the faculty of the Stonecoast Creative Writing MFA Program at the University of Southern Maine. In 2004 he was appointed to be the Chair of the New Hampshire State Council on the Arts.

Jody Lynn Nye lists her main career activity as "spoiling cats." She lives northwest of Chicago with two of the above and her husband, author and packager Bill Fawcett. She has written over thirty books, including *The Ship Who Won*, a humorous anthology about mothers, with Anne McCaffrey, *Don't Forget Your Spacesuit, Dear!* and over ninety short stories. Her latest books are *Strong Arm Tactics* (Meisha Merlin), and *Class Dis-Mythed*, co-written with Robert Asprin (Meisha Merlin).

Nick DiChario's short fiction has appeared in science fiction, fantasy, mystery, and mainstream publications in the United States and abroad, and his work has been reprinted in *The Year's Best Science Fiction*, *The Year's Best Fantasy and Horror*, and *The Best Alternate History Stories of the 20th Century*, among many others. He has been nominated for the John W. Campbell Award, the World Fantasy Award, and two Hugo Awards. His collaborations with Mike Resnick may be found in the collection *Magic Feathers: The Mike and Nick Show* (Obscura Press), and Robert J. Sawyer Books recently published his first novel, *A Small and Remarkable Life*. The author's Web site is www.NickDiChario.com.

Ray Bradbury has said that you must write a million words of crap before you write one good one. This was doubly true in **Tom Gerencer's** case. He started writing 1000 words a day in 1992, and it was not until ten years later that he wrote his first good word. It was "cucumber," and he was exceedingly proud of it. He spent the next ten years refining it (at first, for example, he spelled it 'g-e-o-r-g-e') and eventually wrote others, like for instance, "fiduciary," and "whack." Later, he produced entire stories. This, he claims, is how all good works are written, except for the really long ones, which have to be plagiarized from Dostoyevsky.

Gerencer attended the Clarion workshop at Michigan State in '99, where he learned that it's important actually to write, as opposed to, say, getting up to have a bagel—and yet, in cases where one does the latter, it is crucial to ask the question, "Do I want really want to eat, or only to 'have eaten'?"

He was mentored by the likes of Robert Sheckley and Mike Resnick, who taught him that handling rejection is the single most important step along the path to literary success, second only to actually knowing how to write.

Finally, Gerencer recognizes that he owes a great debt to his parents, without whom he would not have been himself, but possibly someone else, such as Sirhan Sirhan or the Earl of Sandwich.

Michael Swanwick's works have won five Hugos, a Nebula, and the Theodore Sturgeon and World Fantasy Awards. His stories have been included in magazines and anthologies, including *Omni*, *Penthouse*, *Asimov's Science Fiction*, and *The Norton Book of Science Fiction*, and have been translated throughout the world. His books include the novels *The Iron Dragon's Daughter*, the Nebula winner *Stations of the Tide*, and *Bones of the Earth*, in addition to several short story collections. He currently lives in Philadelphia.

Esther Friesner has published twenty-seven novels and has had numerous short stories published in magazines and anthologies. She is also the editor of the popular "Chicks" series, including *Chicks in Chainmail*, *Chicks 'N Chained Males*, and *The Chick is in the Mail*. She won the Nebula Award for Best Short Story in 1995 for "Death and the Librarian," and has received the Romantic Times award for Best New Fantasy Writer and the Skylark Award. She lives in Connecticut with her husband, two cats, and several hamsters.

Gardner Dozois has won fifteen Hugos for best editor of *Asimov's Science Fiction* magazine and two Nebulas for his own short stories, "Peacemaker" (1984) and "Morning Child" (1985). He has also been the editor of *The Year's Best Science Fiction* since 1984.

Jack McDevitt is a Philadelphia native. He has been a naval officer, an English teacher, a customs officer, a Philadelphia taxi driver, and a motivational trainer. In 2004, *Omega* won the John W. Campbell Memorial Award as best novel. Six of his novels have made the final Nebula ballot. His most recent effort is *Seeker*, and *Odyssey* is imminent. The recipient of the 2000 Phoenix Award for his body of work as a Southern writer, he is married to the former Maureen McAdams of Philadelphia. McDevitt and his wife live in Brunswick, Georgia.

Ralph Roberts has sold over ninety books and more than five thousand articles and short stories to publications in several countries. His work includes the first U.S. book on computer viruses, *Classic Cooking with Coca-Cola®*, *Genealogy via the Internet*, and other bestsellers. Roberts is a member of the Mystery Writers of America and the Science Fiction Writers of America. He lives and works in the Blue Ridge Mountains of western North Carolina.

Kristine Kathryn Rusch has written mystery, science fiction, romance, and fantasy books under several pseudonyms. She has won many awards, including the Ellery Queen Readers Choice Award, the John W. Campbell Award, the Herodotus Award for Best Historical Mystery Novel, the Romantic Times Reviewers Choice Award for Best Paranormal Romance, and two Hugo awards, one for editing and one for her story "Millennium Babies" (2001). She is also the former editor of *The Magazine of Fantasy and Science Fiction*. You can visit Kristine on the Web at www.kristinekathyrnrusch.com.

Bill Fawcett has been a professor, teacher, corporate executive, and college dean. He is one of the founders of Mayfair Games. Recently Bill produced and designed several computer games and as Bill Fawcett & Associates packaged over 250 novels and anthologies. Bill began writing with the juvenile *Swordquest* series in the mid-'80s. The *Fleet* science fiction series he and David Drake edited has become a classic of military science fiction. He has collaborated on several mystery novels as "Quinn Fawcett," including the Authorized *Mycroft Holmes and Madame Vernet* mysteries. Recent works include *Making Contact: a UFO contact handbook*, and a series of books about great mistakes in history: *It Seemed Like a Good Idea, You Did What?* and *How to Lose a Battle*.

Josepha Sherman is a fantasy and SF writer/editor and folklorist who has written everything from *Star Trek* novels to a bio of Bill Gates to titles such as *Trickster Tales* (August House). Current titles include *Star Trek: Vulcan's Soul* with Susan Shwartz, the reprint of the *Unicorn Queen* books (Del Rey), and *Mythology for Storytellers* (M. E. Sharpe.) She is editing *The Encyclopedia of Storytelling* for M. E. Sharpe. Sherman also owns Sherman Editorial Services, which handles everything from writing and editing to PR and design. Visit it at www.ShermanEditorialServices.com.

Nancy Kress is the author of twenty-three books, most recently *Crucible* (Tor) and *Nothing Human* (Golden Gryphon Press). Her fiction has won three Nebulas, a Hugo, a John W. Campbell Memorial Award, and a Sturgeon award. She regularly teaches writing and has authored three books on writing for Writers Digest Books. She lives in Rochester, New York, with the world's most spoiled toy poodle.

David Brin used to eke a living from government grants, till he quit research and teaching to become an entertainer. Lacking a singing voice, or other discernible talent, he chose writing. "I discovered a latent gift for making up stuff out of thin air," he explains. "But never had the heart to slander real people. Then I found you can lie all you want…about fictional characters! They can't gripe, or sue, if you strand them in space or marry them off to aliens, or ruin their reputations. What a deal." Other comedic adventures can be found at www.baensuniverse.com.

Walter Jon Williams is an author, traveler, kenpo fiend, and scuba maven. He lives with his wife, Kathleen Hedges, on an old Spanish land grant in the high desert of New Mexico, and is the author of twenty-five novels and two collections of shorter works. His first novel to attract serious public attention was *Hardwired* (1986), described by Roger Zelazny as "a tough, sleek juggernaut of a story, punctuated by strobe-light movements, coursing to the wail of jets and the twang of steel guitars." His fiction has won two Nebula Awards. Walter's subject matter has an unusually wide range, and includes the glittering surfaces of *Hardwired,* the opulent tapestries of *Aristoi,* the bleak science-tinged roman policier *Days of Atonement*, and the comic adventures of the Allowed Burglar, Drake Maijstral. His latest works include the Dread Empire's Fall series of far-future novels. Walter's Web page may be found at www.walterjonwilliams.net.

Joe Haldeman sold his first story in 1969, while he was still in the army, post-Vietnam, and has been a constant writer ever since, with a little time off for teaching. He's written about two dozen novels and five collections of short stories and poetry, and appears in about twenty languages. Since 1983, he and his wife Gay have spent the fall semester in Cambridge, MA, teaching at MIT. His latest novel is *Old Twentieth*, and it was joined in 2005 by *War Stories*, a collection of fiction about Vietnam.

Mike Resnick is the winner of five Hugos, plus other major awards in the USA, France, Japan, Spain, Croatia, and Poland, and according to *Locus* currently stands fourth on the all-time award list. He is the author of fifty-two novels, two hundred short stories, fourteen collections, and two screenplays, and has edited forty-four anthologies. His work has been translated into twenty-two languages. In his spare time, he sleeps.

Harry Turtledove is an escaped Byzantine historian who's spent the last fifteen years telling lies for a living—uh, writing novels and short fiction. He is a Hugo, Sidewise, and Hal Clement Award winner, and a two-time Nebula finalist. He is married to fellow writer Laura Frankos (who puts up with him not least because she has a milder case of the same disease), and has three daughters who are beginning to spread their wings and fly through the world on their own.

Connie Willis has won a total of six Nebula Awards and eight Hugo Awards, including both a Nebula and a Hugo for her novel *Doomsday Book* and a Hugo for her novel *To Say Nothing of the Dog*. Her first novel, *Lincoln's Dream*, won the John W. Campbell Memorial Award. She has also written many award-winning short stories and speaks frequently at science fiction conventions around the globe. She lives with her husband in Greeley, Colorado.

Robert Sheckley has written for radio and television and even worked on a computer game, in addition to producing forty novels and nine collections of his short stories. His first novel, *Immortality, Inc.*, was made into the movie *Freejack*, and several of his other short stories also became the basis for films. Some of his other well-known novels include *Mindswap* and *Dimension of Miracles*, in addition to a three-book fantasy series with Roger Zelazny and a humorous three-novel series about a private detective.